Jacquelyn Benson has always known who she wanted to be when she grew up: Indiana Jones. But since real archaeology involves far more cataloging pot shards and digging through muck than divi   out of airplanes and battling Nazis, she decided instead to de   herself to shamelessly making things up.

  yn studied anthropology in Belfast, Northern Ireland, and
  .d a man from Dublin, New Hampshire. She wrote a thesis
  ·anormal investigators and spent four years living in a
  .n. When not writing, you may find her turning flowers
  .ne, herding an unruly toddler, or hiding under a blanket
  ·ing genre fiction. *The Smoke Hunter* is her first novel.

www.jacquelynbenson.com
Facebook: /jacquelynbensonauthor
Twitter: @JBheartswords
Instagram: @jbheartswords
Goodreads: /jacquelynbenson

Praise for

THE
SMOKE
HUNTER

'Intrigue and suspense aplenty. A refreshing and
original new voice' Scott Mariani

'Fast-paced and action-packed but with a keen eye for detail
[*The Smoke Hunter*] moves from Victorian London to the
badlands of Central America with barely time
to draw breath' Stephen Leather

'Wonderful characters, thrilling action, a social conscience,
mystery and a dash of romance: this is a page-turner with
everything' Iain King, author of *Secrets of the Last Nazi*

'Conspiracy, mystery and a courageous suffragette with an eye
for adventure – a sparkling debut novel from Jacquelyn Benson'
Rob Jones, author of *The Vault of Poseidon*

'Prepare for an intense ride . . . Jacquelyn Benson keeps you
guessing and her smart storytelling weaves thread after thread
to create a thrilling adventure, right up until the last page'
David Leadbeater, author of *The Bones of Odin*

THE
SMOKE HUNTER

JACQUELYN BENSON

HEADLINE

First published in Great Britain in 2016 by
HEADLINE PUBLISHING GROUP

1

Cataloguing in Publication Data is available from the British Library

ISBN 978 1 4722 3834 4

Offset in 10.29/13.74 pt Berkeley Std by Jouve (UK), Milton Keynes

Printed and bound in Great Britain by CPI Group (UK) Ltd, Croydon, CR0 4YY

MIX
Paper from
responsible sources
FSC® C104740

Headline's policy is to use papers that are natural, renewable and recyclable
products and made from wood grown in well-managed forests and other
controlled sources. The logging and manufacturing processes are expected
to conform to the environmental regulations of the country of origin.

HEADLINE PUBLISHING GROUP
An Hachette UK Company
Carmelite House
50 Victoria Embankment
London EC4Y 0DZ

www.headline.co.uk
www.hachette.co.uk

For my family — the whole big, crazy lot of them.
Thanks for never doubting I could make the impossible happen.

ACKNOWLEDGMENTS

Producing a first novel is a bit like giving birth: you can do it on your own, but it's a heck of a lot harder. This book owes a great debt to the following people:

My readers – Jasmin Hunter, Danica Carlson and Andrew Rea – for invaluable feedback and enthusiasm.

Michael Kimball for being one of my first and biggest fans.

My agent, Howard Morhaim, for his advice, support and expertise.

My editors, Beth deGuzman and Caroline Acebo, for falling in love with this story and helping painstakingly shepherd it from a wild mess to the book you see before you.

And most important, my husband, Dan, for his unshakable faith in me, and my daughter, Tula, for having the courtesy to remain in utero until I completed my first draft.

THE
SMOKE
HUNTER

Prologue

FOR THE HUNDREDTH TIME, Friar Vincente Salavert sank to his knees and prayed, begging forgiveness. He knew now that he, and no other, had been the agent of death for thousands—among them hundreds of women and children, the innocent and the helpless.

His prison cell was little more than a hole in the ground, a gated underground chamber at the end of a long, dark tunnel. No sound from the world beyond reached him here, nor a single glimmer of light. In the black and the silence, time stretched and contracted, becoming meaningless. He countered disorientation with the regular rhythm of prayer.

Prayer was all he had left. There could be no escape from this pit. When he next saw the glory of sunlight or the pale glimmer of the moon, he would be marching to his death.

It had begun with a whisper. Salavert first heard it six months ago in the mission of San Pedro de Flores, a primitive outpost on a stinking swamp of a shoreline, plagued by mosquitos and disease. The New World, they called it. Salavert preferred the old, but it was here where God's great work needed to be done. An entire continent deprived of the love of Christ, and Salavert could be the one to bring it to them.

He had crossed the sea, carried by visions of the thriving population of a new continent hungry for salvation. The reality had been starkly disappointing. The villages that sprouted up around San Pedro de Flores like a fungus held only a huddled mass of small, dark people, most of them sick, all of them filthy. The rest of the population of this "New World" was scattered through the thick, humid wilderness that surrounded them. Four days slogging on muleback through the jungle might bring him to a collection of farms with perhaps a hundred souls, most of whom would refuse to hear the Word of Christ, or pretended to listen, only to return to their old gods as soon as Salavert and his brothers had departed.

He had been near despair when the rumors first came to him, stories of a great city hidden in the unexplored vastness of the mountains. Some described a metropolis of marble palaces and gleaming temples, a paradise where even the poor laborers drank from jeweled goblets and the kings slept in rooms tiled with gold. Others spoke of a land of demons disguised as men, horrors that lived on the raw flesh of children, painting the steps of their temples with blood.

Some called it the White City. El Dorado, others said. A place of gold and death.

No one, of course, had seen it for themselves, or even claimed to have met one who had. It was a river of story without a source, something that haunted the jungles of New Spain like the ghost of one who had never lived.

That did not stop it from sinking hooks into Salavert's imagination. Day after day, he worked to bring the light of Christ into the minds of the pitiful groups of natives who found their way to the mission. But if he could find a place inhabited by more than a scattered, impoverished few, imagine what an effect he might have. He would bring God's Word to the heart of a native king, and like a Constantine of the New World, he, in turn, would impose it upon his people. With one blessed act, Salavert could be responsible for bringing thousands of souls to the faith.

He had tried to inspire his abbot with this vision, but the man remained stubbornly blind to its potential. The great cities that peppered the jungles had been abandoned centuries ago, he said. They were all ruins, buried in thick vegetation and avoided by the small tribes of natives, who called the places haunted. Only far to the north, in the land of the Aztecs, had such metropolises remained alive and thriving, though, of course, Cortés had seen an end to that. Now even the halls of Tenochtitlán were silent, save for the beating wings of swallows nesting where princes and warriors once walked.

The abbot believed the rumor was only another dream of the gold-hungry that would drive them to lonely deaths in the wilderness. Try as he might, Salavert could not convince him otherwise. Then God saw fit to call the old abbot into his arms, and the brothers chose one to replace him whose mind was not so closed.

The new abbot gave Salavert permission to seek out the truth behind the rumors, along with two of his brothers in Christ and a dozen new converts to serve as bearers. They trekked north, moving from village to village, following stories of the fabulous city.

It eluded them every time, seeming tantalizingly close, only to fade once more into obscurity, until at last Salavert reached the dark mountains where no Christian foot had ever stepped. What lay beyond was a mystery even to the wildest of natives, and the region was vast enough that he could wander through it for a lifetime and never cross the same path twice.

He had plunged into it, trusting faith to lead him to his destiny, but it seemed that God had abandoned him. Sick and starving, Salavert and his brothers remained lost in a verdant hell for weeks, until at last he had known they must find civilization or die.

Skeletal and sweating, Salavert climbed to the crest of a high mountain ridge. There he fell to his knees and uttered one final plea that he would be chosen for this great work: the saving of an entire city from devil worship and damnation. He put his very soul into the prayer, along with every ounce of his will and the last of his hope.

And he was answered.

In something like a dream, glimpsed through a haze of weakness and desperation, the clouds before him parted and the light of heaven gilded the face of a near mountain, across which wove a dark and distinctive line of stone as black as smoke.

It was the sign he had prayed for. Salavert ran, stumbling, back to his brothers, and told them that they must proceed. The entrance to the city was at their feet. God had pointed the way.

They had doubted him. He read it in their faces. They thought the long weeks of hunger and isolation had finally made him mad.

They were wrong.

He could still remember his first glimpse of the city, how they had staggered out of a narrow ravine to see it glimmering before them, a place even more magnificent than the rumors had promised. Stone towers rose from the dark green of the jungle canopy, shining like the purest white marble. The streets gleamed like rivers of snow. Truly, there was no place on earth so near to paradise.

Or to hell.

They killed the bearers first, opening their throats with blades of obsidian. The ranks of priest-kings in their barbarian finery watched as blood poured down the steps of the temple like a rich red carpet. Salavert was imprisoned with his two brothers in Christ, thrust into a pit where time had no meaning, where all of his awareness was filled with the smell of earth and decay.

They took Brother Marcus first. The light of their torches burned Salavert's eyes, already so accustomed to the darkness. They bound the monk's hands and led him down the tunnel. He had prayed as he went, calling out to the Lady of Mercy to protect him.

Salavert could not say how long it was before they returned for Brother Ignatius. The younger monk had gone mad by then, the darkness seeping into his brain. He leapt at the guards as they entered, fighting them like an animal with teeth and nails as Salavert had pressed himself to the far corner of his prison, an instinctive horror forcing him away from the disfigured faces of the soldiers.

The image remained with him long after the guards had carried Ignatius away, his screams echoing down the tunnel behind him. Salavert knew the meaning of the oozing sores that wept down his captors' cheeks. He recognized the pestilence.

He had been a mere slip of a boy when smallpox had burned through his native Valencia, leaving piles of corpses in its wake. That his expedition was responsible for bringing it here was impossible to deny.

The disease would spread like wildfire. Some would burn with fever, faces swollen and unrecognizable. Others would bleed, life pulsing from every orifice. He had seen what the disease did when it ravaged the villages near San Pedro de Flores. It was murder, carried in the breath or a touch.

But here, in the White City, perhaps it was something else. That he had been called here, Salavert had no doubt. But the people of this place were steeped in a darker wickedness than he ever could have suspected. It occurred to Salavert that instead of the Word, God might have sent him to bring a scourge to this city that would cleanse it of its evil in a way that none could resist or overpower.

The instrument of redemption he had been chosen to deliver was not prayer but death.

Though time was next to meaningless in the darkness of his pit, Salavert felt that the visits of the guards who brought him food and water seemed to be growing further and further apart. The faces of the men who came changed constantly, and increasingly he saw not only the marks of disease on their skin, but fresh wounds, as though they came to him by way of some ongoing battle.

Salavert had long since accepted what his end in this dark place must be. He would join the ranks of the holy martyrs, making the ultimate gift to Christ. But as he waited in that long, unending night, it occurred to him that instead of blood on the temple steps, his fate might lie in a slow death by starvation, forgotten in a pit beneath the earth.

The notion filled him with unspeakable horror.

When at last the light glimmered against the tunnel walls, stabbing his unused eyes with pain, he felt not fear but relief.

He emerged, blinking against the agonizing brightness of the day, to find that the city he had seen when he arrived had gone. In its place was a vision of hell.

Bodies were strewn across the ground. They were not the victims of disease, but of the sword. The air was dense with smoke, an acrid burning that told him both the fields and the dead were aflame. Salavert recalled the wounds on the faces of the men who had been tending to him and realized that God, in His wrath against the people of this city, had visited them with war as well as plague.

His escorts pushed him past the carnage, crossing the square to where the great pyramid temple loomed like a pale ghost in the smoke.

The building was massive. Salavert had seen great monuments before, among them the cathedrals of Valencia and Seville. Next to this, those towering tributes to the glory of God seemed like children's toys, slight and full of air.

When last he had looked upon the temple, its stairs had run red with the blood of the natives who had accompanied him and his brothers from the mission. How long ago had that been? Weeks? Months? It was impossible to say, and hardly mattered anymore.

The climb was endless. He had grown feeble during his long imprisonment and staggered up each step, the guards—weakened themselves by disease—all but carrying him by the time they reached the pinnacle.

A slight figure waited for him there, made larger by the elaborate feather headdress and jade breastplate of a priest.

But this was no priest. It was a mere woman, done up in priest's clothing. Her face was familiar, and Salavert realized he had seen her before, standing at the back of the assemblage of great men who had presided over the slaughter of his bearers. Her place in the crowd was that of some minor functionary, no one of importance, but the jagged scar that marred the skin of her cheek had marked her in his memory.

Now she wore the finery of the high priest, which sat overlarge on her, as though meant for a bigger man—which he was certain was the case. Around her neck hung one of the medallions of dark stone he had seen on the most prominent of the men who had watched over the sacrifices, a symbol of rank he was sure she would never have attained if not for the plague.

The implication was clear: This woman—this girl—was all that was left of that grim assembly. The elders he had seen before, men who had reeked of power despite being demon-haunted heathens, were all dead. The small, scarred woman before him was all that remained of the rulers of this city.

His impure heart revolted at the thought. Was he really to be martyred by a mere female? The notion filled him with disgust. Yet God would think no less of his sacrifice for its being made at the hand of a woman. It was only his pride that rebelled, and pride was sin.

At least the woman would not hold her blasphemous position for long. Her face was flushed with dark purple patches and small pinprick sores, symptoms Salavert knew indicated a less visible but more virulent form of the disease. It would end in blood, her vital fluid hemorrhaging from every orifice—a horrific way to die.

God had not spared His hand in this place.

The woman made a sign, and the two guards pulled a black hood over Salavert's head. The cloth stank of another man's fear, enclosing him once more in the darkness.

He was pushed forward into what must be the narrow sanctuary at the top of the temple, but he did not remain there. Instead, he was dragged along an obscure and tortuous path—up ladders, down sharply twisting stairs, through echoing chambers, and along the length of a long, slippery tunnel. The air around him grew cool, filled with the smell of damp, and he knew he was being taken into the very bowels of the temple.

At long last, they halted. The bag was pulled from his head, and to his profound surprise, Salavert found himself inside a cathedral.

It had been formed by the hand of God from the very earth itself. The cave was massive, filled with soaring pillars and graceful veils of stone. The stone around him glittered in the torchlight, sparkling like stars. Tombs surrounded him, enormous stone sarcophagi engraved with ancient pagan figures. It would have been a sublime vision, if not for the paintings covering the walls.

Their artistry was undeniable. The colors were rich, the figures startlingly lifelike, but the scenes they depicted were images from hell itself, portraits of violence and horrifying decay.

They failed to hold his gaze. Instead, his eyes were drawn to a dark pool that lay in the very heart of the cavern. No, not a pool, he realized. It was a great flat disk of stone. The surface was polished to gleaming perfection, reflecting phantom glimmers of the flames that illuminated the space around them.

It was a mirror. A massive black mirror made of stone instead of glass.

Dark, ruddy stains marked the ground that surrounded its still, flawless surface. With the instinct of a cornered animal, Salavert knew he was looking at the remnants of centuries of blood. The implication was as clear to him as the painted horror on the walls of the cave.

They had made sacrifices.

A primal fear choked him, banishing all his martyr's resolve and leaving in its place only the pure, animal urge to flee.

He screamed, the sound echoing off the delicate frills of stone, but the guards held him fast, dragging him to the mirror's edge as the small priestess began her incantation.

The droning, singsong tones of her chant melded with the fading echo of his terror, the cave transforming her worship and his cry into a symphony.

She took a small, wicked blade of obsidian from a sheath at

her waist, and Salavert began to recite the last contrition, grasping frantically for some semblance of self-control. He must meet his God in peace and acceptance, not howling like a beast at the slaughterhouse. Still, sweat dripped down his body beneath the remains of his cassock, and he stumbled over the words that should have been as familiar to him as his own name.

But the knife did not move for his throat. Instead, the priestess drew it across the skin of her own palm. She whispered something, a few phrases laced with grief and desperation, the tones very like those of a prayer. Then she knelt at the edge of the dark glass and pressed her bleeding hand to the surface.

There was a hiss like water on a hot pan. Smoke welled up from between her fingers. The priestess leaned into it, breathing deeply. Her eyes glazed over.

The air around Salavert seemed to grow colder, and the monk was overwhelmed by the awareness of something at work in that unholy cathedral—something old and powerful. Something that had nothing at all to do with God.

Her eyes still unfocused, the woman extended her free hand, uttering a single word of command. To Salavert, it seemed as though two voices spoke, both priestess and something that was more than an echo.

He wanted to run, but the guards were strong, and they dragged him to her side, forcing him to his knees. He closed his eyes, trying to prepare for the inevitable blow, but instead her small hand grasped the neck of his robe. With shocking strength, she pulled his face into the column of smoke that rose from the place where her blood met the mirror's surface.

The cave vanished.

Salavert was in a place he knew well. Around him soared the elegant walls of the cathedral of Valencia. He stood in the nave, looking down the aisle toward the altar, a rich and glorious monument to the might of God. This was the place where he had been called to a life in Christ, where he had begun to believe that he, the third son of a butcher, might have a greater destiny than anyone suspected.

The pews were deserted. Candles flickered along the aisle, but all the usual quiet activity—the muffled voices and reverent footsteps—were gone. Only silence remained.

Silence, and a woman.

The priestess stood at the altar, holding aloft the Santo Cáliz— the very chalice of Christ, believed by many to be the Holy Grail itself. Salavert had seen it before, during the grandest of church ceremonies he had attended as a child. The finely wrought gold, framing a bowl of bloodred agate, looked even grander now, clasped in the woman's small, dark hands.

Her heathen trappings had been replaced by the robes of a bishop, and her face was free of smallpox sores. She looked as she had when Salavert had first seen her at the temple, solemn and sad as the Holy Virgin.

Some remote, near-forgotten part of his brain knew that he should find this the most profound blasphemy: a woman wearing the garb of a priest of the Holy Church. The thought was only an itch at the back of his mind, overwhelmed by the pensive silence that surrounded him.

The light shifted, and his eye was drawn to the familiar frescoes that decorated the walls. But the images he remembered vividly, the lapis-toned scenes from the lives of Christ and the saints, were no longer there. In their place were scenes of horror like those he had left behind in the cave. He saw knights of the Crusade storming Jerusalem, their swords red with the blood of children. There were women tied to stakes and screaming as the flames licked at their feet, men twisted on the rack of the Inquisition. Massacre, torture, and slaughter surrounded him.

"Where am I?" he demanded, his voice shaking with outrage and fear.

"We are meeting in the heart of something very old and very

dark. A place shaped by will and desire," the priestess replied. There was no wonder in him that he could understand her words. He would not have wondered if the sky had turned around to lie under his feet.

She lifted the cup once more, her eyes closed in fierce concentration, then set it down reverently on the altar.

"It wants me to ask a different question. One that leads to great glory . . . and a greater feast of blood." She seemed to be engaged in some immense effort, her hands clenched, sweat breaking out on her brow. "*I will not ask it.*"

"Ask what? What's happening? Why am I here?"

"So much death." Her face twisted with grief. "Centuries of death. It made us great, but what is greatness? It is a sport for men." Her bitterness was palpable, and for the first time since the dream had begun, she looked to where Salavert stood, helpless and terrified, in the midst of the empty pews.

"It would use you," she accused. "It would make you the doorway to a greater world in which it could satisfy its thirst for blood."

"We are but feeble sinners." His reply was instinctive, and even to himself, the words seemed lame.

She didn't answer. Her eyes slid closed again. She seemed to be gathering herself, concentrating both body and will.

"I would know how to stop this," she cried fiercely, her small frame trembling with power. The call echoed off the graceful arches of the cathedral, filling the silence and resonant with significance.

It seemed to Salavert that something answered her. It came in an uncanny wind, stirring the folds of his tattered cassock and carrying with it the sense of a thousand voices whispering in concert from every corner of that vast and holy place.

She listened, her body held in perfect stillness, her eyes closed. Then the wind moved through, and the silence that descended once more was broken by the harsh bark of a laugh that was very near a sob.

"So that is to be the way of it."

Grief shuddered through her frame. She opened her eyes, her gaze locking onto Salavert once more, direct and forceful as a blow.

"Wake up," she ordered, and he did.

⁓

He came to choking, lying on his side at the edge of the devilish mirror. The priestess was beside him, her arms shaking with the effort of holding herself up.

She climbed painfully to her feet, giving a sharp command to the guards. They responded with a shocked exclamation, clearly doubting the evidence of their own ears, but the priestess's look left no room for debate. Salavert was yanked away from the mirror, back the way he had come.

Hurrying now, he was pushed through a tunnel carved into the rock, the priestess following at a stately pace. They emerged into a room full of wonders. Mysterious objects glittered from tables on every side. In the center of the room, a great gilded weight swung slowly and silently back and forth like the mechanism of some enormous clock. He realized that he had sensed the thing when he had passed through here before, blindfolded and disoriented. It had felt like a whispering, ghostly movement, some uncanny force flying through the darkness around him. He had been blind then, but sure of his martyrdom. That certainty had been whisked away from him, and the unknown that rose in its place disturbed him more than the promise of his own death.

"What is happening?" he demanded.

The priestess did not answer. Instead, she moved to the center of the room. As the great pendulum swung at her, she caught it, halting its regular progress.

The silence that followed had weight, as though filling a space that had never been silent before. He saw one of the guards make a strange gesture and knew on instinct that it was a ward against evil.

The woman approached Salavert and drew her knife once more.

He felt a moment's fear that he had escaped that hellish cavern and the hunger of its dark fetish only to die here instead, but once again the knife moved to her body, not his own. She severed a leather thong at her throat and caught the weight of the medallion in her hand. Seen up close, it looked as though it were made of the same dark stone as the mirror, carved with the image of one of their heathen gods.

She grabbed his wrist and forced the cursed thing into his hand, closing his fingers over it.

He glanced down at it and shuddered. The stone gleamed in the torchlight, undoubtedly the devil's own icon. It felt cool against his palm, uncannily so, given that it had just been worn against the skin of a woman flushed with fever.

He knew that he should toss it aside. He was a man of God, prepared for his own martyrdom. He should not suffer such a fetish to contaminate his holy person.

But he did not. Instead, he clasped it tightly.

The priestess saw his movement and something gave way in her as though a great burden had been set down. She seemed to age before him, the exhaustion concealed by her regal bearing at last plainly apparent.

She looked at him once more, her eyes full of unspeakable sorrow, and uttered a single word. Though he did not know the tongue, he could not mistake its meaning.

Go.

He offered no resistance as the guards hauled him toward a narrow doorway on the far side of the room. Only as he was about to pass out of that strange, secret chamber did he stop and look back.

A grinding echoed through the room. Behind the priestess, the opening in the floor that led back into the nightmarish caves below slid closed. The woman knelt before it, the obsidian knife in her hand. As Salavert watched, she lifted the blade over her head, then plunged it deep into her own chest. She fell to the ground, her blood seeping out across the stones.

After that, Vincente Salavert began to run.

1

Eleanora Mallory sat in the office of Mr. Henbury, assistant keeper of the rolls, waiting to be fired. It was morning, and the narrow, high-ceilinged room was silent save for the drumming of the rain against the tall, thin windowpanes. The shelves that lined the walls were covered in disorganized piles of books and papers. Mr. Henbury's desk was even worse, a mountain of documents where sixteenth-century court proceedings cozied up against bundles of eighteenth-century receipts in a chaos that made Ellie's fingers twitch. Henbury was constantly finding fault with her work but let his own responsibilities sink into shocking disarray. It was high on the rather long list of things about him that infuriated her.

His tardiness was another. She had been summoned here from her desk almost as soon as she'd arrived, but that had been more than twenty minutes ago, and Henbury still hadn't bothered to make his appearance.

She'd been so unsure of how briefly she would be allowed to remain in the building, she hadn't bothered to remove her coat. Of course, the place was also freezing. The Public Record Office was never heated. It was too much of a risk to the precious documents housed within. And on an April morning that felt far more like February, a coat was close to a necessity.

Ellie knew perfectly well that Mr. Henbury had never liked having a woman working in his section—particularly not a young, unmarried woman with a university degree. It was undoubtedly the degree that had gotten her in the door. That and the near-perfect score she had earned on her civil service exams. The degree also meant that she was technically as well educated as Mr. Henbury himself, and more so than the vast majority of her fellow archivists. Mr. Henbury did not like that at all.

She looked around the gray, gloomy office and tried to decide how upset she would be if Henbury did indeed enter gleefully wielding the ax of dismissal. After all, the prisonlike building on Chancery Lane was hardly what she had dreamed of while she'd worked for her degree at the University of London. She had wanted what her cousin Neil—now Dr. Fairfax, she reminded herself—had practically been handed: a position as a field archaeologist. At this very moment, as she sat watching the rain streak dully down the windowpane, Neil was off in the deserts of Egypt excavating ruins and uncovering knowledge lost for millennia. She closed her eyes and imagined the hot sun on her skin, sand sticking to sweat as she worked with a brush in her hand, dusting away the debris of centuries from ancient stones.

Since she was a girl, she'd dreamed of working to recover the past, reading every book and journal on the subject she could get hold of. She had been only nine years old when she decided to conduct her first excavation, digging up the garden in front of their home on Golden Square. She could still remember Aunt Florence's histrionics about her dahlias, which had not been abated by Ellie's assurance that she would put them back once she had determined nothing of importance was concealed beneath them. At that tender age, it had never occurred to her that the life she dreamed of was an impossibility—that no amount of intelligence and determination would overcome the handicap of her sex.

It could have been worse, of course. At least her position as an archivist had enabled her to get her hands on history, if not quite in the way she'd expected. And the money had been very good, or would have been if she had spent any of it. Uncle David had begrudgingly agreed to her taking a job, but the suggestion that she let a room of her own had thrown Aunt Florence into hysterics.

"You'll never find a husband living on your own!" Aunt Florence had wailed. The horror of it had driven her to fan herself vigorously, declaring she was feeling faint. In the end, Ellie had capitulated. She had done it for the sake of maintaining peace with the beloved relatives who had raised her—certainly not because she had any desire for a husband. Marriage would mean the end of any work for her besides "managing the household," which sounded to Ellie like a slow-burning hell.

It might be all that was left to her now. Dismissal from her position would mean the gates of the civil service would be closed to her. What other options were there? Teaching—the last resort of all women unfortunate enough to be educated. The thought was more depressing than the weather.

She checked her pocket watch. She had thought he would have been eager for this particular meeting, given that he'd undoubtedly been looking forward to it for a long time.

Ellie rose and strode over to Henbury's chair, plopping down into it with a happy little sigh of rebellion. This should have been her chair, really. She was cleverer than Henbury, and both of them knew it. And *she* certainly never would have let the assistant keeper's desk become such a muddle. Documents that defied simple categorization often found their way to this disorganized mountain. Not from Ellie, of course, who trusted her own faculties far more than those of Mr. Henbury. Still, the mess did occasionally make for interesting browsing.

She turned idly through the piles of papers, searching for anything intriguing. It seemed that Henbury had a dull to-do list this week, she thought, frowning at what looked like a mess of dry court proceedings. She lifted them up to peek at a pair of ledgers, but the maneuver upset a precariously balanced stack of papers. They spilled to the floor, along with something that landed with a more substantial thud.

Ellie hurried to tidy the mess, all too aware of what it would look like should Mr. Henbury arrive to find her riffling through his papers on her hands and knees. She gathered up the pages, which looked like an assortment of shipping logs, and revealed something wholly unexpected lying beneath them.

It was a psalter—a very old psalter, wrapped in a faded black ribbon. The spine was embossed with gold lettering. Though it had faded with time, Ellie could see that what remained was in Latin. The leather cover was deeply worn, indicating that the book must have been well used before it became part of the records. But that, of course, was the puzzle: Why on earth would someone have included a psalter in the archives?

Altogether, the book posed an enticing mystery. Most of the mysteries Ellie encountered in the records office were far from enticing, like wondering why some long-dead clerk had decided to drop half the vowels from all of his nouns, or why another had chosen to file a count of the royal herds alongside a translation of Geoffrey of Monmouth.

Intrigued, Ellie slipped the book out from under the stack of papers. It was printed in octavo, making it roughly the size of a novel, and felt heavy for its size.

Footsteps sounded, and Mr. Henbury's voice echoed down the hall.

"Tell Edwards that there will be no extension. The calendar will be done by next Friday or I will find someone else to enjoy his position."

There was a mumbled reply. Ellie scooped up the tumbled papers, depositing them on Henbury's desk and hoping he wouldn't notice a change in the clutter.

Her hand paused on the psalter. It seemed to itch under her fingers, begging to be explored. Before Ellie could think further about it, the book had slipped into the pocket of her skirt. She dashed to her seat and quickly arranged herself as the latch clicked and Mr. Henbury entered the room.

He was a shorter man, bald but fighting it desperately by way of a swatch of thin gray hair combed pathetically across his scalp and plastered there with a generous palmful of pomade. It gave the skin between the strands a special gleam, which was particularly noticeable when Henbury stood, as he did now, under an electric light.

"Miss Mallory," he said, then hesitated as he looked toward his chair. He adjusted its angle and dropped himself into it, assuming, to the best of his admittedly meager ability, the mantle of authority. "I imagine it is not a mystery to you why you have been called here today."

Ellie smiled back at him blandly. Henbury frowned in response, which gave his face an even more puggish look.

"It has come to our attention that you were arrested over the course of this weekend," he continued.

"That's correct," Ellie replied. Her calm tone perceptibly deepened Henbury's frown, but now that the storm was upon her, she found herself surprisingly at ease in it.

"To be more precise," he intoned grandly, "you were jailed after chaining yourself to the gates of the Houses of Parliament."

This was the moment. If she chose, she could throw herself on Henbury's mercy, weep and plead for her position, claim a hysterical turn of the brain, and promise nothing like it would ever happen again. He would certainly enjoy that, a display of thoroughly feminine weakness from the implacable Miss Mallory. The thought turned her stomach and steeled her resolve.

"Correct," she confirmed flatly.

Henbury stared at her. She knew he was feeling both bewilderment and irritation at her lack of horror in the face of her circumstances. The thought almost made her smile. She suppressed it with no small effort.

"This is a tolerant organization, Miss Mallory, even of those with obviously misguided opinions. Mr. Barker, as I imagine you are aware, is a socialist. But he is a *law-abiding* socialist. While the Public Record Office can tolerate even a *suffragette*"—Henbury made the word sound like something very unpleasant and possibly infectious—"it cannot house within its hallowed halls a militant agitator."

"I would say I inconvenienced more than agitated," Ellie countered.

"Your opinions have, I'm afraid, been demonstrably proven

unreliable." Henbury huffed. "Our course of action under the circumstances is clear." He shuffled some papers importantly. The self-inflating little gesture struck a nerve, and she felt her temper begin to flare.

"It was only for a night," Ellie interrupted.

"What?"

"My time in jail. It was only a night. And they aren't pressing charges. It in no way impinges upon my ability to perform my duties."

"You chained yourself to Parliament!" Henbury spluttered. "Such behavior is completely unacceptable for a member of Her Majesty's Public Record Office."

Ellie raised her chin defiantly.

"I have a bachelor of arts from the University of London. I am a ranking member of this nation's civil service. And I am not permitted by its government to cast a vote."

"That's what you get a husband for," Henbury snapped.

"I don't want a husband," Ellie said, clearly and firmly.

Henbury pulled a paper from his briefcase, uncapped his pen, and scrawled a signature across the page. He stood, Ellie echoing his movement instinctively. He handed the page to her.

"Your notice of dismissal. Effective immediately. You will not receive a reference. You will collect your belongings and remove yourself from the premises."

Ellie, back straight, reached out and snatched the page from Henbury's hand.

"Good day, Miss Mallory," he said as she turned to go.

"You mean good riddance, Mr. Henbury," she corrected him, then spun on her heel and marched out of the room.

She continued, head high, down the hall to her desk, which sat under a window in the archivists' office. Everything on it was neatly organized, from the ink, blotters, and catalog forms, to the documents she had left that Friday evening.

As she sat down, she heard a quick rush of whispers from across the room. They came, she knew, from Langer and Johnson, whose desks were closest to the door. The pair had never liked the idea of working alongside a woman—particularly not one who was just as well qualified as they were. Better, in fact. Johnson had graduated tenth in his class at Nottingham. Ellie had been first in hers at the University of London, which was a more reputable institution.

What on earth am I going to do?

The thought came unbidden, and she quickly shunted it aside. It had brought with it a sudden trembling in her hands, and she could not afford to show uncertainty, not while hostile eyes were studying her every move from across the room.

She took a deep breath, forcing herself to calm. Then, her movements even and crisp, she lifted her valise and began to remove her belongings from her desk. They were meager enough. The process took only a few minutes. All that remained were her works in progress, which, as always, had been meticulously noted as she went along. Any of the other clerks would be able to pick up where she left off—even Johnson.

That left only one thing. She pulled the psalter from her skirt pocket and allowed herself a little smile of satisfaction at the notion that Henbury would have to do some hunting once he realized he had lost it.

Let him be inconvenienced, she thought.

It was too soon to go. It would look like she was running away, and she didn't want to give Johnson, Langer, Henbury—any of the lot of them—the satisfaction of thinking they had made her scamper off like a scared kitten.

She would take a few more minutes and indulge her curiosity. She carefully removed the black ribbon binding the book and opened it.

Inside she found not a collection of psalms but a mutilation. The center of the holy book had been carved out, leaving a compartment in the now-hollow pages. Within it lay something impossible.

The disk-shaped medallion was made of dark, gleaming stone,

heavy and almost metallic-looking. An odd pattern of notches was carved into its circumference, and a hole was drilled into a peak at the top, as though it was meant to be worn as a necklace or an amulet. But it was the engravings on the surface that riveted Ellie's attention, making her forget the rustling papers across the room and the clatter of traffic outside the window.

A grinning idol was carved onto the surface, its face decorated with slashing horizontal lines. It held a knife in one hand, the other having been replaced by a writhing snake, and angular, batlike wings protruded from its shoulders. A round disk covered its chest, and the whole figure was surrounded by whirling lines, like streams of smoke.

Ellie risked a glance around the room. The rest of the archivists worked quietly at their desks, either oblivious to her presence or purposefully ignoring it. She quickly turned her chair to face the window, which provided better light than the electric lamp and also allowed her to put her body between the artifact and any surreptitiously prying eyes. Then she delicately plucked the strange object from the book.

She stared down at the artifact wonderingly. The reverse side was carved, like its circumference, with deep, deliberately shaped notches. The remaining flat surfaces were inscribed with blocky glyphs. Ellie recognized the style. It resembled the Mayan icons and characters she had studied at the university.

A Mayan artifact . . .

If it was true, then the object she held must be ancient. Though her education at the university had leaned more toward the classical, there had been a series of lectures on Cópan and the other Mayan cities. All of them had been abandoned centuries before the first European explorers had set foot in Central America. It meant that what she had in her hand was almost certainly more than a thousand years old. How on earth had it ended up inside a psalter in the archives of the Public Record Office?

Ellie ran her fingers over the cool surface, filled with wonder. She had read about the relics of past civilizations, studied them in books and drawings until she knew the names of the pharaohs and the caesars as well as, if not better than, those of her class-mates. For all of that, this was the first time she had held a piece of ancient history in her hands. They almost tingled with the sheer awe of coming into physical contact with the forgotten past.

But what was it doing in a hollowed-out book of psalms?

Looking for answers, she forced herself to shift her attention to the rest of what lay concealed in the book. She lifted out a piece of parchment, yellowed with age. She unfolded it, her eyes falling to a few lines of text scrawled elegantly along the back of the page. They were written in Latin, which she translated with ease.

Map indicating the location of the inhabited city discovered by Fr. Salavert of San Pedro de Flores, which may be supposed to lie behind the various legends of the land of El Dorado.

El Dorado?

She knew the story as well as anyone—a legendary city of unthinkable riches, supposedly hidden in the unexplored wilds of Central or South America. The dream of its wealth had led count-less explorers and adventurers to their deaths, including Sir Wal-ter Raleigh, whose imprisonment and eventual execution resulted from his failed mission to find the place.

Unfolding the document the rest of the way, Ellie saw that she was, indeed, holding a map, drawn by hand in painstaking detail. Rivers, marshes, and mountains were carefully indicated. In the center, marked by a small drawing of a stepped pyramid, was a place labeled, in the same flowing hand, "The White City."

It had to be a hoax. El Dorado, after all, was a fairy tale.

But that wasn't what the author of the map was claiming. A city that lay *behind* the legends...was it so impossible a notion? Many myths and stories had their roots in fact, however distantly.

If it wasn't a hoax...

The clock over the doorway chimed. Ellie glanced up and was shocked to see how much time had passed. If she remained at her desk much longer, she'd risk Henbury coming in and ordering her out in front of everyone like a recalcitrant schoolchild. She should return the map and artifact to the psalter and leave it for Henbury to furiously seek out when he eventually discovered it was missing.

She lifted the medallion again, preparing to place it back into the compartment, but as her fingers came into contact with that cool, shining surface, she hesitated, overwhelmed by a sense of possessiveness.

It was not an entirely illogical sensation. She must be the first one in centuries to have found it. If Henbury had opened the book and seen what lay inside, he would hardly have left it lying around on his desk. He would have had it couriered over to the museum. That he hadn't meant it was almost certainly another item that Langer or Johnson couldn't be bothered to properly catalog and that Henbury hadn't so much as glanced at yet.

The notion of leaving the map to that miserable little man filled her with abhorrence. The piece of paper before her could very well be the key to one of the greatest archaeological discoveries in decades.

Henbury was not qualified to investigate such a potential find. But she was. It was exactly the sort of thing she had prepared for through all her years of study—what the world had denied her thanks to her gender. It was as though someone had finally heard her dream and decided to answer it, right here in the gloom and drudgery of the Public Record Office.

Ellie was startled by the sound of a chair scraping. She looked up to see Mr. Barker—Mr. Henbury's generously tolerated socialist— rising from his desk. He was about her age, pale and slightly over-weight. And he was walking toward her.

She quickly closed the psalter, shuffling some folders over the map and medallion.

"Miss Mallory," Mr. Barker said, bowing to her slightly. "I— ah—heard about what happened. I just…that is…"

Ellie waited with barely concealed impatience, forcing herself to smile.

"I wanted you to know that you'll be missed. Here. At the office," he finally managed.

"Thank you, Mr. Barker," she said graciously.

Glancing around himself furtively, Barker quickly leaned toward Ellie's ear. She experienced a sudden terror that he was going to try to kiss her.

"Votes for women!" he excitedly whispered instead. He leaned back, glanced around, then triumphantly pumped his fist in the air.

He grinned, proud of his small rebellion, then returned to his desk.

As soon as he had gone, she unburied her discovery and looked down at the map and medallion.

If she left this with Henbury, it might be lost forever under a mountain of unfiled meeting minutes. The discovery it promised would never be explored, never realized. But if she took it . . .

The thought sparked a quick burst of adrenaline. *Steal it?*

No, she couldn't possibly.

Borrowing it, on the other hand . . .

She would take it only long enough to determine whether the thing was just a centuries-old hoax. A few days at most. Then she could drop it in the mail, and it would find its way right back to Henbury's desk.

And if it was genuine?

Well, that would be another matter entirely—a bridge she would cross when, and if, she came to it.

The medallion gleamed up at her from the desk, darkly compelling and full of promise. Without further hesitation, she plucked it up, dropping it back into the psalter along with the map. She secured it with the black ribbon and slipped it into her valise.

She stood, taking a final look around the room in which she had spent so many laborious hours for the past five years.

She wouldn't miss it.

Jailbird on Saturday, thief on Monday, she thought to herself. If nothing else, at least things were getting interesting.

The Reading Room of the British Library had always struck Ellie as one of the most wonderful places on earth. The great domed ceiling rose impossibly high overhead, sparkling with light even on a gloomy day like today. The many tables were always eloquently quiet, the silence broken only by the soft shuffling of pages and scratching of pens.

But most important, there were the books. The shelves that lined the circular walls of that marvelously vast space were packed with volumes, but that only began to scratch the surface of the possibilities. The collection was massive, a universe of knowledge needing only a circulation number on a slip of paper to be unlocked.

Ellie left her sodden overcoat and umbrella gratefully at the cloakroom and presented her pass to the door attendant. She knew that she was one of the few women in the city to have one, and it had taken no small degree of wrangling to acquire. But every ounce of effort had been worth it.

Once inside, she took a moment to breathe in the intellectually rarified atmosphere. It smelled like home. It was relatively quiet, the rain having kept away all but the most devoted scholars. Ellie made her way directly to the catalogs surrounding the grand circulation desk. She knew precisely what she was looking for, rapidly flipping through the cards and jotting numbers onto her request slip. She handed the paper to the clerk, who accepted it after treating her to the same skeptical glance she got every time she put in a request, despite the fact that she had been coming to the library for years. At this point, it was practically a tradition.

It would take some time before the books arrived, and Ellie used it to more thoroughly examine the papers hidden within the psalter.

The map itself had obviously been drawn with painstaking care. Rivers, marshes, and mountains were carefully indicated. A series of landmarks was meant to show those who followed that they were on the right path. These, on the other hand, were some-times painfully vague. One was described in Latin as "a black pillar which draws the compass." Another was a "great stone, hol-lowed into an arch by the hand of God."

It didn't matter. She'd do the research, see whether anything marked by contemporary explorers seemed to correlate.

Putting the map aside, she turned her attention to the rest of the papers. The two remaining pages constituted a letter addressed to the master of the Dominican order in Rome from the abbot of the mission at San Pedro de Flores.

The contents were astonishing.

The letter told of the arrival at their mission of a brother who had been sent into the wilderness to spread the Word of Christ, along with two of his brethren and a company of native bear-ers. He had returned alone nearly two years later, starving and half-mad. He claimed to have come from a native city hidden deep within the mountains—a city thriving and heavily populated in a region where all such places were supposed to have been ruins long before the arrival of the first Spanish explorers.

At least, it used to be heavily populated. According to the fri-ar's story, which he shared shortly before he died of something the abbot described as "exhausted nerves," he had escaped the place in the midst of disaster. The abbot argued that this would have left the abandoned city ripe for the taking, and he was certain there was fruit there well worth harvesting. Even if short on potential souls, the city would almost certainly be well stocked with gold that could contribute much to the Church's coffers.

The abbot had sent the medallion as evidence, hiding it and the map in the dead friar's psalter, urging that the order fund and equip an expedition to follow the long and dangerous route the friar had described.

But the abbot's message had never made it to Rome. Some-thing must have happened to his emissary—perhaps capture by the English pirates who roved the waters between Europe and the Americas during the seventeenth century, looking for Spanish galleons loaded with treasure. That would certainly be one way in which the psalter might have found its way to her hands, lumped in with other documents from trials involving the privateers.

The implications of the letter made Ellie's head spin. The Mayan cities were all supposed to have been abandoned a thousand years ago, devastated by plague or war or famine. But what if one, isolated in the far reaches of the mountains, had managed to survive?

It would be the find of the century, the sort that would make an archaeologist's career. No scholar worth his salt would be able to ignore it—not even if it had been made by a woman.

It would mean her career. Not the one she'd settled for, but the one she had dreamed of. That impossible hope, the one she'd long since given up on, could be *hers*. No one would be able to deny her right to work as a field archaeologist after making a discovery like this.

It was a thrilling possibility, one that set her heart leaping.

Of course, all of this depended on the map being genuine, she reminded herself. And there was also the chance that someone else had already stumbled across her big discovery.

A rattle and creak alerted her to the arrival of the circulation cart. Acting on quick instinct, Ellie shuffled the psalter and its contents under a volume of Cicero a previous reader had abandoned on the table.

The clerk deposited the books she'd requested with a deliberate thud, giving her a disapproving look for good measure, then pushed his squeaking trolley to the next table.

Ellie eyed the mountain of volumes with determination. Somewhere in those pages, she would find some answers.

~

Ellie had been bent over her reading table for three hours when she made her most significant discovery. Her hands trembling with excitement, she looked down at the page in front of her, which gave a brief history of a small mission in a remote corner of the Spanish New World.

San Pedro de Flores.

The purported source of the map and its history had been a real place.

It was another piece of the puzzle that was rapidly coming together as she scoured the library's collection. She had also determined that the abbot's map most closely resembled a stretch of coastline located about a hundred and fifty miles north of the monastery, in territory that was now part of the colony of British Honduras.

She even knew the name of the river that constituted the starting point for the journey.

The only sour note so far was the medallion itself. She had compared the glyphs and the iconography of its gruesome carving to the illustrations in the latest works on Mayan archaeology and was forced to admit that it wasn't exactly a perfect match. There seemed to be something just a little off about her artifact, though what, exactly, was hard to pinpoint.

Did that mean the medallion was a forgery? She resisted the conclusion. After all, it was supposed to have come from a Mayan city that survived for centuries after the fall of the rest of their civilization. Surely there would have been changes and developments in their language and artistry over such a period of time. If anything, the discrepancy might actually lend more credence to the mapmaker's tale.

She glanced up at the clock. The library would be closing in fifteen minutes. She would have to leave the rest of the mysteries for another day. She had just enough time for one final bit of research, a task she had intentionally left for the last moment. After all, if it provided the wrong answer, it would shatter the dream she had already begun to build up.

She placed the books she had been studying onto the return cart, then moved to a massive tome that rested on its own pedestal directly beneath the library's elegant dome. It was the atlas.

The greatest library of the most powerful empire in the world made it a point to keep the most up-to-date atlas on hand. The

volume below her would display every landmark of any significance that had been discovered and reported in recent history.

Her hand on the cover, she hesitated, aware of an overwhelming fear. What if she looked inside, only to find that her city was
already mapped and surveyed?

Then there would be no use wasting any more time about it, she
thought, and opened the book.

She stared down at the broad, beautifully inked pages, and the
spread of carefully labeled towns, rivers, and plains representing a
part of the world she had never much thought of before that afternoon. It had just become possibly the most important place on
earth to her, because there, where the abbot's map said her city
must lie, was a vast expanse of mountains across which ran a single miraculous word.

Uncharted.

It was still a long shot, almost certainly an exaggeration, a case
of seventeenth-century gold fever overblowing the story of a few
natives squatting in a set of ruins no different from the places
already marked on the pages before her.

But if it wasn't.

If it was what it claimed to be—the last surviving outpost of the
Mayan world, pristine, hidden, and still waiting to be discovered—
then what, exactly, did she propose to do about it?

The question made her collapse into her chair. The obvious
answer was to report her suspicions to the British Museum, or perhaps write a letter to the Royal Geographical Society. She would,
of course, be expected to turn over the map and the medallion,
and it would be questionable whether either organization would
think the abbot's message worthy of further investigation. After
all, both the museum and the society surely received countless
such leads. They couldn't possibly follow up on all of them. Even
if they did decide this lead was worthy of their attention, where
would that leave Ellie?

She would, at best, be thanked for the initial discovery, then brushed aside as her map was handed off to some more seasoned explorer.

Some more seasoned *man*.

The notion almost made her want to toss the psalter and its contents into the Thames, but the idea that no one would ever put its promises to the test was equally unbearable. Surely there had to be another solution, one that didn't involve destroying her find or being left out in the cold.

And like that, the solution came to her, as elegant as it was audacious.

She would go.

It was not so impossible an idea. She had a map. She had money—five years of her eighty-pound annual salary, to be precise, or the greater part of it. It was more than enough for steamer passage, a guide, and equipment.

She would travel light, move quickly. She just needed to get there. To survey the site, make a record of it. And if she did? Then there would be no man alive who could tell her she was any less capable an archaeologist than the rest of them. She would elbow her way into their world by making one of the greatest discoveries of the age: the last living city of the Mayan civilization.

And after all, she was now unemployed. What else did she have to do?

2

CHARLES HENBURY CURSED AS he sifted through a pile of documents for the fourth time. It *had* to be there somewhere. It had to because Henbury had realized he was very uneasy about how the man he was supposed to meet would react were he to tell him that the promised item was no longer available for purchase.

Perhaps it was what he deserved for offering to sell one of Her Majesty's records, though it was hardly a state paper. If anything it was a misfile, packed in with other evidence filed in a trial against a gang of unlicensed privateers taken prisoner off the Azores. No one had ever even opened it, not until that idiot Johnson. If they had, it most certainly would not have been left to gather dust amid a pile of depositions.

Johnson had thought it a practical joke. Henbury wasn't sure he was wrong. But it had looked real enough to make him think it might be the sort of thing someone would be willing to pay for. And Charles Henbury was not the sort of man to give up on a winning ticket, should it happen to fall into his lap.

He had made inquiries—rather sloppily, he recalled with a wince. But after he'd been laughed or terrified out of a few of the more disreputable taverns, his luck had turned. Someone had come to *him*.

The man called himself Jacobs. He was thin and dark but spoke with a flawless English accent despite a physical appearance that seemed suspiciously foreign. From his look, he might have been some East India Company officer's by-blow or, even worse, an *Arab*.

That hint of some less civilized heritage was the only thing untoward about him, but the man had terrified him on the primal level a mouse might feel when confronted with a hungry cat.

Well, he was a criminal, or Henbury assumed he must be. How else would he have heard about the map? Henbury had very little experience with criminals, but he supposed it was possible that all of them exuded that same cold-blooded aura. He vowed to himself that he would make it a point to avoid the type from here on. Just as soon as this little bit of business had come to a close.

It had all sounded simple enough. Henbury was merely to hold the artifact until Mr. Jacobs returned with someone to authenticate it. The sum Jacobs agreed to consider was more than Henbury had hoped for, and the risk—besides further contact with the unsettling man—was minimal. No one was going to miss what they had never known was there. And Johnson was a blessedly thickheaded man who had likely forgotten the whole thing already, the brunt of his attention taken up by the latest football scores.

But the day appointed for their next meeting had arrived, and Henbury had gone and lost the blasted thing. He did not want to imagine what Mr. Jacobs might be like when disappointed.

As though summoned by Henbury's thoughts, Johnson appeared, poking his head into Henbury's office after a brief rap on the door. He let out a low whistle at the sight of the disarray.

"Looks like someone robbed the place," he quipped cheerfully.

"How many times must I tell you—do *not* come into my office without knocking!" Henbury said through gritted teeth.

"I did knock," Johnson pointed out, stepping inside without waiting for further invitation.

"After knocking, you're supposed to wait for permission. Did I give you permission, Mr. Johnson?"

"A bit late for that now, I'm afraid."

Henbury forced back his temper. "What do you want?"

"I was just letting you know I was heading home for the night. Everyone else has already left. Are you missing something?"

Henbury put his hand to his temple, feeling the threat of a headache. "A book. I've misplaced a book."

"If you're a bit more specific, I might be able to help."

Henbury doubted that, but at this point he was willing to try anything. "It's a seventeenth-century psalter. The one you brought to me a couple of weeks ago."

"The one with the clever little whatsit hidden on the inside?"

"Yes, Johnson," Henbury confirmed tiredly, looking underneath a pile of folders for the twelfth time.

"I saw it this afternoon, as a matter of fact," Johnson said, perking up.

Henbury stopped, looking up at the younger man with flat surprise.

"What?"

"Miss Mallory was looking at it just before I left for lunch."

"Miss Mallory?" Henbury stammered. "Bloody woman…" He pushed past Johnson, hurrying down the hall. He stopped halfway down, turning suddenly.

"Johnson?" he called.

"Yes, Mr. Henbury?" Johnson replied from Henbury's doorway.

"Go home."

"Yes, Mr. Henbury," Johnson agreed, putting on his hat and turning in the opposite direction as Henbury nearly jogged the rest of the way to the archivists' office.

He pushed through the door into the room, which was dim with twilight. He turned on the electric lamp and moved to Eleanora Mallory's elegantly tidy former workstation. It took only a moment for him to riffle through the neat stack of documents on the desk, and the drawers were almost entirely empty. He closed the last of them with a rap, then drummed his fingers on the maple desktop.

With a satisfied grunt, he moved down the hall toward the office that held the building's personnel files. Each one included the employee's name, résumé, yearly review—and, of course, home address.

Florence and David Fairfax had lived in their rooms on Golden Square for as long as Ellie could remember. Certainly long before she lost her parents and came to live with them. The square had changed much over the years, its population shifting from black-suited clerks like her uncle to a still respectable but rather more colorful group of inhabitants. It had become a center for the better-off of some of the city's immigrant communities, and on warmer nights, music and laughter flowed easily from the opened windows.

Ellie loved it, but to her aunt, it meant Golden Square was becoming dangerously unfashionable. She had set her sights on Mayfair, clipping out advertisements from the real estate pages of the *Times*, or dropping not-so-subtle hints over tea in the afternoon—"The Robertsons have gotten themselves a lovely set of rooms near Berkeley Square at a very nice rate."

Her uncle would simply grunt and turn the page of his newspaper. He couldn't care less about the social acceptability of his neighbors. He didn't want to move a block farther from his offices on Fleet Street, where he served as chief accountant with the firm of Wesley and Black.

That was fine with Ellie. Golden Square was as much home as she had ever known, which was why she approached it with her guard comfortably down even though the sun had almost completely set and the lamplighters had yet to make their way to her quiet little corner of the city. Her mind was absorbed by thoughts of crumbling temples and untranslatable glyphs as she climbed the steps, so much so that she registered the sound of voices only once she was already inside, hanging her coat on the hook.

"I expect that's her now," she heard. The drawing room door opened and Aunt Florence leaned into the hall.

"Eleanora, darling, there are some gentlemen here to see you."

The thrill of alarm was instinctive, and her first thought was to laugh it away. It was true that she rarely had any callers at all, and certainly wouldn't have expected anyone Aunt Florence would refer to as a "gentleman." For all she knew, it could be nothing more than the representative of a charity canvassing the local spinsters to see whether any would donate their time to his cause.

So why was her heart pounding away in her chest like a steam engine?

Ellie forced herself to remain calm.

"I'll be right in," she said, and watched as Aunt Florence turned away. She slipped her valise behind the potted fern in the hall, pulled off her gloves, and unpinned her hat. She hesitated only one moment longer, taking a deep breath, and stepped into the room, a polite smile fixed to her face.

Uncle David sat in his customary chair, the evening edition of the *Times* held before him like a shield. The cat, Admiral Nelson, an ancient and lethargic tabby, snored at his feet. Beside them, on the chintz settee, were two men Ellie had never laid eyes on before.

The first was older, a man of middling height and build. Both his hair and beard were pale gray, with hints of lingering ginger. He sat awkwardly on the settee as though aware he did not belong there.

The other stranger stood behind him. He was taller, lean and well-built, with dark hair and eyes and a deeper tone to his skin that looked foreign, though not in any way that Ellie could clearly place.

It was the first man who spoke, however, rising hurriedly from the couch and offering a quick bow.

"Miss Mallory," he said.

"Good evening," she replied coolly.

"Eleanora, this is Professor Dawson and his colleague, Mr. Jacobs," Aunt Florence said. Ellie could hear the disapproval in her tone. The hour was unfashionably late for calling, and Aunt Florence was a stickler for custom.

"We came hoping you could help us with a misplaced document. A missing book, actually," Dawson clarified. "An antique psalter. It was last seen in Assistant Keeper Henbury's office. He thought perhaps you might have borrowed it to examine and forgotten to replace it."

How did they know?

She tried to maintain an expression of polite confusion as her brain spun wildly. How did they know about the psalter? She hadn't mentioned it to anyone, had kept it concealed under her papers even on the table in the library. So how had these two strangers sitting in her living room discovered its existence?

And how had they known where she lived?

The younger of the pair, the one Aunt Florence had called Jacobs, was staring at her with the focus of a hawk. It occurred to her that he was analyzing every nuance of her face and posture. He was watching for a lie, and she felt an unsettling certainty that he was very good at detecting them. She prayed her meager skills as an actress would be up to the challenge.

"A psalter, was it? I'm afraid that's not the sort of thing I usually handle."

"One of your colleagues at the Public Record Office—a Mr. Johnson—claimed he saw you handling this one earlier this afternoon." Dawson wiped a line of sweat from his forehead, though the room was, if anything, slightly cool.

"Then Mr. Johnson must have been mistaken." She smiled apologetically. "I'm afraid you've wasted a journey."

Dawson glanced back at his companion as though for instruction. Jacobs said nothing but continued to regard Ellie with unsettling attention.

"I realize this must seem highly irregular," Dawson said, stumbling a bit over the words. "But would you mind terribly if we took a look in your valise? Perhaps you mistook the book for something else and removed it by accident. The document in question is actually quite important. I'm afraid we have to pursue every possible line of inquiry until it is found."

She felt a brief flash of doubt. What if the book hadn't just been a misfile? Henbury might have been holding on to it for some other reason, and perhaps the strangers in her living room had a legitimate claim on its contents.

The notion sparked a flash of anguish. She didn't want to let the map go, she realized desperately. She already thought of it as *hers*. To come so close to a dream she had very nearly given up on, only to have it snatched away from her was unbearable.

No, she thought, forcing herself to be rational. That couldn't be right. Henbury only handled *public records*. These men were trying to intimidate her into giving herself away.

Well, they wouldn't find it that easy.

"My valise? Of course," Ellie said agreeably. "I entirely understand. I'll fetch it for you." She turned to the door, then paused. "I'm sorry— but what branch of the office was it you said you worked for?"

Dawson looked at her blankly, then glanced to Jacobs, who merely raised an eyebrow.

"I'm just a little curious, you see. I'm quite certain I haven't seen your faces before, and I thought I knew everybody in the building."

"We're not actually employed by the office," Dawson said.

"You aren't?"

"No. We're just—ah—lending some assistance with this particular incident." Dawson lifted a cup of tea from the tray on the table and sipped it. Ellie had the distinct impression that he wanted to hide behind the porcelain.

"I'll just go fetch my bag," she said, and, keeping a deliberately normal pace, stepped out into the hallway.

She picked up the valise and plucked the psalter from inside it. Without a moment's further pause, she slipped the book into the Chinese umbrella stand beside the potted palm, then walked calmly back into the room.

"Here you are," she said pleasantly, handing the valise to Dawson. It took him only a moment to examine the contents. When he closed it and returned it to her, he looked relieved. But behind him, Jacobs gave her an unsettlingly easy smile that dispelled the tiny flame of triumph Ellie had begun to allow herself.

"Thank you, Miss Mallory," the professor said, standing and

wiping his sweating palms on his trousers. "We're sorry for disturbing your evening. You have been most helpful."

"I'll show you out," Aunt Florence offered, and rose, leading the pair back to the hall. Ellie heard the door close a moment later, and Uncle David returned to his paper with a harrumph.

"Inconvenient hour for calling," he muttered.

Aunt Florence ducked into the room. "I'll see if dinner is ready," she said, then moved away again.

Acting on instinct, Ellie hurried up the stairs to her room, which looked out over the square. There, in the light of the gas lamp across the green from the house, two figures stood talking. Ellie could see the professor gesturing vehemently. Almost—to Ellie's eyes—pleadingly. She saw Jacobs, apparently unmoved. He turned toward where she stood, and despite the distance, she could see the cool, assessing look in his eyes.

The realization was like a blow to the stomach—a sudden certainty that he *knew*. He knew she had what they were looking for. He knew she had lied to him, and he didn't care. Jacobs's look was that of a man who had no doubt that he would achieve his aim and was indifferent as to the method.

He would be back. And Ellie suspected that those methods would be something less scrupulous next time. Whoever the pair were and however they had found her, there was an aura of danger around them that she felt certain wasn't imagined.

She knew what the sensible course of action should have been. She should have simply handed them what they were looking for. Or if not them, then she should have returned it to Henbury, whose desk she had gotten the blasted thing from in the first place.

The idea repelled her. Henbury didn't deserve it. Neither did these strangers, whoever they were. Perhaps the book wasn't technically hers, but in that moment her instincts told her with utter certainty that Professor Dawson and Mr. Jacobs had no real right to it, either.

This was her chance—very likely the only one she would ever have—to make the life she'd dreamed of a reality. She would not simply hand the psalter over to the first thug who showed up and demanded it.

But she could not let Aunt Florence and Uncle David get drawn into this. She would have to make it clear that they had no part in this business. As she stood in the window, watching the professor lose whatever argument the pair had been having, she realized there was only one way for her to do that.

Ellie raced down the stairs, grabbing her coat and tugging it on as she passed the hook. She burst into the drawing room, her guardians looking up at her, startled.

"Where on earth do you think you're off to?" Aunt Florence demanded.

"Out," Ellie replied breathlessly. She kissed her aunt on the cheek, then quickly clasped and shook Uncle David's hand. "I'll wire," she promised.

"Wire?" Uncle David asked, confused.

"But you're not wearing a hat!"

Ellie ran to the hall, Aunt Florence's cry ringing behind her.

Plucking the psalter from the umbrella stand, Ellie dashed out the door and down the front steps. Then she lifted the book over her head and gave what she knew to be an exceptionally loud whistle.

Across the square, Gilbert Dawson sighted the slight, feminine figure waving her prize over her head. His stomach sank like lead.

Not again, he thought to himself. *Please don't let this turn out like Ostrask.*

Ostrask.

The name haunted him. A collection of hovels in a desolate corner of the Carpathians, Ostrask hardly deserved to be called a village. But Dawson would remember that miserable place until he died. How could he forget it, after what he had seen there?

Such horror.

It would all have been fine if he could just be left to his library, to his books and journals, his notes and sketches. That was where he flourished, where he truly belonged. Once, perhaps, he had nurtured ambitions to distinguish himself in the field, but even before he had begun work for his new employer, those had largely languished in favor of a preference for his comfortable easy chair, his glass of port in the evening, and a cozy fireplace to drink it by.

His new employer. How could he really have believed that working for such a man would be nothing but books and journals? It had been clear enough the moment they had met in a cell beneath the Edinburgh jail.

Dawson, the distinguished professor of ancient history, had sat in that dark filth awaiting the hangman's noose—justly awaiting it.

He had never thought himself capable of murder, and certainly not the hot, berserk slaughter of someone he had once loved.

There was nothing in his history that pointed to this capacity for violence, hidden inside of him. Dawson had never been involved in so much as a brawl. He barely raised his voice during the most frustrating and heated academic debates.

Drink. That was the culprit he grasped upon. He had never been a heavy drinker, but that night, the two—or was it three?—glasses of whiskey he consumed had resulted in an unusual intoxication.

Perhaps that was all it took. Perhaps there was an animal lurking under the civilized facade of every man, waiting for its moment to emerge.

It was a terrifying notion.

Dawson had tried to resign himself to the death he knew he deserved. Then a man walked in and offered him a second chance.

He was an utterly unremarkable figure, middling in height and slightly balding, with a comfortably bulging stomach under his plain waistcoat. Only his eyes revealed something deeper, a sharp and penetrating intelligence.

He had offered Dawson a deal: his life, in exchange for agreeing to work as his employee for an indefinite time. When Dawson asked after the nature of the work, he was told merely that it would be a research position. The matter of his studies was to be kept private. There would be no publishing, no discussions with his fellow academics. Discretion was a primary requirement for the position. Could Dawson be relied upon?

Dawson could. What did he care for journal articles and conferences when his life was on the line?

He had consented with little more than a moment's thought. Only three days later he had been released, the case against him dismissed. When he stepped outside the door, he had expected the man from the jail to meet him. But it was Jacobs who bundled him onto the train to London, Jacobs who delivered him to the town house there that had been prepared for him. From that day to this, Dawson had never again been graced with the presence of the man who saved him. He continued to live in almost complete ignorance of who had pulled the strings that gained him his release. What he knew could be counted off on a single hand.

He was powerful. No simple man could free a murderer from prison with the snap of his fingers.

He was ruthless. Ostrask had taught him that.

And the interest that drove that power and ruthlessness was both bizarre and specific.

Dawson's work—the employment for which he had been liberated from a just execution—consisted of a series of research assignments. Jacobs would arrive on his doorstep at irregular intervals, carrying a plain yellow envelope. Inside, Dawson would find a typed note with some frustratingly obscure request. He was to provide details about a particular artifact, or dig up the roots of a little-known myth. Magical cauldrons, legendary swords, kings with godlike powers . . . the assignments crossed cultures and eras, skipping around history like stones on the surface of a pond. The only thing that connected them was their strangeness.

But what did Dawson care? He was a researcher by both trade and inclination, and thrived on digging out secret threads of knowledge. It was only the mystery of it that nagged at him. Why had these pieces of ancient trivia been worth the trouble of organizing his exoneration? What did they say about the man who now controlled his destiny?

His lingering ignorance about his employer was the only dark mark in what had otherwise proved a remarkably pleasant existence.

Dawson was given what every scholar dreamed of: seemingly unlimited resources to acquire whatever texts he desired. Was there a rare tome on Egyptian hieroglyphics available only at Sotheby's for a prohibitive reserve? He merely need mention it, and a few days later it would arrive at his door. He had an entire town house to himself with a set of taciturn but dependable servants. There were crackling fires and a choice of easy chairs. After a few weeks, he had found himself so comfortable that when he spotted a small article in the newspaper about the execution of a foreign itinerant convicted of murdering one Anne Dawson, he felt only a quick pang of guilt that someone else had suffered the punishment Dawson justly deserved. The feeling was largely overwhelmed by a shaking sense of relief. In that moment, Dawson had discovered an uncomfortable but undeniable truth about himself: He was, in his essence, a profoundly selfish man.

After all, whether he worked for a criminal mob or a determined and unorthodox collector, Dawson was alive. A bit of mystery and the death of one poor Russian peasant whom he'd never so much as set eyes on seemed a small price to pay.

He knew better now.

Before Ostrask, it had never occurred to Dawson to question what the consequences might be should he decide he no longer wished to continue his employment. Why should he? The job was an academic's dream.

Ostrask changed all of that. After what he witnessed there, Dawson wanted nothing more than to escape, to get as far from Jacobs and his master as he possibly could.

That was when he realized *there was no escape*.

A man who was capable of saving Dawson from the gallows could just as easily return him to them, or deliver him to an even viler fate.

No polite letter of resignation would end this contract. Dawson was as much a prisoner now as he had been in Edinburgh. Those months spent in the cozy confines of his library were an illusion. His captivity was comfortable only by default. At any moment he could be yanked from that familiar world and thrown into a nightmare.

But the worst part of all was that *it didn't matter.* Dawson was still a coward. He knew he would do anything—*anything*—to cling to the life he'd been granted. To survive.

Even if it meant living in hell, with a devil beside him.

When Jacobs arrived on his doorstep that afternoon, Dawson had known, with a sinking, terrified feeling, that his world was about to be shattered once again.

Just authenticate the map, he had said. *A short excursion to The City.*

But after their meeting with Henbury, Dawson had jogged along behind Jacobs to the telephone office, where Dawson had sat on a bench between a large-bosomed woman with a squalling infant and an elderly man with a prodigious snore while Jacobs made and received a round of calls. In what seemed to Dawson a surrealistically quick amount of time, he had received new orders from their superior. The day's work was far from over, and they began the trek to Golden Square.

He saw the look in Jacobs's eyes as they riveted themselves on the figure of the girl, standing there boldly on the doorstep with the book in her hand, daring them to come for it. Dawson had an unwelcome suspicion that the night was going to get even more unpleasant before it was over.

"This what you're looking for?" she shouted across the green.

Then, to Dawson's horror, she dropped it into her pocket and dashed down the pavement away from them in a sprint that was not the least bit ladylike.

Jacobs was after her like a hound on a fox. Dawson made a futile effort to follow but was immediately outpaced. He fell back, hands to his thighs, panting.

"God help her," he muttered grimly.

Ellie could hear the pounding footsteps behind her and knew with a sinking heart that she would not be able to simply outrun her pursuer. She was going to have to lose him, and quickly.

Dodging a pair of carriages, she dashed onto the road and turned toward the glow of bright lights a few short blocks away—the shining shop windows of Regent Street.

She burst onto a wooden pavement packed with bodies. She forced her way into the crowd between a pair of grande dames clutching spaniels in their arms, followed by footmen staggering under the weight of a dozen packages. A street urchin skidded out of her path as she ran forward, slipping nimbly through ephemeral gaps in the press of bodies fashionable and rough, old and young. Hawkers flashed their wares at her, calling in high voices, and gasps of indignation followed her as she used her shoulders to wedge her way through the crowd.

She risked a glance behind her. She could see Jacobs doing the same, the bodies in his path seeming to part more readily. He was gaining on her.

She vaulted over a vendor's crate of young, yapping poodles and stumbled off the pavement onto Regent Street itself. She heard the shout of an angry coachman and stepped nimbly out of the path of heavy wheels.

At this time of night, traffic on the street was near a standstill, and for once Ellie was grateful for it. She dodged among the carriages, surprised faces gesturing at her through windows, giving herself a bit more of a lead on Jacobs—a lead she knew was temporary.

She caught sight of a glittering facade—Liberty, Regent Street's most luxurious emporium, its windows glittering with silk kimonos and graceful Oriental tables. Wheeling abruptly, she ducked past the attendant, who was holding the door for a pair of elderly, top-hatted gentlemen, and ran inside.

The grand atrium soared overhead. Its glass ceiling was dark now, but Ellie had seen it by day, filling the impressive space with light. It was still impressive in the dusk of evening, the sunlight replaced by the gleam of hundreds of electric lamps. It was also far too open.

Shouts sounded behind her, and Ellie dashed into the ladies' department. She raced past glass-topped counters with displays of gloves and leather wallets.

There was another bark of protest from the atrium. Ellie knew what it meant. Jacobs hadn't missed her maneuver. He had followed her into the store.

She looked around frantically. She needed someplace to hide, but ducking behind a Chinese armoire full of silk scarves didn't seem like it would fool Jacobs for more than a moment.

Her eye lit on a more promising possibility: a heavy damask curtain hanging across the far wall. The colors nearly blended into the beige silk of the wallpaper, making it almost invisible at first glance.

She ran for it as the outraged exclamations of the wealthy matrons browsing the front of the department told her Jacobs was getting closer.

A thin young shopgirl clutched her arm, eyes wide, as Ellie reached the curtain.

"Miss, you can't…"

"Please," Ellie begged. She pressed a coin into the girl's hand, then slipped behind the damask before she could make any further protest.

She peered anxiously through the narrow gap between the curtain and the wall, watching as Jacobs stalked into view. He paused, scanning the space. She saw his gaze linger on the armoire, then move on to the shopgirl, who stood gaping at him.

"Did a woman come through here?" he demanded.

The shopgirl raised her hand and pointed to the rear of the store, a warren of fabric samples and cutting tables.

Ellie felt her shoulders sag with relief, then detected an odd, muffled murmur behind her. She turned and saw an array of equally surprised faces staring back at her. It seemed she had selected the brightly lit shop window for a hiding place. A little girl, her cheeks stained red from the lollipop she held, waved at her. Ellie flashed her a nervous smile, then ducked back into the store.

She paused by the shopgirl.

"I had a beau like that myself," the girl said before Ellie could speak. She shuddered. "Best hurry."

Ellie swallowed the instinctive retort that Jacobs was nothing remotely approaching her "beau."

"Thank you," she muttered, then moved quickly back the way she had come, slipping amid the shoppers crowding the grand atrium.

She made her way to the door just as a clatter and raised voices resounded from the ladies' department.

The door attendant's eyes widened with recognition as Ellie approached, and she saw him open his mouth to protest. She was gone before he could call, slipping into the crowd that packed the wide pavement.

She let the river of movement carry her forward. She knew her chances now depended on blending in. She needed to look as much like one of the crowd as she could while hatless and flushed from a chase.

It was a fine sort of torture, forcing herself to move with the plodding pace of the crowd, refusing to glance back and see whether she was safe, or if Jacobs stalked behind her like a tiger after a gazelle.

Just to the next corner, she made herself swear. It seemed to take an eternity, but when at last she reached it, she took a neat step to the side, ducking behind a carriage stopped to unload a gaggle of giggling debutantes.

She peered around the side of the coach and was rewarded with a glimpse of Jacobs standing by the entrance to Liberty.

He looked up and down the street with clear frustration, then turned abruptly and punched the lamppost, earning a surprised look from a pair of nearby loungers. He stalked away in the opposite direction, fading into the crowd.

Ellie let out a breath she hadn't realized she was holding and stepped back into the press of bodies as the carriage pulled away. She remained hidden in the ranks of fashionable shoppers until at last she reached Oxford Street, and waved her hand to hail a passing hackney.

The driver frowned at her, and Ellie realized how she must look, her face red from exertion, hair wild, and hatless.

"Stanwick Gardens, Bayswater." She pulled out a coin and pushed it into his hand. "You can keep the change."

The driver shrugged and she climbed in, sinking back against the worn upholstery with relief.

The hackney rattled to a halt at a quiet corner lined with the tall, graceful forms of town houses with early flowers springing from window boxes. The driver opened the door for her, his attitude having improved with his tip and her destination.

The very air smelled cleaner, the lamplight seeming to shine with greater elegance. She could hear the sound of chamber music echoing from one of the houses, accompanied by laughter and voices. A stately carriage rolled down the street, and a pair of well-dressed older gentlemen strolled by, their walking sticks tapping evenly on the pavement.

She walked past the entrance to Stanwick Gardens, slipping instead into the mews that ran behind the great houses. She moved along in the gloom until she found a familiar spot in the brick wall adjoining one of the carriage houses. She grabbed the gaps that formed such ideal handholds in its surface and hauled herself up. It was comforting to know they hadn't changed in the ten years or so since she'd last used this entrance.

She paused at the top of the wall, listening for the voices of the footmen. The coast looked clear. She swung her legs over, turned, and let herself down onto the soft, still-damp spring grass.

The garden was quiet. Ellie avoided the places where light spilled through the windows, keeping to the shadows until she reached the house. Stooping, she picked up a pebble from the path and threw it with sharp accuracy at an upstairs window.

The sash was raised a moment later and a very pretty blond head appeared, peering out into the darkness with a little frown.

"Who's down there?" she demanded.

"Constance!" Ellie whispered.

"Ellie?"

Ellie stepped to the edge of the shadows, and her friend's face shone with a bright grin.

"What a delightful surprise! Do tell me you've gotten yourself into trouble. Preferably the sort involving a man."

"For the love of…can I come inside before the coachman sees me?"

"I'll be right down," Constance promised. The blond head vanished from the window, and a few moments later the back door opened, Constance motioning to her from inside of it.

Ellie hurried across the lawn and slipped in after her friend. Constance put a warning hand on her arm. Her hair was braided loosely, and she wore a silk-embroidered dressing gown over her lace-edged nightdress.

"Robert has a load of MPs over to dinner. I pleaded headache and slipped off to pack—lucky for you. They're dreadfully boring," she whispered.

Ellie had never quite gotten used to Constance's habit of referring to her father—Sir Robert Tyrrell, CMG, and deputy chairman of the Department of Inland Revenue—as Robert.

She held back as Constance scouted down the hall, returning a moment later.

"They're in the library at their port," she said, her tone more relaxed. She grasped Ellie's hand. "Come on."

Constance led her down the hallway, creeping past the door leading to the light, clatter, and voices of the kitchens. They skirted around a fern and up the darkened, narrow servants' stairwell. The smaller girl motioned Ellie back as she scouted the upstairs hall, then stepped quickly past a row of ornate brass wall sconces with electric lights illuminating ancient oil paintings and tapestries, finally half shoving her through one of the doorways. She closed it behind them and, taking a key from her nightstand, turned the lock.

The room was a maelstrom of feminine disarray. Several trunks littered the floor, spilling out lacy undergarments and khaki jackets, satin gloves and parasols.

"Packing," Constance said by explanation with an idle wave of her hand as Ellie took in the chaos. "You heard about Robert's promotion?"

"Promotion? No," Ellie said, distracted. She sat down on the only uncluttered spot on the bedspread.

"Financial adviser to the khedive of Egypt," Constance announced proudly. "Isn't that marvelously exciting?"

"He was there before, wasn't he?" Ellie recalled.

Constance nodded. "Before he went to India. Now he'll be running the finances of the entire country and—more important—I get to go with him. Can you believe it?" Constance clasped her hands, practically hopping with excitement. "He was dead against it, of course, especially my missing a season and all, but I managed to convince him. I'll be there for the year. Then he plans to ship me back to Aunt Cat to see if she can have any luck marrying me off."

"You could be married anytime you like," Ellie pointed out.

"I imagine I could, if I didn't mind saddling myself with someone who would bore me for the rest of my days. I swear to you, every eligible man in this city is interminably dull. The whole lot of them. It's an epidemic."

She sighed, tossed aside a stack of hats, and collapsed elegantly onto her dressing table chair.

"Egypt for a whole year—isn't that magnificent? But I'm letting myself get entirely distracted. This can't be simply a social call. I haven't had one of those from you in months, and they weren't generally made in the dark over the garden wall."

"I know. I'm terribly sorry. I've just been so busy. . . ."

"Sod that. I'm not admonishing you. I'm glad at least one of us can do something worthwhile with her time."

"What about your book?" Ellie asked. The ease of chatting with her old schoolmate kept distracting her from her own strange situation.

"Blocked!" Constance exclaimed, throwing up her hands. "Blocked for months. I'm entirely in a rut. It's dreadful."

Since Ellie had met Constance Tyrrell while at Dame Mary Nottingham's School for Girls, her friend had one sole and overriding ambition: to write novels. She was determined to oust H. Rider Haggard as the preeminent adventure writer of her age. Of course, Ellie had yet to read anything Constance had written. It seemed very little survived the fireplace, where she wrathfully resigned her inadequate drafts.

"Enough about that. I demand to know what you've gotten yourself into."

Wordlessly, Ellie removed the psalter from her pocket and opened it. She placed the black medallion in Constance's hand.

"What on earth is it?" the other woman asked wonderingly, examining the strange object.

"There's this as well," Ellie said, and unfolded the map on the floor. Constance knelt down beside it, eyes wide.

"Is this really . . . ?"

Ellie nodded. "I checked it out in the library. It's entirely possible it's a hoax, but I can't prove that it isn't, either."

"An honest-to-God treasure map," Constance finished.

"I wouldn't say 'treasure,'" Ellie protested.

Constance ignored her. "Where on earth did you get it?"

Ellie felt a slight wave of guilt. "I stole it," she admitted.

Constance clapped her hands together with delight. "Oh, fantastic!"

The rest of the story spilled out of her, from the theft of the book to her flight up Regent Street. Constance listened with rapt attention.

"I didn't know where else to go," Ellie admitted. "But I know I wasn't followed. I wouldn't have come anywhere near here if—"

"Oh, stop. It's a good thing you did come here. It sounds like you're truly up to your neck in this one."

"No," Ellie said, shaking her head. "Not necessarily. I could still give it back."

"They'd kill you anyway," Constance asserted boldly, throwing herself down in her chair.

"Kill me? Don't be so dramatic. Killing is far more trouble in real life than it is in novels. Even if those men are some sort of ruthless criminal types, I don't see that they'd bother if they have what they want."

"So that's it, then." Constance visibly drooped with disappointment.

"Hardly," Ellie replied, her voice clipped. "I said I *could* give it to them. I didn't say I would." She stood and began to pace the floor, picking her way absently through the few spaces not cluttered with fashionable debris. "How would those men have even known the thing existed?"

"That's obvious," Constance asserted. "Your Mr. Henbury was clearly planning to sell it to them."

"Henbury? Selling Crown property?" Ellie found the concept difficult to believe. It was not so much that Henbury seemed like the scrupulous type, but more that she couldn't imagine him being bold enough to even think of such a thing.

"Ellie, just look at this!" Constance's gesture took in both the map and the medallion. "Even a dolt can see it's the sort of thing someone would be willing to pay for. Possibly a rather large sum, if it's as promising a piece as you say it is."

"It would make sense," Ellie admitted.

"And when he found that the item was missing, he offered them the next-best thing. You," Constance finished proudly. "How else would they have known your address? Henbury must have guessed that you took the map and told them exactly where to find you."

"The devil…" Ellie cursed, feeling a quick burst of outrage. She knew Charles Henbury had no fondness for her, but the notion that he would turn her over so readily to a set of criminals made her rather indignant.

"Eleanora…"

Her friend's tone had changed, and Ellie forced her mind away from dire musings on what she would do to Henbury if she ever got her hands on him.

Constance was gingerly lifting the black medallion from where she had set it down on the bedspread. But it was not coming alone. A small collection of hairpins had adhered themselves to its black surface. Constance gave it a small shake, but the pins stayed put.

"Your stone appears to be magnetic," she announced, raising an eyebrow.

Ellie frowned, coming over and taking the medallion from Constance's hand. She pulled loose one of the pins, then brought it gradually closer to the dark disk. When it got within an inch, the pin leaped from her fingers to join its brethren on the carved surface.

"You're right," she said wonderingly, turning it over in her hands.

"This is getting more intriguing by the minute," Constance asserted excitedly. "And these men of yours—who do you suppose they are to want the map so badly? A ring of ruthless antiquities thieves, perhaps?"

"I doubt it's anything so dramatic," Ellie said, forcing back the sense of wonder the discovery of the strange properties of the medallion had evoked in her. She plucked off the hairpins and returned the disk to the safety of the hollow psalter. "Even ordinary thieves would see the potential for a tidy profit if they were able to find the right buyer."

"So what are you going to do about it?" Constance demanded.

The question made Ellie sink down into a chair.

"I don't know," she said helplessly.

Instead of replying, Constance brushed aside a stack of poorly folded blouses and pulled out a thick blue book. She flipped it open and browsed nimbly through the pages before stabbing one triumphantly with an elegant finger.

"Brilliant. Positively ideal."

"What is?"

"The steamer timetable. You'll leave tomorrow morning."

"Leave for where?"

"British Honduras, of course. That is where you said this map of yours picks up, isn't it?"

"Yes, but—"

Constance raised an eloquent eyebrow. "Don't tell me you weren't considering it."

"Of course I was considering it," Ellie retorted. "But an expedition to the deep jungle is not to be undertaken lightly. There are preparations that must be made. Equipment, supplies. . . . I was hoping to take a few weeks as a research period to refresh my knowledge of Central American prehistory. My degree focus was primarily on Egypt and the classics, you'll recall. And there are physical exercises I should undertake to prepare for—"

"Bollocks." The word sounded particularly shocking coming from such a pretty mouth. Constance crossed her arms, determination clear in every inch of her frame. "You have a degree in ancient history. That's as much as any man would have before setting out on an expedition. You can buy your equipment when you arrive in Central America. And it would appear that a traveler's boutique has exploded in this room. I can supply you with a complete traveling wardrobe. Aunt Cat is still convinced I'm three inches taller, or else expects me to wear impossible heels. There are piles of things she's given me for Egypt that will fit you perfectly."

"What about a guide?"

"You're hardly going to find a guide to the unexplored jungle here in London."

"Funds," Ellie offered, scrabbling for an objection Constance couldn't just brush aside. "I have money in the bank, yes, but I can hardly withdraw it at five in the morning. That steamer will leave with the outgoing tide."

"I'll fund you. I've got a stack of circular notes in that desk. You can pay me back when you return, if you like. Or not. You may have a bit of cash squirreled away, but Robert has piles, and you're hardly going to be a major investment. You'll simply have to credit me as your sponsor when you find this delicious city of yours."

"There's no guarantee it even exists."

"The mystery is half the fun."

"It will be dangerous."

Constance sighed. "And that's the other half of the fun. After all, you're hardly defenseless. It was rather handy for that college chum of your cousin's to have boarded with the Shaolin monks, and being amenable to sharing a few of those clever maneuvers they taught him with a lady."

"Wushu," Ellie filled in absently. Her cousin Neil's friend, Trevelyan Perry, was the sort of man women deliberately fainted in front of. He wasn't exceptionally tall, but what he lacked in height he more than made up in charm. With his dark hair, regular features, and devastating smile, Ellie was sure he made more than a few knees weak every time he stepped into a society ballroom.

Her own interest in Mr. Perry had nothing to do with his smile. When he had casually mentioned that the martial arts he had learned in China were as easy for a woman to perform as a man, Ellie had immediately perked up. It had never seemed fair to her that a female had to resort to weapons in order to prevent herself from being accosted, should she be so foolish as to wish to exercise her right to walk the city without a man or a gaggle of lady escorts. During his stay at Golden Square, Ellie had taken every opportunity available to pull Perry out into the yard and demand he teach her everything he knew.

She shook her head. "If Neil had any idea what we were up to..." She glanced over at Constance. "You still remember those moves I showed you?"

"I make Edwards practice with me every Tuesday," she replied.

Ellie felt a momentary flash of sympathy for the Tyrrell family but-
ler, though being on the receiving end of Constance's martial arts
was probably not the worst of what the long-suffering Edwards
was subjected to.

"You realize I'm dreadfully jealous, don't you? I thought Egypt
sounded like an adventure, but what you're about to do will make
Cairo look like a stroll through Hyde Park." Constance's tone grew
serious. "You can do this, Ellie," she said quietly.

Ellie stopped her pacing, looking down at the map.

"I really could, couldn't I?" Ellie replied wonderingly. "What a
fantastic notion that is."

"Don't even begin to pretend it was my idea. You knew the minute you saw that map that this was the way it would go. I'm just the
angel on your shoulder."

"Are you sure you're the angel?"

Constance flashed her a wicked grin, then sobered.

"Be careful, Ellie. But not too careful." She clapped her hands.
"Now, let's kit you out."

Ellie gave in, throwing up her hands. "As you wish, Miss
Tyrrell."

Constance's eyes brightened. "This is going to be ever so fun!"

While the rest of the city contemplated another half hour in bed,
the West India Docks shrieked, shouted, and whistled. The tide
had turned at five, and the outgoing ships did not want to miss
their chance to let the current carry them to sea. Ellie's hackney
had to fight its way through streets already bustling with vendors
crying their wares to men and women hurrying to shifts at the
docks, factories, and warehouses that crowded the Isle of Dogs.

She sat against the cushioned seat, her heart pounding in her
chest. She hadn't slept, spending the remainder of the night with
Constance getting outfitted for the journey. Part of that outfitting
had involved an impressive sum in circular notes, which meant
that Ellie would now be traveling as Miss Constance Tyrrell.

"Which is just as well, anyway," Constance had mused as Ellie practiced her signature. "If they're checking ships' registries, it's best they don't see your name."

"You think they'll check?"

"Certainly," Constance asserted. "But not for a while. You are still a woman. They *will* underestimate you. You have that on them, as well as your lead."

There had been only one more stop to make before heading to the docks—the Central Telegraph Office. It had been Constance's idea.

"Bournemouth. We'll tell David and Florence you've gone for a bit of a holiday. I've got a cousin there. I'll have her send the telegram, so it will look right if anyone is checking. That should buy you a few more days."

It would also save her aunt and uncle quite a bit of worry, Ellie thought. The concern she knew they would feel if they discovered where she'd truly gone was the only thing impeding her growing excitement as the wild notion she had formed in those last moments at the British Library became more and more firmly a reality.

Ellie watched as her trunk—Constance's trunk—was hoisted up the gangplank, headed for the berth Constance had just secured for her, happily paying full price. There was time only for the pair to share a brief embrace before Ellie had to board.

"Have a magnificent adventure," Constance said.

"Thank you," Ellie said sincerely, grasping her hand. Then she turned and hurried up the gangplank. A moment later it was pulled in, and the dock lines were loosed. The great boat whistled its way from the pier. Ellie watched a small blond figure waving to her from the dock. Constance blew her a kiss, then stepped back into the waiting hackney.

She remained by the rail long after Constance had departed, watching as London receded behind her in the rosy light of dawn. The stink of the Thames began to lighten into the salty freshness of the shore, and Ellie felt something stretch and open inside of her. It grew greater as the river gave way to the wide blue sea that would take her to her destination—one step closer to the life of her dreams.

3

The Imperial Hotel, Belize City, May 2, 1898

ADAM BATES WAS EXHAUSTED, mosquito-bitten, and covered in what he hoped was mostly mud. He had spent the morning shouldering a mule out of a fetid sinkhole. It was hardly his ideal way of passing the time, but the long dry season had left water levels low, and the ground under his usual path through the marshes had given way. It was get in and push, or leave the animal for the vultures. Last time Adam had gone into the bush, he'd lost three mules. If he came back short this time, he was fairly certain Frederico would refuse to rent to him again.

He knew he looked like hell. He felt like hell, so in all honesty it was only fair. As he watched a very respectable-looking family flee the serene, palm-lined oasis of the Imperial Hotel's lobby at the sight of him, his slight twinge of regret was quickly overwhelmed by the desire to get to his room and stop moving for a while. And then there was the Imperial's bath: gorgeously tiled in cool white with the big, enameled tub full of piped-in hot water. At the moment, soaking his trail-sore bones in that tub sounded like paradise.

The hotel's owner, Augustus Smith, emerged from his office and stopped short at the sight of Adam standing in his lobby.

"For the love of Pete..." Smith's accent was thick Northumberland, though his tan made it clear he was far from new to the tropics.

"Sinkhole," Adam explained. "I was only three miles out. Nearly lost a mule."

"Frederico would never have leased you another. Not after—"

"I remember," Adam interrupted.

Smith regarded him resignedly.

"Couldn't you have rinsed off in the harbor or something before you came up? Or at least put that broadsword of yours into your pack?" Smith glanced unhappily at the machete Adam wore in a sheath at his belt. Since it was covered in muck like the rest of him, Adam thought it was rather less conspicuous than usual, but he didn't bother to argue.

"It's been a long trip."

Smith limited his response to a disapproving sigh, then handed Adam a key from the rack behind his desk. After the fifth time Smith had been forced to call a locksmith to get Adam back into his room, he had insisted the key be left at the desk when Adam went on one of his expeditions.

"Has anyone—"

"God, no," Smith said, anticipating the question. "No one's cracked the door, not for so much as a dusting. Not after last time."

"Sorry about that." Adam grimaced.

"You did warn us," Smith admitted. "Oh! Your mail." He pulled out a stack of letters and passed them to Adam. A quick glance showed him that all of them were return-addressed to San Francisco, which told him clearly enough what they would contain—missives from his mother berating him for wasting his time in the jungle when he should be preparing to take over the family business. Adam mentally pictured himself walking into the boardroom of Robinson, Bates, and MacKenzie in his current state, and smiled. It would almost be worth the trip to see the look on his father's officers' faces.

Smith called to him as he turned for the stairs.

"Put your dinner clothes out and I'll have them brushed for you."

"I'll be decent," Adam promised, then crossed to the steps, leaving a trail of flaking mud behind him.

Ellie Mallory was feeling marvelous. She was wearing Constance's dressing gown, a long affair of silk embroidered with gorgeous peacock feathers in a bright, rich aqua. She sat on the cushioned stool, feeling comfortably rested, and pulled the last pin from her hair, relaxing it gloriously with her fingers.

She had not expected to find such a luxurious space in a remote colonial town that hardly qualified as a city, whatever the pretensions of its name. The hotel's bath was beautiful, from the blue-and-white-tiled walls to the frosted glass that let in the light of the afternoon sun without risking any immodest peeks from the outside world. A shelf was packed with soft freshly laundered towels. A towel rack stood beside the tub, a piece of gleaming, polished chrome, so that she could wrap herself up as soon as she emerged from her soak. And then there was the tub itself: massive, claw-footed, and currently filling with steaming-hot water from a modern tap.

She even found lavender-scented soap on the little table beside the sink. She had added some of the flakes to the tub, and they were currently covering its surface with fragrant bubbles.

It was everything she hadn't known she wanted when she had left her cabin on the steamer *Salerno* earlier that morning, making her way through Belize City's admittedly relaxed customs building to the shore, where the owner of the hotel had been waiting to escort her. Accommodations on the boat had been comfortable enough, but fresh water had been in short supply, limiting washing to ablutions at a basin. It was all well and good. Her aunt and uncle didn't have the luxury of a separate bathroom in their suite at Golden Square. But the fact that one was readily available at the hotel had made her aware of a griminess and exhaustion she hadn't known she was feeling.

It was just one of a series of delightful experiences she'd had since arriving. The warmth of the air, the way the breeze caressed her skin even through the linen of her traveling suit—the broad turquoise blue of the bay and the rich colors of the flowering vines draped over walls and fences—all of it was intoxicatingly lovely. Even the hotel itself—which would at best have been called "modest" in London terms—had a number of charming features beyond its remarkable bathroom. The long wooden building fronted the street, separated from the light traffic by a shoulder-height fence. Beyond the fence lay a narrow strip of grass, palms, and flowering shrubs, lending a tropical air to the shaded patio that lay outside the doors to the ground-floor rooms. A similar patio bordered the rooms on the reverse side of the building, though these looked out over a small but luxuriously verdant garden. A broad veranda ran the full length of the upper floor of the building on both the rear and street-facing sides. Ellie's room opened onto it with airy French doors. Stepping outside provided a view of the garden and the ramshackle houses beyond. Farther off, at the very edge of the horizon, Ellie could see the hazy green of the mountains, soft as a watercolor brushstroke against the blue of the sky. The sight had called to her, sirenlike, promising mystery and adventure.

The tub gurgled, warning her that the water had gone as high as the overflow drain would allow. She stepped over and closed the tap, the sound of the last drops echoing softly off the tiled walls. She reached for the tie of her robe, readying herself to step in, then paused as a flicker of movement tickled the corner of her eye.

She looked down at the water, frowning. The surface was covered in suds, wafting the light scent of lavender to her nose. As she watched, the bubbles rippled. Then a sleek black form cut swiftly through the foam, and a narrow black head lifted from the water. Yellow eyes gazed into her own, and quite in spite of herself, Ellie shrieked.

Adam had been about to turn back to his room, frustrated by the Occupied sign outside the bathroom door, when the sound of a very female, very alarmed scream stopped him in his tracks. His response was instant and instinctual. Pulling his knife from its sheath, he steeled himself, raced toward the door, and broke it open.

The woman inside whirled at the sound. Her slender form was covered only by a light silk bathrobe, her chestnut hair falling in loose tendrils around her shoulders. Pale gray eyes stared at him with an expression of mingled horror and surprise.

In an awkward moment of epiphany, Adam realized what he must look like to her—a filth-covered stranger in tattered shirt-sleeves and bare feet who had just broken through the door to the bathroom, wielding a twelve-inch machete.

Maybe he could have planned that better.

Please don't faint, he thought desperately.

"What the devil do you think you're doing?" she demanded, her surprise quickly replaced by righteous indignation. The tone threw cold water on Adam's brain, reminding him why he'd made the intrusion in the first place.

"What was it?" he asked, moving into the room, knife ready.

"What was what?" she retorted.

"The thing you were screaming at," he elaborated with forced patience.

Her sense of outrage seemed to be rising exponentially. Ignoring his question, she pointed imperiously toward the door.

"Get out."

"Listen, lady," Adam drawled, preparing to offer her a quick lecture on worrying about the rules of propriety in an emergency situation. But a small splash from the tub, and the way she immediately jumped and turned toward the sound, told him where he would find what he was looking for.

He moved forward swiftly on his bare feet, putting himself between the woman and the tub. He grabbed hold of her elbow, steering her toward the corner, the machete ready in his other hand as he studied the surface of the water. The woman would have had to fill the thing with soap bubbles, of course.

"Let go of me," she demanded, squirming in his grip.

"Stop moving," he ordered.

Ellie felt her temper flare.

Stop moving?

Who the devil did he think he was? The man had broken down

the door and come barreling into the room as if he owned it. To top it off, he looked as though he had recently crawled out of a swamp. Every inch of his body was covered with mud, save for a pair of sharply contrasting blue eyes. Who else but a lunatic would be wandering around the halls of a hotel looking like *that*?

She felt a quick flash of outrage. Giving off one alarmed squeak at the sight of something unexpected splashing in her tub hardly justified being manhandled. Well, she knew how to take care of that.

Gripping the man's wrist, she executed one of Trevelyan Perry's wushu maneuvers.

Though she was admittedly a bit out of practice, Ellie was pleased with how easily the skill came back to her. She felt the intruder's center of gravity shift. The tension on his hands forced him to release his grip on her arm. Then she instinctively added the final touch—a sharp, quick blow to the small of his back.

The stranger lurched forward, falling ungracefully into the tub.

Ellie froze. She looked on in horror as he emerged, sputtering, from the water, his knife clattering against the ground. He immediately went still as well, his eyes glued to the bubble-obscured surface.

It was as if time held its breath. Everything seemed to slow— the wash of the spilled water across the floor, the waves roiling the foam-covered surface of the bath. She felt the heavy, regular thud of her pulse in her throat, pounding in time to the slow drip of water against tile. She found herself wondering absently, and with horror, if she had just inadvertently killed a man.

Then his arm flashed out, and he grasped hold of an oily black form, which he promptly tossed across the room.

He thrust himself out of the tub, taking most of the rest of the water with him, and grabbed the nearest thing to hand—the chrome towel rack. Whirling it like a javelin in his grip, he thrust it at the black form, which was already recovering itself in the opposite corner. The bar of the rack pinned the creature's neck, and it let out a hiss of rage, baring a pair of fangs that made Ellie's stomach quiver.

He peered down at the snake, and Ellie waited, barely able to breathe, to see what he would do next. Try to crush it? Order her to get help?

Instead he smiled, then set the towel rack aside.

She watched, horrified, as he bent over and picked the animal up, handling it with deft comfort.

"Gave us quite a scare, didn't you?" he said, talking, Ellie could see, to the snake and not to her. She began to think that her first impression had been correct: This man actually was completely insane. She took an edging step toward the door as he held the creature out toward her, sliding his hand along the whipping body to hold it straight.

"Orange stripe. Not yellow. She's a cat-eye, not a moccasin. Harmless. Aren't you?" he said as the snake coiled around his arm, giving him another irritated hiss.

He turned and carried it through the doorway. Ellie followed him hurriedly, wrapping Constance's robe around her, though it was soaked from the tidal wave that had followed the man's plunge into her bath. She watched as he moved to the end of the hall and stepped through the door onto the patio. Once there, he tossed the snake into a stand of lush palms and flowering hibiscus. An elderly couple walking past stopped and stared. The old woman's grip whitened on her husband's arm.

He wiped his hands on his trousers and strolled back inside.

Now that the better portion of the muck that had covered him was washed away, Ellie could see that his face was rather startlingly well put together.

"They like the heat," he said.

"Excuse me?" she stammered, brushing aside the thought that underneath two days of stubble, his chiseled jaw rather resembled that of a statue of Apollo she had admired at the British Museum.

He didn't answer. Instead he stared at her, his sudden stillness making her wonder for a moment whether he hadn't gotten himself a poisonous bite after all.

Then again, she was standing in the hallway in nothing more than Constance's blue silk bathrobe. A wet silk bathrobe, which was clinging rather tightly to her body.

She crossed her arms over her chest protectively, and he seemed to snap out of it.

"Cat-eye snakes. They like the warm water. You should check the tub before you fill it."

"I think I would have noticed—"

"And while you're filling it," he continued. "It's rare to find the dangerous ones here in the city, but it's not unheard-of. And you do not want to cross paths with a moccasin. It's lucky I was here."

"Lucky? Just who the devil do you think you are?" she demanded.

"I think I'm the man who just saved you from a snakebite," he said pointedly.

Saved her? She felt her temper flare.

"You broke down the door."

"You screamed," he countered.

"That wasn't an invitation," she snapped.

"Were you planning on dealing with that yourself? Forgive me for saying so, but you don't look like someone who's had a lot of experience with snake wrangling."

"If I had needed help, I would have gone myself to acquire it," Ellie shot back. "I certainly didn't require some filth-covered madman to batter through the door!"

"Sorry I wasn't quite up to your standards of hygiene when I came to help you."

"This has nothing to do with hygiene!" she exclaimed.

She stared at him with astonishment. Was he really that thickheaded?

"Listen, princess," he said, stepping toward her. "In this part of the world, you don't wait for an invitation. In case you hadn't noticed, you're not in jolly old England anymore. Most of the local animal life here is harmless, but there are more than a few of them that will have you dead before you get a chance to think about it. You hear somebody scream, you err on the side of caution, whether or not it's in the bathroom."

She felt her fury rise. *Princess?* Who the devil did he think he was, talking to her as if she were some kind of privileged ninny? She might not be able to recognize different species of snake off the top of her head, but she was hardly about to hop into the tub with the bloody thing when the oaf in front of her had decided to bash his way inside.

"I didn't need your help," Ellie said tightly. "I was perfectly capable of handling that situation myself without being manhandled by a knife-wielding thug."

"Knife," he repeated numbly, his hand going to the empty sheath at his waist. He pushed past Ellie into the bathroom and retrieved the huge blade from where it lay in a muddy puddle by the tub. He wiped it off on his sleeve, then returned it to its place at his side.

"Are you quite done?" she demanded, exasperated.

He turned to respond, then stopped, frowning. He stepped toward her.

"What's that around your neck?"

Ellie's hand flew to the place where the shape of the medallion pressed through the thin, soaked silk. Then she grasped hold of the madman's pointing finger and twisted it. He let out a yelp as she forced him into another one of Perry's holds, then pushed him out the bathroom door. She slammed it firmly in his face, throwing the bolt, which, since she'd relied on the latch before, was still intact. She wished for a moment she'd had the foresight to use it in the first place. She would have been interested to see him try to break through that. Though with that thick head of his, he might have succeeded.

She half fell into the chair, her fingers brushing against the cold black stone under her robe. They trembled as she moved them. But it wasn't her close call with the snake that had her knees weak. It was the idea of how near the stranger had come to seeing the secret she wore over her heart.

4

ELLIE FIXED A LAST pin into her hair and considered her reflection in the vanity mirror. It was going to have to do. She had scoured Constance's wardrobe on board the *Salerno* and knew that while the daytime clothes she had sent along with Ellie were pleasantly practical, her evening wear was far prettier and less comfortable than what Ellie was used to. It was also significantly more revealing—the muted green dress she wore now was the most modest she could find, but the squared neckline was still much lower than she would have liked, and not just for reasons of habitual propriety.

She had started wearing the black medallion her first day at sea, stringing a piece of spare ribbon through the hole at its apex. It hung low on her chest, concealed beneath the bosom of her shirts.

After her encounter with Mr. Jacobs on Regent Street, she had found herself uncomfortable with the notion of leaving the artifact in her room. It wasn't that she suspected her enemies were on the *Salerno*. Ellie was confident that Constance's audacious plan had enabled her to give them the slip. Even if they guessed that she'd had the courage and determination to try to follow the map herself, they had no way to know where it would lead her. She was also traveling under an assumed name. Jacobs would be looking for Eleanora Mallory, not Constance Tyrrell.

However, there was still a chance that some member of the crew might stumble across it while servicing her cabin. It simply seemed like a sensible precaution to wear the object instead, and by now it was habit. There was something comforting about feeling its cool weight against her skin, a constant, tangible link to the place she sought.

Perhaps its constant presence was responsible for her dreams.

They had started shortly after she left London. Before, Ellie's dreams had generally involved bizarre but relatively harmless phenomena, like finding herself swimming through a pool of eighteenth-century tax records, or holding a debate about the differences between the male and female brain with Admiral Nelson, Aunt Florence's fat tabby.

These were different.

Some were wonderful. In one, Ellie had been in the desert, overseeing a team of fellahin as they excavated the entrance to a pharaoh's tomb. In another she had lectured to a group of students, an even mix of men and women who scribbled notes assiduously as she spoke.

But the others...

She had dreamed of standing on a podium in front of the ruins of Whitehall. The prime minister had sat beside her, bound in chains. A crowd of women chanted before her, their fists in the air, screaming with the adrenaline of victory. There had been blood on their hands and skirts, but the most terrifying part of the vision had been what Ellie herself had felt in that moment.

Power. Excitement.

There had been a woman behind her holding an ax: a massive Viking of a female with arms like a dockworker. As Ellie soaked up the cheering voices of the mob, she had motioned to the bound man beside her, and the ax-wielding giantess had stepped forward.

Ellie had woken from that one in a cold sweat, sure that for the first time since she started her journey across the sea, she was going to be ill.

It was probably the motion of the boat. She'd heard people say before that being on the water did strange things to one's sleep. She hoped things would be better now that the ground wasn't rocking beneath her feet.

The medallion was a more likely culprit than the motion of the waves for the other strange thing about her dreams: the common element that united them.

That element was a woman. She was small and slender, delicate like Constance but dark where Constance was light. There was something ageless about her, though if she had to guess, Ellie would have put her at perhaps ten years older than herself. Her face was sad and lovely, save for a single blemish, a jagged scar that cut across her cheek.

She had appeared in the dreams dressed like any other Londoner, in a simple blouse and tailored skirt. Ellie would catch sight of her in the midst of the desks that filled her classroom, or at the back of a crowd of admirers asking her to sign books for them. There was something uncanny about seeing her standing at the far end of an Egyptian wadi or in the middle of a mob of screaming women. She never spoke. Never moved. Her very stillness and silence, her solemn watchfulness, made her stand out like a beacon. The memory of her face would continue to tease at Ellie's awareness long after the rest of the dream had faded into the fog of waking.

Now that Ellie had arrived in British Honduras, she recognized the particular cast of the woman's features. Her strong nose and earth-toned eyes made her resemble one of the natives of the place in which she now found herself, the descendants of the Mayans who had built the ancient cities of Copán and Palenque.

She supposed that the small, still figure was the way in which her dreaming mind had decided to embody the adventure she was embarked upon.

Putting her dreams aside, Ellie turned her attention to the more substantial matter of her wardrobe. She was very tempted to throw convention to the wind and simply wear her tailored suit, but a glimpse of the other guests strolling through the garden below told her quite clearly that dinner in British Honduras was, if anything, an even more formal affair than at home. It was as if being so far from civilization made people here want to cling to its vestiges that much more ferociously.

She sighed and gave the lace of her bodice one last tug. Then she picked up her clutch, peeking inside to see the medallion nestled beside her handkerchief, a few spare pins sticking to its surface. Snapping the bag closed, she turned down the lantern, letting the room slide back into near darkness.

Ellie stepped out onto the veranda. She instantly felt the warmth of the sun on her skin, even though it had sunk low on the horizon, painting the rooftops around her in gold and flame. Tufted heads of palm trees rose from between the buildings, and the dark shadows of gulls cut across the sky. But it was that horizon that drew her, marked by the distant charcoal line of the mountains.

Somewhere out there lay the secret she had crossed an ocean to find.

Ellie felt the breeze brush against the exposed skin at her collarbone and admitted to herself that while Constance's gowns were certainly of a lower cut than she preferred, they offered a distinct advantage in terms of ventilation. It was so rare in London that her skin actually felt the brush of open air. She relished it for a moment, then stepped back, pulling the French doors closed behind her.

The other guests were filtering into the Imperial's dining room as Ellie descended the stairs. She caught sight of the hotel's owner, Augustus Smith, returning from seating a French family she had seen earlier.

"Miss Tyrrell," he said, bowing as she approached. "You look very nice this evening," he added, quite genuinely.

Ellie was pleased in spite of herself. "Thank you. That's very kind."

"May I show you to a seat?" he offered.

She caught his arm, stopping him. "Actually, if I might speak to you for just a moment?"

Smith nodded, holding back.

"I wanted to ask you if you knew of a reliable guide to the interior."

Smith frowned and stepped aside as a pair of young gentlemen moved past him into the dining room.

"Where is it exactly that you're looking to go?"

"To the mountains in the Cayo District."

Smith looked at her with concern. "I must tell you, Miss Tyrrell, the mountains are almost entirely unexplored and the journey is quite hazardous, particularly for a young lady."

"I'm sure that it would be. I have no intention of going." She smiled through the lie, as much as it galled her. After all, why shouldn't a woman be just as capable as a man of making the trek, if properly outfitted and guided? But she had admitted to herself on the passage to Central America that revealing her intent would only raise eyebrows, and Ellie felt no desire to draw any undue attention to herself. A cover story was an annoying necessity.

"I'm simply making preparatory inquiries for my brother," she said. "He should be joining me here shortly. He's a geologist in the employ of a mining firm potentially interested in making a purchase here."

"I see. Well, I'll make some inquiries. Did you want me to hold a room for him? We're getting rather full here at the moment."

The offer caught Ellie off guard. She forced a quick recovery. "Oh, no—I wouldn't want you to do that till I have confirmation from him on his arrival. He's dreadfully unpredictable, I'm afraid. I'll let you know as soon as he's made definite arrangements."

"Very good," Smith said, and motioned her inside. He led her to an empty chair at a round table already mostly filled. "Will this do?"

"Of course. Thank you," she said.

He held the chair for her as she sat down, then headed through the doorway into the kitchen. A server approached with a carafe of wine, and Ellie nodded, letting him fill her glass. She took a heavy sip, hoping it would calm the rush of nerves Smith's offer of a reservation for her nonexistent brother had sparked in her.

"Rotten lot," the portly gentleman beside her was saying. He wore a suit of light linen, sharply tailored, with a bright blue handkerchief neatly folded in his pocket. His accent flowed with the easy drawl of the Southern United States. "That's what they sold you. I'd say it was probably a surplus from someone else's shipment that was sitting around on the docks for a few weeks."

"My agent should have noticed the difference," said the small, dark-clad man across from him, who wore a very morose expression.

"As regards that, I would consider whether perhaps some money might have changed hands," the portly gentleman pointed out. "Don't rule it out. It's the sort of thing that happens all the time here."

"Seven crates of rotten oranges. That's what they delivered. Seven," the dour man emphasized sadly.

"You were right to come see about it yourself," the other man confirmed. Then he turned his attention to Ellie, giving her a warm smile. "Will your traveling companion be joining you, miss? I would gladly move to another chair so that the two of you might sit together."

"That's very kind, but it won't be necessary," Ellie said.

"I see. Well, that being the case, perhaps I might take the liberty of making your introduction to the table. With your permission."

"Granted." She smiled at him politely.

"I am Major Jeremiah Tucker," he announced with a flourish.

"Major? In what army?" said the young man beside him. He wore an expensive suit and spoke with a distinctly aristocratic accent.

"That of the former Confederate States of America."

"You're a Confederate?"

"I am," Tucker acknowledged with a nod.

"So you fought on the side of the slave owners?" the young man said pointedly, gesturing with his spoon as a bowl of soup was set down in front of him. Ellie leaned back as another was placed for her.

"This is Mr. Galle," Tucker said to Ellie. "He and his companion, Mr. Tibbord, are touring Central America. They spent the last

month in the Yucatán and have just arrived here in British Honduras." He shifted his attention back to Mr. Galle. "If I'd been fighting
to preserve the institution of slavery, then tell me why I would have
chosen to emigrate to a place where it has been illegal for well over
a century." He took a spoonful of soup and nodded his approval.
"Very nice. Now, then—I fought on the side of self-determination,
young man. And of our nation's Constitution, which quite clearly
states that the affairs of a locality should not be imposed upon by
the will of a far-off government."

"So you moved to a place run by an even farther-off government?" said one of the table's other occupants, a pale, dark-suited
man with a thick Scottish brogue.

"Point taken, Reverend. But your Crown doesn't stick its nose
into business here until it's necessary. They're content for the most
part to leave well enough alone. Ah—the Reverend Markham, my
dear. And his sister, Frances," Tucker said to Ellie. "The reverend
has a Presbyterian mission in the interior, outside Orange Walk.
They come into town periodically to supply themselves with a few
comforts from the homeland, and I've had the pleasure of crossing
paths with them twice now."

The reverend nodded at Ellie and smiled. His sister moved her
glare from Ellie's face to the neckline of her gown. Frances, apparently, had plenty of high-necked dinner dresses in her wardrobe.
Ellie suspected most of them were in shades of stiff gray or black.

"And this is our unfortunate fruit dealer, Mr. Burgess, who is
joining us from Liverpool." Tucker gestured to the owner of the
rotten oranges.

"How do you do?" Mr. Burgess said morosely.

"Ah—and our final companion for the evening arrives, a com-
patriot of mine—Mr. Adam Bates. A pleasure to see you again, sir,"
Tucker said to someone who had entered the room behind Ellie.

"As always, Major."

Ellie felt herself stiffen at the familiar rumble of his voice. She
turned to confirm it but had to look twice. The tall, broad-shouldered
gentleman in a finely tailored navy suit was barely recognizable as

the mud-covered, snake-wrangling intruder who had burst into her bath earlier that afternoon. With his sandy hair neatly combed and his face clean-shaven, he almost looked respectable. At least, he would to anyone who didn't know better.

He finished shaking Tucker's hand and moved to the empty seat across from Ellie.

"Mr. Bates would know where to find the ruins you're after, Mr. Galle," Tucker offered. "Though I doubt he'll divulge. He keeps his finds close."

"It's that or watch them get looted," Adam said grimly, holding out his wineglass for the server's carafe. He cast the two younger men an appraising look and seemed unimpressed. He nodded politely at the reverend and his sister. Then his attention fell to Ellie and stuck. Ellie found herself very aware of how blue his eyes looked against the deep tan of his face, and she felt an unwelcome heat rise into her cheeks at the memory of the state she had been in the last time he'd seen her.

"You now have all of us at a disadvantage, my dear," the major said kindly from beside her, jolting her out of the hold Adam's stare had on her.

"I'm terribly sorry," she apologized, and flashed a smile. "Constance Tyrrell. It's very nice to meet all of you."

She accepted a nod of acknowledgment from Mr. Galle's companion, Tibbord. The slightly overweight man was sporting a pink sunburn and spectacles, through which he gazed at her slightly reverently. When he realized she was looking back at him, he seemed to catch himself, jumping slightly, and turned his nervous attention to Adam, who sat beside him.

"So you know where we could find some ruins?" he said.

"You'd have seen the best of what's accessible in the Yucatán," Adam replied, sipping his wine.

"What's that mean, exactly—accessible?" Galle cut in.

"It means what it sounds like. In the Yucatán, you've got post-card vendors next to the temples. The ruins here are extremely difficult to get to even if you know where you're going."

"We're hardly amateurs," Galle said archly. "We just spent a month in the bush in Mexico, and managed quite well."

"Did you?" Adam said. Ellie saw him glance over at the plump-cheeked Tibbord.

"We don't mind a bit of discomfort. I'm actually fond of 'roughing it,' as they say. I think it's quite invigorating in a masculine sort of way—if you'll forgive the expression, Miss Tyrrell."

Ellie refrained from commenting.

"Take my word for it," Adam said. "The bush here isn't like the bush in the Yucatán. It's about a hundred years behind when it comes to roads or trails, and half the men posing as guides are looking to rob you and leave you out there."

"You'd best listen to what the man is telling you," the reverend spoke up. "Mr. Bates is the colony's assistant surveyor general. He knows the conditions out there better than almost anyone."

"You're the assistant surveyor general?" Ellie blurted, unable to contain her surprise. Adam's gaze drifted over to her, and she felt suddenly self-conscious.

"That a surprise?"

"Well, yes. You're American. Surveyor general is a civil service position. You've got to be English to be in the civil service."

"They make exceptions in the colonies. But I am English, technically. I was born in the Cotswolds."

"I didn't realize you were acquainted with Mr. Bates, Reverend," Tucker said.

"He assisted us in our journey to the mission," the reverend replied. "I must admit, without him we would have been in for a rather difficult time."

"I was headed that way," Adam said.

"Lucky for us you were," the reverend added firmly.

"And where are you headed now?" Tibbord asked, a bit timidly.

"Nowhere. I'm eating my dinner," Adam replied as the main course was set down in front of him. Ellie leaned back to make way for her plate, which was loaded with a richly spiced fricassee. She realized she had barely touched her soup when Smith lifted the bowl away, giving her a slightly disapproving look when he saw its contents. Judging from the figure of his wife, Smith was a man who preferred his women eat heartily.

"He means your next expedition, obviously. I think Mr. Bates isn't interested in company, Tibbord, if that's what you were getting at. Am I right, Mr. Bates?" Mr. Galle said.

"Go to the cays," Adam said, spearing a piece of chicken with his fork. "Easy boat ride. Nice beaches. Pretty girls. It'll make for a fine chapter in your book."

Tibbord's eyes widened.

"How did you know we were writing a book?"

"Your type are always writing a book," he replied around a mouthful.

"*He's* writing a book," Galle corrected. "I'm just putting my name on it and providing all the interesting anecdotes. If it were left to Tibbord, it would be a travelogue of life at nice hotels." He accepted a refill for his wineglass and leaned back in his chair. "I do wonder if Mr. Bates's disinclination for travel companions extends to young ladies. Our Miss Tyrrell, for example."

"Me?" Ellie blurted, taken off guard.

"Forgive my eavesdropping, but I couldn't help overhearing your asking Smith about a guide to the interior on your way in. What do you say, Mr. Bates? Would you break with your principles for the lovely Miss Tyrrell?"

Adam studied her sharply. Ellie forced herself to stay casual.

"You're going to the interior?"

"I was making the inquiry for my brother, actually. Oliver," she said, quickly inventing the name. "He's in mining and hopes to survey a potential site in the Cayo for his company."

"What's he mine?" Burgess asked, the merchant in him perking up at the sound of business talk.

"Silver," Ellie said, then coolly turned her gaze to Adam. "But you needn't be baited by Mr. Galle, Mr. Bates. My brother and I are making our own arrangements."

"Oliver not feeling well?"

"Sorry?"

"Your brother," Adam clarified flatly.

"Oh." Ellie smiled. "I certainly hope not. He's finishing up work on his last site and will meet me here once it is complete."

"You'll be joining him in the Cayo?"

Ellie felt Adam's eyes on her, studying her reaction. She schooled it carefully, flashing him a light smile.

"Perhaps."

"We'll look forward to meeting him," the major said. "About those oranges, Mr. Burgess..."

Ellie felt the weight of the air shift as Adam's attention moved to the mousy fruit dealer, who leaped on the opportunity to share more of his frustrations, regaling the reverend with a description of different types of citrus rot.

She was grateful for the dull turn to the conversation. Even mold was an improvement over the intensity of Adam's stare. Surveyor he might be, but Ellie had determined she would happily do without his advice. She was sure Smith had sufficient knowledge of the men of the colony to know the reliable ones from the thieves. Adam Bates, she decided firmly, was someone she'd happily limit her acquaintance with.

Ellie managed to excuse herself before dessert. She hurried back to her room, closing the door and leaning against it gratefully. Being alone again was a relief. Dinner had made her feel like she was performing on a stage. Well, it had not been dinner itself. It was more specifically the presence of Adam Bates that had imposed the pressure. The way the man looked at her had made her feel as though he were searching for a crack in her armor. Tomorrow, she decided, she would ask for dinner in her room. It would be simpler to stay out of the way for however long it took for her to find her guide.

The room had cooled since she had left it. Though she had closed the French doors, she left her window open. After all, it was still as warm as any summer night in London. She sank down onto the chair and opened her clutch, pulling out the medallion.

She ran her fingers over the surface. It felt cool, as it always did, even in the thick tropical heat. The weight of it filling her palm was oddly comforting, and looking at it helped settle her. It was so solid, so very real. It had to have come from somewhere just as real. And she would find it.

She heard the click of the door handle and started. It had to be one of the maids trying to get in to tidy things before she returned from supper. She had only enough time to bury the black stone under the hat on her vanity table before the door opened the rest of the way.

"I don't actually need . . . ," she began, then stopped short as she turned and saw not the thin young chambermaid but the looming figure of Adam Bates.

He shut the door behind him and stood, arms crossed.

"So how about you tell me what you're really up to?"

"Don't you ever knock?" She shook her head, realizing the futility of that line of inquiry. "Not that it's any of your business, but I believe I already did."

"If you've got a brother named Oliver, then I'm your aunt Mabel."

"You're calling me a liar?"

"Didn't say you make it a habit. You aren't that good at it."

Ellie felt a welcome flare of righteous indignation. Well, perhaps not entirely righteous. After all, he was right about the brother. But she was hardly going to admit that. She drew herself up to her full height and pointed an imperious finger at the door.

"Get out," she ordered.

"Now, that looks familiar. Listen, princess—"

"Why do you keep calling me that?" she demanded, exasperated.

"It fits better than Constance," he said with a wry look. "I don't know what sort of scheme you've got up those pretty sleeves of yours, but take it from someone who spends far more time there than he ought: The bush is no place for a lady. Even," he continued, cutting off her protest, "a relatively resourceful one. There's not a lot of fine-bred women who would've made the trip across the water in that tub on their own. But a busted excuse for a freighter is one thing. The jungle is another. There are things out there a lot meaner than the one I pulled out of your bath this morning, and some of them walk around on two legs. If you know what's good for you, you'll take the same advice I gave those boys in the dining room: Have yourself a nice holiday. Then head back to England, where you belong."

"Why is it, exactly, that you think my affairs are any of your business?" she asked, frustration rising.

"There's enough of the gentleman left in me to want to keep a woman from putting her neck on the line."

"Gentlemen knock, Mr. Bates," she said meaningfully.

Adam's eyes narrowed. "If you won't take that piece of advice, at least listen to this one. What I told Lewis and Clark down there was true—particularly for a woman. Any decent guide is going to refuse to bring you out there unaccompanied, especially when, any day now, it's going to start raining. Getting through the bush in the rainy season is no picnic. And that means," he added, stepping closer to her, "that anyone who does agree to take you is probably planning on robbing you or worse. I can tell you don't want to hear this, but if you don't have a man accompanying you, you're setting yourself up for some serious unpleasantness."

She hated what he was saying. And she hated even more that it was very possibly true. From what she had seen, the local men were, if anything, even more strict in their notions of what was and wasn't appropriate behavior for a woman, and she was fairly sure that archaeological expeditions did not fit under that particular umbrella. She fought fear with sarcasm.

"What's that, then? An offer or a threat?"

Adam laughed, shaking his head. "Miss Tyrrell—whoever the hell you are—I probably am the only man in this country crazy enough to do what you're asking. But I'm not going to partner with someone who won't come clean about what she's after. You also don't strike me as the type to follow orders, and from my experience, that's a pretty quick way to get yourself killed out there."

"Are you quite finished?"

He studied her for a moment. "Reckon so," he said finally.

"Then kindly remove yourself," she said coldly.

"Don't say I didn't warn you," he shot back, then turned and stalked out, leaving the door open behind him.

She ran over to shut it and was unable to resist the urge to shout after him, "Maybe you should spend a little less time out there, Mr. Bates. You might remember to behave like a civilized person."

"Sweet dreams, princess," he drawled in reply, continuing on his way.

Ellie slammed the door and set the lock, adding the chain for good measure. She should have done that the moment she'd returned from dinner—though then again, she hardly expected anyone to come waltzing in as if he owned the place.

She went back to the vanity, tossing aside the hat, and gripped the medallion. She pressed it to her chest, as though hoping its cool solidity would help banish the doubts Bates had put into her head. It wasn't possible that every guide in this colony would be as backward and pigheaded as he implied—that not one of them would think her capable. She'd let them put her to the test, if that was what it took to convince them. One way or another, she'd find a way to get where she needed to go, and to hell with Adam Bates.

5

Professor Gilbert Dawson was in hell. His suit clung to his skin, heavy and damp with sweat. He thought longingly of the cool greens of Saint Andrews, the soft gray skies that arched over the campus. Right now, the air in Fife would be crisp, a steady breeze freshening the lecture halls and the offices with their book-lined shelves. Instead he was here in the devil's armpit of Central America, taking orders—he, Gilbert Dawson, a tenured professor of ancient history—from a half-foreign street thug.

Jacobs seemed unaffected by the climate, undoubtedly a gift from whatever part of his heritage lay behind his dark complexion. He never had to stop to wipe sweat from his face with a handkerchief, as Dawson had to do quite frequently.

There had been a telegram waiting for them at the customs office—coded, of course. Jacobs had provided the decryption, though the message it contained was hardly any clearer than the jumble of code he'd first seen.

Candidate for Tulan Zuyua, it read. *If present acquire Smoking Mirror.*

Tulan Zuyua...Dawson knew there was something familiar about the words. Hopefully one of the texts on Central American history he had brought with him would provide more insight. As for the Smoking Mirror, Dawson's only clue as to its significance had come, humiliatingly enough, from Jacobs.

"That's what we bring back," he had said, when Dawson had managed to cough up the nerve to ask.

The reply had chilled him, even in the thick tropical air. It reminded him all too well of Ostrask.

There, too, all of their efforts had been directed at acquiring a single object, no matter what the cost.

He remembered what the cost had been in Ostrask. He hoped desperately it would prove otherwise here. But he supposed that would depend upon the girl.

She had proven surprisingly capable. Dawson had to admit that much. But Jacobs had been more so.

It had been another revelation, an additional piece of the puzzle of who exactly Dawson was working for. He supposed he shouldn't have been surprised. It had taken significant influence and resourcefulness to arrange Dawson's salvation. His life had been forfeit, every piece of evidence pointing—rightly—to the fact that he was a violent murderer. Yet another life had been found to replace his own, evidence manufactured out of thin air, judge and jury as compliant as a basket of kittens.

Now he could add to those feats his employer's ability to muster a vast and mysterious network of informants. After Jacobs had lost the girl, a few more telephone calls had set this machine of information in motion. Within two days, they had learned that Constance Tyrrell, a schoolmate of Eleanora Mallory's, had suddenly booked herself passage on a steamer to British Honduras.

While the girl herself could still be seen through the windows of her father's house in Bayswater.

If that idiot Henbury's description of the map was to be trusted, British Honduras was not an illogical place to begin the search for the promised city. The girl had clearly decided to pursue the route herself. Of course, that simple fact still boggled Dawson's mind. That a woman—a young, unmarried woman—would voyage to a remote and dangerous colony, apparently intent upon trekking alone to an unknown location in the deep jungle, would never have occurred to him.

She was either remarkably brave or entirely insane.

The possibility had clearly occurred to his employer, however.

Why else would he have checked ships' manifests, not just for the girl's name but for that of any person she had associated with over the past ten years?

Dawson and Jacobs had been dispatched posthaste. The Jamaica steamer, the next boat that would put them in the vicinity of British Honduras, had been full. It hadn't mattered. Two passengers had failed to arrive at the docks that morning, and Dawson and Jacobs had been given their rooms. Dawson had stood and watched as an absurd amount of equipment was loaded into the hold, including an item he had almost jokingly included on a list Jacobs had once demanded he make of materials that might be needed for an expedition to remote, uncharted territory.

It had all been purchased, all been packed and made ready. And now it was here . . . and so was the woman.

Finding her had been as simple as a chat with the customs agent. The colony didn't often receive unaccompanied female visitors, and he remembered precisely where she had gone for accommodations.

Dawson looked at the hotel ledger. There was no entry in the "checked out" column beside the scrawled feminine signature. The girl was still here.

He prayed she would prove more cooperative this time. He knew with a dread certainty just how far Jacobs would be willing to go to get what he wanted.

The afternoon was at its height when Ellie returned to the hotel. It was the hour when most of the city sought escape from the thick, wet heat in shady hammocks or the cool confines of the cantinas. She was ready for a nap herself, her spirits plummeting after the result of her latest interview, this one with the last on the list of potential guides Mr. Smith had given her.

The interview had gone as she had expected, not as she'd hoped. He had refused, claiming that he could not in good conscience take her where she wanted to go. It was too dangerous for a lady. He couldn't be at peace knowing he was putting a woman's life at risk.

Ellie wanted to retort that he did that every time he impregnated his wife, but she politely thanked him instead. That wasn't a battle she would win today.

It had been the same story with the six other men she had tried to convince to lead her expedition. Either her gender proved an insurmountable obstacle, or the imminent arrival of the rainy season provided their excuse.

It had been hard for her to take the threat of a bit of rain seriously at first. After all, she was a native of London, a place where rain was more common than pigeons on St. Paul's. But here in the southern latitudes, it was a different story. The colony's rainy season was notorious, washing out even the most established and well-traveled roads and flooding the rivers. She had been assured, time and again, that it particularly made passage to the wilder areas of the interior virtually impossible.

The rainy season lasted for months. If she wasn't able to find a guide before it set in, she might very well be stuck in Belize City until the fall.

Six months. Far too long for her cover story of a holiday to Bournemouth to keep Aunt Florence and Uncle David from worrying. They might report her missing, and Ellie had to admit there was a chance her relatives wouldn't be the only ones looking for her.

She might have escaped Dawson and his companion, Mr. Jacobs, back on Regent Street, but they still knew who she was. How determined would they be to acquire the map? There was no way to know.

The thought was an unsettling one, until Ellie reminded herself that she was traveling under an assumed name. There was no way they could guess where she had gone.

Unless, perhaps, they had six months to do it.

She felt a headache coming on. As she trudged into the lobby, she saw Mr. Smith standing behind the front desk.

"Good afternoon, Miss Tyrrell. Will you be joining us for dinner?"

The thought of keeping up appearances for another hour seemed exhausting, especially given her latest disappointment. And there was always the chance that Adam Bates would turn up. She felt certain he would be able to read her failure from the mere set of her shoulders, and the thought of giving him the satisfaction of knowing he had been right was a galling one.

"I'm feeling a bit under the weather," she said. "Could you have someone bring a tray up to my room for me?"

"Certainly," he replied.

Ellie moved toward the stairs, mounting them wearily.

It was not the end of the line, not by any means. It was just a disappointment. There were bound to be more of them. But it did not mean that Bates's dire prediction would prove true. She would get more names from Smith. Somewhere in this colony, she would find a man willing to work for a female.

As she reached the top of the stairs, she nearly collided with Mr. Tibbord. He visibly jumped at the sight of her, then settled himself with a quick flutter of his hands to lapels, hair, and glasses.

"Good afternoon, Miss Tyrrell," he said politely.

"Good afternoon," she said. Trying to move past, she was stopped as Mr. Galle stepped into the hallway from a neighboring room.

"Miss Tyrrell!" he said. "Tibbord and I are going bathing. Want to join us?"

Ellie watched Mr. Tibbord's face flush a rather extreme shade of red.

"But, Galle, she can't...she's..."

"Bosh. We're off the map; she can do as she likes. No one would know. It'd be a lark. Might as well take full advantage, that's what I say. Eh, Miss Tyrrell?"

"I don't think so, Mr. Galle," she replied coolly.

"If you change your mind...," he offered with a wink, then headed down the stairs.

"Sorry...sorry about that," Mr. Tibbord said. Ellie gave him a tight smile, and he stepped carefully around her to follow Mr. Galle.

A dip in the cool blue water did sound heavenly, but Ellie was hardly going to indulge with a pair of overgrown schoolboys as audience.

She reached into her pocket, then stopped as her hand encountered nothing but a tear in the linen of her skirt.

Ellie cursed herself. She had noticed the hole days before, when she had last worn the garment, but she had been hurrying out for another interview and promptly forgot about the need to repair it. Now the key to her room was probably lying on the street somewhere between here and the harbor.

There was no point in trying the door. She had started to set the lock by default since Adam Bates's intrusion a few nights before.

Cursing floridly under her breath, she turned back for the lobby. She would have to ask Mr. Smith to let her in, which was likely to involve small talk about how her interviews were progressing. Ellie could hardly explain that every one of the recommendations he had made for a guide had refused her. At least, not without admitting that it was Ellie, and not her imaginary brother, who needed the help.

The dreadful awkwardness of it stopped her in her tracks. She scrambled for a way to avoid it, and inspiration struck in the shape of an unremarkable door on her left.

It opened onto the veranda. Ellie had closed the French doors leading from the veranda to her room before leaving, of course, but they were held closed only by a simple hook-and-eye latch. A little work with a hairpin should be enough to lift it and gain her access without Smith's assistance.

She stepped out onto the wide, weathered planks. The light was softly golden as she moved past the rows of glass-fronted French doors, her feet tapping lightly against the wooden planks. As she reached her room, she paused, drawn in spite of herself by the beauty of the view. The light was warming the tiled rooftops, painting the wide stretch of marshland that lay beyond them vividly. On the horizon, the dark line of the mountains was almost invisible, lost in the haze of late afternoon. Somewhere in their midst lay the goal of her map, the possible location of a stunning archaeological discovery. However far away those peaks might look today, they were there, and that meant they could be reached, one way or another. The thought reassured her.

Then she heard the voices.

"It's not here, either," the first said. It was close by, barely muffled, and there was something familiar about it, something that set the hairs on her forearms tingling.

"Jacobs?" it said again, and her skin went cold. The image came to her sharply—the pale, bearded man, sitting on Aunt Florence's settee, and his companion, lean and dark-haired with eyes like coals.

Quickly, silently, she moved away from the railing, ducking behind a tall fern that stood next to the doors to her room. She pressed her back against the weathered siding. As she did, she heard the floorboards creak just inside the doorway and knew, quite suddenly and surely, that Jacobs was standing just inside, gazing out through the filmy curtain. She found herself furiously trying to remember how she had approached moments before. Had her feet creaked on the boards? Would he have heard her?

How had they found her?

She pressed herself flatter against the wall as the doors opened.

Through the fronds of the fern and the glass panels of the door, she could see Jacobs's profile as he stepped over the threshold. His gaze drifted over the landscape, attentive but unhurried. For a moment, she thought that he must know she was there. That he was simply toying with her and would turn and look directly at her pathetic hiding place.

But he didn't turn. She watched him, the glass panes amplifying the oppressive heat of the afternoon. Sweat trickled between her breasts and down her back as she saw him cross to the edge of the veranda and kneel down. Reaching through the railing, he ran his hand along the underside of the platform, as though searching for something that might have been secured there.

All he had to do was glance her way, and she would be exposed like a butterfly pinned in a case, her pale skirts perfectly visible through the glass panes of the French door. But the alternative was to turn and flee down the veranda, a move certain to catch his attention. Ellie remembered racing through the press of bodies on Regent Street, Jacobs rapidly closing the distance between them. He was faster than her, and there was no busy department store here for her to duck into and lose him.

Her best chance was to stay perfectly still and hope that by some miracle he failed to look her way.

She waited behind the door, barely daring to breathe and feeling as trapped as an animal in a snare.

Jacobs stood, looking out over the garden to the distant green haze of the mountains. He seemed perfectly calm, not the least bit like a man breaking into and searching someone else's hotel room. He wasn't afraid of being caught, she realized. He wasn't afraid at all.

As though he knew, with certainty, that he was, in fact, the most dangerous thing in this hotel.

Then he turned and looked at her.

Jacobs's gaze was directed exactly where Ellie stood. Only the thin pane of glass separated them.

Ellie closed her eyes, waiting for his hand to clamp around her arm and drag her to whatever fate he had in mind for her.

Then she heard his footsteps pass evenly by as he returned to the room.

The sun, she realized. The same light that gilded the landscape must have been reflecting off the glass, making it opaque. It had hidden her.

She shuddered with relief but forced herself to remain still.

"She has it on her," he said.

Her hand rose to the medallion, tucked into her blouse, its weight resting against her bosom.

"We don't need it," the professor replied. His next words hit her like a fist. "We have the map. And there's nothing written here about the artifact. I think it's safe to say it was sent along merely as a token to add validity to the story. As far as I can see, we've got what we came for."

It suddenly occurred to her that the professor was frightened. It was subtle, no more than an undertone in his voice. But given the fear she was feeling herself, she recognized it clearly.

"Our employer doesn't like loose ends," Jacobs said flatly.

"I'd hardly call the artifact a loose end."

"I wasn't speaking about the artifact."

The words were cold, matter-of-fact. Ellie realized they referred to her. She was a loose end. And what happened to loose ends?

They get cut.

Ellie felt a clear, animal fear sing through her. She pressed herself, slowly and silently, closer to the wall.

"I should get back to the room, get started transcribing this. Unless you require, ah, assistance—"

"I'll handle it."

"But how will you know when she's—"

"The doors, please," Jacobs interrupted smoothly. Ellie heard Dawson's heavy tread and caught a glimpse of his sweating face as he leaned out to catch the doors, pulling them shut.

She heard Dawson's footsteps retreating quickly. Then silence.

It was a thick silence. A waiting silence. It stretched, becoming impossibly tense, until at last she heard Jacobs's lighter, more even tread moving slowly through the room.

She could see him in her mind's eye, passing from the bed to the vanity, taking one last, leisurely look at the space where she slept, at the gloves and stockings she had left draped over the chair, the hairpins scattered across the table.

Then, finally, Ellie heard the sound of the door closing and, a moment later, the click of the tumblers of the lock.

She waited another breath, fiercely studying the silence of the room, then finally forced herself to move. Tense, half ready to turn and sprint the other way, she stepped up to the doors.

The room was empty.

Her hand shaking, Ellie pulled a pin from her hair and lifted the latch that held the doors closed.

She stepped inside to survey the damage. The room seemed untouched, everything exactly as she had left it. The illusion was so complete, for a moment she found herself wondering whether perhaps she'd hallucinated the whole business. Then little things began to leap out at her—the angle of her hat on the table, the arrangement of the nightclothes she had left draped over the chair.

Ellie fell to her knees and lifted the lid of the trunk. She slid back the panel of the secret compartment Constance had shown her back in London—a clever little hiding place, impossible to find unless you knew exactly where to look. She gazed down into it, her heart sinking.

It was empty. The map was gone.

She closed the lid, forcing herself to do it slowly instead of slamming it down. She had to be calm, not shaking with panic or outrage. She couldn't afford either. She had to *think*.

How had they found her? The notion that they had simply guessed was too far-fetched. They hadn't seen the map. Even if they'd been capable of supposing that she had started on the track of the city on her own, they wouldn't have known where she had begun.

If they hadn't guessed, they must have *known*. The implications of that were frightening. To know, they would have had to discover her friendship with Constance, which meant they had learned her history right back to her school days. They must have had access to the registry of every ship leaving London, as well as have the manpower to check them not just for her name but for that of anyone she might have trusted.

It would have been an immense undertaking, one that required access to who knew what resources. What was more, it would have to have been accomplished in a matter of days. Dawson and Jacobs had arrived here on her heels, practically speaking.

Who the devil could organize something like that?

Ellie realized, with a sinking in her stomach, that she had gotten herself entangled in a web far larger and more dangerous than she had suspected.

It was a sobering thought. Whomever Dawson and Jacobs worked for was someone truly powerful—and ruthless.

Our employer doesn't like loose ends.

Was she really prepared to oppose someone like that? Did she even have a choice? If Jacobs's words were anything to go by, she was already a liability they planned to eliminate.

She felt a rush of indignation. They would find that more difficult than they thought. She had just learned what she was up against. They were yet to find out.

They had the map. There was nothing she could do about that. But she could see to it that they were exposed for the thieves and criminals they were. If she could get word to Constance's father, Sir Robert Tyrrell. With his connections, he could see to it that an investigation was launched. She'd bring the entire weight of the British government down on these thugs.

But she would need information. All she had so far were two names that could very well be false. That was hardly an auspicious start. She needed more—particularly the name of the person or persons her enemies were working for.

She cursed herself inwardly, fighting the urge to kick the travel trunk. She should never have been so careless as to leave the map in her room. It should have been with her always. She would not make a mistake like that again. The success of their intrusion galled her. They had walked in and taken what they wanted.

She would simply have to do the same. They were bound to have something useful in their rooms—papers, letters, something that would give her a clue as to who was behind all of this. Of course, she'd have to figure out a way to get in there without getting caught.

The solution to that was simple enough. They were looking for a young Englishwoman. She would just have to become something else.

Ellie stepped onto the veranda. She carried a canvas bag over her shoulder. It was the plainest of the pieces of luggage Constance had given her in London, a simple pack with two straps, meant to be worn over her back.

The afternoon was falling toward evening, and she knew it would not be long before the rest of the guests returned from their excursions to dress for dinner. She could see one of them in the garden below her, an elderly man who appeared to have fallen asleep on a wicker bench. She hoped the soft snores she could hear rising from him were genuine. She could not afford to be watched for the next few minutes.

She made her way down the weathered boards, moving closer to the sleeping gentleman. She paused in front of the last set of French doors before the entrance that led back into the hotel. The room before her was, she calculated, the same one from which Mr. Tibbord had emerged when she encountered him earlier that afternoon.

She looked up and down the length of the veranda, then gave another glance at the dreamer on the wicker bench. Satisfied that she was unobserved, she took a chance and cupped her hands to the glass, peering into the dim interior of the room.

It looked empty.

She checked the next door down as well, just to be certain, but it appeared that Mr. Galle and Mr. Tibbord were yet to return from their swim.

Ellie pulled a pin from her chignon and slipped it into the space between the French doors to Mr. Tibbord's room. Lifting the latch was easier this time. She stepped inside, pulled the door shut behind her, and looked around.

She would have to be quick. There was no telling when the pair would return. Dropping her bag on the bed, she moved to the wardrobe. She flipped through Mr. Tibbord's clothes, picking out a long pair of khaki trousers and a light field coat. Though Mr. Galle was closer to her in girth, he was a few significant inches shorter. And there were her additional curves to consider. Tibbord's over-size gear seemed far more likely to create a successful illusion.

She pulled her dress off, tossed it aside, then nimbly unlaced her corset. Tugging off her stockings, she wound the silk length of them around her chemise, flattening her bosom.

Steps sounded on the boards of the veranda. Voices accompanied them, closer by far than Ellie would have liked.

"I want to change first."

Mr. Tibbord's words were close to a whine. Ellie ducked beside the wardrobe. Its bulk would cut off the sight of her through the glass of the doors but would do nothing to conceal her once Mr. Tibbord stepped inside.

She glanced down at herself. She was wearing nothing but her chemise with stockings wrapped around it, and held his trousers in her hand.

How could she possibly explain this?

A lower voice rumbled back. It must be Mr. Galle.

"I don't want a pint. I want a nap," Mr. Tibbord said distinctly.

Ellie closed her eyes, reaching frantically for a passable excuse.

I'm terribly sorry, but I just stumbled into the wrong room....

In her underwear.

It was impossible.

She heard Mr. Galle make a muffled retort, then Mr. Tibbord's indignant reply.

"I most certainly am not a . . . Oh, very well. You win."

There was a scuffle of shoes on the boards of the veranda, and the voices moved away.

Ellie began to breathe again, and decided to get dressed. Quickly.

The trousers were a bit long and loose, but turning up the cuffs and the addition of a leather belt solved both problems aptly enough. She pulled on a white cotton shirt, then moved to the washbasin.

Mr. Tibbord's trimming shears sat in the stand next to a shaving brush and razor. Taking a handful of her long brown hair, Ellie lifted the scissors.

She hesitated, feeling a momentary fear at the irrevocable nature of the step she was about to take. But it was a necessary part of her plan, and anyway, all that hair was too much bother in the heat.

She started snipping.

A few minutes later, she set Mr. Tibbord's straw hat onto her cropped hair, slipped on the field jacket, and glanced into the mirror. She smiled. It was really quite an impressive illusion.

Only one problem remained: Mr. Tibbord's boots were far too big. Her own, though fairly sturdy, looked distinctly feminine.

She pulled open the door adjoining the rooms and stepped into Mr. Galle's chamber. It was much messier than Mr. Tibbord's. It took her several minutes to locate his boots, hiding under a pile of discarded towels beside the vanity.

She sat down in the chair and pulled one onto her foot. It fit. Thrusting her toes into the other, she cursed roundly as she stubbed them against a solid, heavy object. She upended the boot, and a plain wooden box slid out onto her lap. Curious, she opened it, and stared down at the contents in shock.

The box contained a small, heavy revolver. The well-oiled steel gleamed in the light through the window, resting against a bed of red velvet. Gingerly she lifted it out, keeping her fingers well away from the trigger. The cylinder gave way with a click, rolling open to reveal a circle of gleaming brass bullets.

She felt a wave of annoyance. Ellie didn't know much about firearms, but she knew better than to leave them lying around fully loaded. She carefully shook the cartridges out into her palm and slipped them into one of her pockets. Then she closed the cylinder and dropped the weapon into her bag.

She certainly had no intention of shooting anyone, but given what she was planning, even an unloaded pistol could come in handy.

Quickly, she gathered up her clothes and the locks of hair from the washbasin, tying it all into a bundle. She took a few coins from her purse and tossed them onto Galle's nightstand. If she had to be a thief, at least she could be a fair one.

She closed the French doors behind her and made her way down the veranda, casually tossing the bundle of her clothing over the railing as she went by. It landed in a thick stand of hibiscus.

She was lucky enough not to encounter any of the other guests as she made her way to the lobby. That space, too, seemed happily deserted. Ellie hurried through it toward the front entrance. She had nearly reached the door when a voice from behind stopped her in her tracks.

"Good afternoon, Mr. Tibbord."

Smith stepped out of the open doorway behind the desk, one she presumed must lead to the back office. Ellie glanced at him out of the corner of her eye but didn't turn around. Instead, she raised a hand, giving him an awkward wave, and then hurried out into the street.

Once through the door to the Imperial, she nearly tripped on a small boy who sat on the hotel steps. He was a slim, dark child, dressed in rough clothes, much like any of the other youths of the city she had seen dodging among the mules and run-down carriages. But this boy wasn't playing games or asking for coins. He looked up at her with sharp, watchful eyes, and Ellie had the distinct suspicion that he was looking for something.

Or someone.

His gaze moved from her boots to her hat, and he turned away, quick eyes roving along the street before them. Ellie forced herself to walk past him without another look, knowing that her disguise had just passed a second test.

The heat was breaking, a breeze from the harbor carrying it back to the swamps that surrounded the city. It breathed life back into the sleepy town. Children chased one another across the dusty pavement with sticks and stones as snatches of song rose from opened windows. Standing at the edge of the street, Ellie scanned the colorful rows of buildings, painted in pale pastel hues and overhung by palms and pepper trees.

She saw what she needed just across the way—a roofless structure across the road on a diagonal from the hotel. The new, unfinished wood had a rosy hue in the evening light. A group of men were leaving it, tool belts slung over their shoulders, a construction crew headed home after their day's work. She leaned against the shoulder-high fence that separated the hotel property from the street, trying for all the world to look like an arrogant young gentleman with nothing better to do, and waited until they had moved past her and disappeared around the corner. Then, with a glance to make sure the boy's attention was elsewhere, she hurried across the street and jumped up through the entryway.

The interior was open, the walls that would divide it into rooms only roughly framed. She made her way up the staircase to the second floor, then stepped into a room on the corner that faced the hotel.

Only half the wall had been planked, leaving an opening from floor to ceiling. She dropped to the ground beside it and pulled out Constance's field glasses. She put them up to her eyes and turned the dial to bring the Imperial into focus.

She studied the rows of French doors lining the veranda at the front of the hotel. The sun had begun to dip down behind the far side of the building, which meant that these east-facing rooms would be getting dark. And there was no point conserving lamp oil when it was already part of the fare. She scanned the panes of glass, waiting.

As she watched, light began to bloom behind the thin curtains, illuminating the figures of the men and women within. There, in the room that she calculated would lie directly across the hallway from her own, was what she had been looking for—the solid shape of Dawson, bent over a table, scribbling.

She closed the glasses, storing them back in the bag, then settled into a more comfortable position. She could see the shape of the man at the table well enough with her own eyes. All she had to do now was wait.

6

I⊤ WAS WELL INTO sunset by the time the light in the room winked out. Raising the field glasses, Ellie focused on the still-lit windows of the lobby and caught sight of the well-dressed figures mingling inside. A pang in her stomach confirmed that the dinner hour had arrived. Even the watcher on the steps had absconded, presumably headed home for his evening meal.

She stashed the glasses and gathered her bag, hurrying down the stairs and back outside.

Ellie walked along the Imperial's fence. She took a quick look up and down the street. Confident that it was deserted, at least for the moment, Ellie slipped the canvas bag from her back and dropped it over the fence. Then she followed, scrambling over and landing on the narrow strip of garden that ran along the rooms of the lower floor. It was a maneuver that would have been impossible in skirts. She smiled at the thought.

She collected the bag and hurried toward the south end of the building, as far from the lobby as she could get. Once there, she slipped through a door that opened onto another stairwell.

At the top, Ellie paused, glancing down the long, dim length of the hallway. All was quiet, the guests all enjoying a five-course repast in the dining room, on the other side of the hotel. Still, her route lay elsewhere.

Ellie pushed through the door leading out onto the veranda lining the front side of the hotel.

Compared to the silent hallway, her current position left her feeling painfully exposed. Walking along the veranda, she was visible to anyone who looked up from the street below. Ellie forced her pace to remain even as she slipped her trusty hairpin out of her pocket.

With her other hand, she reached into the canvas bag slung over her shoulder and pulled out the revolver. She held it against her body, concealing it from the view of anyone below. Praying that no one would come onto the veranda in the next minute, she pushed the pin into the crack between the doors, felt it bump up against the latch, and lifted.

It stuck.

The fear was quick and urgent. She couldn't afford this. At any moment, a guest could—almost certainly *would*—come out for a breath of air and see her, apparently a man in ill-fitting clothes, holding a gun and trying to pick a lock.

Please just work, she prayed silently. Taking a deep breath, she inserted the pin again, gave it another firm push, and felt the metal bend in her fingers.

Ellie pulled the crooked hairpin out of the door and stared at it in dismay. It was the only one she had saved from the massacre of her feminine locks.

She rapidly considered her options, but her awareness of how vulnerable she was standing in the open like this made it hard to think. Could she come back later? Steal the spare key from behind Smith's desk? No, there was no other time she could be sure that Dawson and Jacobs would be out.

She had to get inside and find something that would tell her who her enemies were working for—something that might also serve as a bargaining chip if Jacobs decided to trim his "loose end."

She looked from the clear pane of the French door to the solid steel weight of the revolver in her hand. Before she could stop to question the impulse, she drove the nose of the gun through the glass.

It shattered with a soft tinkling that sounded, to Ellie's ears, roughly like a bomb going off. She reached carefully around the remaining shards of glass and felt for the latch.

A nail had been driven into the wood of the frame just above the hook, a crude but effective method of ensuring the latch couldn't be lifted from the outside. Ellie wrestled with it for a moment before finally managing to wrench it loose. She pushed open the door and slipped inside.

The room was tidy save for a clutter of books and papers on the table, but as her eyes adjusted to the darkness a few other objects registered in her mind—a cluster of gear in the corner. Picks, ropes, brushes. A set of gaiters. A half-packed rucksack.

They had come prepared for an expedition, she realized, the thought filling her with anger. They had been that sure that they were going to get the better of her.

She moved to the desk, dropping the pistol to sift through the papers, holding them to the remaining light coming through the glass to see what they contained. There must be something here that would tell her more about Dawson's employer, some piece of evidence she could pass along to Sir Robert Tyrrell to see that these men were brought to the justice they deserved.

She riffled through useless journal articles, her frustration mounting, until something more promising caught her eye, half-buried under a treatise on pottery types.

It was a telegram. The message was a garbled assortment of seemingly random letters and numbers, a bundle of nonsense. But the message had originated in London, and no one paid international rates to send gibberish to the far ends of the earth.

There was something about this particular gibberish, something that struck her as startlingly familiar. . . .

Then it came to her, as impossible as the insight was. The message was in a code. Not just any code: one that Ellie knew.

It was a standard cipher, one used by agents of the British Foreign Office during the Napoleonic wars, seventy-five years before.

A box stuffed with coded documents had been one of the more enjoyable items Ellie had cataloged at the Public Record Office that year. Of course, they had been intended as a lesson in failure. After all, how was she supposed to properly categorize papers she couldn't read? It had been Henbury's idea of a joke, a way to take Ellie down a notch.

Well, she had shown him.

A few days' study, and a bit of rather brilliant research, had uncovered the secret of the cipher. Ellie had neatly translated the documents, placing both the originals and her decoded text in their proper places. It had been a thoroughly satisfying endeavor.

And now she held the same code in her hands.

It was impossible that the document had actually come from the Foreign Office. No agency worth its British salt would use the same cipher for seven decades. Ellie suspected these codes were changed as frequently as horses on a mail coach. Yet she recognized the call numbers for the London office where the telegram in her hands had originated. It was the Westminster office, just down the road from Whitehall.

Where the Foreign Office was located.

Ellie could see only two possible conclusions she could draw about the strange document in her hand. The first was that the Foreign Office was somehow directing Dawson's and Jacobs's activities.

That made no sense. Legitimate government employees did not lie, steal, and threaten innocent lives. Besides, what interest could the British government possibly have in a map to a ruined city? That was the territory of antiquities thieves, avid collectors, or organized criminals.

But what crime network would know a secret government code, even an obsolete one like this?

Perhaps the contents of the message would be more enlightening. Ellie grabbed a pencil, pressed the telegram to Dawson's desk, and began to work.

It took her only a few minutes to decipher the brief message, but the true contents of the telegram were just as confusing as the coded text had been.

Candidate for Tulan Zuyua.
If present acquire Smoking Mirror.

Ellie looked at the call letters for the London telegram station. Perhaps someone there would remember sending the message. It was unusual enough to be memorable. Coded telegrams weren't generally sent from public offices. She was certain the various government departments used their own lines for secret transmissions. The message in front of her would surely have struck the clerk who tapped it out as odd. It was possible he might remember something about the man—or woman—who had sent it.

Ellie tucked it into her pocket. The lead, slim as it was, would have to do. There was nothing else of promise on Dawson's desk, and she couldn't afford to waste much more time.

Then a familiar sight caught her eye. It had been shuffled under a stack of books on Central American history, only the corner peeking out, blending with the mess on the desk.

The map.

She stared at it, stunned. It had never occurred to her that Dawson might be so foolish—so utterly confident—that he wouldn't take the document with him when he went to dinner. He had left it here, certain it would remain undisturbed while he enjoyed his fillet of sole and apple tart.

Ellie snatched it, upsetting the pile of books in the process. She winced as they hit the floor with an audible thud. She carefully folded the map and was about to add it to her pocket, beside the telegram, when she heard the sound of a metallic scratch against the lock.

Someone was at the door. Someone with a key.

Her hand moved instinctively to the revolver. There was no time for anything else, and no place to hide. She pointed the gun at the door as the lock clicked and it opened.

Dawson froze in the doorway. For a moment all Ellie could feel was relief that it wasn't Jacobs, but she knew the professor's partner wouldn't be far behind.

"Inside, and close the door," she ordered.

"Miss Mallory? What on earth have you done to your—"

"Now," she added sharply.

Dawson's eyes moved from her cropped hair to the gun, and he stepped inside, closing the door behind him.

"You are making a very grave error," he said calmly. Too calmly. Ellie felt the cold weight of the gun in her hand and was suddenly very aware that the bullets were stuffed into her other pocket. If Dawson decided to call her bluff, the best she could hope to do was knock him over the head with it. She cursed her moral superiority. But then, if the gun had been loaded, could she really have pulled the trigger? Even against a man she knew would do her harm if he could?

She didn't have the answer to that question, and it hardly mattered anyway. What she needed to do now was escape.

"You have no idea who you're trifling with. *What* you're trifling with," Dawson said.

"Do I look like I'm trifling?" Ellie shifted her grip on the gun, hoping she looked fiercer than she felt. "Who are you working for?"

Dawson gaped at her.

"Your employer. His name." She pulled back the hammer of the revolver. Going by Dawson's expression, it made a satisfyingly intimidating click.

"I don't know."

"I said—"

"I don't know!"

Ellie stared at the older man. His face was pale, his hands shaking. There was no doubt that his fear was real.

She had the distinct impression that it wasn't entirely due to the weapon in her hand.

Something shifted in Dawson's expression. For a moment he looked almost desperate.

"Listen to me—please. If you want to live, let this go and get back to England."

His tone surprised her. His concern sounded almost genuine. Not that it mattered, she reminded herself.

"I'd still be a 'loose end' in London," she spat back.

Dawson winced. "Then for God's sake, just disappear."

"That's exactly what I had in mind." She kept the pistol pointed at him as she backed through the French doors.

Ellie stepped onto the veranda, trying frantically to plan her next move. Then a shout sounded below her. She looked down to see the boy from the steps staring up at her, recognition clear in his gaze. He called again and turned, dashing into the building.

He was going for Jacobs, which meant there was only one strategy left to her.

Ellie turned and bolted down the veranda, all pretension of blending in abandoned now. She reached the far end of the building and skidded through the door to the interior.

The back staircase lay before her. She pounded down it, trying to calculate her best chance of escape. She needed to disappear, quickly. It was her only chance of surviving long enough to make a better plan.

She would be too exposed on the street, but the verdant, shadowy foliage of the back garden could offer cover, and the fence that surrounded it wasn't too high to climb. If she could scale it and pass into the warren of yards and alleys behind the hotel, she might be able to slip away.

But to where?

She would worry about that later, when she wasn't running for her life.

Ellie reached the ground floor and heard shouts echoing down from above. She had less time than she'd thought.

She burst through a door that opened onto the patio that ran beneath the veranda at the rear of the hotel. In the falling light, the length of it was cloaked in deep shadows.

Ellie's eye lit on a shed that might provide an easier way over the fence. She dashed toward it along the patio. She dodged around a massive potted palm and promptly slammed into a dark, solid object.

A powerful hand gripped her arm. She felt a burst of panic. All her wushu maneuvers went out of her head. The only thing she could think to do was swing the heavy bulk of the revolver, still gripped in her hand, in the vague direction of her captor's head.

There was something familiar about the loud, creative string of curses that followed the gun's impact. The weapon fell from her fingers as she was yanked into a pair of iron-strong arms.

"Let go of me!" she said desperately, and found herself looking up into the surprised face of Adam Bates.

They stared at each other in shock for a moment. Then Ellie winced at the sound of more shouting from above.

"That for you?" he asked. He shook his head, not waiting for an answer. "Inside."

"But I—"

He cut her off by half tossing her through the opened doorway behind him, a pair of French doors much like her own on the floor above. He paused to collect the gun, tucking it into the back of his trousers, then crushed out the stub of his cigar. He quickly closed the doors behind him.

Inside the room, Ellie clambered to her feet, fury mixing with fear. She lunged, trying to push past him. Adam caught her easily, lifting her off the ground.

"I will not let you—"

He silenced her with a hand clamped over her mouth. He pulled her up against the wall, out of sight of the French doors, and Ellie stopped fighting as she heard the sound of footsteps on the patio outside.

Ellie froze, her pulse pounding, letting Adam hold her.

"Check the garden."

The voice belonged to Jacobs, and it sounded from just beyond the fragile glass of the doors. "Thoroughly," he added.

Adam's grip on her remained firm until the sound of Jacobs's steps had faded.

"Promise not to do anything stupid if I let go of you?" he murmured.

Biting back the retort that leaped to her lips, Ellie merely nodded tightly.

He released his grip, stepping away from her. With a yank, he closed a heavier set of curtains over the French doors. Then he moved to the table and turned up the lamp.

Ellie let the canvas bag slip from her shoulder, momentarily transfixed by her surroundings. The room was a glorious chaos. Every flat surface—including the floor—was covered with stacks of books and papers. Crates of yet-to-be-cataloged pottery shards teetered precariously on top of one another. Sketches and photographs lay in piles on tables or the seats of chairs, and maps, old and beginning to yellow, were tacked to the elegant paper covering the walls. In every corner lay some bizarre assortment of equipment: picks, shovels, mosquito netting, even a pair of broken hammocks. It reminded her of the basement of the British Museum, a place she'd been to only once and had been dying to get back inside of since.

Adam let out a low whistle.

"Hell of a new look you've got going there."

She resisted the urge to put a hand to her newly cropped hair. Instead she treated him to her best glare, though she was admittedly somewhat distracted by the impact the sight of him had on her concentration. He was in his shirtsleeves and looked as though he hadn't shaved in a few days. The golden grizzle marking his features combined with an angry red mark on his left cheekbone to give him a rather dangerous air. Then Ellie realized who was likely to blame for that soon-to-be-vicious bruise, and winced.

"I need to get out of here."

"How about first you tell me what sort of trouble you managed to get yourself into?"

"And why should I do that?"

He shrugged. "Because I might be able to help."

"I can do without your—"

Adam cut in before Ellie could finish her retort.

"It looks to me like you could use a friend right now, princess, and I don't see anyone else lining up for the job. So how's about you hold whatever it was you were going to say and think for a minute?"

Ellie closed her mouth. Her eyes traveled over the layered pages on the walls, and a thought—not a particularly welcome one—forced its way into her mind.

She had the map. She had stolen it back, and that meant there was still a chance she could find the city. After all, Dawson had told her to disappear, and what better place to vanish than into the bush?

But she wasn't foolish enough to believe she could do it alone. As much as it galled her, she needed someone to guide her. And the only person in the colony who'd admitted to being that crazy was standing in front of her.

"Whatever you're thinking right now, it looks interesting," he commented wryly.

She stepped over to the table and looked down. On top of it were a pile of sketches—very good sketches—of ruins surrounded by thick rain forest.

"Are these yours?" she asked.

"Just—don't touch anything." He gently removed her hand from the papers. Her eyes drifted to the huge map on the wall, an amalgamation of sketches like the ones on the table, prints, and notes, all tacked onto the surface with strings running from one place to another. She let her eyes follow the course of rivers, the detailed drawings of mountain peaks.

"You've been to all these places?"

"Most of them," he confirmed.

She turned to him, steeling herself. He raised an eyebrow.

"Do you even realize it when you're glaring like that?"

She frowned, then caught her reaction and forcibly cleared her expression.

"You once told me you were the only guide in this city who would take a woman into the bush," she said. "Did you mean that?"

He regarded her evenly.

"Depends on the woman, and what she's after."

She could feel how precariously the situation was balanced. However little she liked the form it happened to be taking, Ellie knew that this was her chance—possibly her only chance. But if she was going to convince him, she needed to make an impression, and she knew of only one way to do it.

She could feel the medallion's cool weight against her chest.

Steeling herself, she slipped the ribbon over her head and pulled off the dark circle of stone. She handed it to Adam.

He stared at it, then carried it over to the lamp and turned up the flame. He sat down and looked at the piece in the light.

"Excellent craftsmanship. Unusual material, though. Not obsidian…"

She took the bent hairpin from her pocket, held it near the medallion, and released it. The pin flew to the stone and adhered to it with a soft click.

"Magnetic," he said wonderingly.

"Hematite," Ellie said. "It can become magnetized under certain conditions. Though for a piece this large to achieve this degree of pull…"

"I'm aware."

She tried not to let that gall her. "It's Mayan, isn't it?"

Adam frowned down at the dark surface. "I don't know what the hell it is."

"Not Mayan?" The notion made her stomach jolt. Ellie was so surprised, it took her a moment to realize that Adam had just cursed at her.

Well, not *at* her, precisely. More like in her vicinity. But it wasn't something Ellie was accustomed to. Gentlemen—there was at least something of the gentleman about Adam Bates—did not use foul language in front of ladies.

Which either meant that the medallion had impressed him into forgetting himself, or he had decided, somewhere between the patio and the room, that Ellie wasn't the sort of lady he had to keep up pretenses for.

She wasn't sure quite what to think about that.

She shook it off, returning her attention to the greater revelation Adam had just given her.

Not Mayan.

Did that mean she'd come all this way for nothing? She wanted to sit down, but Adam was occupying the only chair.

"It's the carvings. The figural representations are off. I mean, this one here," he said, tapping the disk, "he looks a lot like Schell-has's God F to me. See the lines decorating his face? But this decal? The mirror? You don't see that with God F. That's classic God B."

"God B?" she echoed.

"Not their real names," Adam said wryly. "We don't know what the people who worshiped these gods called them. That knowledge was lost, along with whatever else had survived of the Mayan civilization, when the priests of the Inquisition arrived in the New World and decided to have a bonfire with their books."

Ellie's scholarly instincts flared.

"There were books?"

"Thousands of them. And at the time the Catholic missionaries were arriving here, there were still plenty of people around who knew how to read them."

"But I thought the written Mayan language was dead," Ellie protested. She'd learned as much in the lectures she'd attended at the university.

"It is," Adam confirmed. "But not of natural causes. The missionaries couldn't read the Mayan books they found. And what they didn't understand, they figured was probably the work of Satan. They gathered up every Mayan text they could get their hands on and systematically burned them. They made writing in the old glyphs a criminal act. So people stopped doing it, and within a generation, maybe two, the knowledge was gone."

Ellie felt outrage well up in her as though Adam had just told her about a massacre. She had assumed the key to the meaning of the Mayan glyphs was simply lost, something that had faded away over time. The idea that the answers to so many compelling questions about the builders of the great ruined cities might have been at their fingertips, if not for the fear and superstition of a few small-minded men, was horrific.

Adam traced a line of tiny, elegantly carved symbols on the medallion's surface. "A few years ago, an amateur linguist in Germany came up with a system for classifying the depictions of gods in Mayan glyphs. The wings and the serpent you see here? Those are associated with God B. He oversees life, creation. But these strong horizontal lines marking the figure's face? That's God F. War and sacrifice. Life and death, creation and destruction— these aren't symbols you're supposed to see together on a single icon. And then there's this." He tapped the round circle on the chest of the grinning idol. "That's not even Mayan. It's the Smoking Mirror."

"Smoking Mirror?" she echoed involuntarily. Her thoughts went straight to the telegram in her pocket. Dawson had been ordered to acquire a Smoking Mirror. Did that mean the medallion?

Something told her the answer wasn't that simple.

Adam elaborated, oblivious to her confusion, his attention still riveted by the artifact.

"The Smoking Mirror is an Aztec deity. Tezcatlipoca. The god of prophecy. The Aztecs claimed he possessed some kind of magic glass through which he could see anything he wanted—the past, the future. The thoughts and ambitions of rival kings." He paused, frowning. "Or maybe Tezcatlipoca was the mirror? Damned if I can remember. Aztec mythology isn't my area."

"So that symbol isn't Mayan?"

Adam rubbed a hand through his hair distractedly. "Strictly speaking, no. But the Mayans did use mirrors for ritual purposes. Not mirrors like we know them. No glass. They used polished disks of obsidian. I've seen them depicted in Mayan carvings with waving lines like these around them." He pointed to the marks on the medallion.

"Like smoke."

"Maybe. But then again, we know next to nothing about their glyphs. It's all guesswork."

She leaned over Adam's shoulder, looking down at the dark, fierce figure carved into the stone.

"So is it Mayan, or Aztec?"

He shook his head slowly.

"Beats me. It doesn't look like any Mayan or Aztec artifact I've ever seen. But it sure as hell doesn't look like a forgery, either. Where did you get this?"

"Call it a family heirloom," she said quickly, hiding her uneasiness. "And there's more."

Adam raised his eyebrow, waiting.

"There's a map."

"A map," he echoed flatly.

"It claims to show the location of a city hidden in the mountains."

"Of course it does."

Sarcasm? That was hardly the reaction she'd been expecting. Ellie felt her temper start to flare.

"What's that supposed to mean?"

He leaned back in his chair. "Look, princess—this is a hell of an intriguing trinket you've got here. But I've heard this story a hundred times. You can pretty much bet the farm the thing is either a hoax, or somebody else—probably the guy who drew your map—has had plenty of time to get to those ruins and clean out whatever treasure you think you're going to find."

"I'm not looking for treasure. And they weren't ruins."

"What do you mean, they weren't ruins?"

"The city was inhabited."

"Maybe by a few squatters..."

"By a kingdom. A flourishing one. In 1632."

He crossed his arms. "So this is supposed to be a map to an Aztec city."

"The location it points to is nowhere near Aztec territory."

"The Aztecs were the only Central American civilization with inhabited cities in the seventeenth century."

She walked over to the map on the wall. It was a beautiful piece of work, showing everything from rivers and villages to the terrain itself. There were plenty of ruins marked there as well—more, she realized, than she had seen in the atlas at the British Library.

"The location is deep in traditional Mayan territory. It's nowhere near Aztec lands," she said.

"There were no Mayan kingdoms in 1632."

"None that anybody knew about," she countered evenly. "But for all I know, it could be something else. The map just calls it a white city."

Adam went still.

"The White City. This map of yours claims to show the location of the White City."

"It could just be a descriptive term," Ellie offered, sensing the rise in Adam's tension.

"It's a blasted myth, is what it is. Another El Dorado. Cortés wasted a lot of money looking for it—and a lot of lives."

He stood silent for a moment, and Ellie could practically hear the gears turning inside his head. She waited, afraid that anything she might say would push him the wrong way. Finally he sighed.

"I have a feeling I'm going to regret this, but what the hell. Show it to me."

She felt a flash of alarm. "Show what to you?"

"Your diary. What do you think? The map."

Of course he would want to see it. But now that the moment had arrived, she found herself reluctant to hand it over. The reason came to her clearly: Give it to him, and he would hold all the cards. He was the expert, after all. The experienced surveyor with intimate knowledge of the territory, and certainly more knowledge of Central American cultures than she could claim. Where would that leave her? She'd be so much extra weight.

No, she thought. This was her adventure. The map and its secrets had fallen into her lap, no one else's. She wasn't going to hand it over that easily. But she had to show him something. He was far from convinced, and whether she liked the idea or not, right now he was her only hope of getting where she so desperately wanted to go.

The solution came to her quick and bright, like a spark. She didn't pause to second-guess it, just pulled the map from her pocket, walked to the desk, and then stabbed the parchment with Adam's letter opener.

"What the hell are you doing?" he protested as she yanked the blade down through the map. It cut cleanly, and she finished the job with a tear. She handed the bottom half to Bates, tucking the rest neatly back into her pocket.

"That should be enough to start with."

"To start with? What about the rest of it?"

"The rest is my insurance policy," she replied coolly.

"Insurance against what? If I were out to steal it and feed you to the crocodiles, keeping it in your corset isn't going to stop me."

"We can skip the references to my corset," she said tightly, flushing. "I wouldn't be offering to bring you in on this if I thought you were going to rob me. I trust you that far. What I don't trust is that once you have what you need, you won't treat me like a piece of baggage instead of a partner, or pack me back to London out of some convenient sense of chivalry. So until we're well on our way, the rest of the route stays with me."

They stared at each other across the room, the tension thick. Ellie suddenly realized that she was very afraid he might refuse—that he'd hand back the map and tell her to go to hell. She forced herself to meet his gaze without showing a hint of her unease.

"Where's this city of yours supposed to be? *Approximately*," he added as her posture quickly turned defensive.

She hesitated only a moment, then walked over to the map and laid her finger on a place in the Cayo District, a stretch of mountains labeled, *Uncharted*. Adam came beside her, gazing at the spot she indicated. She risked a glance at his face, trying to read his expression. It didn't look good. She felt her stomach sink.

He turned to her, their closeness making him loom. She hadn't noticed how very *large* he was before. She also found herself noting that he smelled—not unpleasantly—of cigar and whiskey. It was a distracting detail.

"Let me make one thing perfectly clear. If I agree to help you with this insanity—which I haven't yet—*I'm* the one who calls the shots. I tell you duck, you duck. Run, you run. And not after you've asked me thirty damned questions, or called me a chauvinist good-for-nothing. Where you want to go, there are a whole lot of things that could cut the both of us down. It's dangerous, and whatever you think, until you've been out there you can't pretend you know what you're doing."

"If I did, I wouldn't be offering to do this with you," she retorted.

"Seems to me I'm the one doing the offering, princess."

She jumped at the sound of voices in the hall. Adam's eyes narrowed, and he motioned for her to duck behind the door. The knock came a moment later. Adam picked a glass half-full of amber-colored liquid up from the table, then opened the door as Ellie pressed herself into her hiding place.

She peered through the narrow gap between the door and the wall and glimpsed Augustus Smith, looking harried and apologetic.

"I'm terribly sorry to bother you, Mr. Bates, but we're checking with all the guests. This is Mr. Jacobs. His room was robbed earlier this evening. We're wondering if you've noticed anything amiss."

Jacobs.

Smith stood in the doorway, taking up the entirety of Ellie's narrow band of vision. Jacobs would be behind him, only a few inches from where she stood. The thought made Ellie want to shrink into the carpet. Her hiding place behind the door seemed unaccountably feeble. She felt certain he would know she was there, would step forward and catch sight of her through the gap between the hinges, or smell her out like some small prey run aground. She pressed herself back against the wall.

"Not a thing."

Adam's reply was utterly easy. The man was a decent actor. *And liar.* Ellie made a note to remember that.

Smith continued, sounding as though he did so against his inclination.

"It also seems that Miss Tyrrell has gone missing. She wasn't at dinner and isn't in her room. We're obviously rather concerned. Have you seen her within the last few hours?"

"Pretty. Brunette. Talks too much." The boards creaked as Adam leaned against the frame of the door. "Afraid not."

There was an awkward silence. Jacobs's voice broke it.

"Mr. Smith would like me to take a look around your room."

"He would, would he?"

"Mr. Jacobs has told me he has some experience with these matters," Smith explained. Ellie watched him tug nervously on his ear.

"I might notice something you've missed," Jacobs offered smoothly.

"I see. That's very considerate of you."

The tension between Jacobs and her unexpected protector was thick enough to cut, and Ellie risked a closer peek through the crack in the door. Adam was just visible, reclining against the door frame with his whiskey glass in his hand. He reminded her of a lion, all lazy power and implied threat.

"Smith, tell Mr. Jacobs. Does anyone come into my room?"

"Mr. Bates keeps his things in a very particular order and expressly requests that nothing be disturbed."

"Which is how I'd know if anything was missing. Besides which, I've been inside all day. I probably would have noticed if any thieves or mouthy women decided to drop in."

"Of course," Smith hurried to assure him. "We're sorry to disturb you, Mr. Bates."

"Don't worry about it," Adam drawled. "Mr. Jacobs."

"Mr. Bates," Jacobs acknowledged coolly, and Ellie heard their footsteps continue down the hall.

Adam watched them for a moment longer, then finally closed the door. Ellie tried not to slump with relief. He said nothing but raised a finger to his lips. She nodded as they listened to the footsteps move away, followed by the sound of knocking on a farther door.

He reached out and fingered a curl of her butchered hair.

"You really went whole hog, didn't you?"

She stepped back, tugging her coat more closely around her shoulders.

"I didn't steal all this from his room, if that's what you were thinking."

"Of course not. That's Tibbord's jacket. I'm surprised you fit in his trousers."

She felt her face burn.

"I had to belt them."

"I expect you did," he drawled. "You going to tell me what the story is with Mr. Friendly?"

Ellie struggled briefly, realizing what the truth would sound like—implausible at best, or worse, like a whole lot of extra trouble. The lie was instinctive and automatic.

"He's an agent of my uncle's. When I left to come here, Uncle David sent him to bring me back."

"Your uncle a nice guy?"

"Of course," Ellie replied instinctively.

"Then why did he hire someone like that to take care of his niece?"

"Mr. Jacobs is very thorough," she blurted in response.

"I can see that. So why doesn't he just tell Smith he's looking for a wayward ward?"

She opened her mouth to reply, closed it, and flashed what she hoped was a disarming smile. "I'm sure he's hoping to avoid embarrassment for the family."

"Family like that brother of yours?"

Ellie felt her face flush. She lifted her chin, crossing her arms over her chest. "I don't have a brother."

"I figured as much." He studied her face. "Anything else you're leaving out?"

She felt a brief flash of guilt. *Quite a lot, actually.* She shook her head. "That's all of it. Now, are you in, or shall I take this to someone else?"

He chuckled. "You got cojones, princess. I'll grant you that."

"What exactly is a cojone?" she demanded.

"Maybe I'll tell you later."

"Is that a yes?"

She could see him hesitate. She fought against panic. *If he refused...*

Well, she would worry about that when—if—it happened. Not that she'd blame him. It wasn't much to go on—even the parts that were true.

"Look—this isn't the sort of thing I usually worry about, but under the circumstances..." He ran a hand through his hair awkwardly, and Ellie felt her heart sink.

This was it. The snag, the perfectly rational objection she wouldn't be able to talk her way around.

"You see, we go ahead with this, it's just going to be the two of us. I don't drag a team out for this kind of initial survey. There's no funding for it, and I don't like wasting people's time. We won't be bringing an expedition. Which means you're going to be traveling alone with a strange man, possibly for weeks. Now, I've never been one to give much of a damn for my reputation, but I've also never been considered a debaucher of proper young ladies. I'm not sure that's a distinction I'd like to earn."

Ellie stared at him in shock. This turn of the conversation had taken her completely by surprise—but shouldn't have.

That Ellie had come to British Honduras alone would have raised an eyebrow or two, but women traveled to the Caribbean for health reasons often enough, and the Imperial was a reputable hotel. As for the rest of it...

If she had ended up securing one of the men Smith had recommended as her guide, she doubted anyone would have thought twice about it. But those had mostly been native men, many in their forties or fifties. In the eyes of society, there was quite a difference between them and a man like Adam Bates. One look at him would start tongues viciously wagging. But then again, those tongues were a very long way off.

She caught herself. Was she really considering this an obstacle?

Ellie Mallory, suffragette, modern woman, shying away from the opportunity of a lifetime because of an outdated, oppressive concern for her reputation?

No. It was ludicrous. If this was her chance, she was going to take it, and to hell with the consequences.

After all, how bad would those really be? If their quest did turn out to be a false one, then no one would need to know about her "indiscretion." Belize City was hardly crawling with acquaintances.

And if the map was genuine? Then she would hope the reputation she would have gained as a scholar would outweigh a bit of spiteful gossiping.

If she were a man, no one would think twice about her decision to undertake such a venture. It was just another way the world tried to keep her sex at home, docile and bored to insanity.

To hell with all of them, she thought boldly.

Of course, it didn't sound as though Adam was going to share that enlightened opinion.

She could feel the pressure of the moment. If she couldn't convince Adam to help her, she was in trouble. Big trouble. What she'd said in spite to Dawson was, after all, true—she'd still be a "loose end" in England, and her enemies had already proven their ability to dig up even the most obscure corners of her life. How long did she really think she could hide from them?

She needed this man to agree to her proposition, and now. With a rush of adrenaline, she realized that her life might actually depend on it.

There was only one thing to do: lie. Fast.

"That's not a problem," she said breezily. "I'm already debauched."

He stared at her, obviously shocked.

She stumbled to elaborate.

"I mean to say that I'm married. Was married. I'm a widow," she concluded firmly, then clamped her mouth shut before it could do any more damage.

"You're a widow," Adam echoed slowly.

"Yes," she said with more sureness now, daring him to contradict her. And he clearly wanted to—she could see the desire in his expression. But she lifted her head, meeting his gaze steadily. After all, what could he do? Cross-examine her for details about her departed husband? Accuse her outright of making it up? If she was, in fact, a widow, that would hardly be the gentlemanly thing to do—and it seemed that Adam, whatever else he was, occasionally felt obliged to play that part.

He studied her for another tense moment, his skepticism warring with his sense of decency. Then the tension in him broke.

"Maybe you are. Either way, I suppose it'll have to do."

"Does that mean you agree?"

Ellie's heart pounded as she waited for his answer.

She could see him thinking, felt her fate hanging in the balance. He moved to where his map hung on the wall, gazing at the place Ellie had pointed out, right above that single penciled word— *Uncharted.* He turned from there to the table, where the medallion lay glittering in the lamplight. He picked it up, testing its weight in his hand, then shrugged.

"What the hell? It sounds more interesting than anything else I've got on the agenda." He turned to her. "You need anything else from your room?"

She couldn't quite believe it. It was a moment before she remembered to shake her head.

Adam glanced at the canvas bag on the floor. "That's it?"

"That's it."

"You pack light. Good. That much less we'll have to get rid of. Oh. Almost forgot."

He pulled the gun from his belt and held it up. The lamplight glinted off the well-oiled steel of the barrel.

"You know how to use this?"

Ellie pushed back the flicker of nerves, tilting her chin firmly. "Well enough."

Adam studied her for a moment before spinning the gun nimbly in his hand. He held it out to her, stock first, and she hesitated only a moment before taking it.

"Where we're going, you might want to keep it loaded."

Ellie glanced down at the weapon. How had he known it was empty? Just by *feeling* it?

He pulled back the curtain and opened the French doors to the garden. He bowed gracefully in a startlingly good imitation of a proper society gentleman. "Ladies first."

"We're going now?"

"Unless you want to wait here and see if your Mr. Jacobs comes back for another inspection."

Ellie stuffed the revolver in her bag, then held out her hand expectantly.

Adam hesitated for a moment, turning the dark circle of stone around in his hand, then finally handed it back to her. Ellie slipped it around her neck, feeling an unexpected relief to have it back where it belonged. She glanced at Adam's now-empty hands.

"Aren't you bringing anything?"

"Everything I need is already with *Mary Lee*."

"Who's Mary Lee?"

"My boat," he replied. He leaned over and blew out the lamp.

They stepped outside. The night had turned peaceful once again, quiet and jasmine-scented. Adam gripped the railing and hopped over it into the garden, Ellie following.

"This way," he said, leading her down the pathway. He stopped at an exposed area of fence at the far end.

"Need a boost?" he offered.

Ellie shot him a glare. She tossed her bag over, then pulled herself up. She dropped awkwardly into the dirt on the far side. Adam chuckled, then climbed over himself, landing far more gracefully.

They were in the quiet, well-kept rear garden of the house beside the hotel. Adam strolled through it, Ellie following, until he reached a door at the back. Unbolting it, he led her out into a narrow alley that ran between the buildings. She found herself wondering why he had need of a secret way in and out of the hotel. She was fairly certain she would rather not know the answer to that question, but it made her suddenly aware of how little she knew about the man she had just agreed to partner with. It should have been a terrifying thought, but all she could feel was a wild exhilaration.

They moved down the dark space between the fences and buildings until at last the alley ended. She stepped out onto the street that led to the harbor, the night sky spreading wide and dark above them. Ellie could hear music and voices coming from the more ramshackle buildings nearby. Already, the danger of the hotel felt years behind her, impossible in the peaceful stillness.

The harbor was glowing, stars and the slice of moon reflected off the water. The soft light was broken only by the shadowy, rocking shapes of boats, the line of the waterfront marked by the occasional orange glow of a lit window.

Adam strolled down the dock, Ellie following after, her feet pattering hollowly against the boards. They moved past tall-masted sailing ships and weathered fishing sloops to the outer reaches of the marina.

"Here we are," Adam said at last. He hopped off the dock onto a small, shallow-draft steamboat with a pair of paddlewheels at her sides. The boat had obviously seen better days. The wide, low deck was gray and worn, practically begging for a new coat of paint, as were the rails, which rose to about waist height. There was no cabin, only a canopy, slightly tattered at the edges, aft of the stovepipe. A few crates and bundles were piled beneath it, and a coal box in the stern was nearly full. Along the side, barely legible, were painted the words *Mary Lee*.

"You sure it's not going to sink?" she asked warily.

"She's seen a lot more of the bush than you have," Adam countered.

Ellie gave the boat another skeptical look, then shrugged inwardly. She tossed her pack onto the deck and climbed after it.

"Welcome aboard," Adam said, and grinned at her.

7

THEY STOPPED FOR THE night after a few hours, anchoring in a sheltered cove, and Ellie made up for her missed dinner with a tin of beans heated on the boiler. She had been tempted to lick the bowl. Afterward, she was too tired to protest when Adam hung a pair of hammocks under a white drape of mosquito netting on opposite sides of the canopy, and she realized just how close the two of them would be sleeping. She'd never been in a hammock in her life, but the sling of fabric proved remarkably comfortable. Before she knew it, she was asleep, and by sunrise she felt remarkably rested.

They returned to puttering past the thick tangles of mangroves that lined the coast. At first, the forests were sometimes broken by crescents of white sand or the rickety dock of a fishing outpost, but by midmorning there was nothing but thick gray and green meeting the turquoise water.

It was stunning. Ellie felt washed away in the brightness of the blue sky, the calm sea, and the flashing yellow-green of the mangrove leaves. Everything seemed so wide, so warm, so bright—so decidedly different from London, she realized. The thought sent a thrill racing through her.

She watched as a pair of pelicans rose from the shore and lifted into the air. They sailed over *Mary Lee*'s wake, apparently mistaking the small steam launch for a fishing boat likely to throw them some extra bait.

"Will we see the mouth of the Sibun, or is it overgrown?" she asked, breaking the long silence.

Adam glanced at her from the tiller, impressed.

"You know where we're going?"

"I studied a few maps back in London. It's how I knew to start where I did. The shape of the rivers matched."

"It's a big river," Adam said. "We'll see it." He reclined in his seat, shirtsleeves rolled up to his elbows. His eyes matched the color of the water, contrasting brightly with his deeply tanned skin, and his sun-bleached hair ruffled in the light breeze. Only a dark, vicious bruise on his cheekbone marred the classic lines of his face. Ellie remembered with chagrin that she was responsible for that.

She realized she was spending a bit more time than was justified studying that particular aspect of the scenery. She had never been one to moon over supposedly dashing men, however much Constance had tried to impress the habit on her. She was too aware that pretty faces usually entailed insipid conversation and an irritating smugness to enjoy the pastime. And there were better things to do—books to read, lectures to attend. Why her current traveling companion should suddenly prove an exception to that rule was beyond her.

She pulled her eyes away forcibly and directed them to the water. She could see through it to the white sand of the seafloor, speckled with shells and stones. Occasionally some bright-colored fish would skirt past, surprised out of its hiding place by the churning of the paddles.

She let her hand hang over the side, trailing her fingers in the water. It felt delicious, just cool enough to refresh against the heat of the sun on her skin. Checking to be sure that Adam's attention was still focused on piloting the boat, she dipped her hand farther down, then rubbed it against the back of her neck, nearly sighing aloud at the feeling of the water against her skin.

She dipped her hand in again, then froze as a massive gray shape drifted slowly beneath the *Mary Lee*.

"Mr. Bates?" she called, unable to take her eyes away from the shockingly large . . . something. Then a great, whiskered head rose from the water, its snout pushing against the palm of her hand.

She felt a rush of fear, certain she was about to lose a limb to some ferocious sea monster. She held herself perfectly still, terrified that a sudden movement would provoke the beast into opening its sure-to-be-ravenous jaws and snapping off a piece of her.

"It won't bite," Adam called to her easily. "Manatee."

Ellie forced back her panic and looked down into the small, soft eyes that framed the whiskered face. They stared up at her, liquid and warm, and the wet muzzle nudged her hand once more. Then the creature turned, diving elegantly back into the water and disappearing under the boat. Three others followed it, darting beneath them, massive shadows moving across the white sands.

"He was hoping you had food," Adam said.

"For a minute I thought I was the food," she admitted.

Adam chuckled, shaking his head. "Sailors used to think they were mermaids. That'd be one ugly mermaid." He roped off the tiller and stood to add another shovel of coal to the boiler. "You can put your hands back in the water. I'll let you know when to take them out."

"And when will that be?" she asked as he dropped easily back onto his seat.

He flashed her a white grin.

"When we get to the crocodiles."

Ellie saw the reality behind Adam's warning not long afterward as they reached the mouth of the river. There, she was startled as a rotting log drifting past their boat suddenly raised a pair of beady yellow eyes out of the water. The crocodile stared at her as the *Mary Lee* steamed past, and Ellie instinctively moved closer to the center of the small craft.

The boat chugged steadily as the day wore on. The tidy fields gave way to a wilder landscape of tangled green leaves, trees, and vines thickly bordering the high banks of the river. By the time the sun began to drift toward the horizon, it had been hours since Ellie had seen any sign of human presence. There were only the lizards, the bright birds, and the thick wall of green on either side of them.

~

When the sky began to change its blue for purple, Adam rounded a bend in the river and drew the *Mary Lee* in closer to the trees. With an echoing rattle, the launch's engine slowed to a stop. The pent-up steam was released with a forlorn whistle. The sound raised a cacophonous cry from a flock of birds startled out of the branches of a massive overhanging oak. They rose up, dark, fluttering shapes calling in irritation to one another against the richly colored dusk.

Ellie rose as Adam banked the fire. She stretched, her limbs protesting. She glanced forward and felt her heart jump. There, visible between the break in the foliage afforded by a straight stretch of the river, were the mountains. They rose up, shadowy and close— so much closer than they had seemed when they were a green haze in the distance from the veranda of the Imperial. They seemed near enough to touch.

Her hand went to the medallion, hidden beneath her shirt. They were that much closer to the mysterious place it had come from.

If it's real, she reminded herself.

She jumped as Adam brushed against her side, slipping past her to the anchor. He tossed it over the bow, letting it draw out its line, then secured it tightly.

"Where are we?" she asked.

Adam popped open one of the crates and pulled out a tin cylinder. He unscrewed the top and removed an oilskin bundle. Inside was the map. Unfolding it, he laid it down on the deck, smoothing out the creases. Ellie came over to look.

"Right about...here," he said, pointing. He took another map out of the oilskin, this one much more detailed and obviously modern. As Ellie looked down at it, she realized it wasn't printed.

"Is this hand-drawn?" she asked.

"Yup," he confirmed, studying it.

Fear bubbled up, sudden and primitive. She wanted to tell Adam to fire up the boiler, to keep moving.

No.

She fought for calm. There was no point panicking, not when she didn't *know* anything...except that there could be no going back to the city. Whether she met them in the harbor or on the river, Dawson and his cold companion would be waiting for her. And they would not let her slip away again.

She would have to find an unimpeachable reason why there was no choice but to push forward.

Ellie reminded herself that it was entirely possible she wouldn't have to. After all, the *Mary Lee* might be able to navigate the caves just fine. It was better not to risk rousing Adam's suspicion unless she had to.

She'd also have had several hours by then to think up a good excuse.

The thought left her feeling uneasy. She seemed to be doing quite a lot of lying lately, particularly to Adam Bates. She'd lied about the origin of the map, lied about Jacobs...He didn't even know her name, she realized. He still thought she was Constance Tyrrell.

She knew she couldn't remedy that without unraveling the rest of it, but that didn't stop her from feeling a sharp pang of guilt.

She pushed it back.

"Let's give it a try," she said firmly, and was relieved when Adam accepted her answer with a nod.

"So after we get through the caves—if we get through—we're watching for this rock."

"'A black pillar which draws the compass,'" Ellie said, translating it from memory.

"Must be magnetic, like that bauble of yours." Adam ran his finger along the torn edge of the old map, then glanced up at her meaningfully. "Any other landmarks I should know about?"

Ellie shifted awkwardly. "A few. I'll show them to you when we get closer."

"Still don't quite trust me, huh?" He gathered up the two maps, folding them together and sliding them into the cylinder.

"That's not . . . It isn't precisely . . ."

"Relax. I know the deal. Just don't leave it too long, all right?"

She nodded, and he returned the cylinder to the crate, taking out a pair of tins. He set a pot on the still-hot boiler, punched them open, and poured out a thick mess of beans. They started to hiss against the hot steel.

"We'll have canned food while we're on the boat, but it'll be different once we start cutting cross-country," he remarked. He opened the firebox, using a pair of tongs to remove one of the glowing coals. He touched it to the wicks of a pair of lamps, blowing the flames to life, then tossed it into the water. The landscape around them was growing dark quickly, and the lamps added a welcome glow to the little world of the boat.

"I can't imagine it being worthwhile to carry tins," Ellie commented. Her stomach rumbled. She was surprised. It seemed like all she'd done that day was sit in the bow, yet she was starving.

"We'll bring some dry goods for emergencies, but for the most part we'll have to find what we need as we go. There's usually fruit this time of year, and we'll try for game. I don't suppose you're any good with a rifle?"

"We don't do much shooting in central London."

"I'm pretty handy with the express." He nodded toward the large gun that leaned against the rail. "We'll find game. But you should know that some of what will be on hand won't be quite what you're used to."

"Like what?" she challenged. As hungry as she felt now, it was hard to imagine anything she wouldn't eat.

"How do you feel about termites?"

She frowned thoughtfully. "What do they taste like?"

"Kind of nutty."

"Doesn't sound bad," she concluded.

Adam took a pair of bowls from one of the crates and ladled out the beans. Ellie accepted hers gratefully, though it was almost too warm for her to set on her lap. Adam dipped the pan into the river, set it aside to soak, then sat down beside her on the deck with his own bowl.

They ate in silence. Then, her hunger somewhat sated, Ellie's thoughts turned to the question that had been dancing at the back of her mind all day as they'd chugged along the slow, remote waters Adam obviously knew so well.

"How did you come to this?" she demanded, setting her bowl aside.

"Eating termites?" Adam asked around a mouthful of beans.

"No," she dismissed. *"This."* She waved her hand, taking in the thick forest overhead, the dark river—all of their remote and beautiful surroundings. "Was it something you always knew you wanted?"

"No. I didn't figure this out until pretty late in the game. Mostly I just knew what I didn't want to do."

"And what was that?"

"What my father does," he replied flatly. He reached over and collected Ellie's empty bowl, then leaned over the side to give everything a wash.

"And what's your father do?" she called, turning awkwardly away from the admittedly nice view of him leaning over the rail.

"He owns a very successful insurance firm. Robinson, Bates, and MacKenzie of San Francisco," he recited.

"Robinson, Bates... I've heard of that," she realized, surprised, then explained. "My uncle works for a shipping company—he's their chief accountant."

"They mostly cover shipping," Adam confirmed. "Since I was a boy, both my parents assumed I would take over the company. I'm pretty sure my mother still thinks that," he added dryly.

"But you didn't want to," she finished for him.

"No. It's all... keeping clean-shaven, playing nice. Not rocking the boat." He shook his head, distant. "I know there are plenty of people who'd think I'm crazy, walking away from a life like that. There's a hell of a lot of money, and all the things that go along with money. But the whole thing's just a puppet show. Everybody going through the motions, pretending to like people they can't stand, looking for a chance to stab their friends in the back. It's business."

"Not everyone feels that way about it," she pointed out.

"Of course not. I know that. My brother, Robin—he's great for it. Reliable, and he loves playing the game. He would've been happy with it. But I'm the older son." He looked thoughtful for a moment. "I suppose he is happy with it, now."

"You don't hear from them?"

"My mother writes. I send her a letter every now and then. But it's always the same thing—come home, be responsible. When am I going to grow out of this."

"And your father?"

"He doesn't much like it when people don't do what he tells them." He glanced over at her wryly. "So you might be able to guess how well we got along. To be honest, I think he'd given up on me long before Cambridge."

"Cambridge?" Ellie perked up, frowning. "As in the university?"

"That's the one." He stretched his legs out in front of him, crossing them lazily.

"You went to Cambridge? But you lived in . . ."

"San Francisco," he filled in.

Her eyes widened. "That's halfway across the world."

He shrugged. "My mother insisted I go to her father's alma mater. And my cousin Arch was going to be there at the same time." He shook his head. "Thank God he didn't turn out to be a stuffed shirt—I was sure he would be, when I went over there."

"Why?"

"Because he's the Fourteenth Earl of Scarsdale."

Ellie stared at him as he tugged off one of his boots, then the dirty sock beneath it, baring a set of somewhat filthy toes.

"Your cousin is an earl," she said dumbly.

"And a genuinely down-to-earth guy, which is the surprising part."

"So your...grandfather...?"

"Was the twelfth earl."

"Tell me you're joking," she said flatly. Adam raised an eyebrow and shook his head. She burst out laughing. "I'm sorry, really. It's just...well, you're probably the last thing I'd expect in an earl's grandson."

"I'll take that as a compliment. Arch fits the bill—he's head-to-toe the proper nobleman. He was just lucky enough to be born with a sense of humanity."

"So, heir to an insurance empire, earl's grandson, Cambridge—then British Honduras?"

He laughed. "Well—you can blame Fairfax for that part."

Ellie felt her heart skip a beat.

"Fairfax?"

Adam continued, oblivious to her startled tone.

"I met him in a mathematics course. He talked me into coming with him to his Greek history lecture. Fairfax is that kind of guy—too earnest to say no to. I got hooked."

"Hooked?" Ellie echoed numbly. He couldn't possibly be talking about her cousin Neil, the man she'd essentially grown up with. But...*Fairfax. Cambridge*. Her mind reeled.

"Suckered. I couldn't get enough of the stuff. Greece, Rome, ancient China—didn't matter where. I'd never felt like that about anything before—never wanted more of something. It was always less. Less rules, less formality, less bull." When he looked at her, his eyes were bright. "He converted me, is what it comes down to. And I wasn't the only one. He lured Arch into it, too, and another classmate of his—guy by the name of Perry. Trevelyan Perry."

At the sound of the name, Ellie twitched. There was no use denying it now, no hoping Adam was talking about some other Fairfax from Cambridge. She knew Perry, had sat and listened to him and Neil discuss excavation reports, picking apart their lecturers. She had stood in the back garden and mimicked Perry's strange and elegant movements until she could put Neil into a stronghold with little more than a twist of her body.

"All lovely girls should know how to take care of themselves," he had said with that heart-fluttering smile.

And on some of his visits home, she realized, she had heard Neil mention *this* man—the stranger she had unwittingly teamed up with halfway across the world. The Yank, he had called him. *The cowboy.*

She'd traveled across an ocean to a distant continent and ended up on a boat with her cousin's school chum.

Neil was going to kill her.

If he ever finds out, she silently amended. As far as Adam Bates knew, she was Constance Tyrrell, a girl from London with no connection to him or anyone he knew. And there was absolutely no reason it couldn't stay that way.

Adam was still talking, fortunately oblivious to the turmoil in her brain.

"History was what started it, but for all four of us it was archaeology we really fell for. And of course, Cambridge wasn't much use for that. Too new a discipline. What we wanted to know, we had to learn on our own. So we did," he concluded. "Made ourselves an unofficial club. Met once a week in a room over a pub on Magdalene Street."

"Yes, it was the same at London," she murmured absently, her mind still whirling from the revelation. "No official course for it."

Adam frowned, suddenly alert. "Are you talking about the University of London?"

Ellie felt a quick panic. She should backtrack, she knew, invent a cover. But something in her rebelled at the notion. Why shouldn't he know she was educated? They were equal partners in this expedition. He might as well be aware that the woman he traveled with was well qualified for the undertaking.

"Yes," she replied tartly. "The University of London. I graduated five years ago."

"I should've figured as much."

She felt a flash of temper.

"What's that supposed to mean, exactly?"

"Just that you've got the right sort of chip on your shoulder," he replied easily.

"A chip on my shoulder," she echoed coldly, feeling her fury begin to rise.

"You got a better word for it?"

"Bluestocking, perhaps? Harpy? Battle-ax—that's a nice one. Virago. Harridan. I suppose there are any number of appropriate terms for a woman who fights her way into an education the rest of society thinks she should be forbidden. Bitch—that's a particular favorite, I think."

"Hold on to those horses just a minute," he said gently. "Let me set the record straight before we go any further. As far as I'm concerned, a woman should have as much right to an education as anyone else, if that's what she wants."

"How very forward-thinking of you. And magnanimous, since the common trait of those who go through with it is apparently a recognizable degree of shrewishness."

Was that hurt that slipped into the end of her clipped tones? She desperately hoped not. After all, what did she care if this man thought she was a shrew?

He sighed, running his hand through his hair.

"I'm sure I'm going to step into something here, but what the hell... Princess, there's a certain sort of attitude a girl acquires when she's gotten so used to everybody telling her what she can't do, she walks into a room ready to roll over anyone who looks at her sideways."

"And I strike you as the type?" she retorted.

"How exactly would you describe your state of mind just about every time I've had the pleasure of running into you?"

"I don't really see how—"

"How about 'hostile'?" he cut in with a drawl.

She felt the rebuttal spring to her lips, the quick instinct to cut as harshly as she could. She bit it back, forcing herself to calm.

It was true, of course. She had been spitting mad at Adam just about every time they'd been in each other's company, up till the moment he'd agreed to help her. Not, she countered inwardly, that she had been entirely unjustified. Though she also had to admit that however uncouth his methods, his various invasions had been made with the intention—misguided or not—of helping her.

"Don't get me wrong," he continued. "It's not unwarranted. I can't guess half of what you've gone up against to get where you have, but I'd reckon it'd put just about anybody on the ornery side."

"You reckon," she echoed a bit numbly, struggling to take it all in.

"It's got to be hard enough just getting through the door, never mind what sort of attitude those smug public-school types would've given you. I got a taste of that myself before they realized the uncivilized Yankee wasn't afraid to give them a jab in their well-bred kidneys."

The image made her smile in spite of herself.

"So London. Did you specialize?"

She nodded. "Natural science and ancient history."

"Figures," Adam said, mouth pulling into a smile. "And what about after?"

"After what?"

"University. You said you finished five years ago. What've you been doing since?"

"Not what I would've liked," she said quietly, looking at the wild, foreign world around them. The night was rich, trees thick with birdcalls and animal hoots, the river lapping warmly against the hull. There was not so much as a glimmer of lamplight breaking the darkness that surrounded them. No human voice, no smoke or clopping of hooves. They were alone in a true wilderness, a new and strange territory. It was what she had yearned for since she was a girl, listening to Neil's stories of discoveries in far-off lands. This was Adam Bates's life, and from what she could read in the easiness of his posture, it fit him as comfortably as an old shoe.

"You still haven't told me how you ended up out here," she said.

"Not much to it. Perry convinced me to take the civil service exam and they offered me the spot."

She tried not to let the words hurt. Of course it had been that simple. Even if he hadn't been a Cambridge scholar and the descendant of nobility, all he needed was a decent score on his exam to get where he belonged. He was a man.

Well, she admitted—perhaps he would have to have done a bit better than "decent." The position of assistant surveyor general wasn't one they would have handed out lightly.

She found that the implication did not surprise her. She must finally be breaking the habit of underestimating Adam Bates. It was both a warm and an unsettling realization.

He stood, yawning widely.

"We should get some sleep. Long day tomorrow."

"Of course," she agreed. She slipped past the mosquito net and climbed up into her hammock, somewhat ungracefully. Adam reached up and turned down the flame of the lamp, letting the warm darkness enfold them. The *Mary Lee* dimmed into a softer moonlight and the jungle gleamed.

"Good night, princess," he said, the ropes of the hammock creaking as he shifted, settling in.

Princess. She realized that the term had ceased to grate on her, as it had back in the city. It had become something warmer and more comfortable.

"Sleep well, Mr. Bates," she replied.

8

THE DREAM STARTED LIKE the others.

She was standing on a platform in the courtyard of Burlington House, the headquarters of the Royal Society. A sea of reporters was in front of her. Flashes burst with puffs of smoke, cameras whirring and clicking. A stuffy little man stood at the podium in front of her, wiping a bit of sweat from his forehead with a handkerchief.

"And now, I am honored to introduce the society's most eminent new member, the explorer responsible for the discovery of the final resting place of Atlantis—Miss Eleanora Mallory."

Ellie knew what she should have been feeling as she stepped forward to a roaring cheer: exultation, victory at achieving at last the recognition she deserved. But as the reporters began to shout their questions, scrambling over one another for her attention, she found her gaze wandering to the back of the assembled crowd.

She knew what she was looking for—whom she was looking for. She found the scarred woman standing alone in the center of the busy London street, the traffic moving around her as if she were a rock in a tumbling stream. Her slight figure was dressed not in the plain blouse and skirt Ellie had seen her in before, but something far more exotic. It was a gown made entirely of feathers in bright hues. Red mingled with blue, gold, and green, covering the whole of her tiny frame, making her look finer, Ellie thought, than any English aristocrat she'd ever seen.

As Ellie's admirers began to chant in her honor, she called over them to where the scarred woman stood, solemn and silent.

"I'm dreaming again, aren't I?"

She nodded, and the carriages, the crowd—even the Palladian facade of Burlington House—shattered and spilled to the ground, dissolving like water.

Aunt Florence was making a racket again. It tore painfully through the veil of Ellie's sleep, an irritating screech and clattering. Ellie winced against the noise and reached, eyes still shut, for her blanket. Instead, she found herself grasping the front of her shirt—or rather, the front of Mr. Tibbord's shirt.

Not London. Not Aunt Florence.

She sat up abruptly, opening her eyes, and the clan of monkeys in the tree overhead went quiet for a moment, looking down at her. Then they rapidly resumed their chattering and swung off through the canopy. She watched them go, then shook her head, trying to clear the last vestiges of sleep from her brain.

She had been dreaming again. It had been something good, something wonderful. She tried to grasp the memory, but the fragments of it dissolved, replaced by a far less enticing reality. Dawson and Jacobs, the map, the boat . . . Adam Bates. She looked around. The other hammock was empty, as was the rest of the deck. She felt a quick rush of fear.

"Mr. Bates?" she called. Only the fluttering of a few birds answered her, and for a moment her mind was flooded with images of a massive jaguar slipping on board, or an ancient crocodile emerging from the water to clap its jaws around the man's head.

Or perhaps he's gone to find breakfast, she ruefully corrected herself, forcibly noticing the absence of such crocodile or jaguar attack indicators as blood or severed limbs. She wondered how far he had gone.

"Mr. Bates!" she shouted as loud as she could. *"Helloooo!"*

Her call echoed neatly off the far bank and inspired a renewed burst of whooping from the apparently not-so-distant monkeys.

But there was no answering call from the man himself. For the moment, it seemed she was on her own.

She looked down at her rumpled, stained clothing and grimaced. She suspected she was even worse off herself. After all, she hadn't been able to do so much as wash her face since before her encounter with Jacobs and Dawson. In fact, the last time she'd had a bath had been... Her brain filled with the image of Adam Bates, his wet, mud-soaked shirt clinging to his taut, muscular chest. She pushed it aside hurriedly.

It had been long enough, anyway, and the water around her looked cool and inviting, especially in the already rising heat of the morning. If he was out of earshot, she probably had time for a quick dip.

Ellie pulled off Tibbord's shirt and trousers, stripping down to her chemise and drawers. She hopped over the side of the boat, bringing the clothes with her as she landed in the water with a splash.

It felt even more glorious than she'd imagined, clean and refreshing. The current was slow, nothing she couldn't overcome with a lazy paddle. She gave her clothes the best scrubbing she could, then flung them over the rails. She tried to give herself the same treatment, ducking her head back to massage her scalp with her fingers. She felt a quick burst of shock as she realized that the long locks she was used to had vanished. She had only a short, cropped mess to work through, which was admittedly a much easier task.

She was as clean as she could get in the absence of a bar of soap, but delayed climbing back onto the boat. The water felt utterly delicious. Floating in it was like a dream. On her back, she looked up at the immense trees rustling softly overhead. Bright, quick birds flitted from branch to branch, chirping cheerfully. For a moment, her thoughts drifted back to the gray, prisonlike dreariness of the Public Record Office, and she nearly laughed out loud. Why would anyone ever choose to spend their days in London when there were places like this in the world?

A thud sounded against the planks of the deck, and a shadow fell over where she floated in the water.

"Sorry to disappear...." Adam's voice trailed off, and Ellie looked over to see him standing on the deck, staring down at her dumbly. She realized what she must look like floating on the surface, wearing only her wet, translucent underclothes.

She might as well be naked.

She submerged herself with a splash, attempting to cover herself with her arms, sink up to her chin in the water, and still not drown.

"Turn around!" she ordered, glaring at him over her shoulder.

Adam stared at her numbly for a moment, as though the words were taking longer than usual to penetrate his brain. Abruptly he obeyed, putting his back to her.

"I heard you shout for me."

"I was trying to see how far away you were."

"You weren't that specific."

Ellie saw him peek back at her. She answered him with an irritated splash of water.

He responded with a grin.

"Now that I think of it, that looks like a great idea."

Her eyes widened.

"Don't you *dare*..."

Adam kicked off his boots. Then, with a running start, he leaped over the side of the boat and landed in the water with the impact, roughly, of a tidal wave. He surfaced a moment later and shook his head like a wet dog. Ellie gaped at him, so shocked she nearly sank.

"You can't come in here like that!"

"We're outside, princess," he corrected her. Then he casually pulled off his shirt and flung it up beside hers on the rail.

The move was so shocking, Ellie almost forgot to keep swimming.

Adam had been in a state any other gentleman would have considered dishabille pretty much since the moment she had met him. The sight of him without a jacket, his shirtsleeves rolled up to expose tanned wrists, or soaked through to expose . . . well, many other things . . . had been unsettling enough. But *this* . . .

His arms, chest, and shoulders were all deeply tanned, just like the parts of him she had already seen. It didn't surprise her, but it should have. It meant that Adam spent the better part of his time outdoors without so much as a shirt to cover all that firm, rippling muscle.

Apparently merely rolling up his sleeves had been a concession to her feminine sensitivities.

Adam drifted into a lazy backstroke, as though the situation did not disconcert him in the least.

Ellie, on the other hand, was acutely aware that she was in her underwear, sharing a river with a half-clad man.

"I'm in the middle of a bath," she choked out, reaching for a way to get the inappropriateness of their circumstances through to him. "Not that it bloody well stopped you last time," she acknowledged with a grumble. She decided to direct her efforts toward keeping her body as low in the water as possible.

"Trust me. You'll be glad I did this by the end of the day."

She shot him another glare, then began paddling toward the boat. Then she hesitated, struck with the realization that she did not have the foggiest idea how to get back on board.

The *Mary Lee* had a relatively shallow draft, but the top of her rail was just out of Ellie's reach. The paddlewheels on either side of the boat looked like deceptively promising handholds, but she could only imagine how easily they would turn should she try to grasp them—and how ridiculous she would look falling headlong back into the water.

Never mind what Adam would see of *her* while she made the attempt.

The bow of the boat looked far more promising. The anchor line ran from there down into the water, and might give her something to hold on to while she tried to scramble back on board.

It was also farther out of Adam's line of sight.

She started swimming toward it.

"I wouldn't do that if I were you."

Ellie stopped, seething, but refused to turn around.

"I'm hardly going to get back in on this side with *you* here," she retorted.

"See that log?" he said. She glanced over and saw it, lying in the river near where she had planned to cross under the rope. "That's just the sort of place you'll find a water snake."

"I'll be careful," she replied coldly.

"They don't care how careful you are," he drawled. "Besides, how exactly are you planning on getting up there?"

The deck seemed much higher than she had thought it would be.

She felt a brush of water against her back and realized he had swum up behind her. She jumped.

"I'll give you a lift," he said.

"You will *not*," she countered.

He moved around her and gripped the deck. She watched the muscles in his shoulders bunch as he hauled the full length of his body up, swinging gracefully over the side. His wet trousers clung mercilessly to his physique, and Ellie felt an entirely unwelcome heat suffuse her body. He leaned over the side and extended an arm.

"I'll look away."

"You'd better," she said threateningly.

"Promise." He grinned at her.

She scowled back, then reached up and took hold of his hand with both of her own. He pulled her easily from the water, catching her around the waist when she was at his level and swinging her over the rail—an act that left her body pressed flat against his.

Her mind went numb. All that separated them was a pair of soaked trousers and the all-but-translucent silk of her chemise and drawers. She could feel every plane, every ridge of his body as though there were nothing between them at all.

The shock of it overwhelmed the possibility of response. All Ellie could do was stare at him blankly.

"See?" he said, his face inches from her own. "Not looking."

He released her and stepped back, turning around. She took a moment to make sure her knees weren't about to give out, then hurried over to the rail and pulled on her shirt and trousers.

When she turned back around, he was staring at her strangely, his wet shirt limp in his hands.

"Are you all right?"

He snapped out of it, pulling the shirt back over his head.

"Couldn't be better," he mumbled, then bent over to build up the fire.

They passed the fork in the river a few hours later. Adam glanced in her direction, raised an eyebrow, then steered them toward the smaller tributary that led to the caves. They moved up the winding path of it for several hours, passing high banks covered in lush greenery. At times the canopy overhead met from either side, covering the sky and creating a cool, dappled underworld through which they glided.

Finally they rounded a bend in the river and saw their obstacle. Arching over the water was a tall ridge of rock covered in thick jungle. The river vanished into a black hole in the heart of it.

Adam cut back the throttle, tied off the tiller, and moved to the bow beside her. He looked forward to the cave, narrow-eyed. The interior was impenetrably dark.

"What do you think?" she asked, looking over at him. She tried not to let her voice show just how much was riding on the question.

If he tried to bring them back to the city . . .

She watched him, heart pounding, as his sharp gaze moved from the stack of the steam engine to the dark mouth of the cave. Her heart sank as she saw him slowly shake his head.

"I don't want to risk it. We'll go back and get my friend's launch. It'll only add maybe four days to the journey."

"We could leave the boat. Start overland," she suggested quickly.

He raised an eyebrow.

"You have any idea how long it takes to cut your way through virgin jungle? You're lucky to make two or three miles a day. You're talking about adding weeks to the trek for the sake of saving four days."

"How do you know it would only be that long? Your friend might not be around. He might have taken his boat and gone off on an excursion."

"The only excursions Eduardo brings his boat on are up the river for a day's fishing. He'll be around."

"What about the rains? You said yourself we can't afford to waste any time."

"We can't afford to take off the top of the boiler. I'd rather risk the rains than the engine."

She felt panic rise, and with it a sense of powerlessness. But was she really powerless?

It's my map, she reminded herself. Crossing her arms, she stared at him defiantly.

"I vote we go forward."

"Since when is this a democracy?" Adam drawled in reply.

"Since I said it is," she countered. "It's my expedition, after all."

"It's my boat. And I'm not too keen on risking it in some cave full of God knows what kind of debris."

Ellie felt her desperation rise.

"We can go slowly. We'll watch for obstacles. If there's something we can't get past, we'll just turn around."

"We might not be able to turn around. The cave might be too narrow."

She felt a flash of inspiration and assumed a sympathetic air.

"Oh, I see. You're not sure you've got the skill to pilot through it."

"Very clever," Adam said, eyes flashing. "Challenge my manhood and you think I'll jump, do you?" His expression shifted, becoming serious. "Why are you so set against going back?"

She felt herself on the brink of exposure and grasped at one final straw.

"I'm not against going back. It's just that you said yourself the water is as low as you've ever seen it. Maybe it won't be by the time we go to the city and come back. The rainy season could start any day now, couldn't it?"

"If the rains hit, we're going to have more than a flooded cave to worry about."

"All the more reason to push forward now. This might be our only shot to get through. Honestly, I'm surprised you're not more keen on taking it. After all, the other side of this cave is a big, blank spot on that map of yours. I'd think you'd be eager to fill it in." She paused musingly. "Of course, I'm sure someone else will get to it eventually."

"You're baiting me."

"I'm just stating the facts."

He glared at her for another moment, then stalked to the prow. He studied the entrance to the cave silently. Some instinct told Ellie to bite back the urge to keep pushing him. Instead she waited, hiding her desperation, as he considered.

"If we take down the canopy, it'll buy us another foot."

She felt relief wash over her but tried not to let it show on her face.

He stopped as he moved past her and flashed her a smile.

"Can't have someone else filling in my map, can I?"

Ellie had thought that, once decided, they would simply head forward, but Adam apparently had a few precautions in mind. The canopy of the steamer was a mere sheet of canvas suspended on steel poles. It took only a few minutes for Adam to pull it down, and Ellie could see that the change bought them a bit more clearance.

Next, he stripped down to his trousers—an act that once again filled Ellie with a distinctly uncomfortable awareness of just what years of trekking through the wilderness could do for a man's physique. Diving from the deck, he swam to the steep banks of the river, where he cut free a slender, straight sapling with a swipe of his machete.

With a smooth, powerful push, Adam hauled both himself and the sapling over the low rail of the *Mary Lee*. He stood, the water cascading down his body and soaking the deck, then began what looked to Ellie like a perfectly bizarre construction project at the prow of the boat. When he was finished, a long plank extended several feet out over the water before them. Adam's sapling had been fitted into a notch at the end of the plank, lashed securely with rope. The top of it pointed toward the sky, stopping a few inches higher than the stack of the steam engine. The bottom disappeared into the water.

Satisfied with his efforts, Adam dived once more into the water, this time disappearing under the surface, his machete in hand. The sapling quivered dangerously as he worked at it beneath the river. Finally he emerged, treading water beneath the prow.

"Come out here," he ordered.

"Out where?"

"Slide out onto the plank."

She started. He wanted her to lie on that thing, suspended out over the water? She thought of the crocodiles she'd seen the day before by the mouth of the river. But surely Adam wouldn't be swimming if there were man-eating reptiles in this water.

He was waiting for her, a bemused expression on his face, as though guessing her thoughts. Fear turned quickly to a determination not to let him see her waffling like a nervous schoolgirl.

She crawled out onto the plank, then farther as Adam continued to wave her forward.

"Good. Now grab the tree, right in the middle. That's right. You comfortable enough?"

How comfortable was she? She was lying on an eight-inch plank off the end of a boat.

"I'm fine."

Reaching a fist out of the river, Adam gave the sapling a sharp blow.

"Feel that?"

She nodded.

"If we do clear the entrance, there's no telling what might be hiding under the water. If we hit something that puts a hole in the hull, it'll be a long swim back—in the dark. And an even longer walk back to civilization. This staff should encounter it before the boat does. If you feel it shake like that again, you shout. You're our warning system."

With a few long strokes, Adam reached the side of the boat, then pulled himself back up onto the deck. He strode over to where Ellie lay plastered to the plank, his sharp blue eyes moving from the top of the sapling to the smokestack.

"Hold on," he said.

Hold on? What was he planning to . . .

The thought cut off as Adam leaned out over her body, his machete in hand. She could feel water dripping from his chest onto her back. Grasping the sapling, he lopped off the top of it with the machete as Ellie clung to the shaking plank beneath him, biting back a curse.

He stepped back.

"That looks better."

He returned to the stern, taking the wheel. Ellie noted that his focus on the task ahead had apparently caused him to forget to replace his shirt.

This time the curse came out. Adam ignored it.

"Here goes," he said, and gently pushed the throttle.

The *Mary Lee* moved forward with painstaking slowness. Ellie had to fight the impulse to squeeze the sapling. She needed to feel for vibrations, not hold on to it like a lifeline. The water rippled beneath her, and she was unable to avoid awareness of how vulnerable her position was, hanging off the front of the boat like a piece of bait.

They approached the mouth of the cave. All was darkness within, the water fading after just a few feet of rippling obscurity into a complete void. She reminded herself that they were bringing at least a little light with them—the lantern was hanging just behind her, casting a comforting if small glow out over the water.

She could see it would be close. She chanced a glance back. Adam's face was creased with concentration as he studied the rock overhead, but she noticed that he kept his hands light on the wheel. It was reassuring to see that he had enough discipline not to put a potentially dangerous white-knuckled grip on his only means of control over their situation.

She felt a quick pang of doubt. What if she had pushed him to the wrong course? If the boat sank, both of them might very possibly die out here in the wilderness. Aunt Florence and Uncle David would wonder why their beloved niece never returned from Bournemouth. She'd simply disappear, leaving them grieving and uncertain.

Well, they would have been grieving and uncertain if she'd let Adam take her back to Belize City and gotten herself loose-ended, she thought.

Then the gaping stone was upon them, and after one tense, cringing moment, they were through.

The sapling—and the smokestack—had cleared the stone by only a few scant inches, but once inside, the cave widened to a degree that almost made the journey feel comfortable. Adam maintained a slow pace regardless, for which Ellie was grateful. Just because things looked clear above them didn't mean there weren't dangers concealed beneath the black surface of the water.

They passed from spaces of complete darkness into regions where rifts in the rock let shafts of light spill down to the water. Vines dangled down thickly from such openings, dripping jungle moisture onto Ellie's back as they chugged slowly past.

The walls of the caves were worn smooth almost to the ceiling in places, making it clear just how high the river must rise during the furious rainy season. Sometimes the *Mary Lee* passed under long pillars of stone, stalactites that dangled down from the roof like teeth in hungry jaws. Occasionally the glow of the lantern revealed the dark, skittering forms of massive cave spiders clinging to the walls. When she wasn't starting at those sudden, skin-crawling movements, Ellie watched the water carefully for any sign of obstruction, uneasy about what might lie concealed under the black surface.

Adam piloted the boat in tense silence, his eyes working to penetrate the dark beyond the feeble flicker of the lantern. When she dared, Ellie glanced back at him, a stern and shadowy figure in the gloom.

They passed briefly into light again, then through another dark mouth. The blackness here seemed even deeper than what they had moved through before.

"Look up," Adam ordered.

Ellie followed the direction of his gaze to see a log jammed against the cave roof. It was huge, obviously the remnant of a very tall and ancient tree that had fallen victim to floodwaters. That it hung suspended above them was a testament to the power of the rains.

As she stared up at it, the launch shuddered abruptly. Ellie felt a quick burst of panic. Had they hit some sort of obstruction in the water? She hadn't felt so much as a quiver from the sapling. Then she realized that the engine had stopped. The boat drifted slowly backward with the current.

"What's wrong?" she asked nervously.

"Hold on for a minute," Adam replied. He steered the drift of the boat toward the wall of the cave. He quickly tied off the wheel, then grabbed a rope and looped it around the rail. He stood, staring mysteriously at the darkness to the right. Then he stepped up onto the rail and, with a leap, vanished into thin air.

Ellie clung to the deck as the *Mary Lee* seesawed after the sudden change of weight. As soon as it settled, she hurried to the rail where Adam had disappeared.

There hadn't been any splash, which meant he wasn't in the water. It hadn't looked like he was falling into the river anyway. He had simply been swallowed up by the darkness.

"Mr. Bates?" she called tentatively. Her voice echoed eerily.

The rope beside her went taut, the boat swinging sharply back. A chorus of squeals shattered the quiet of the cave. Above her, a swarm of black bodies erupted from the wall. They were bats, hundreds of them, all screeching, flying wildly around the narrow space of the cave. Ellie ducked, pressing herself to the deck of the *Mary Lee*, feeling the rush of disturbed air moving over her neck.

Then they were gone.

"Sorry about that."

Ellie climbed to her knees and looked up. Adam was a few feet above her, leaning out of a hole in the wall of the cave. It was just visible in the light of the lantern, now that the boat had been yanked back to rest parallel to it.

"I must have disturbed a colony. Didn't notice them until I stood up. Pass me the lantern?"

He held out his hand. Ellie was tempted to throw the lamp at him but resisted, passing it to him with a glare instead.

The light began to fade as Adam moved farther away, leaving her in darkness.

"Bates!" Ellie cried. The light stilled, and a moment later Adam's shadowy form loomed out of the tunnel above her. He knelt and extended his arm.

"Come on," he said.

"Come on where?" Ellie protested, her heart still pounding in her chest.

"I think I've found something."

Even in the near-darkness, she could see the glimmer of excitement in his eye.

"What kind of something?"

"How about we find out?" he asked, grinning at her.

The urge to snap at him was overwhelmed by a growing curiosity. Ellie extended her arms. Adam grabbed hold and helped her climb from the rail of the deck up into the cave opening.

He collected the lantern and lifted it, giving Ellie a look at the strange space he had discovered. They were in the mouth of some sort of tunnel. The ceiling was high above them, almost indiscernible in the weak glow of the lamp. The floor rose smoothly beneath them.

"This way," Adam ordered, and set off with the lantern, Ellie close behind him.

They advanced along the tunnel through twists and turns, narrow gaps and wide openings. Adam moved carefully, making sure of his footing on the cave floor before advancing. Ellie followed nimbly, keeping to his track, though her attention was constantly drawn to the wonders she could see in the flickering light of the lantern. She felt a rush of excitement as they moved forward. This was what she was made for—exploring new territory, discovering its secrets. At last, she was finally doing it, not just dreaming about it while she shuffled papers in a gray London office.

She suppressed a squeak as a massive spider skittered across the ground in front of her.

Adam climbed through a high gap in the stone, taking the light with him. Then she heard him laugh.

He put his head back through the gap, grinning down at her.

"You're going to love this."

He extended a hand and helped her up. She scrambled through, then stood, brushing the dust from her knees. Raising her head, she gasped.

The space around her was massive. The walls and ceiling soared, cathedral-like, and every surface seemed to glitter, throwing shards of light through the vast, flickering space.

"The walls are glowing," she exclaimed, breathless.

"It's the crystal," Adam said. "These hills are limestone. That's why they're so easily hollowed out by the river. With the right geological conditions the limestone crystallizes. There are pockets like this all over the mountains."

He moved ahead, following some instinct toward the center of the cavern, where he knelt, examining the ground. Ellie picked her way over to where he crouched.

There, scattered before him in a slight depression, was an assortment of pots, some whole, others cracked or shattered. A short distance away were signs of scorch marks, remnants of old fires edged with bits of ash.

She knelt beside him.

"It's a ritual site," she said, awed.

Adam looked over at her, surprised and approving.

"The Mayans believed caves like this were entrances to Xibalba."

"Xibalba?"

"The land of the dead. Supposedly there were twelve gods there who ruled over every form of fear and destruction. It's described as a series of caverns like torture chambers—rooms of ice, knives, bloodthirsty jaguars. A regular carnival. This space would have been seen as a gateway. The dead would pass through it on their way to Xibalba, and plague and suffering would come out. The Mayans would have offered sacrifices here to keep the death gods happy." Adam nodded toward the wall of the cave. "There's one of them over there."

In the flicker of the lantern, the walls, ceiling, and floor of the cave seemed to sparkle with a thousand stars, making it hard at first to see what he pointed to. Stepping closer, she realized that the walls of the cave were decorated with paintings. The images were faint, long faded with time. There were primitive scenes of hunting and dancing, but other scenes were more elaborate. One in particular leaped out at her, seeming darker and more detailed than the rest. It depicted some sort of beast, a massive figure with black wings, claws, and jagged fangs.

"Is that supposed to be a bat?"

"They called them Camazotz," Adam said. "Sort of like bloodthirsty monster bats. They were one of the guardians of Xibalba. Take a look at this." He drew her attention away from the paintings and down to the little pile of ashes. She crouched beside him as he brushed aside a bit of cinder, revealing a small bunch of half-burned, wilted flowers.

"Someone's been here recently."

"Who?"

"Some of the local Maya, I'd imagine."

"But I thought they were all Christians now," she said, surprised.

He gave her a wry look.

"Some of them like to cover all their bases." He stood, raising the lantern and looking around.

Ellie was still transfixed by the artifacts. She brushed her fingers over the pottery shards, lifting one and examining it.

"How long do you think this has been here?"

"Pretty damned long," Adam said. "Take a look at this."

She stood and moved over to where he knelt near a slight hollow in the ground. The lantern light revealed the glittering, icelike form of a human skeleton.

"My God," she said quietly, kneeling beside him.

The figure looked as though it had been half swallowed by the ground. The exposed bones were thickened, bristling with a sort of stone fur that sparkled in the moving light.

"She's calcified," Adam said, gently brushing his fingers along the surface of a shoulder blade.

"She?"

"It's a female. A young female—probably about twelve or thirteen."

Ellie could see a broken area at the top of the long-dead girl's skull.

"A sacrifice?" she asked.

"She wouldn't be down here if she weren't," Adam replied.

She felt a pang of sympathy. The girl had been barely more than a child.

"She was so young."

"You want to appease the gods, you give them something precious."

The emotion passed, overwhelmed by her growing curiosity.

"How long has she been here?"

"At a guess? About a thousand years or so. That calcification doesn't happen overnight."

"A thousand years," she said wonderingly, looking down at the skeleton. The crystal made it look as though the girl were built of diamonds, sparkling in the light of the lantern.

She leaned back, eyes scanning the wide chamber. What else might be hidden here, waiting for centuries to be discovered?

She turned to Adam. "Will you come back here? Conduct an excavation?"

"No."

"Why not?" she asked, surprised.

"Two reasons. One, there's no funding for it."

"That's absurd."

She found it hard to imagine that something as petty as money would destroy a chance at sharing such a find with the world.

"It'd take more than a few bones in a cave to get either of our governments to open their pockets."

She absorbed this quietly. It was something she had never considered before. But then, she should have. She had heard Neil talk about the constraints funding put on his excavations in Egypt, and that was in a region private patrons loved. Few knew or cared about this obscure corner of the empire.

"You said there were two reasons. What's the other?"

"They're still using it," Adam replied. He moved toward the exit and made a gentlemanly sweep of his arm. "After you."

With a last look back at the chamber, she moved past him through the gap.

9

Ellie felt a new sense of security. The stretch of river they now navigated was officially off the map, and the *Mary Lee* had only just managed to make it through the low tunnel into the caves that had led them here. Few other boats would be able to do the same. It seemed impossible to imagine that anyone could follow them here, even if they'd known where to look—and Dawson and Jacobs didn't, she reminded herself.

All she had to worry about now were venomous snakes, man-eating jaguars, and the imminent arrival of the rainy season. That, of course, and the tanned, chiseled man behind her steering the boat, the virtual stranger who also happened to be the only one with the knowledge to get them through the jungle to their goal.

It was practically a walk in the park.

Nothing like the challenge of finding the next landmark the map marked on their path. It was described as a black pillar, one that drew strangely at the needle of a compass. Something magnetic, like her medallion. The pillar would signal the end of their leisurely boating expedition and the beginning of a long, hard trek through the bush.

There was nothing simple about finding a black stone in a landscape of gnarled tree trunks, hanging vines, and wild greenery. Her only hope was that Adam's compass would give the stone's presence away. She sat in the bow, holding it in her hand in front of her, afraid to do more than blink lest she miss some telltale twitch of the needle.

By the time Adam brought the launch to the bank and tied it off to the trunk of a fallen oak, she was thoroughly exhausted. The engine rattled to a stop, and she both gratefully and reluctantly put the compass away, stretching her painfully cramped muscles as Adam pulled out the battered tin pan and bowls. He took another tin from his crates and poured out the contents. Ellie winced when she saw them.

"Is that all you've got? Beans?"

"No idea," Adam replied. Tiredness crept into his tone as well. It had been a long day. "The cans weren't labeled when I bought them. Got a discount." He gave the pan a stir, then sat down wearily and stretched out his legs.

Ellie looked out into the darkening world of thick, veiled foliage. Strange birds called to one another distantly.

"Should we have found it by now?" she asked quietly.

Adam shrugged tiredly.

"It's hard to say. The map's not exactly to scale. Of course, it might not matter if you'd let me see the rest of it."

Ellie's eyes narrowed. She was instinctively wary. "The rest doesn't matter until we find the stone."

"Princess, do you know what's going to happen once it starts raining?"

The quick twist in the conversation caught her off guard.

"We get wet?"

Adam wasn't amused. "This lazy stream we're puffing up turns into a torrent. It completely floods that cave we just passed through, blocking off our route home. The ground turns into mud. Cutting overland through the jungle is hard work even at the best of times, but add a torrential downpour and it turns downright treacherous. Mudslides. Sinkholes." He shook his head. "If we don't find your pillar in the next day or two, we might need to think seriously about heading back to regroup."

The idea sparked a sharp panic.

"You can't know the rains are coming that soon."

"I can't know that they *aren't*." He sighed. "Look—if you show me the rest of the map, there's a chance I might recognize one of the other landmarks. It would save us traveling up and down the same stretch of water looking for something that might have fallen into the river a hundred years ago. Right now we really can't afford to pass up a shortcut."

She could sense his irritation and knew it wasn't entirely unjustified. But the notion of handing over her last bargaining chip still frightened her.

"I checked the maps back in London. There was nothing on there. You can take my word on that."

"I can, can I?" he drawled, eyebrow raised.

She felt a flare of temper.

"I'm perfectly capable of reading a map."

He crossed his legs. "Doesn't matter how good you are at reading it if the map's out-of-date."

"The map wasn't out-of-date," she scoffed.

Adam shrugged. "Things change pretty fast around here."

"I was in the British Library. I hardly think they're going to stock out-of-date maps."

Adam chuckled derisively. Ellie felt a rush of nationalist indignation.

"The British Library is the foremost—"

"For the love of— Can I just see the damned map?" Adam burst out. "I've spent an awful lot of time out here. I might know a thing or two more about the ground we're covering than the British Library."

Ellie shot him a glare but closed her mouth. He was right, of course. It was men like Adam who had made the map she'd studied in the library's atlas. How could that bound and printed book reflect everything out there, when new discoveries were being made all the time?

If she withheld the rest of the map now, Adam would think it was out of spite or suspicion, not logic. And he'd be right.

Swallowing her fear, Ellie reached into the pocket of Mr. Tibbord's jacket and pulled out the other half of the map. She offered it to him without a word.

He went to the crate, removing the tin cylinder and unscrewing the cap. He shook out the first half of the map along with his own hand-drawn version. Laying them out, he crouched down over them, considering. He shook his head, chuckling.

"What's so funny?" Ellie demanded. She half tossed a bowl of beans onto the deck beside him, then sat down with her own on the opposite side.

"I think we're going the wrong way," he said evenly.

"What?" She stopped with her spoon halfway to her mouth.

Adam pointed. "See this?"

His finger tapped a series of strange markings that ran alongside the curving line that led to one of the map's other landmarks, an arch labeled, *Bridge hollowed by the hand of God*.

"I think these are cataracts."

"You mean rapids?"

Adam shuffled the yellowed page aside, revealing the newer map.

"See this?" He pointed to a curving blue line.

"Is that another river?" Ellie asked, looking.

"Tributary of the Belize," Adam replied. "Some logging scouts reported it. Said this whole stretch was taken up with rapids."

"The Belize? That's the river that passes through the center of the city."

"Yup," Adam confirmed, leaning back with his beans.

"But this branch of it wasn't on the other maps," she protested weakly.

"Probably because they only found it last season."

She studied the route and felt her stomach sink

"You're sure that's the same river?"

He answered her with a raised eyebrow as he lifted a spoonful of beans, and Ellie admitted defeat.

"We should have taken the Belize," she said.

"Mmm-hmm," he replied around a mouthful of dinner.

"It would have brought us…"

"Within two or three days' hike. *If* the map is accurate."

Ellie sat back, repressing the urge to curse. She didn't want to give Adam the satisfaction. She closed her eyes.

"Should we go back?"

He shook his head. "We're too far along now. But it does mean that we don't have to find that pillar to know where we're going. We could follow the river up another fifteen miles or so, then cut overland until we hit the tributary. But if we don't find it," he added pointedly, "you might seriously want to consider whether it's worth it."

"Worth it?"

"I can't be sure how many miles we'll have to bushwhack to get to that tributary. Could be five. Could be twenty. We're talking up to a week of hard travel through uncharted jungle. And like I said, the rains could start any day, which is going to make getting back a hell of a lot more complicated. You've got to ask yourself whether the risk is justified, if this whole thing could turn out to be a wild-goose chase."

Her dismay must have been visible. Adam's features softened.

"We could come back, you know. Wait out the rains, then hit it again. Put a small survey team together. If this city of yours exists, it's been sitting out there for centuries. It's not going anywhere."

It wasn't an option, but how could she make that clear without admitting the danger that might be waiting for her back in Belize City?

She felt the trap closing around her, Adam's doubt and common sense on one side, Jacobs on the other. If only she'd let him see the whole map to begin with. They would have been at the rapids by now, could have been looking up at the stone arch that would prove the abbot's map correct just as surely as his damnable black pillar.

An urge rose up to crawl into her hammock and let sleep wash away the rather unpleasant feeling of being wrong.

Not wrong, she corrected herself fiercely. She had done what she had to in order to protect herself. She couldn't have known for certain that Adam would be true to his word. She was a woman traveling alone, and the world she moved through—whether here or in London, as she had learned long ago—was a hostile one. It was better to watch her back than get caught with her defenses down.

Adam picked up the two halves of the map, rolling them up together. He leaned over, frowning.

"What's this?"

Ellie glanced back and saw him looking down at a scrap of paper that had lain unseen under the map. She recognized it instantly as the telegram she had taken from Dawson's desk.

Alarm shot through her. She had all but forgotten about her little piece of evidence, tucked away with her half of the map. She sought for a convincing explanation for its presence, but the one her worn-out brain offered was painfully feeble.

"Oh—that's nothing. Just a scrap of paper I picked up at the hotel desk. I don't know how it got rolled up with the map."

She smiled in what she hoped desperately was a disarming manner.

"At the hotel desk," Adam echoed skeptically. "Pretty strange coincidence that you'd just happen to find this there."

"I don't see why. Anyone receiving a telegram at the hotel would get it at the desk. They must have left it behind after it was read. I used it to make a few notes."

"Notes about Tulan Zuyua?"

Adam glanced from her to the telegram, and Ellie was painfully aware of how suspicious it must look. He must be able to see that the message was written in some sort of code. She only hoped that her excuse would make him think the penciled words were, in fact, just scribbled notes, and not a translation.

If he started to doubt her story, what else might he start to question? Her assumed widowhood? Her name? Who those men were, chasing her through the hotel? She realized that she had constructed a fragile edifice, one that could very easily be brought crumbling down—and then what? What would he do with her if he learned that she'd been lying to him this entire time?

There was only one line of defense she could think of that might just distract him from the mystery of the paper's existence and get him talking about something else. Though it galled her, she decided to admit ignorance.

"I remember seeing the name in one of my books. I wrote it down to remind myself to look it up later. I'm afraid I don't have the foggiest idea what it means."

She saw his expression shift. Doubt was forgotten in favor of the chance to enlighten Ellie on the finer points of Mayan folklore.

"You've heard of the Popol Vuh?"

"Popol Vuh…" The words had a rich, exotic sound on her tongue. "No. What is it?"

"The Mayan books might have been lost in the Inquisition, but what they couldn't write down, they could still talk about. The myths, the old stories—they survived, for a while. Some of them lasted long enough that a Dominican priest with the intelligence to realize what was on the verge of being lost was able to write down a Spanish translation. The Popol Vuh."

"So—Tulan Zuyua?"

"It's part of the Mayan creation myth. The Popol Vuh describes it as a city on a mountain, a place they also called Seven Caves. The Mayans went there on some sort of pilgrimage because they wanted the people who lived there to give them gods."

"*Give* them gods?" Ellie echoed.

Adam shrugged.

"That's the story. Apparently the people of Tulan Zuyua could hand them out like sweets at a birthday party."

"So they were gods themselves, then?"

"Perhaps. The Popol Vuh isn't exactly clear on the subject. It's a myth, after all." He leaned back, stretching his legs out before him. "It's funny, actually. The Aztecs have a similar story. They even use the same name for the place—Seven Caves. It's where they say their people began. The rest is a sort of Garden of Eden scenario—paradise turned sour. They eventually fled to set up cities of their own outside its influence."

"So the Mayans and the Aztecs shared the same creation story?"

"No. The creation myths are totally different."

"But they both involve a city called Seven Caves."

"Now you're getting it."

Ellie absorbed this, her mind humming with potential implications. *Candidate for Tulan Zuyua.* Why had Dawson's telegram contained the name of this obscure piece of Mayan mythology? Tulan Zuyua had never been mentioned during the lectures she'd attended on Mesoamerican history at the university; nor had the Popol Vuh. And those courses had been taught by an expert in the field. Not someone as expert as Adam Bates, of course, but still a tenured professor with a laundry list of books and journal articles to his name.

Yet someone had connected her White City with that obscure piece of mythology—and another, she reminded herself. The Smoking Mirror, the mythical object Adam said the symbol on the idol of her medallion resembled.

The city and the medallion. References to pieces of Mayan and Aztec folklore only a handful of people in the world would recognize.

Someone had sent them to Dawson. Someone with a purpose, one they disguised with code, hiding it from casual eyes, yet sent from the Westminster telegram office. The combination was as bewildering as it was unsettling.

The message had to have come from Dawson's employer. Not a colleague or a research assistant. Ellie was *sure* of it.

But that meant that Dawson's employer knew both Foreign Office codes and more about Mayan history than anyone Ellie had ever met . . . except for the man sitting across from her.

The reasons others would be interested in her map should have been obvious: Gold. Treasure. A wealth of priceless artifacts that would be quickly swallowed by a black market hungry for antiquities. The telegram didn't reference any of those things. It was as specific as it was obscure.

Why would Dawson's employer care about the Smoking Mirror?

She pushed the thought aside. There would be time to worry about it later. First she needed to disarm any suspicion Adam might still be harboring about the origins of the telegram.

"I knew I must have remembered it for a reason," she said cheerfully. "I suppose I hardly need a library with you around."

She reached out for the telegram, but Adam paused, looking up at her meaningfully.

"Anything else you'd like to tell me?"

Ellie forced a smile. "Fine. I admit it. Your knowledge of Central American history is remarkable." She extended her hand for the telegram, the smile plastered firmly on her face.

After only the briefest hesitation, he handed it over. Ellie tucked it back into her pocket and inwardly cursed herself for having been so careless with it before. The flash of doubt she'd seen in Adam's eyes had frightened her.

Why wouldn't it? If he realized she'd been hiding the truth from him, he might abandon the search and head back to the city. Why would he want to maintain a partnership with someone who kept feeding him lies?

That wasn't all of it, though. Her fear of how he might react went beyond losing her guide to the interior. The notion of how he might look at her if he discovered the truth made her feel ill.

She would fix it, she determined. Just as soon as she had the chance.

She prayed she would know what that "chance" might look like.

~

The next day's journey should have been easier. With Adam's knowledge of their ultimate route in mind, Ellie was no longer dependent on the movements of the compass for success. But instead of relaxing and taking in the wild beauty of the world they moved through, she kept her eyes glued to the needle. Finding the mysterious pillar described on the map would prove to him that the trail they followed was genuine and put to rest any more arguments about whether she had led them both on a "wild-goose chase."

As they traveled, the landscape around them transformed. From even plains, the ground rose up into steep-sided hills wearing thick coats of vivid green. The banks of the river grew harder, replacing silt with smooth-worn stones, and at certain bends in the stream, Ellie looked up to see towering peaks appear through gaps, looking startlingly close. By midday, she knew they had truly entered the mountains.

The first few sets of rapids they encountered were small, and Adam was able to skillfully pilot the launch up and over into calmer waters. But finally, late into the afternoon, they rounded a bend to see the river end in a wall of hissing water pouring from a shelf of rock ten feet over their heads.

"Looks like the end of the line," Adam called to her over the rush of the falls. He cut the throttle and the boat's momentum quickly dropped, countered by the force of the rushing water. They drifted forward slowly, and Ellie could feel the cool mist on her skin. She rose, moving to where Adam stood by the tiller, his eyes closed as he tilted his face toward the spray of water. He smiled, relishing the feeling of it. He looked down at her.

"Anything?"

"I could have missed it," she said, glancing down at the compass. She snapped it shut and handed it to him. "The river forked several times over the last few miles. Maybe it's on one of the other branches."

"It doesn't matter. I can get us there. We'll backtrack until we can find a safe place to hide the boat, then head north." He looked down at her. "If you still want to do this."

She glared back.

"What is that supposed to mean?"

Adam was unmoved.

"That it's going to be a hard walk from here, and it's entirely possible we won't find anything at the end of it."

"Is that what you think? That there's nothing there?"

"I'm admitting that it's a possibility," he countered. "But I've followed plenty of false leads before. I'm used to disappointment. I just don't want you to—"

"You think this is a false lead," she cut in coldly.

"Come on, princess—you have to admit that's what it's looking like at the moment."

"Don't call me that," Ellie said, gritting her teeth.

"What do you want me to call you?"

"How about my—" She stopped, catching herself with a wince. He didn't know her name, of course. And the notion of demanding he call her by a false one was something less than comfortable. She shook it off. "How about you just put me ashore, and then you can take yourself back to the city."

The boat had turned with the current as they argued, the stern now soaked with the spray of the cascade. Adam had to raise his voice to be heard over the noise of the water.

"What?"

"I don't want you to waste any more of your time," she snapped at him.

"For the love of— You're not wasting my time," he shouted back. "Besides, you wouldn't last ten minutes out there on your own."

"If you think I'm going to let you come with me out of some backward sense of chivalry—"

She was cut short as he grabbed hold of her shoulders and threw her down with him onto the deck. Behind them, a huge piece of debris tipped over the falls and smashed down onto the stern. Ellie heard wood splinter and lifted her head to see a heavy, waterlogged limb tilt, then drag itself under the boat with a loud cracking sound.

"Are you all right?" Adam demanded.

"I'm fine."

He looked her over as though not entirely trusting her word, then rose to his feet and went to survey the damage. Several boards at the top of the transom had been cracked, but the breach was still well above the waterline. Adam reached over the side into the river, exploring with his hands. Then he sat up, shaking off the water.

"Hull feels fine," he announced. "Can't say the same for the rudder."

"What do you mean? What's happened to it?"

"It's not there anymore," he replied. He sat down and stretched out his legs.

"Can you fix it?"

"Nothing left to fix. I'll have to build a new one."

"So what do we do?"

"Go wherever the river decides to take us," he replied. He reached into a bag near his feet and pulled out a ripe piece of fruit. He took a bite and sat back, chewing casually. He held it toward her. "Want some?"

"So we just . . . sit here," she said, ignoring the fruit.

"The current will bring us up on the banks eventually. Once I can tie her up, I'll be able to see how bad the damage is and figure some way to rig things back together."

"And how long will that take?"

"Who knows? We're just along for the ride."

Underneath them, the boat had turned, pushed by the current to head back downriver. Ellie fought a wave of frustration and moved to the bow, wanting to get some distance from Adam before she grabbed the piece of fruit out of his hand and threw it at his head. Then she went still, staring out over the water ahead of them.

"We're going the wrong way," she said.

"The river only goes one way."

"No, I mean—this isn't the same river. We've taken some kind of branch." She pointed, watching as the spit of land that divided the two streams slipped past them

"They all go our way. Quit worrying about it and sit down."

She obeyed, but the uneasy feeling remained. Something tugged at the edge of her awareness, a detail calling disproportionately for her attention. She frowned, confused.

"That's funny."

"What is?" Adam called to her from the stern.

"The waterfall," she said. "We're moving away from it, but I swear it sounds like it's getting louder."

"Sound travels funny sometimes in the mountains," Adam said dismissively.

Ellie looked ahead of them down the river. She stood.

"Bates?"

"I said quit—"

"There's something wrong with the river," she cut in.

Adam frowned and came forward. He stood beside her and looked out over the water. Then his eyes went wide.

"Waterfall," he mumbled. He grabbed her shoulders, turning her toward him, and pointed at the low wall of mist covering the water a hundred yards ahead of them. "Waterfall!"

Ellie stared forward at it and felt panic rise in her chest. Adam sprang into action. Grabbing his pack from under the canopy, he quickly tossed a few items into it, then cinched the tie and lifted it. Swinging it over his head, he let it fly into the trees lining the banks. He tossed Ellie's smaller pack into her arms.

"The maps!" he ordered, then raced to the stern, whipping out his machete. With a quick, practiced motion, he pried up one of the boards of the deck, revealing a hollow space beneath. As Ellie grabbed the tin cylinder from the crate, Adam reached in and pulled out a clear glass bottle full of a dark, amber-colored liquid. He hurried to her, shoving the bottle into her pack and throwing it around his shoulders.

"What is that?" she demanded.

He ignored the question. "Can you swim?"

"I suppose. We used to summer at the lake and—"

Her words were cut off as Adam shoved her over the rail and she plunged into the cold, rushing water.

The river swallowed her, the current sweeping her along with terrifying speed and robbing her of her sense of which way was up.

Fear paralyzed her. Ellie knew she had only moments before she was swept over the falls. She had to get to the surface, but if she swam in the wrong direction, she would expend her energy effectively to drown herself—or get washed over a cliff.

Her lungs screamed for air, her mind howling for action. Then a hand grabbed her shirt, hauling her up.

She exploded through the surface, gasping. Adam shoved her toward the bank, not directly, but diagonally.

"That way! Use the current; don't fight it," he ordered.

She began to swim furiously, stifling the powerful instinct to turn toward the bank, which seemed so close, instead letting the current propel her as she pulled for safety. At last she reached out and felt her hand close around a slick, protruding root. She gripped it, and the force of the water crushed her into it, nearly knocking the breath out of her chest. Then Adam was beside her, hitting the tree with a thud. He hauled himself up, then reached back and pulled her up after him.

They tumbled onto the bank and lay there, breathless, exhausted, the pack on the ground beside them. Slowly Ellie rolled over and looked back to the river.

The brink was frighteningly close to where they lay, and from their vantage, Ellie could see that the waterfall was dizzyingly high. The sight of it made her stomach drop. As she watched, the *Mary Lee* reached the edge, spun, and toppled over. A few moments later she heard a distant crack from the ground far below.

She glanced over at where Adam lay beside her, his eyes still closed.

"That was my boat, wasn't it?"

"I'm afraid so," Ellie replied quietly.

She waited for the burst of rage she felt sure must come. After all, they were now lost in an unexplored wilderness on the brink of the rainy season with no way back to civilization.

Instead, he started to laugh.

It was contagious. Ellie felt it bubbling up inside of her, spilling out so ferociously it made her eyes water.

"How are we going to get back?" she asked between moments of hysteria.

Adam wiped his eyes, slowly sobering.

"I don't know. We might be able to hitch a ride after we get to the Belize. There will be traffic on that river, even this time of year."

Ellie felt the mirth start to rise once more.

"I still can't believe..."

Her words trailed off as she realized that Adam was no longer listening. He was looking down at his belt.

The sheath of his machete was acting strangely. Instead of lying flat against his leg, as it was supposed to, it had lifted away from his trousers, and was pointing, quite insistently, at a stand of brush a few yards away.

They exchanged a look, and Adam leaped to his feet. Moving forward, he pushed the tangle of vines aside and revealed a massive, grotesquely carved pillar of night-black stone.

10

Watching Adam Bates set up camp was a humbling experience.

Ellie had always thought of herself as a competent woman, but compiling the means of survival out of the pitiful arrangement of gear they'd had in the two bags they'd rescued from the *Mary Lee* was, she had to admit, as far beyond her capability as flying.

Watching him start their fire, rig a fishing line, and easily identify the edible portions of the myriad plants that surrounded them brought home to her how utterly dependent she was on this man. His skills and knowledge were what would get them back to civilization again. Had she been foolish enough to venture out here on her own, she would probably have poisoned herself with her first breakfast.

Once his aromatic stew of fish and wild yams was bubbling in a pot over the fire, Adam at last turned his eye to the object that had, Ellie was sure, been calling to both of them since they'd reached the shore.

The black pillar was more than just a stone. It was a stela, a painstakingly carved and deliberately placed memorial. Ellie had read about such monuments in her studies. They were often found near Mayan ruins, though no one knew whether they served as altars, icons, or three-dimensional histories. This one was different. It stood alone in the middle of the jungle, with no sign of ruin or habitation nearby.

It was also an enormous magnet.

Every piece of metal in the camp had scuttled across the ground to the stone, unless it was tied up or weighed down with fish and yams.

The front of the monument was taken up with a larger, more elaborate version of the medallion's idol. His face was crossed with horizontal lines like paint on a warrior, giving him a fierce, inhuman aspect. The icon of the black disk, with its weaving lines of smoke, rose over the idol's head this time, like a dark moon. It was surrounded by rows of glyphs.

"Can you read any of it?" Ellie asked.

"I might be able to decipher some of the dates, if it were Mayan."

"But it's not?"

He shook his head.

"The glyphs are similar to Mayan writing. I've seen enough of it to recognize the symbols. These are different."

"Then what is it?"

"Wish I knew, princess."

She studied it, absorbing the grotesque figure of the god and the monstrous shapes that surrounded him.

"It's the Smoking Mirror again."

"Tezcatlipoca. Or his close cousin," Adam confirmed.

"What else do you know about him?"

"Tezcatlipoca was a god of sacrifice. There was a lot of that around here before the conquest. For both the Mayans and the Aztecs, blood was power. You offered it up, either your own or someone else's, and received gifts from the gods in return. Fortune. Glory. Or, in the case of the Smoking Mirror, visions of prophecy."

"You mean the mirror might have been an actual ritual object."

"Ever heard of scrying?" Adam asked. "It's an old European folk tradition, the notion that you could see the past or the future by studying the surface of a pool of still water. Or a mirror."

"The Grimm brothers," Ellie said abruptly.

Adam gave her an odd look.

"German folklorists," she hurried to explain. "They collected old stories. My father gave me a book of them when I was a girl. I don't think he realized that they weren't really fairy tales for children. There was a story in there about a girl named Snow White whose wicked stepmother owned a magic mirror that would show her whatever she desired to see." Ellie frowned, remembering. "That mirror wanted a sacrifice, too. The girl's heart, brought home in a box."

"It's funny how so many of these myths turn up on opposite sides of the world. But then again, I can't really be sure exactly what we're dealing with."

"Something very important to the people who put that here," Ellie concluded.

She gazed at the enigmatic figure on the dark stone. It was offering no answers.

"Come on," Adam said, interrupting her reverie. "Let's get some dinner."

Ellie hadn't realized how hungry she was until Adam set the steaming bowl in her hands. His simple stew smelled more delicious than the finest meal she'd ever eaten. It was funny what a near-death experience could do for the appetite.

"You'll have to use your fingers," he apologized. "Damned if I know where the spoons went."

Ellie suspected they had probably joined the rest of their metal objects, gluing themselves to the pillar, but didn't want to stop eating to suggest it.

When they'd finished, Adam tightly covered the pot, weighing down the lid with a heavy stone.

"We'll still find some bugs in there in the morning," he warned. "Just pick them out if they bother you."

Given how hungry life in the bush seemed to make her, Ellie felt certain she wouldn't be bothered.

With the camp safely set and her stomach full, she felt weariness begin to creep in. It had, after all, been a rather long day.

But they'd found the pillar.

The thought exhilarated her. It had proved beyond a doubt—and not just to Adam—that the map they followed was genuine. She realized that she had been harboring a quiet fear that her discovery would prove to be little more than a seventeenth-century joke. Finding the stela had done away with that, making it clear that everything she had risked to pursue this course was justified.

She yawned involuntarily. Even the excitement of knowing for certain that they were on the right track wasn't enough to completely counter her exhaustion.

"Anything else we need to do before we sleep?"

"Damp out the fire a bit," Adam said. "And then there's this."

He reached back and pulled a glass bottle from behind the log he sat on. He gazed at it appreciatively.

"That's what you saved from the boat," Ellie said, remembering the extra seconds he had taken to retrieve it from its hiding place under the planks of the deck.

"And thank God for small miracles; she made it here in one piece." Adam used his machete to neatly pry out the cork, then returned the knife to his belt, careful to fasten it back into place lest it take flight for the nearby monument. He inhaled luxuriously at the nose of the bottle.

"What is it?"

"The finest rum in the world. Possibly the last existing bottle of it. It was made by the grandmother of a friend of mine. She had a still on her farm in Jamaica. I've tried for years to pry the technique out of her, but she swore she'd take it to her grave. She was old then, and that was ten years ago, so I'd be surprised if she's still bootlegging."

"You've had that bottle for ten years?" Ellie asked, shocked.

"Yup. Been saving it for a special occasion."

"But you're drinking it now. What's the occasion?"

He lifted the bottle and smiled.

"Not being dead."

He took a swig, then leaned back with an expression of bliss. He glanced over at Ellie and offered her the bottle.

"Oh, no. I don't drink rum."

"We can't take it with us. As you'll soon learn, every extra bit of weight counts in what we're going to do. It's drink it tonight or tomorrow we make this a very lucky piece of dirt. But you can rest assured that I will get myself mighty drunk before I sacrifice this stuff to the ground. So we'll all be better off if you do your part."

Tentatively Ellie reached out and accepted the bottle. She sniffed at it. The aroma was admittedly enticing—all heat, spice, and caramel.

"I'm not even sure that I'll...I mean, I've had sherry, of course, and wine every once in a while...."

"Just drink it," Adam ordered, and she lifted the bottle.

The taste burned, rich and gorgeous. Her mouth erupted with heat and vanilla, sweetness and fire.

"My God," she exclaimed wonderingly.

"Told you," Adam retorted.

She drank again, then somewhat reluctantly handed the bottle back. Adam swigged, and a comfortable silence settled over them. Then Ellie felt a quick pang of guilt.

"I'm sorry about your boat," she said. "Had you had it long?"

"Pretty much since I got here."

"And that was?"

"About ten years ago."

"Right after you graduated," she surmised.

He leaned back and took another swig from the bottle.

"Never graduated."

"What do you mean? Why not?"

"Spite, mostly," he replied. He saw the confusion in her look and sighed. "In my last semester, my parents came to England and showed up at Cambridge. My father told me they'd pay a visit to my uncle, Lord Scarsdale, then return to collect me and bring me back to San Francisco to take up my position with the firm."

"And you said no," Ellie finished for him.

"Careful," he warned. "Sounds like you might be getting to know me." He took another swig and offered her the bottle. She accepted it.

The stuff was *good.*

"So what did he say?" she asked, after the warmth had made its way down her throat.

"He made all kinds of threats—cutting me off, disowning me—most of which, to his credit, he did follow through on."

"He disowned you?" It seemed unthinkable to her that a father could take such a step.

"Not officially. But I haven't spoken to him since."

"I hope he comes around."

"I won't be holding my breath." He noticed her shock, and his look softened. "Look, princess—some types of people just aren't meant to get along. I'm sure you can think of a few examples."

"But he's your—"

"I'm aware," he said, stopping her with a raised hand. "But family doesn't guarantee compatibility. George Bates and I are two very different men. The only surprise in the whole business is that it took as long as it did to come to a head. I've still got contact with my mother—for better or worse—and my brother, Robin, is an all-right sort. Much better suited to a life in the company. He'll thrive doing what they had planned for me. It's worked out for the best, but my father will never see that." He shrugged. "He doesn't have to."

Ellie quietly absorbed this.

"It still seems sad to me. I would give quite a lot to have had more time with my parents."

"They died?" Adam guessed.

She nodded.

"My mother died in childbirth, along with the baby that would have been my sister. My father passed away shortly afterward. His heart gave out. My uncle David—my mother's older brother—and his family took me in."

"I'm sorry."

"I was very young. I honestly don't remember them all that well. Certainly not well enough to miss them. It's more . . . I would have liked the chance to have known them, if I could."

"Understandable. And I know mine a little too well."

There was a comfortable silence, the fire crackling between them. The rum felt warm in Ellie's stomach, loosening both her muscles and her mind.

"So—graduating?"

"I didn't see the point in taking my last exams. Who did I need to prove myself to? I knew what I knew. My father wanted me to have that degree, and I wanted to tell my father to go to hell. The rest is history."

"You really don't think he'll ever change his mind?"

"Oh, I don't know," he admitted. "I suppose my mother might keep working on him till I'm safely back in the fold. Not that I miss it. And I don't need the money."

"Now, really—" Ellie said, half laughing.

He raised an eyebrow.

"You may not have noticed, but I'm a man of rather simple needs."

"That," she said pointedly, "is an understatement."

She took another sip of rum. Adam looked at her wryly as she drank.

"You approve."

"It's quite lovely," she admitted.

"Best in the world," he asserted, gently taking the bottle back.

"What if money could buy you more of this?" she challenged.

"It can't," he replied, unmoved.

She gazed at him thoughtfully for a moment, an unexpected question rising in her mind.

"You're not married, are you?"

Adam spit rum.

"Good God, no. Where did that question come from?"

She shrugged.

"I just realized I had never asked. You might feel differently about the money if you had a wife and children."

"I have no intention of acquiring either."

"Why not?"

"You're honestly asking me that?"

"Yes."

Adam took another slug from the bottle. "I'm not the marrying type."

"That's a thin excuse."

"A woman might pretend she doesn't mind my spending months at a time in the jungle. But give it a year or two, and it's going to be, 'Why can't you find work that'll let you stay home?' and, 'Why can't we move somewhere with more shops?' Then there's babies," he added. "However good I am at what I do, it's a risky line of work. What woman is going to let me keep at it and chance that she'll be left on her own if something happens to me?"

"What makes you so sure there'd be children?"

"Women always want children," he muttered.

Ellie felt her hackles rise.

"I don't," she countered.

"Come again?"

"They're the quickest way for a modern woman to lose what little freedom she has." She felt herself warm to the topic. "Do you know—if I'd even gotten engaged to be married, I would have been dismissed from the civil service? It's one thing to be removed because you were arrested—"

"Arrested?" he cut in. Then the other implication dawned. "You were in the civil service?"

Ellie winced at her slip—at both of them. It must have been the rum, she thought. It seemed to be making her tongue a bit loose.

Well, there was no denying it now.

"I was," she replied stiffly.

"Sorry I seem so surprised. It's just hard to imagine you in a typing pool."

"I was not a typist. I was an archivist in the Public Record Office."

She could see his surprise. He leaned back, considering her, and Ellie felt the instinct to defend herself begin to rear its head.

"You must have really knocked their damned socks off."

She stopped, feeling her face heat. Was she blushing? She pushed the notion aside.

"My point was—"

"No, really," he interrupted. "You had to have aced your exams. I can't imagine them giving that position to a woman otherwise."

"I'm not sure whether to be complimented or offended right now," she stammered.

"Be complimented."

There was a quiet moment as she accepted this. *He thinks I knocked their socks off.* The notion made her feel a warm glow. Then again, perhaps that was just the rum.

She cleared her throat and pressed on.

"What I meant to say was, for a woman who wants something more than the life of a housewife, children—marriage, even—are as good as a jail sentence. But not for you. You could have all of it, if you wanted."

"It's never that simple," he countered.

"Why not?"

"Because people aren't simple. No woman is going to be happy with the kind of life I live."

"I would be," she blurted, then went still, slightly horrified.

Adam looked at her skeptically.

"Even after nearly going over a waterfall?"

"Well, that part was a little terrifying. But also...exhilarating." She extended her hand for the bottle. "And finding that stela..." She nodded toward where it lay, hidden in the darkness beyond the glow of the campfire. "It's a piece of a vanished civilization, and we're the first ones in hundreds of years to lay eyes on it. It's wonderful."

He watched her as she took a healthy slug from the bottle. "You're a rare breed, princess."

She smiled. "Is that another compliment?"

He shook his head. "I'm still working that out."

She laughed, and he grinned, and the sight of his tanned face in the firelight made her heart do an unexpected flip. His next question did nothing to help matters.

"So how about that arrest?" he drawled.

"Oh, dear."

"Come on—you can't let a nugget like that drop and not expect me to pick it up."

She felt a quick flash of nerves but caught herself. This wasn't the Public Record Office. She was in the middle of the jungle. What did she have to lose?

"I chained myself to the gates of Parliament."

Adam choked on a slug of rum. "What?"

"It was during a suffrage rally. Things were getting rather heated, and someone—I can't actually recall who—called for a blockade. I suppose I was caught up in the spirit of it."

"You chained yourself to Parliament."

"Yes," she replied, meeting his gaze evenly.

He leaned back, shaking his head. "They really broke the mold with you, didn't they?"

"Perhaps they did," she replied, smoothing the legs of her trousers demurely. She glanced over at him and felt something shift in the atmosphere, a sudden thickening. She was caught in it, eyes locked with his, powerfully aware of a quickening in her chest. The sensation was foreign and utterly overwhelming.

She wanted him. *Dear God.*

Everything the temperance people said about drink was true. Here she was, just halfway through that golden bottle, and she had gone from a rational, modern woman to a primitive, lustful savage. Her brain burned with possibilities—the way that tanned, muscular chest of his would feel under her hands. How the scruff on his face would burn against her skin. What he would taste like.

It was abominable. These were not the notions of a logical mind. Adam's dangerously delicious liquid was transforming her into an animal. What was more, there was really nothing to prevent her from acting on her impulses.

The realization set her heart pounding, but it was perfectly true. They were in the middle of the remote jungle. The only prying eyes around them were those of insects and the odd sloth. What happened between them in this moment need never find its way back to civilization. She could act on her wildest desires without fear of any of the social consequences.

And at that moment, her desires were unspeakably wild.

She looked over at him and felt their gazes lock. His eyes blazed with an emotion that amplified her own ferocity. Beyond thinking, she felt herself lean toward him. Her impulses bloomed, becoming irresistible.

I'm going to do it, some lingering shred of her rational mind realized. *I'm going to put my hands on him, and I don't even care about the consequences.*

Then the silence of the night was shattered by a roar. It echoed off the trees, shocking the jungle into silence.

Ellie stood up. "What is that?"

Adam had risen beside her. She noticed that he had picked up the rifle from where it lay on the ground beside him. He held himself in an uncanny stillness as he listened.

The silence was broken by the sound of crashing some distance away from the camp.

"Jaguar," he concluded.

She felt a flash of alarm. "Are we in danger?"

He shook his head, slinging the rifle back over his shoulder.

"No. It won't come near the fire. I'll build it up before we go to bed."

That last word lingered awkwardly between them. Ellie thought of what she'd been about to do when the jaguar had called, and felt her face flush.

"Yes. Well. Good night, then," she said stiffly, then turned briskly and marched over to the hammocks, not daring to look back until she was safely within the ghostly embrace of the mosquito netting. Only then did she glance over to see him tossing logs onto the embers of the fire. The easy strength of his movements sent another jolt through her. She turned deliberately away from him, staring up at the dark shadow of the canopy, painfully aware of how close she had just come to throwing her virtue to the wind.

Ellie had certainly never considered herself a proper lady. No female collegiate or suffragette would claim that title. But she'd at least assumed she had a certain moral core. Now she knew that to be nothing but an illusion. All it had taken was a few sips of rum to send her decency shrieking into the abyss. She had been that close to throwing herself at a man she had known for only a few weeks. A virtual stranger.

If not for that jaguar . . .

Ellie walked through a strange jungle, a thick fog obscuring the trees and shrubs around her. No, not fog—it was smoke, she realized. Thick and heavy, it crept across the ground like a living thing.

She moved forward blindly, pushing past the vines and palms until she felt her feet contact stone instead of the soft jungle floor. She looked down and saw that she was on a road. It was wide and cleanly swept, the paving stones expertly wedged together. She began to follow it, walking steadily through the smoke.

It was a little while later when she saw the first of the dead. A woman lay sprawled across the stones. There were sores on her face, and her throat had been cut, the blood blanketing the road in a still, black pool.

Skirting carefully around the corpse, she continued walking, aware now of the sounds around her—the clashing of metal, shouts and rustling footsteps. There was also a smell in the burning, something rich and fat. It brought bile into her throat and she tried to push the awareness of it from her mind.

The path rose and she walked into the city. It was beautiful and strange, with pyramid temples and long, columned palaces, all built of the same gleaming white stone. She approached a row of arches that led into a shadowy interior, drawn to it even as it repelled her.

It was filled with the dead, bodies stacked upon bodies like cans packed into a pantry. She saw the marks of disease on them and recognized it: smallpox. A plague to be feared, quarantined, and fled from. It had taken all of them, these stacked and stored lives.

She turned away and quickly followed the road up onto a raised platform. It proved to be a courtyard, wide and splendid. The temples sat on either side of it, three small and one massive, looming over the others. Smoke still hung over everything. The vast space was empty as a tomb, echoing with the distant sounds of screaming and conflict.

No—not empty. Not abandoned yet. A lone figure stood in the center of the plaza.

It was her, the scarred woman, resplendent in the gown of feathers Ellie had seen her wearing before. Her stillness seemed utterly out of place in this jungle battlefield, where the clamor of fighting still echoed through the streets around her.

As Ellie met her gaze, the sounds of violence seemed to fade into the background, replaced by a thick, tense silence, like snow or the muffled aftermath of a blow to the head.

Then, for the first time, the woman spoke.

"Listen. Can you hear it?"

Ellie listened, and it seemed to her that there was something sliding beneath that uncanny silence, a hush like the low murmur of a thousand voices, moving through the air around her.

"It sings to you. Whispers possibilities, dreams of blood and power."

"Who are you?" Ellie demanded.

"The echo of a sacrifice," the woman replied. The words were plain, but something hummed beneath their surface, a deeper sadness.

The landscape around them, the gleaming courtyards, the pale ghosts of the palaces and temples, flickered like the flame of a lamp on the verge of guttering. She saw shadows out of the corner of her eyes, the beating of great black wings.

"And this place?"

"Is a line of communication, open to those who bear the key."

"What key?"

Her glance moved to Ellie's chest, and Ellie lifted her hand to feel the cold weight of the medallion against her skin.

"But what does it open?"

The woman shook her head.

"There is a more pressing question. One that everything hangs upon."

"And what is that?"

"*What do you want?*"

The whispering rose, and Ellie felt it like a call, a thousand voices urging her to taste, indulge.

See what we can give you, they seemed to say. *Just a little closer.*

Then the world dissolved into darkness, and she knew no more.

Ellie sat up with a start and immediately wished she hadn't. The movement had awoken a ferocious pounding in her head. She winced with each throb, then realized they were coming in time with her own heartbeat.

Moving more slowly, she carefully swung herself out of the hammock. It took her longer than usual to get her balance. By the time she slowly ducked under the net, she had a fairly good idea of what was wrong. She'd either caught some sort of jungle disease, or she was experiencing, for the first time, the legendary after-effects of an excessive consumption of alcohol.

The memory of the night before came back to her in a queasy rush. Horrified, she recalled the thoughts that had danced through her unruly mind—thoughts she had very nearly acted upon.

At that moment, her guts churning in uncomfortable time with the pounding in her head, Ellie determined to become an ardent teetotaler.

She looked quickly to the hammock next to her. It was empty. Adam was crouched by the fire, bringing last night's stew up to a lively bubble. Seeing her up, he gave her a casual wave, then returned his attention to his task.

He didn't *seem* to be acting any differently. Perhaps he hadn't noticed that she'd been about to throw herself at him.

The thought calmed her. She reached for her boots, but her trembling hands refused to work properly. One of the pair slipped from her fingers, landing on the ground with a thud and tipping onto its side. Ellie barely repressed a shriek as a horrid-looking centipede well over four inches long scurried out of it and slipped away across the dry leaves.

Pushing aside the netting, she stepped gingerly over to the fire. Adam looked none the worse for wear. The thought was galling. He had to have consumed just as much, if not more, of that blasted stuff as she had. Surely he deserved to be suffering at least a little. But no—his eyes lacked even a hint of redness, and his movements were just as sure and easy as ever.

He turned to look at her as she approached, and winced. Apparently the signs of her own damage were a bit more obvious.

"Sit," he ordered, pointing to one of the logs by the fire. Ellie was too uncomfortable to protest. He grabbed a large green object and set it onto a flat stone, then began hacking at it with his machete, pieces of it flying off until a chop revealed an opening in the fibrous exterior.

Ellie knew it was some sort of seed or fruit. She'd seen its like hanging under the fronds of palms back in the city.

"Drink it," he said, handing it to her.

"What is it?"

"Coconut."

"But coconuts are brown." She had seen them often enough at the exotic grocers.

"Not until they're dry. Now drink."

"Drink what?"

Thinking seemed to be something more of a challenge than usual.

"This," Adam explained, shaking the coconut. Ellie could hear liquid gently sloshing around inside.

She took it and glanced up at him skeptically.

"It'll help with the headache." With a few swift slices of the blade, he chopped his way to a hole in another nut. He lifted it to his lips, drinking deeply and with obvious satisfaction.

Ellie tentatively imitated him. The liquid that poured into her mouth tasted light, cool, and slightly sweet. Her eyes brightened.

"That's good!"

"Finish it and have another," he directed.

A few coconuts and some leftover stew later, Ellie was feeling remarkably recovered. She rose and walked over to where Adam sat, quickly but carefully completing a sketch of the stela in his journal.

It was beautiful, every detail of the carvings captured with eloquence. Apparently Adam could add drawing to his list of talents.

Here and there, he had copied larger versions of some of the glyphs, annotating them with his thoughts. He glanced up, noticing her attention.

"I'd copy all of them, if we had time."

"We can spare a few hours, surely."

Adam shook his head, closing the book. "Any flexibility we might have had in terms of time went over that waterfall with the *Mary Lee*. If we're going to get back to the city, we've got to hitch a ride. And once the rains hit, we'll be hard-pressed to find a boat anywhere on the Belize, possibly for months."

He wrapped the book in oilskin and stashed it in his bag, then turned his attention to breaking down the camp.

It didn't take long. Everything they had fit neatly into the two packs. Adam shouldered his, tightening the straps, then moved to Ellie. He stopped just short of her, and something about the unease in his expression made her pulse skip.

"I need to adjust the straps," he said, nodding toward her bag.

"They're fine," she countered nervously.

"They won't be an hour from now. Hold still."

Bracing herself, Ellie obeyed. Adam's hands ran over the woven straps with a practiced air, tugging here and tightening there. Ellie tried desperately to ignore the quick rush of sensation the brush of his hand elicited against her side.

He gave the bag a final wiggle and stepped back.

"That should do it," he concluded, then quickly turned away. "You ready to move?"

She nodded, then realized he was looking the other way.

"Yes."

He glanced down at his compass, hefted the machete, and led her into the wilderness.

Ellie thought the pace was slow at first, but after a few hours she appreciated why Adam had kept them from sprinting ahead. The humidity, the rough terrain, and the burden of the pack all added to the difficulty of moving forward. And she wasn't the one hacking their path through the thicker areas of brush.

Adam wielded the machete with an easy, swinging motion that let the sharp blade slice through the vines and shrubs blocking their way. He also carried a stick he'd cut early in their trek, which he used to shake out areas of leaves before moving through them. Ellie had her own, which she wielded to push aside certain plants Adam warned her of as they passed.

"Thorns," he would say, lifting the vine with his stick, or, "Poisonous."

"How do you mean, poisonous?" she'd asked.

He smiled thinly. "You'd rather not find out."

He stopped only once. It was abrupt, a sudden coming to attention that reminded Ellie of a hunting dog. He held up a hand in a clear signal for silence, and Ellie halted. She waited for a full minute before her curiosity finally overcame obedience, and she demanded an explanation.

"What is it?" she whispered.

"Thought I heard something," he murmured.

"Something like what?"

He remained still for another moment, then shrugged and started forward.

"Probably nothing."

"But what did you think it was?" she demanded.

"We're not the only ones in this jungle, princess. Uncharted doesn't mean uninhabited."

He slashed cheerfully at the brush, Ellie staring after him.

By noon, the sun had reached its zenith and the moist heat penetrated even through the thick canopy. She could feel exhaustion approaching. It made her slow to recognize the low buzzing ahead of them. But it grew louder as they approached, suddenly registering in her awareness with a thrill of danger.

"What on earth—"

"It's fine," he assured her with a strange look. "Follow me."

The sound, like the swarming of giant bees, grew until at last they stepped out into a clearing. In the center of it was a massive tree dripping with ripe fruits. Many had fallen to the ground and split open, revealing pink flesh. Around the tree, the source of the buzzing could be seen flitting and hovering—a flock of hummingbirds sipping the sugary juices. Both jewel-toned males and dully camouflaged females moved dizzyingly fast around the tree and its bounty.

The sight was stunning. For a moment, Ellie stood transfixed. Then Adam moved past her.

"Lunch," he announced.

She gratefully lowered the pack from her shoulders and followed him. He pulled down one of the fruits.

"Don't eat the seeds," he cautioned. He sliced it in half and handed it to her. The interior of the strange-looking fruit was a soft pinkish-red, and the flavor, when she bit into it, was gently sweet, refreshing after the long morning hike. She dug in greedily.

The hummingbirds had fled as they approached but gradually returned as they sat and rested, buzzing around them. Then, halfway through her second fruit, the tiny jewel-like birds suddenly rose and raced away into the jungle. Adam frowned, casting a sharp eye around the clearing.

Across the way, the bushes suddenly rustled. The hairs on her neck rose warningly.

"Stand up, slowly. Put on your pack," Adam ordered, his voice a low murmur. She obeyed as the brush rustled again. Adam slowly reached behind him and slid the rifle out from where it was strapped to his back. He leveled it as two small creatures suddenly burst from the brush and tumbled into the clearing. To Ellie, they looked like piglets covered in soft, gray fur.

She felt a flash of relief, realizing the pair were obviously young and were mainly interested in rooting among the fallen fruits.

Beside her, Adam cocked the express.

"They're just babies," she protested.

"It's not them I'm worried about."

The brush rustled again, more loudly than before, and a much larger creature pushed through. It sported a pair of wickedly curving tusks, and its small, dark eyes moved from Ellie and Adam to the pair of infants gamboling at their feet.

Adam cursed under his breath and raised the gun, readying himself for the shot.

The boar screeched and was answered with a great shaking of foliage. Adam lowered the gun, his face pale, as a series of grunts and screams sounded from the brush before them. A moment later, four more of the hulking, black-bristled monsters blasted out of the greenery and stood glowering at them.

"Walk backward. Slowly," he ordered. They took a tentative step back, then another. "If you see them move..."

With a roar, the biggest of the boars leaped into motion. Adam shoved Ellie by her pack.

"Run!"

She didn't need to be told twice. Oblivious to the weight on her back, she flew through the forest, vines and branches snapping as she raced past. She could feel Adam close behind her and could hear the outraged screams of their pursuers—screams that were getting closer.

She picked up her pace, leaping nimbly over tangled roots and fallen branches. Then she burst through a thick wall of ferns and the ground beneath her vanished.

She twisted forward, unable to stop her momentum, grabbing hold of one of the thick vines that spilled down from the branches of the overhanging trees. The instinct saved her, halting her with one foot still resting on solid ground.

Then Adam pummeled into her.

She slipped, feet tripping out over the edge. With a crack, the vine loosened from its lower anchor and they swung out over the abyss.

The ground spun beneath them. The treetops below were so far away, they looked like a distant green carpet. She was hanging over an immense bowl sunken into the earth, surrounded by cliffs of sheer, jagged limestone.

Her hands, sweaty from the chase and slick from the fruit, slipped on the smooth surface of the vine. With a sickening feeling in her stomach, she felt herself drop by a foot. Adam's own grip on the vine stopped her fall, but the move put her face-to-face with him as he quickly twisted the vine around his leg, locking himself into place.

"Grab onto me," he barked.

Ellie felt her face flush.

"I couldn't possibly—"

"I can't hold you and the vine. Grab on!"

She obeyed, switching her sliding grip from the vine to Adam's shoulders.

"Put your arms around my neck and hang on," he directed her.

The grip his instructions gave her did feel more secure, but her legs still dangled loosely, and she knew she would not be strong enough to hold her weight for long. So did Adam.

"Wrap your legs around my waist."

She stared at him, shocked.

"Princess—" he growled in warning. With a silent prayer to the gods of mortification, she wrapped her legs around him.

"Higher. Settle your thighs on my hips. That's better," he said.

With the solidity of his body beneath her, she could take some of the weight from her already aching shoulders. But, as she was entirely too well aware, the position also forced their bodies together in a way that was unsettling, to say the least. The broad expanse of his chest pressed against her, and his waist was trapped between her thighs. Her mind was momentarily filled with the image of him standing, shirtless and soaked, trousers clinging, on the deck of the *Mary Lee*.

It was almost enough to make her let go.

The edge of the cliff was perhaps ten feet away. It made safety seem tantalizingly close, but the distance might as well have been a mile. As Ellie looked at it longingly, she watched their pursuers crash out of the jungle, skidding to a stop before the drop. Slowly turning as she dangled, she saw the frustration in their eyes as they pawed, bellowing, then retreated, huffing, making their way back into the bush.

Painfully aware of the feeling of Adam's body radiating heat between her thighs, Ellie forced herself to study the landscape around them. The cliffs marked off a roughly circular area of land. It seemed nearly a half mile across, the ground hundreds of feet below the level of the rest of the jungle. She could see birds flitting under her feet, colorful specks against the distant green canopy.

"It's a sinkhole," Adam offered. She could feel the warmth of his breath on her cheek as she clung to him. "Probably an underground lake that drained and collapsed."

His face looked pale. Ellie realized that his breathing had also grown shallow, and she felt a quick burst of panic. Was he hurt? If something had happened to him in their race through the jungle, maybe an encounter with one of those poisonous shrubs he'd shown her carefully to avoid . . .

"What's wrong?" she asked, unable to keep the panic from her tone.

"Nothing. I'm fine."

He was clearly not fine.

"Have you been poisoned?" she demanded.

"I'm afraid of heights," he said with forced deliberateness.

"Oh." Ellie looked down. The ground was rather far away.

"We need to get back to the ledge."

"How do we do that?"

He didn't answer. Another look told her why. His face seemed to have entirely drained of blood.

"Open your eyes," she ordered sharply.

"I'm not sure that's a good idea."

"Open them, and look at me."

He obeyed, and she realized just how close his face was to her own.

"Isn't that better?" she asked weakly.

"Marginally."

Even with his eyes open, Adam clearly wasn't going to be much use. If they were going to get out of this, Ellie would have to be the one to do the thinking.

The vine spun slowly over the abyss. As it turned, the ledge came back into view. It seemed dishearteningly far away, and was, if anything, slightly above the level at which they currently dangled.

We're like a pendulum, she thought vaguely.

A pendulum. The answer came to her in an instant, slipping from her mind out onto her tongue.

"We just need to swing."

"Swing?" Adam echoed, and the implications of her little stroke of genius settled in. Ellie knew perfectly well what sort of motion would start their vine arching back and forth, but the idea of doing—well, *that*—with her legs wrapped around Adam's midsection was worse than a whole case of bootleg Jamaican rum.

Adam adjusted his grip on the vine and swallowed thickly. He didn't look good. She glanced down at the drop that awaited them. She could feel the strain in his shoulders, the muscles taut like cords.

There was no time to think of another option. Ellie swallowed the remaining shreds of her propriety.

"Please don't take this personally," she said.

"Take what— Oh, dear God."

She shifted her hips from one side to the other, furiously ignoring the fire of sensation the action aroused in her. Their vine began to arc farther out over the sinkhole, then fly back toward the safety of the ledge. She moved in complement to the rhythm, adding her weight to it and increasing the length of their swing.

They moved faster. The wind whipped through her hair, and she wondered vaguely just how well anchored the vine was from above.

Her stomach lurched, and they flew back toward the ledge, their trajectory turning just over the top of it.

"Next time, we let go," she called to Adam. His eyes were shut again, beads of sweat dotting his forehead. She wasn't entirely sure he could hear her.

The vine swung back along its course, and when it reached the outer limit, she felt Adam release his hold. She followed suit, tumbling with him into a stand of massive ferns.

Ellie remained still, wondering whether she was really still alive.

"You all right?" he croaked.

Ellie realized that she lay sprawled across Adam's body. She rolled off of him abruptly and stumbled to her feet.

Adam followed more slowly, then, frowning, moved toward her. Ellie had the distinct and unsettling impression he meant to check for himself whether she had survived the adventure whole.

"I'm fine," she quickly assured him, dancing back. She narrowly avoided twisting her ankle on a fallen limb.

"Can you walk?"

"Certainly. Absolutely." She paused. "Why?"

"We have to keep moving. Get out of that herd's territory," he said. He sounded almost as tired as she felt. She suppressed a groan.

"How are your straps?" he asked, coming to check them. She darted away. She was beginning to fear her own reaction to him, which was growing increasingly intense every minute.

"They're fine. Honest. Let's just get moving, right?" She stepped forward, ready to trek.

"This way," he said, nodding in the opposite direction. He unsheathed the machete and led them back into the wilderness.

11

HOW MUCH TERRITORY DO these pigs have?" Ellie called ahead to Adam. He was swinging the machete unrelentingly, trudging steadily forward as the midday sun turned even the shaded air under the canopy to a sweltering blanket.

"They're like hunting dogs." He severed a palm frond. "I want to get past where they'd care to follow our scent."

Ellie was exhausted. Her pack, which had seemed absurdly light when they left camp that morning, had grown exponentially in weight until it felt as though someone had stuffed it full of rocks. Her body was pouring sweat, her shirt and trousers soaked with it, and the day seemed to be getting nothing but hotter.

She had long ago ceased to notice the rich color and strange beauty of the world they moved through, her entire awareness instead taken up with the effort of putting one foot in front of the other. When there was any extra energy to spare, she used it to think of creative ways to murder her slave-driver companion.

Not that she ever asked him to stop or slow down, of course. That would have meant admitting weakness, and she'd be damned if she did that in front of Adam Bates.

She was so absorbed in their march, she failed to notice when it halted. It took physically bumping into Adam's back for her to realize he wasn't moving anymore. He caught her as she stumbled back.

He looked her over. "You're beat," he concluded.

"I can keep going," she insisted dully.

"Well, you won't have to. Take a look at this."

He stepped aside. Before them, the jungle broke open into a

wide expanse of field. Ellie recognized the dark stubble of recently harvested corn.

"It's a *milpa*—a Mayan farm. Which means there's probably a village nearby. Let's see if we can't find ourselves some decent grub and a good night's sleep."

The prospect noticeably lightened Ellie's step as she followed him out into the open space of the clearing.

A flash of movement caught her eye. A quick brown form dashed across the edge of the field. The figure was that of a boy. He could be no more than fifteen, Ellie judged. He emerged from the bush a hundred yards away and raced soundlessly along the shadowy verge of the field, his feet bare. She clutched Adam's arm instinctively, startled by the sight of another human being after the long walk through the wilderness.

"Who is that?"

"Probably the one who's been following us," Adam replied evenly.

"Following us? For how long?"

"The last four or five hours. Maybe more."

"Why is he running?"

"I expect he's preparing our welcoming committee."

Ellie felt her nerves jangle.

"What kind of welcome should we expect?"

Adam touched her back lightly, pushing her forward.

"Come on, princess. We'll be fine."

On the far side of the field, they followed the course of a winding footpath that led them up the side of a hill to the village. It sat in a stretch of cleared land: a cluster of palm-leafed houses surrounded by fruit trees and gardens. She heard a rooster crowing a warning as they approached, and a pair of young girls in colorfully embroidered dresses came rushing out of a nearby doorway. They stopped in the path and stared at Adam and Ellie, eyes wide, then turned as one and dashed away.

By the time they reached the first of the houses, the girls had returned. They brought a small army of children, who gazed in rapt silence as they passed, then promptly formed a noisy gaggle behind them, following as they made their way along the path.

"They must not get many visitors," Ellie commented.

"There aren't a lot of our type who'd venture this far out in the bush, beyond maybe timber scouts or the odd missionary. Most likely we're something of a novelty."

As they walked, Ellie caught sight of other observers, the faces of women peering from the darkened doorways, whispering to one another. She felt more than a few of their gazes move across her body, taking in the female form under the men's jacket and trousers. Every one of them was wearing a femininely embroidered shirt and skirt, and sported long, straight locks. Novelty indeed, she thought, aware of her short-cropped hair.

As they neared the center of the cluster of buildings, Ellie caught her first sight of Adam's "welcoming committee." Every man in the village must have been gathered there, a crowd of perhaps sixty. They wore homespun shirts and trousers dusty from the fields and were standing in a cluster, engaged in some sort of urgent debate. It silenced abruptly and conspicuously as they approached. Behind her and Adam, their train of young followers also quieted, the children melting into the doorways of nearby houses, from which they continued to watch the action with rapt curiosity.

Back in the city, several of the guides she interviewed had waxed poetic about Mayan hospitality. But there was nothing friendly about the looks she and Adam were receiving.

Adam didn't seem to notice. He paused for only a moment before giving the group of men a wave and addressing them in a language Ellie didn't recognize, a rich flow of syllables she could tell did not fall completely easily from his tongue.

The response was silence. The men continued to stare at them, faces darkly suspicious.

"Maybe they're Q'eqchi'," he muttered, and tried what she guessed was another dialect. The faces before them remained stony. She began to wonder nervously what they had just walked into, then heard someone chuckle.

It was an old man—the oldest there, by far—who sat on a stool at the edge of the clearing between the houses. His build was slight and wiry, and he was entirely bald save for a few tufts of white hair. A long, obviously old scar ran across his forehead, jagged like a lightning bolt. Ellie wondered what accident had put that there. Then again, perhaps it had something to do with the necklace he wore: an oddly gruesome arrangement of jagged, needle-sharp teeth.

He shook his head as he laughed, then spoke in perfect, if accented, English.

"Your Q'eqchi' is almost as bad as your Mopan."

She saw the surprise flash across Adam's features. It was quickly replaced by his usual easy grin.

"I'm out of practice."

"Were you ever in it?"

"Not particularly," Adam admitted.

The old man stood and ambled toward them, the other villagers watching him silently. Adam extended a hand.

"Adam Bates."

"I am Amilcar Kuyoc. You are looking for a place for the night?"

"We'd be obliged."

"You would be welcome as my guests. Please follow me."

Ellie realized that Adam had neglected to introduce her as well—then remembered that the name he would have given to their newfound host was Constance Tyrrell.

He still didn't know who she really was. The reminder left her feeling distinctly guilty.

Kuyoc turned and said a few words to the group of men. They dispersed. The thick tension had broken with the old man's laugh, and the scene before her looked more like a slice of ordinary life than a ripening threat. Their host briefly shooed away the band of children, who scattered, shrieking joyfully.

Kuyoc led them down a well-worn path through the village until the bulk of the houses were behind them. As they walked,

Ellie caught sight of a small shack set in a hollow in the hillside, some distance from the path. While the rest of the huts had either a curtain for a doorway or nothing at all, this one had a sturdy wooden door with a padlock.

"What's in there?" she asked.

"That is where we keep the dynamite," Kuyoc replied easily.

"Dynamite?" Ellie echoed.

The old man's bright eyes moved from her to Adam, whose face had creased into a puzzled frown.

"Good for removing stumps," he said, punctuating it with a slightly toothless grin. He turned and continued walking, calling back to them, "This way. Just a little farther."

The path led to a house set beyond and above the outskirts of the rest of the village. A small boy sat on the threshold, clutching a hen to his chest like a sleeping cat. He watched them approach with wide, wondering eyes.

"My grandson, Paolo," Kuyoc said. He pointed to the hen. "And that is Cruzita. He named it after his mother, who is not happy that her son chose a good meal as a pet."

The boy got up as they approached and dashed around the side of the house, feet nimbly moving around the bunches of greens in the garden.

"Shy," their host explained, and motioned them inside.

The doorway was low. Ellie could barely enter it standing up, and Adam had to duck. Inside, the air was noticeably and welcomingly cooler. A row of hammocks hung from the roof. The furnishings otherwise were sparse—a battered tin lamp, a collection of baskets. A door at the far end led to what looked like a kitchen.

"You must both be tired. Why don't you nap until supper?" Kuyoc waved toward the hammocks, which looked heavenly to Ellie.

"If you're sure you don't mind," Adam said.

Kuyoc smiled. "Rest. I will tell Cruzita that you are here."

Ellie was too tired to pretend politeness. She dropped her pack and climbed into the hammock. A moment later she felt a tugging at her ankles. She cracked open one of her eyes to see Adam pulling off her right boot.

"Your feet need a rest, too," he explained.

"I'm perfectly capable—" she began, but cut herself off with a yawn.

"Sure you are." He smiled wryly, tugging off the other shoe. She gave up, lay back, and in a moment had slipped away from consciousness.

Ellie woke to a clatter of pans from the kitchen to see a pair of large, dark eyes gazing at her with rapt attention. Amilcar Kuyoc's grandson, Paolo, sat on a stool he had pulled up near her hammock and was staring at her. The stare got bigger as he realized she was looking back at him.

"Hello, there," she said.

"Hello," the boy replied.

She smiled, surprised.

"Grandfather teach me English."

"I guess he does!"

"Little English." He held his fingers up in a pinch to illustrate. "Where you from?"

"London."

"Near Belize City?"

"No—it's very far from there."

"Near San Pedro Siris?"

"I don't know that place. London is in England, on the other side of the sea. Mr. Bates is from San Francisco, in America."

"How do you know San Pedro Siris?"

Ellie turned, surprised to see Adam standing in the doorway. She saw that he was frowning, and the smile that had instinctively leaped to her lips faded in confusion.

Paolo stared at him as though not understanding.

"Who is from San Pedro Siris?" Adam repeated.

A crash sounded from the kitchen, and a female voice called, quick and irritated. Paolo's hen scurried, squawking, from the doorway. The boy snatched her up and then ran out the front of the house.

Ellie looked to Adam.

"Is something wrong?"

"No. Everything's fine," he assured her evenly.

But the uneasiness she had felt before, under the watchful and suspicious eyes of the village men, had returned.

Ellie sat between Adam and their host at a low wooden table eating what tasted like the best meal she'd ever had in her life. The food was simple but mouthwateringly good, a richly spiced chicken stew with soft corn tortillas and a heaping crock of rice and beans. Ellie ate enough for two, not even realizing how hungry she was until the smell of the food met her nose.

"Where's Cruzita? She can't still be cooking." She wanted to thank the woman, whom she had yet to see, for the miracle in her mouth.

"She eats later, with the women."

"The women eat separately?"

"Yes," Adam answered her with a warning look, which of course only deepened her irritation. She glanced around the table and realized it was true. Besides the three of them, there were only Kuyoc's two stoically quiet sons, returned from their day at work in the *milpa*. She looked at the now near-empty pot, thought of her own outrageous appetite, and felt a wave of guilt.

"What will they eat?"

"They'll have saved some for themselves," Adam said around a mouthful of tortilla.

"They don't want to eat with the men. If they do, they couldn't gossip." Kuyoc smiled, eyes twinkling.

Ellie forced aside her unease at the notion that the women of the family weren't present at the table, but it was replaced by an odd epiphany—that to the people of this place, she was considered a man. The thought stopped a piece of chicken halfway to her mouth.

It was something she'd fought for all her life: to be let into that exclusive fraternity, treated as equal with them. And she'd found it in stolen trousers in an obscure place thousands of miles from home.

There was another crash, and a clamor of shouting and squawking from the kitchen. Kuyoc chuckled.

"One of these days, that bird is going to end up in a stew pot."

Ellie could hear the bright voices of the women at their meal as she and Adam sat on a pair of stools in the garden, watching the last rays of sun disappear over the horizon. The sky was moonless, and the stars beginning to emerge were brighter and more numerous than she had seen since her childhood trips to her parents' cottage by the lake.

Amilcar Kuyoc emerged from the doorway carrying two cups in his hands. He passed one to each of them.

"Careful. It's hot."

She took hers and inhaled. The scent was rich and warm, exotic yet familiar.

"Chocolate, the Mayan way," Kuyoc explained.

"Thank you," Adam said, and sipped.

Ellie did the same, and nearly melted. The taste was divine, bittersweet and chili-spiked.

Kuyoc settled down beside them, looking as though he had done the same every night in this place for decades.

Their seats were perfectly positioned to take in the view, a gentle slope of cleared land leading down to the clustered houses of the village and the wide, dark expanse of the wilderness beyond.

"Nice place," Adam said.

"It is," their host agreed.

"And quiet. I didn't know it was here."

"You know where the other villages are." It was a statement.

"Most of them, I'd expect. I'm the assistant surveyor general for the colony. It's my job to know where things are."

"Ah. A mapmaker," Kuyoc said. "And is that why you are here? To make maps?"

There was something strange in his tone, but when Ellie looked, his expression betrayed nothing but a benign calm.

"Not this time," Adam said. He nodded toward the fang-spiked necklace revealed by the open throat of the old Mayan's shirt. "Those don't look like jaguar teeth."

"They're not," Kuyoc replied.

There was an awkward pause where the rest of the story should have been. Kuyoc rolled a cigarette with a pinch of tobacco he took from a pouch at his waist.

"Tell me, mapmaker. If you are not here to map, then what does bring you to this place?"

"Something you might be able to help us with, as a matter of fact. We're looking for a ruined city I'd estimate should be about four or five days' walk from here to the northwest. Can you read a map?" Adam asked.

Ellie jolted at his words. Was he really about to share their secret so casually, with a man they hardly knew? She wanted to protest, snatch the document away from him as he pulled it from the tin in his pack and spread it out across his knees. But how could she? The damage was already done.

Her hand moved instinctively to her shirt. She could feel the medallion, safely hidden there against her skin.

She felt Kuyoc's sharp eyes on her. They flickered from her face to her hand. She forced it down to her knee, and after another moment the old man turned his attention to the parchment in Adam's lap.

"We're just about here, you see?" He looked up for confirmation, then moved his finger. "These ruins should be somewhere right around here. You ever heard of anything like that?"

Kuyoc stared silently down at the map for so long that Ellie began to wonder if he'd lied about being able to read one. When he stopped staring, it was not to answer Adam's question. Instead he stood, stepping away from them into the garden. His gaze was directed past the sloping hillside and the village to the dark, misty shapes of the surrounding mountains.

"No," he said at last. "No one from this village has gone there. And none of them would, not if you paid them to."

"Why not?" Ellie asked.

The old man turned, his gaze cold and unblinking.

"Because Death lives there. Death and the rest of the old gods. And he and his servants feast on the flesh of those who trespass in their realm."

Ellie felt a chill at his words and wondered for a moment whether their host was mad. Then his face cracked into a smile.

"That is what they say, at any rate. There are stories of those who have gone into that region of the jungle, never to be seen again. Or who come back raving about angels with the teeth of jaguars and a thirst for blood. Perhaps there is some truth to it. The jungle has many dangers, does it not? The one that lives in that place may be real, even if the stories told about it are fanciful."

Ellie thought of their close call that afternoon. When she had tried to anticipate some of the trials she might face on her journey, she had never dreamed of "pig attack."

"I'm afraid you will find no guide here. Nor anywhere else for that matter. Only a madman would venture into unknown land during the rains. And they are coming. You can smell them in the wind." He lifted his face as though searching for the scent, and Ellie found herself following suit. It seemed she could almost detect what he was describing—a sort of freshness in the cool evening breeze.

She shook it off. The sky overheard was perfectly clear. They still had plenty of time before the rains set in. The old man was simply a good storyteller.

"If it is ruins you are after, there are those we can show you. Spectacular ruins only a short way from here."

"Thanks, but I think we'll stick to our plan," Adam said, folding up the map and returning it to the cylinder.

"What treasure is it that you hope to find in this city?"

Kuyoc's tone was casual, almost joking, but when Ellie looked, she could see a hardness in his gaze that belied his words.

"We're not looking for treasure," Adam said.

"No? Then what are you looking for?"

"Knowledge. We want to know who these people were. What happened to them."

"You want to know what happened to the people of the dead cities?" He swept an arm expansively over the vista before them—the twinkling lights of the village. "They are right here."

They absorbed this in silence as Kuyoc took a long draw on his cigarette, exhaling in a dragonlike stream of smoke.

"That's a nasty scar you've got there," Adam commented. "Must have come from a hell of a fight."

"You could say that."

Ellie thought she detected the ghost of a smile crossing the old man's face.

"Was it in San Pedro Siris?" Adam asked, his tone careful.

"No," the old man replied.

"But you were there."

"I was." He took another draw, calm and slow, his gaze still cast out over the peaceful landscape before them.

"And the rest of these people?"

"They were here, working the land their ancestors have worked for a thousand years."

Ellie looked from Adam to the Mayan and felt a wave of irritation. There was a conversation happening here that she did not understand and was being left out of. But even as she thought it, she felt it shift, Adam leaning back on his stool and extending his legs out before him.

"I didn't come here to draw any maps. But I can. If I put this village on one, it would bring trade, connection to the rest of the colony. Or I can pretend I never saw it. What do you think the people here would want?"

Kuyoc was quiet, his eyes focused but distant, as though he looked at some far thing none of the rest of them could see. Ellie sensed a tension in him, a sort of fierce determination that seemed to break as she watched, shattering into resignation. He shook his head, suddenly looking older.

"Tell me, Mr. Bates. Do you really think it would matter? Where one foot has tread, others will follow. It is foolishness to think it can be stopped. The whole world will be laid bare eventually, all its secrets dragged out of their hiding places and set down on your maps." He stopped, catching himself. "You must excuse me. I am old and tired. Very tired."

He crushed the remnant of the cigarette under his sandal.

"Cruzita made up your beds in the guesthouse." He gestured to a shack nearby, then turned abruptly and left them.

"Come on," Adam said, and led her to the building. Inside they found a pair of bunks built on elevated platforms of wooden boards. They looked less comfortable than the hammocks in the main house, but instinct told her that in this place, these would be considered privileged accommodations. Adam dropped down easily onto one of them and started tugging at his laces.

"What happened out there?"

"Ghost stories."

"Excuse me?"

"Ghosts of the past. Ghosts of the future."

"What's San Pedro Siris?" She felt snappish, impatient about being left out of the conversation.

He sighed, leaning forward with elbows on his knees. He looked weary.

"About fifty years ago there was some trouble with the logging camps in the north part of the colony. Conflict between natives who figured these were their ancestral lands and loggers who didn't give a damn. There were rumors of abuses."

"What kind of abuses?"

"Forced labor, mainly."

"You mean slavery? But that's illegal."

His only answer was a raised eyebrow. Ellie felt the quick heat of outrage but said nothing, letting him continue.

"There was an uprising. One of the leaders—guy by the name of Marcus Canul—based himself in the village of San Pedro Siris, a little way from Orange Walk. About a hundred miles to the north of here, as the crow flies. His raids got a bit too successful and the local troops decided to retaliate. So they burned the village. It's not a pretty piece of history."

"And Kuyoc?"

"Must have been involved somehow. Maybe a follower of Canul's. He's old enough. And when it all went to hell, the survivors scattered to who-knows-where. This is as likely a place as any for one of them to end up."

"What are you going to do?" she asked.

"About what?" He lay down on the pallet, stretching himself out comfortably.

"Will you put it on your map or not?"

"Princess, how would you describe the welcome we received when we got here? Personally, I'd call it tense."

She didn't disagree, recalling the faces of the men gathered in the center of the village.

"Mapping this village would bring trade. Modern amenities, medicine. Maybe a mission school. But there's a cost. Her Majesty's government doesn't recognize native land rights. I saw mahogany in the bush outside the village. Once the loggers figured that out, they'd claim the whole place for themselves. Maybe the villagers and the logging company could come to an agreement, share the land. But somebody who's seen what Amilcar Kuyoc has seen would have a hard time looking on that particular bright side."

There was a silence as Ellie absorbed this.

"We didn't come here for mapmaking," Adam finally finished. He rolled over. "Get some sleep. We've got another long day tomorrow."

The wooden bed was only marginally less uncomfortable than she had anticipated. She shifted on it and thought longingly of the comfort of her hammock. But at least here she wouldn't have to worry about a jaguar sneaking up on her in the middle of the night. This was probably her best chance at a decent rest for a long time.

She thought of what Kuyoc had said—that he could smell the rains. She hoped he was wrong.

Just a few more days, she prayed as she drifted off to sleep.

12

Ellie woke feeling oddly rested. For the first time in what felt like ages, her night had been dreamless. It was a relief, though why she should feel relieved to escape from dreams of fortune and glory was beyond her. But by the time the village faded behind them, the benefit of a decent night's sleep was overcome by the rising heat of afternoon.

Ellie's irritation rose with the humidity as the sweat poured down her back, soaking the shirt she wore under Tibbord's field jacket. She envied Adam, who she was fairly certain hadn't worn a jacket in days. It didn't seem to matter. His shirt, too, was soaked, either from sweat or from the moisture constantly dripping off the leaves of the thick foliage they moved through.

"Why is it that you're always in the lead?" she demanded, following behind as Adam trudged along, hacking at the brush.

"Because I know where we're going."

"I'm just as capable of reading a compass," she retorted.

"Probably not so handy with a machete, though." Adam severed a vine, which fell to the ground in front of him with a thud.

"It looks rather straightforward. Walk and hack at anything that has the misfortune to be in your way."

"It's a bit more complicated than that, princess. Just like navigating the bush means more than reading a compass."

"You could at least let me try."

"Maybe later."

"Why not now?"

"Because I'd like to cover some distance before nightfall, not stand around watching you saw at the underbrush."

"I know better than to saw," Ellie huffed.

Adam held up his hand.

"Quiet."

The retort died on her lips, and she felt a momentary fear that they were about to encounter another herd of angry boars. Then Adam grinned.

"Come on."

He pushed through the brush to his left, and Ellie hurried after him.

The undergrowth was particularly thick in this part of the jungle. She moved blindly, keeping Adam just within sight ahead of her. Ferns brushed against her face, leaving cool trails of moisture behind, but it was more than that relieving the unrelenting heat. The air itself seemed to be growing fresher, and she realized she could hear a soft rushing underneath the more immediate rustle of the foliage.

Then she stepped out of the brush, and the rushing turned to a roar.

She stood on the banks of a stretch of ferocious rapids. Water leaped and splashed over tumbled boulders, the spray turning to a cool mist that grayed the overhanging branches of the canopy.

Ellie held out her arms, shamelessly relishing the feel of the spray on the skin exposed by her rolled-up cuffs. Adam stood beside her, eyes closed, an expression of deep satisfaction on his face.

"This might be heaven," she admitted.

"Pretty sure it's a tributary of the Belize. We've wandered back onto the map."

The idea was surprisingly uncomfortable.

"Is that a good thing?"

He glanced over at her, sensing the shift in her mood but misinterpreting the reason.

"We're right where we're supposed to be. We'll follow this to another fork, then cut overland to the northwest and look for that ridge."

The "river of smoke." Ellie remembered the enigmatic description from the map. The "river" was supposed to mark the face of a cliff that signaled the hidden entrance to the city. She hadn't the first idea what a river *on* a cliff might look like, but she would find out. Soon.

The idea was as breathtaking as the view.

Adam cut a path for them along the course of the rapids. It made the walk far more pleasant. Being soaked to the bone was a relief compared to sweltering in the deeper jungle, and Ellie would happily put up with being virtually deafened by the rushing water to enjoy it. With conversation reduced to an occasional shout over the roar to watch out for a slippery patch of ground, there was little for Ellie to do but watch her footing and enjoy the view. Somehow the sight of the muscles moving under the soaked fabric of Adam's shirt and trousers continued to draw more of her attention than the soaring trees and mist-shrouded water. She forced herself to look elsewhere. Just because she was in the deep jungle didn't mean she had to give in to base animal instinct.

She was putting such a concerted effort into ignoring Adam, she didn't realize he had stopped moving until she nearly walked into him. He stood at the edge of a rise, looking at a stunning trick of geography. A natural arch of stone hung over the river, covered in tenacious ferns and trailing vines.

A bridge of stone. *Hollowed by the hand of God.*

It was just as the map had described. It framed the view beyond, a broad curve where the rapids seemed to end, the water mud-hued but calm.

And thronged with boats.

Ellie counted three enormous steamships. A small fleet of rafts and canoes paddled back and forth between the steamers and the riverbank, ferrying men and crates of supplies. A large herd of mules was braying from the animals' place in a makeshift corral, and tents covered the shore like a patch of toadstools.

It was an expedition. A very large expedition, from the look of it. Voices called back and forth, and the blast of a steam whistle shook a colorful explosion of birds from the trees.

But who would mount an undertaking like that with the rains just around the corner?

"Get back into the bush," Adam ordered, his voice low but absolute. Ellie felt the first pang of fear and took a step backward.

Something hard and cold pressed against the back of her neck.

"Stay very still, now. You don't want to give me a reason to pull this trigger."

Adam whirled. She saw his hand flicker toward the machete, and the pressure on her neck increased.

"Uh-uh. Hands in the air, if you want the lady to stay pretty. You can come out, Flowers!"

The brush to Adam's right shifted, and a very large, dark-skinned man emerged. He pointed a shotgun at Adam.

"Afternoon," he greeted them amicably. "Should I ask for his rifle, Mendez?"

"What do you think?"

"Do you mind?" the big man asked politely. Ellie saw Adam's eyes move from their captor's shotgun to his face, and then to Mendez, who stood behind Ellie, his gun barrel prodding sharply against the back of her head. With a smooth, resigned movement, he swung the rifle off his shoulder and handed it over.

"Don't forget his bag, and that knife," Mendez ordered.

Ellie felt her own pack yanked from her shoulders as Adam released his machete and bag to Flowers.

"We're just passing through…," Ellie started lamely.

"Now you're 'passing through' to the *jefe*," Mendez retorted.

Ellie contemplated their chances of escape, but the feel of cold steel against her skin quickly overruled the idea.

As though he sensed her thought, Adam met her gaze steadily.

"It's all right, princess," he said. His voice was calm, but Ellie could see the sharp tension in the line of his shoulders. In a way, it relieved her. He would think of a way to get them out of this, whatever it was they had stumbled into.

"Walk," Mendez ordered, jabbing her with the gun. Ellie stumbled forward, coming to Adam's side as Flowers led them through the jungle toward the camp below.

"The damned rapids," he said, his voice low and angry.

"Sorry?"

"I would have heard them coming if it weren't for the rapids. The water drowned them out."

His words surprised her.

"You can hardly expect yourself to have predicted something like this...."

Her voice trailed off. From the expression on his face, that was exactly what Adam believed. She sensed the futility of trying to talk him out of it.

"Just keep quiet and leave the talking to me."

"I'm perfectly capable of—"

Adam shot her a warning look.

"Fine," she whispered in agreement.

Then Mendez was at her back, forcing them down the slope.

Their captors marched them to the far side of the camp, which already stretched for some distance along the riverbank and was continuing to grow. Ellie counted at least thirty men at the site and was sure there were more still on the boats or concealed by the tents.

What could it be? An official expedition of some sort? But given her own difficulties securing a guide, it seemed impossible that any government department would have put something so substantial together when the rains would set in any day. Yet who else but the government would be responsible for such a massive undertaking?

It was not a comforting thought.

With a rifle at their backs, they wove through the crowd. The population of the camp appeared to be a genuine melting pot. She saw men of all colors from the city mingling with the slight forms of Mayans, like the people of the village they had left that morning. She heard English and Spanish spoken alongside something that sounded both like and unlike French, along with other languages she couldn't recognize at all. She even saw a small group of Chinese, keeping to themselves by one of the campfires.

Whatever the object of this massive undertaking, it was as well equipped as it was thoroughly manned. Ellie saw piles of crated goods and ammunition. There was even a stack of steel canisters, the sort used to hold the gas at soda fountains. But surely they weren't here for mixing beverages. She got a closer look as they moved by, catching the letter painted onto the side of the cylinders: *H*. For hydrogen.

She had no time to think about it. They passed the tanks and reached their destination, a large tent on the far end of the encampment. The smaller of their two captors—the one called Mendez—lifted the tent flap and motioned them inside.

The crates within were obviously in the process of being unpacked, their contents half-spilled out in every corner. A field desk had been set up, along with a folding camp chair. But it was the pile of gear beside it that caught her eye: a pair of trowels, a pickax, a canvas roll of brushes of various sizes. An archaeologist's kit.

Whoever was behind this, they had come to excavate. But excavate what? The implication sent a chill through her, which only deepened as she looked to Adam and saw from his expression that he had drawn the same conclusion. She saw the unspoken accusation in his eyes.

Who else knew?

The flap behind them rustled, and the answer stepped into the room.

It was Professor Dawson.

Ellie's heart lurched, and her eyes flew to the exit. But what would she do if she got outside? There were dozens of men between her and escape. And Jacobs would be out there somewhere. She was sure of it.

Dawson was looking at her with what seemed remarkably like dismay.

"I told you to disappear," he blurted.

"I tried," she snapped in reply.

"You know this guy?" Adam demanded.

The realization hit her like a slap, and one fear was quite suddenly replaced by another. Ellie saw what was coming, but there was no possibility of avoiding it.

Dawson's look went from his face to hers, his eyes wide.

"You didn't tell him?"

"Tell him what?" Adam demanded.

"This is dreadfully awkward. We are... Well, I suppose you would call us the competition."

"Competition," Adam echoed. He turned to Ellie, his expression cool. "Would have appreciated knowing about that."

She felt a quick spike of fear, and fought it.

"There wasn't anything to know." She turned her glare on Dawson. "You didn't have the map. You shouldn't be here."

"I had already transcribed the route onto a modern map when you relieved me of the original. Of course, once I did so, I saw that there was a better route than the one the monks had taken, coming up the Belize instead of the Sibun."

"Your map wasn't from the British Museum, I'm guessing," Adam said dryly.

"No. I acquired it at the colony's survey office. It was the most up-to-date...." Dawson's voice trailed off as Adam started to laugh.

"My own damned map." He shook his head.

"I'm sorry—your map?"

"The one he drew. He works for the survey office," Ellie said flatly. The irony of it left her feeling vaguely numb.

Dawson blinked rapidly. "I'm sorry—but you are...?"

"Adam Bates."

He stared at Adam wonderingly.

"Adam Bates who drew the map. Adam Bates the Mayanist."

"You've heard of me?"

Dawson ignored the irony Ellie could hear in Adam's tone.

"I read your report of the excavation of Actun Punit. Your conclusions were remarkably insightful."

"Nice of you to say so."

Ellie fought the impulse to intervene. Something had shifted in the room. She could feel it. Dawson appeared to be making some sort of furious calculation, one that reached a conclusion as the tent flap behind him lifted and Jacobs stepped into the room.

Ellie tensed, but before he could make a move, Dawson was speaking.

"Ah! Mr. Jacobs—you've heard, undoubtedly, that our young friend has returned. And she has brought with her, as it happens, the premier Mayanist this side of the Yucatán."

Jacobs's gaze moved smoothly from Ellie to Adam, then back to Dawson again.

"But I've been terribly remiss." Dawson hurried over to Adam, offering his hand. "Professor Gilbert Dawson, formerly of Saint Andrews. Very pleased to make your acquaintance. And this is my colleague, Mr. Jacobs."

"We've met," Adam said, frowning.

"You have?"

"When I was searching the hotel," Jacobs offered placidly.

"Oh, yes. Of course. I suppose Miss Mallory must have spun quite a story for you about that little mess."

"Mallory?" Adam's frown deepened as the bottom dropped out of Ellie's stomach. She looked to Dawson and saw first bewilderment, then comprehension, and finally something even less expected: a flash of sympathy.

"Oh, dear," he said

"Who's Mallory?" Adam demanded.

Ellie could feel it coming and knew it was unavoidable. She braced herself as Dawson answered.

"She is. That's her name. Eleanora Mallory."

The room was awkwardly, painfully silent. Adam turned to her. "That true?"

That look in his eyes—it was a coldness she had never seen in them before. Fear shot through her, stealing her voice.

Dawson spoke for her, rambling and awkward.

"Tyrrell—that's what she must have told you, of course. Constance Tyrrell is an acquaintance of hers in London who abetted her escape the first time she stole the map. Our map," he added with a quick glance at Jacobs, who was watching the exchange impassively.

Ellie felt the ground slipping out from beneath her feet as she saw the suspicion growing in Adam's face, and the anger. She scrambled for some semblance of control over a situation that was rapidly growing dangerous.

"I only 'stole' it from them when I took it back after they robbed it from my room."

"Recovered it," Dawson countered. The retort seemed transparent, but when Ellie looked to Adam, his expression was closed. She realized what was happening. This was a battle, one for Adam's trust. It was her against Dawson—though God only knew why he felt any need to win that particular prize. But what would happen to them if she lost?

"Then where did you get it?" Adam demanded.

Ellie knew there was nothing else for it. She would have to tell the truth, and hope like hell he understood.

"I took it. From the Public Record Office, where I worked." She glared at Dawson, daring him to contradict her. "It didn't belong to anyone."

"We had sent it there for authentication—to an acquaintance of our employer, a Mr. Henbury," he explained, more smoothly this time, ready with the lie.

"Henbury couldn't authenticate his way out of a paper bag." It was a ludicrous suggestion to anyone who had known the man, whose skills Ellie knew ended at taking cigar breaks and delegating.

"He is the assistant keeper of the rolls in the department charged with caring for the archives of the kingdom," Dawson countered.

"They're lying," Ellie asserted. She stared at Dawson, challenging him with her eyes. But her enemy was only growing more confident.

"My dear girl," he said. "We are not the ones in this room using false names."

It hit her how perfectly she had set the trap for herself. She had lost before she walked into the tent. It was impossible for Adam to take her word over theirs when she had been revealed as a liar over the most fundamental things: the history of the map, the presence of enemies—her own name.

She didn't want to look in his face, to see the mistrust that must be taking root there. The betrayal and disappointment. All because she hadn't trusted him, even after everything he'd done to prove to her that he was worthy of it. Instead she turned from Dawson, who had manufactured a very believable expression of pity, to Jacobs, who was watching the whole exchange with a sort of wry amusement. Catching her look, he raised an eyebrow, as if challenging her to find a way out of the mess she had gotten herself squarely into. But Dawson's next words only sealed the trap still more closely.

"I presume you still have the map. You may certainly hold on to it if you like—my copy was very carefully made. However, there is one other part of our property that I would like returned, if at all possible. A black medallion, rather intricately carved."

Of course they would know about it. If Henbury had hoped to intrigue them into a sale, he would hardly have neglected to leave out the most enticing proof in the bargain. But Adam would not know that. To him it would only make Dawson's story sound all that much more plausible.

"If you do still have it, Miss Mallory...," Dawson continued awkwardly.

"Give it to him," Adam said coldly. The words hit her like a knife thrust. She turned to him, shocked, but he did not meet her eyes.

Her hand went to the medallion. She clutched it beneath the fabric of her shirt, then forced herself to take a breath. She had to hold herself together. What good would the medallion do her if both of them were dead?

Forcing herself, she calmly pulled the ribbon over her head, then strode over to Dawson and placed it in his hand.

As it touched his palm, he looked down at it with apparent surprise. Ellie saw his fingers move over the dark, shining surface wonderingly, and it seemed as though he had to remind himself that he was not alone in the room.

He gave an awkward cough, then continued speaking as he tucked the dark stone into the breast pocket of his jacket.

"The saddest part of it, Mr. Bates, is that she may not even realize she's lying when she does. Are you familiar with the works of a Mr. Freud? He describes a condition called hysteria, one peculiar to females, particularly those who are too long unmarried."

"Not a widow then, either," Adam commented.

Ellie felt her cheeks burn, but there was more at stake than Adam's discovery of her true marital status. She was familiar with Freud's works, of course. What self-respecting woman wouldn't arm herself with knowledge of the man who was trying to pathologize their struggle for equal rights?

"I am not a hysteric," she asserted sharply.

Dawson ignored her objection.

"The symptoms are manifold. Pathological lying is among the foremost, but the others include paranoia, delusions...." He cleared his throat awkwardly and cast a look over her male attire. "And promiscuity. Of course, many hysterics are also quite charismatic, which I believe we can all agree applies to our Miss Mallory."

He was complimenting her? The sheer gall of it was overwhelming. She had to find some way to fight back against this, before it was too late. She drew on every reserve of self-control she could, forcing her tone to remain calm and even, knowing Dawson would seize upon any sign of emotional excitement.

"Bates, you can't trust anything these men are telling you."

She chanced a look at his face, hoping to see some sign there of wavering, some hint that he was still with her. But the feeling etched plainly on his features was not what she'd hoped. It was doubt. Suspicion. Betrayal.

"My case in point, sadly." Dawson gave her a lingering, sympathetic look so convincing it made her wonder, just for a moment, whether maybe she had dreamed the whole thing up. Perhaps the

map had been theirs to begin with, and this whole business had
been nothing but a great misunderstanding.

Then she remembered the words she had heard while hiding
outside her room at the Imperial, the look on Jacobs's face as he
chased her through the crowds on Regent Street. It was not the
look of an outraged man trying to reclaim what was rightfully his.
It had been the cold expression of a cat stalking a wounded bird.

"I am terribly sorry for all the inconvenience this must have
caused you, Mr. Bates," Dawson went on. "You could hardly have
been expected to know....Mr. Jacobs will be happy to arrange passage back to the city for you on one of our steamers. It's the least we
can do. But I do hope I can prevail upon you to stay for the night.
Perhaps join me here for dinner. As to Miss Mallory..." Dawson
gave her a look she imagined must have been well practiced on his
students, an elegant expression of disappointment. If he had ever
actually had students, of course. Formerly of Saint Andrews, her
left foot. "I must insist that she remain with us. I know it must seem
strange, after all the inconvenience she has put us through, but I'm
afraid I feel a certain sense of responsibility for the poor creature.
I will see her back to London personally, once we have completed
our expedition."

"Very kind of you," Adam said flatly. Once again, she struggled
to find any hint of ambiguity in his tone, but there was nothing
beyond cold disappointment.

She was struck with a realization that left her dizzy: He was going
to leave her here, with Jacobs and Dawson. Jacobs with the employer
who did not like "loose ends." How easy would it be for some unfortunate accident to ensure that she didn't make it back to the city?

And what about Adam? Surely they wouldn't want to risk his
going back and telling the tale of how the find of the century was
swiped out from under his nose, all thanks to some lying female.
No doubt they considered him as much of a loose end as her.
Which meant that Dawson had no intention of letting him steam
his way back to safety. They were being separated so that they
could be neatly and tidily removed from the picture.

She had to fight the urge to scream, to grab Adam by the shoulders and shake him into understanding the danger he was in. But that would only reinforce Dawson's claims. Her mind whirled.

"And dinner? You will stay, I hope?" Dawson was saying.

"Fine," Adam agreed. The word flooded her with relief. He was staying. They certainly wouldn't kill him tonight, not when it would be so much simpler once he was isolated on the steamer. She had one night to find some way to prove to him that Dawson and Jacobs weren't what they pretended to be.

She would find a way. She would think of *something*. And in the meantime, she'd let them think they'd gotten the better of her.

She suddenly remembered what she had seen as they had walked up to the tents—the shining cylinders of the hydrogen tanks. An idea began to take shape as Dawson continued to exchange pleasantries with the man he undoubtedly planned to destroy.

"Splendid. I'll arrange accommodations for you. I'm sure that our foreman, Mr. Velegas, would be willing to sacrifice his tent for the night."

"I'll sleep with the men, if it makes no difference to you," Adam said. "I'm used to roughing it."

"Of course. As you please. Mr. Jacobs will see to Miss Mallory. Someplace comfortable but secure. I'm sure you understand, given today's revelations, that it would be unwise to permit her the freedom of the camp. I expect it would take her little time to make her way back into the jungle. That she survived there so long already is, I'm certain, due entirely to your diligence."

"Something like that," Adam grumbled. Ellie didn't let his tone upset her. Her mind was already busy with the plan. She would find a way to show him, beyond doubt, what he needed to see.

"Very well. Six o'clock, then? For dinner? Until then, please let Mr. Jacobs know if there's anything else you require."

"I'll be fine," Adam said. He accepted Dawson's outstretched hand, shook it, and walked out of the tent without a backward glance. Once he had gone, Jacobs approached her, reaching for her arm. She pulled it back.

"I'll walk, thank you." She held her head high. She might be playing along—for now—but that didn't mean she'd hand over what was left of her dignity. Jacobs shrugged, unperturbed, and motioned her through the flap back out into the camp.

He marched her to a small tent near the camp's center, the quarters of the foreman. Ellie vaguely remembered seeing the man when they had arrived, a short, wiry mestizo standing on top of a crate and shouting orders, aptly organizing the chaos around him. Inside the tent was a narrow, simple cot, and another desk, this one covered in papers showing manifests of men and supplies. Jacobs gestured to one of the men and he hurried over, gathering up the pages and carrying them outside. Then Jacobs turned and left, without so much as another threat.

He didn't need to threaten. She understood her situation perfectly.

She hurried over to the flap and peered through the gap without moving the canvas. Jacobs was speaking to the two men who had captured them in the woods. She saw the smaller one—Mendez, she had heard him called—nod, then set himself down on a log across from the entrance to her tent, his rifle resting on his lap. The larger of the two, Flowers, kept his gun slung over his shoulder and leaned against a nearby tree, whistling tunelessly.

Her guards, undoubtedly.

Certain that Jacobs was now out of earshot, she stepped back from the flap and gave the cot a sound kick, letting out a stream of curses. Of course, her fit of pique earned her nothing more than a stubbed toe. She sat down, nursing it. However frustrated she was now, it was temporary. She had a plan. All she needed to do was wait until dark.

13

THE WOMAN HADN'T EVEN told him her damned name.

The thought ran in circles in Adam's mind as he moved through the camp, stealing his focus and leaving some rather less comfortable emotions in its place. She had lied about her name, about the map, about the rivals who were on her tail—and she was certainly not a widow.

Not that he'd ever really bought that last one.

The discovery stirred up a regular maelstrom of emotions—anger, frustration, and no small degree of hurt. The anger and frustration he could deal with. They were good, straightforward feelings. The sense of betrayal was something else, dragging with it all kinds of uncomfortable associations, like why he should care so much that the woman hadn't seen fit to trust him.

He had to put it out of his head, however difficult that was. There were more immediate concerns he had to deal with, like determining exactly what his situation was in this camp.

He turned his attention toward finding a good spot for his hammock. He still had his pack, luckily, though he hadn't failed to notice that his machete and express rifle hadn't been returned. They must be in the hands of the two men who had captured him in the bush, or whoever acted as their supervisor.

He spotted another pair of armed men patrolling the perimeter where the camp bordered the jungle. It wasn't exactly typical for an excavation—nor did it seem to be an isolated case with this particular camp. Most of the men strolling around or resting by the fires were armed in one way or another.

They also didn't look much like the usual expedition crew. When Adam collected a team for an excavation, his own bearers and assistants were just as varied as these in their race, languages, and clothing. They were also admittedly a rough lot. But this wasn't the same sort of rough, he thought, stopping to let by a man whose ripped shirtsleeves revealed biceps that made him look strong enough to crack a coconut barehanded. Or a skull.

He watched as he walked, absorbing as much as he could of the place and its inhabitants. The camp had been set up on a wide riverbank that Adam suspected was probably underwater during the height of the rainy season but for now formed a firm, flat, clear surface for the massive array of tents, mules, crates, and men. Most of the hired bearers would be sleeping rough, as he was, in hammocks with mosquito netting strung between trees on the higher side of the bank. The animals had been penned into a temporary corral closer to the water, and men were still unloading equipment and supplies from the big steamboats anchored nearby.

The sound of the cataracts was a constant static in the background, and the stone bridge shadowed the water only a hundred or so yards away, lending an eerie, almost ritual feeling to the place.

There was no doubting it. The stretch of river was the tributary of the Belize he'd added to the map the previous year, after a group of logging scouts dropped by the survey office and left a report of their explorations. A map the professor had apparently consulted.

Bested by my own damned map. He tried not to let it rankle him, but it was hard. If the woman had just trusted him enough to show him the whole map from the start, they would have been here days ago, long before Dawson and Jacobs arrived.

Then again, she hadn't even trusted him with her name.

He caught sight of the slight figure he'd seen when they came in, calling out clipped, authoritative orders. It must be Velegas, the foreman. The man wasn't anyone he recognized, and Adam had thought he knew every potential expedition leader in the colony.

The whole place raised his hackles, as did the realization of how quickly it must have been thrown together. Had someone been organizing an outfit like this while he was still in the city, he would have heard about it. It wasn't that big a town. But there hadn't been so much as a hint, which meant that Dawson and Jacobs hadn't started organizing until after he and Ellie had left. Using the more direct route up the Belize would have saved them only a day or two. Even taking into account the power of the steamboats cluttering the river, that meant that the pair had pulled this whole expedition together in no more than two days.

That was a startlingly short time frame for mounting an effort of this magnitude. It meant that whoever was running this show had some serious cash to throw around, and enough influence to keep the local authorities from asking too many questions.

Adam couldn't even start to think who would have that kind of power.

As he began tying up his hammock, he wondered just what the hell Miss Eleanora-Constance-Tyrrell-Mallory had gotten him into.

Adam had almost finished setting up camp when he finally saw what he'd been hoping to find since he'd arrived: a familiar face. Charles Goodwin was a lanky native of Belize City and a regular addition to Adam's expedition teams. Though his education was basic—public school offerings in the colony being limited, particularly for the city's poorer black inhabitants—he was a quick-thinking, sensible man, as Adam had more than once had occasion to appreciate. When he strolled into view, he was a very welcome sight.

Charlie stopped just short of Adam's site. He leaned against a thick palm, taking out his papers and tobacco.

"Got yourself into a bit of trouble?" Charlie's tone was low and even. He rolled himself a cigarette.

"Not entirely sure yet."

"You came in with a woman, didn't you?"

Eleanora Mallory's image flashed across his mind.

"Yeah."

He expected a laugh. Charlie wasn't the type to pass over a chance to rag on him.

But the other man merely lit his smoke.

"You joining the crew?"

"More like making a guest appearance."

"Then the woman might not be your biggest problem."

Adam paused only a moment at his task of hanging the mosquito net. He realized that Charlie hadn't looked at him since he'd come over. To anyone else watching, it would seem that he was just having a solitary smoke.

It wasn't like Charlie. Adam felt a warning thrill.

"Care to clue me in?"

Charlie took a drag. The ember of his cigarette glowed at Adam.

"Haven't seen too many familiar faces around here, I'm betting."

"Not as many as I'd expect."

"This boss seems to look for a different sort of qualifications. Most of these guys are in exports. You following me?"

Adam followed. Like most places far from government's watchful eye, the black market flourished in British Honduras. Poached hardwoods, bootleg liquor, and more than a few archaeological artifacts found their way out of the colony's ports, while other illicit goods made their way in. The men who ran the trade were known for their discretion and their ruthlessness. They were the sort of people you hired if you didn't want the colonial offices hearing what you were up to. The sort who didn't balk at a bit of unpleasantness, if it became necessary.

It only confirmed what Adam had already come to suspect— that there was nothing routine, or legitimate, about the expedition he had stumbled into. The knowledge wasn't comforting.

"So how did you end up here?"

"A connection." Charlie shrugged. "And they're paying better than you do. The wife wants a new wardrobe."

"With me, you're on government wages."

"There's others here making more," Charlie added significantly. Adam waited for him to continue. "That man Jacobs has been offering some of them three-times pay."

"For what?"

"Being ready to do whatever he needs them to do. And the ones he's asked . . . Well, he has an eye for the sort who don't draw much of a line at what they won't do."

"Sounds nice."

"Just letting you know what you walked into." The unsmoked cigarette continued to burn in Charlie's hand.

"What about the bosses? What do you know about them?"

"That the professor might make like he's running the show, but it's the other one who holds the reins." Charlie rose. He stamped the cigarette out under his heel, then spoke again without turning to look at Adam.

"You've got me and Lavec. One more in a pinch."

Lavec. Adam pictured the grizzled French Canadian. He was surly and smelled like a hibernating bear, but he was a good man to have at your back.

Charlie, Lavec, and one more. It wasn't much. Charlie seemed to agree.

"Try not to let it get to a pinch," he finished, then strolled away to where the evening campfires of the rest of the men were springing to life.

Adam got the picture. And given what Charlie had told him about the crew of this particular expedition, he had no desire to put things to the test.

Not that he'd necessarily have much choice. He was learning that where his traveling companion was involved, things had a tendency to get complicated whether he liked it or not.

He might as well try to dig up a bit more information about what he was up against. And judging by the golden angle of the sun against the trees, it was nearly six o'clock. Which meant it was time for an appointment that might give him a clue.

Dawson's tent was empty when Adam stepped inside. Its contents had been tidied since he had been there that afternoon, all except the desk, which was covered in papers. A stack of books rested on top of them. Adam moved over for a closer look. He saw a primer on Aztec glyphs, a volume of *American Anthropologist*, Lewis Gunkel's travesty of a study on Mayan deities. What a mess that was.

A glance into the trunk on the floor told him that Dawson had packed a significant library. Adam tried to recall whether he had ever carried a book into the bush with him, besides his field journal.

He dropped the lid and stood just as the tent flap lifted and Dawson himself stepped inside. He pulled off his pith helmet and daubed a line of sweat from his forehead.

"It's damnably hot even this time of the day," he complained. "Sorry you had to wait. I meant to be here when you arrived."

"Don't worry about it," Adam replied. He kept his tone neutral, unsure of exactly what he was in for.

"I see you aren't standing on ceremony. Do you mind terribly if I do the same?" Dawson indicated the khaki field jacket he wore. Adam, who brought a jacket into the bush about as often as he did a book, shook his head.

Dawson shrugged out of the coat gratefully and hung it on the back of the chair. His shirt was stained with sweat.

"I must apologize for the awkwardness of your reception here this afternoon. I'm afraid Miss Mallory took all of us rather off guard. For whatever it might be worth, let me assure you that she is both comfortable and secure, and will remain so."

Adam nodded an ambiguous acknowledgment.

Dawson moved to another of the trunks and pulled out a bottle.

"May I offer you a little refreshment? A donation from our foreman. I'm assured it's quite good."

Adam's thoughts flew back to the liquid gold he had rescued from the *Mary Lee* and the memory of sitting by the fire, the warm heat of it in his throat and the woman at his side.

Eleanora. Eleanora Mallory.

"You go ahead. I'll pass."

"I'm not actually much of a drinker," Dawson replied. He gave an awkward, nervous smile, then returned the bottle to its place. "I realize all of this must seem highly irregular. I can only beg your excuse based on the knowledge that what we seek, if it exists, is entirely extraordinary. However much I might wish that Miss Mallory herself had chosen a safer course, I must admit that I find your arrival here quite fortuitous. There is much I would love to discuss with a fellow scholar, and they have been in rather short supply, as you can imagine." He paused. "What I am saying, Mr. Bates, is that I hope you can put this afternoon's events behind you and let us start tonight with a clean slate. Is that too much to hope for?"

Adam took a moment to reply, occupied in concealing his bewilderment. As far as he was aware, the red-faced, uncomfortable man in front of him held all the cards. So why did he feel like he was being courted?

Maybe there was an ace he didn't know he was holding. If that was the case, he might as well see what the game was.

He gave a nod toward the trunk where Dawson had stashed the bottle.

"Maybe I'll have a glass after all."

Dawson flashed him a smile that looked distinctly relieved and produced a tin mug.

"Will this do?"

Through the walls of the tent, Ellie saw lights beginning to flicker to life around the camp, sparks of yellow against the darkening canvas. They were her signal. Night was falling, and it was time to make her move.

She put her eye to the crack in the canvas again and saw that Mendez and Flowers were still at their posts. It didn't matter. The way she planned on going, they weren't going to see her.

She stepped quietly to the back of the tent, holding the spring she had managed to work loose from the mattress of the cot. The end was sharp, ragged from where she had broken it off of the frame. It easily pierced through the stitching that held the floor of the tent to the back wall. She muttered a prayer against any noise she was making and began working loose the thread, using the spring when she came up against a place that wouldn't give way under her fingers. Before long, she had created a gap roughly three feet wide. It was more than enough. She tossed the spring aside and flattened herself out on the ground. Lifting the canvas, she peered outside.

It was just as she had hoped. Jacobs had assigned guards to watch only the front of the tent. The back opened up onto a stack of crates—tins of ham, from the look of it.

She had never been quite so grateful for tinned ham.

She wriggled through the gap, climbing silently to her feet on the far side. She waited in the shadow of the crates for a moment, getting her bearings. Most of what surrounded her were piles of supplies. The bearers were camped farther up the bank of the river, nearer to the jungle where the trees stood thickly, providing plenty of places to hang their hammocks. She could hear the sounds of their evening filtering down to where she hid—chatting men, crackling campfires, and braying mules. Underlying all of it was the rush of the nearby rapids and the clamor of the nighttime jungle, with its birdcalls and hooting monkeys.

She waited until a pair of men had strolled past before dashing across the open space on the far side of the crates, nearly tripping over the handle of a shovel as she tucked herself into the shadows of a stand of palm trees. She kept to the dark, watching for obstacles as she worked her way toward her goal.

Ellie slipped past a stand of ferns and found herself staring at the stack of hydrogen tanks she had seen earlier that afternoon. She took hold of one of the cylinders and lifted it.

She promptly dropped it on her foot and bit back a curse. It was heavier than she'd anticipated. She was momentarily grateful for the sturdy quality of Mr. Galle's boots.

She eyed the distance to the river, taking in the dark, silent forms of the steamboats. Then she grabbed the handles at the top of the tank and started to drag it, keeping carefully to the shadows of the stacked crates and scattered trees. As awkward as it was to maneuver on land, she knew the tank would be buoyant once she was in the water—easy enough to swim with.

Adam cleared the last bite from his plate. The fare hadn't held a candle to Cruzita's meal the night before, but even canned beef and beans was appreciated on a day's empty stomach. He would have welcomed anything even vaguely approximating food.

One of the bearers came in to clear their plates. He was a rough-looking sort to be playing waiter, but from what Adam had seen of the camp, there wasn't much else on offer.

The man vanished through the tent flap, leaving him alone with Dawson, who offered him the bottle of rum again.

"Another sip?"

Adam saw that his mug was empty. The stuff might be a far cry from the bottle he'd left by the river, but it seemed to be going down easily enough. He would need to be careful—but not look as though he were. He held out his mug for a pour.

"You sure you won't have any?"

"I'm afraid it doesn't agree with me," Dawson said, his tone oddly stiff. He countered it with a quick smile. "So tell me, Mr. Bates, what do you make of the chimera we're pursuing?"

"If it's not a hoax?" Adam shrugged noncommittally. "Hard to say."

"You haven't any theories?"

None he felt like sharing, he thought to himself. "I usually like to see a thing before I start trying to figure it out."

"An entirely rational position," Dawson acknowledged. "I'm afraid I am somewhat less disciplined. I find it hard to resist making guesses, particularly when the subject is as intriguing as this." He leaned back, a gleam in his eye. Adam thought he caught a glimpse of a far less sweltering Dawson holding court over a room-ful of students. "What do you know of La Ciudad Blanca?"

"The White City was another El Dorado—a rich and power-ful kingdom supposedly hidden in the jungle. Cortés wrote to King Charles promising him the place would prove to be richer than Mexico when he found it. Which he never did. Just another gold-fever dream."

"And yet here we are, in the deep bush, chasing a rumor of a city thriving at the time of the conquest. A city described as being built of gleaming white stone."

"I had an opening in my calendar," Adam replied dryly.

Dawson smiled but did not give way.

"The White City, El Dorado, Cibola—as far south as Patagonia, we hear of the City of the Caesars, a rich country inhabited by a people of immense wisdom. All these tales of a singular place, sacred and hidden, full of both riches and power."

"When men are treasure-hungry, they'll see gold anywhere they can," Adam countered.

"Perhaps. And yet there were rich and thriving cities here during the time of the conquest. Aztec cities. Why make it sound so much like myth when there is a plausible reality on offer?"

Adam paused. It was a strange idea, one that had never occurred to him before. The feeling it evoked was unsettling. He shrugged it off.

"They saw ruins. It's natural enough to imagine someplace sim-ilar still intact."

"A viable explanation," Dawson allowed. "What about the City of the Seven Caves? Tulan Zuyua—that's the native name, I believe."

Adam bit back a curse, thinking of the telegram that had slipped out of Eleanora Mallory's pocket with the other half of the map. He should have figured that story, too, would turn out to have been something less than the whole truth.

Just a few notes to look up later, she'd said.

The telegram must have belonged to the man who sat before

him. He tried to remember what it had looked like and recalled a bunch of gibberish with those unexpected words scribbled over the top.

Tulan Zuyua. The Smoking Mirror.

It must have been some kind of coded message sent from London to Belize City. But from who? Who the hell in London would be wiring coded telegrams about a wildly obscure piece of Mayan mythology?

Adam kept his expression cool.

"Your pronunciation is off."

Dawson smiled. "Well, Mr. Bates, my knowledge comes entirely from books. I must make do with my own feeble ear. If I remember my reading, the City of Seven Caves was the place where the first tribes of the Maya gained knowledge of fire, agriculture, and magic. It was the birthplace of their civilization, an ancient city of powerful men advanced far beyond those around them. Now tell me—were you a gold-hungry conquistador, how would you remember hearing such a story, were it told to you? As an account of a city full of precious metals and jewels, perhaps?"

Adam felt a wave of irritation. He was being led, but in spite of himself, something in the tale Dawson was spinning was damnably intriguing.

"You're saying that the tales of El Dorado and Cibola were European interpretations of the Mayan and Aztec origin myths."

"I am suggesting that it is a possibility." He paused.

In the silence, Adam could feel that night had fully descended outside the walls of the tent. The jungle around them was coming alive with chirps and buzzings.

"Let me change the subject for a moment. In your opinion, as one who has had his hands in many of their ruins and settlements, what is the oldest civilization in Central and South America?"

Adam considered the question.

"Well, the Maya predate both the Inca and the Aztecs."

"And predating the Maya?" Dawson prompted.

"There's no concrete evidence that anything did."

"But there are suggestions that would support it, are there not? Indications that there may have been cities here before the Maya. A people with a distinct artistic and architectural style—a very ancient people who may have influenced the development of the Mayan culture."

"That's conjecture," Adam countered flatly.

"But is it ludicrous? Or do you recognize a plausibility? Could the Mayan stories of an origin city not refer to the metropolis of an earlier and more powerful culture?"

"It's a nice theory with very little evidence to back it up."

"Perhaps that is precisely what we are on the trail of, Mr. Bates. The evidence."

Adam thought of the medallion, the strange carvings that were both recognizable and foreign, incorporating elements of Mayan and Aztec styles but seeming something else entirely—something simpler and more essential. It had been the same with the stela—a sense of an artifact both familiar and exotic.

"There is no account of Tulan Zuyua falling," Dawson pressed on. "Nowhere in the myth does it say that it has ceased to be. And then we have native accounts of someplace that bears an uncanny resemblance to it, right up through the start of the seventeenth century." He leaned forward, his expression fiercely earnest in the lamplight. "What if this city we're chasing survived the Mayan collapse because it wasn't Mayan at all, but *something else*? The last relic of a more ancient people."

The room went silent. A moth had managed to slip into the tent. It fluttered dully around the lamp on the table, wings beating hypnotically as it was drawn toward the light.

"Why are you telling me all of this?"

"Because I wish to intrigue you," Dawson replied. "My knowledge of Central American civilizations comes entirely from books and journals, most of which I read only on the voyage here. You have spent years on the ground, discovered and surveyed these ruins, spent time with the remnants of their people. Your knowledge would be an invaluable addition."

"You want me to be a part of this?" The notion was so startling, Adam nearly choked.

"I do not believe our interests are necessarily incompatible. This expedition is of a rather unconventional nature."

"And how's that?"

"My employer is very focused in his interests."

Adam suppressed a sigh. "So he's a collector."

Collectors were the bane of his existence. They were men of passion or madness, feverish for artifacts that fit their particular fetish. For some it was Egyptian relics. Others lusted for Damascene swords, Ming dynasty porcelain, or plump goddess figurines. Adam wasn't sure what drove such men to want to possess pieces of history when others were content to study, observe, or—like himself—discover. But it was collectors who fueled the black market in antiquities, a trade that incentivized the poor of the colony to ravage the graves of their ancestors. Collectors were the ones responsible for the devastation Adam encountered every time he stumbled across a new site, only to find that thieves had already been there before him.

While most collectors cared about the legitimate provenance of the artifacts they acquired, there were plenty of others who were willing to overlook a little dubious legality to get their hands on the objects they craved. Adam had run into the type before, but this was something else.

An entire expedition, better equipped than any he'd ever seen, mounted at an instant's notice. Adam was intimately familiar with the colony's permitting process for such endeavors. It moved slower than a glacier. There were certainly plenty of men who avoided that particular tangle, but they weren't renting three massive steam launches right under the eyes of the government offices. An expedition this size wasn't something that could be put together quietly.

That meant whoever was behind this was capable of pulling

some serious government strings—or of paying obscene bribes to a whole lot of colonial authorities.

And it had all been done just to fulfill the whims of an obsessive.

"What's his flavor, then? Gold? Weaponry?"

"No," Dawson replied shortly. "Not gold. My employer's interest in this matter is focused on a single artifact."

A single artifact.

All of this—all the equipment, the men, the supplies that surrounded him—had been mustered on the chance of acquiring *one artifact*?

Adam was familiar with the mania of collectors. This was something else.

He didn't have to ask what artifact lay behind Dawson's employer's particular madness. The answer had already been spelled out for him, in Eleanora Mallory's penciled handwriting.

The Smoking Mirror.

But he had always thought of the mirror as an allegory. It was the name of a god, a mythic personality, not a real, physical object.

Apparently whoever had employed Gilbert Dawson had a different idea.

"How do you even know this artifact of yours will be there?"

"We don't," Dawson replied shortly.

Adam sat back.

All of this, the whole effort, had been made just on the *chance* that the artifact they sought would turn out to be in the city—if it was even real to begin with.

"What about the rest of it?"

"I suppose that is what we are discussing."

He could hear the significance in Dawson's tone. It took him back to the days he was forced to sit in his father's office, listening to threats levied and deals being struck.

"I'm listening."

"If this city is as important as it might be—if it truly is a surviving relic of a lost civilization that lies behind all of what is known to date about Central American prehistory—it will need to be surveyed and excavated. Promptly, if scientists are to acquire the site before looters move in and clear it out. I am not in a position to conduct that excavation. Besides, I'm an old man, and field-work seems far more exhausting than exciting a proposition. But for someone like you..." He leaned forward across the table. "For a young archaeologist with a promising career ahead of him, the chance to discover and interpret a city out of myth would be an unparalleled opportunity. Would it not?"

Adam's head was spinning. First there had been the revelation that the entire expedition was aimed at retrieving a single, possibly mythological artifact. Now it sounded distinctly like Dawson was trying to bribe him.

What the hell is going on?

"Are you making an offer, Professor?"

"I believe I am, Mr. Bates. A generous one."

It certainly was, Adam thought. If Dawson was right about the city, then it very easily represented the most important archaeological find in the hemisphere. That was a lot to simply hand over to another scholar.

Time for the catch.

"So what do you get out of the deal?"

"Your assistance locating the artifact we are here to acquire. Your familiarity with the layout of Central American ruins far surpasses my own. Having your expertise at our disposal would save us significant time and effort. And as I said, I'm not a young man anymore. If your involvement would speed my return to the comforts of home, I welcome it."

That's it?

Adam couldn't believe it.

He *shouldn't* believe it, he realized. Dawson's story was so outrageous, Adam had stumbled into taking it for the truth—a mistake he'd been making far too often lately.

He was being lied to. The problem was, he had no idea how.

There was only one way for him to find out: He had to keep Dawson talking.

"That's a lot to offer for help finding just one artifact," he said skeptically.

"It's nothing I have any desire to keep. The task of excavating Tulan Zuyua is not for me, Mr. Bates. But it could be yours."

"And if this artifact you're after turns out to be a false lead, what happens to our deal?"

Dawson shrugs. "I see no reason why it would not stand."

"After you've ripped the place apart trying to find it."

Dawson was unperturbed. "The search must be thorough enough to satisfy my employer. That does not mean it cannot be undertaken responsibly. And if at the end of that time we have no evidence that it is there to be found, then my colleague and I return to England and leave the rest in your capable hands." Dawson stood, tidying away the bottle of rum, his tone brisk and businesslike. "I do not expect an answer from you tonight. In fact, I insist that you take at least until the morning to consider it fully. If you should decline, then Mr. Jacobs will arrange passage back to the city for you on one of our boats."

Adam hesitated, then asked the question that was burning too intensely in his mind to be ignored.

"This is a hell of a lot of trouble to go to for one artifact. Why does your employer want it so badly?"

"It isn't my place to inquire, Mr. Bates. I simply follow orders. But that is my offer. Help us find the artifact—if it is there to be found—and the rest of Tulan Zuyua is yours. Will you consider it?"

"I'll think about it," he replied at last.

Dawson smiled, looking relieved.

"That's all I ask," he said, and the table shook as beyond the canvas walls of the tent, the night exploded into day.

14

HIDDEN IN THE REEDS and soaking wet, Ellie watched the men of the camp flood toward the river, hastily organizing crews to paddle out to the steamboat that sat listing in the water, flames shooting out of the holes in its crumbling deck. She was less concerned with the efficacy of the bucket lines and far more interested in the position of two very specific figures. She found Jacobs standing at the water's edge, staring calmly at the destruction as if having already seen that efforts to save the burning steamer would be futile. She kept scanning the chaos until she found his companion. Dawson was hurrying toward the banks, followed closely by a larger figure. It was Adam, of course. She must have interrupted their dinner. The sight of his concerned expression in the flickering light of her fires struck a guilty chord in her stomach—but she was doing this for his sake, after all. And now that she knew where Dawson and Jacobs were, it was time to get down to the real business of the evening.

She hurried along the banks of the river, sticking close to the reeds and the camouflage they afforded. Then she cut away from the water, moving among the crates and piled equipment to Dawson's tent. She paused at the entrance, struck by a momentary fear that she had miscalculated. What if there was someone still inside? One of the men left to watch over Dawson's belongings?

A pair of guards trotted out of the jungle beyond the tent, rifles in their hands. Their eyes were on the blaze on the river, but Ellie knew it would take only a glance in her direction to expose her. There was no time to play it safe.

She lifted the flap and slipped inside.

The tent was empty. A table had been set, chairs pushed back as though the men who had sat in them had left abruptly.

Probably because of a nearby explosion.

Dawson hadn't even bothered to put on his coat. Ellie could see it draped over one of the chairs. While that wouldn't have surprised her coming from Adam, she somehow doubted the professor often indulged in such informality.

She spotted the half-empty mug on the table and picked it up, giving it a quick sniff.

Rum. While she was shut away like a prisoner, Adam had been toasting her nemesis.

She felt her indignation flare. How dared he consort with the enemy like that? But the anger was extinguished by a quick flood of guilt and fear. He could do it because she had broken his trust. He didn't owe her anything anymore, so why shouldn't he get friendly with a fellow archaeologist and scholar?

If Adam was falling for Dawson's charm, she had no one to blame for it but herself.

She moved to the field desk. It seemed the most likely spot for her to find what she was looking for, though she couldn't have said what precisely that might be. That was fine. She trusted she would know it when she saw it.

The surface of the desk was a jumble of notes, books, and papers. It seemed that Dawson could give Mr. Henbury a run for his money when it came to organization, which was even more impressive when she considered that he had managed to make the mess in only a few hours. All of this had been packed when she had been here earlier that afternoon.

She riffled through the pages quickly, painfully aware of how exposed she would be should anyone come inside. Her distraction held their attention for now, but it would not last forever.

The top of the desk seemed hopeless. All she could see were scribbled notes about city layouts mingled with far drier equipment manifests and inventories. And how likely was it, really, that he would leave anything incriminating out in the open like that?

Now, the locked drawer at the center of the desk—that seemed like a far more probable spot to keep secrets. Unfortunately, Ellie's skills as a lock pick were limited to the simple latches she'd loosened back at the Imperial. She considered breaking into it—the letter opener on the desk looked like it could do the job—but quickly dismissed the idea. If it was clear someone had been inside, who was the first potential culprit they'd suspect?

No, she needed to leave no trace. There could be no battered locks. But if she could find the key . . .

Her eyes roamed the space, falling on Dawson's jacket.

Perhaps it was that simple. And sure enough, thrusting her hand into the pocket, she felt her fingers brush against a cool brass key.

It fit the drawer perfectly. Inside, she found a smaller jumble of papers. Most were travel documents. She was disappointed to see that all of them bore the name of Gilbert Dawson. She supposed it was too much to hope that her enemy had also been using an assumed name.

As she moved them aside, her fingers brushed cold steel.

Ellie stared down at the revolver. It was larger than the one she'd taken from Galle's room back at the Imperial, heavy and lethal-looking. She picked it up, opening the chamber, and was unsurprised to find it loaded.

A loaded gun, here in her hands. It was a sore temptation, but Ellie had seen the number of armed men roaming around the camp that surrounded her. One revolver wouldn't do much to get her past an army. And there was no point holding on to it for a future opportunity. Dawson would surely notice it was missing and would know where to look for it.

Reluctantly, she set the weapon back into the drawer and turned her attention to the most promising item it contained: an unmarked yellow envelope.

It looked like just the place to hide one's most dangerous secrets.

Ellie lifted the flap, the glue having dried to uselessness long ago. But inside she found only a pair of yellowed newspaper clippings.

Newspaper articles? Why would Dawson go to such lengths to conceal something that was part of the public record?

Then she started reading.

Foul Murder, ran the headline. And foul it was, Ellie discovered as she read on. The clipping described in lurid detail how the wife of a prestigious university professor had been killed where she slept, strangled so violently that her throat had actually been crushed beneath the hands of her assailant.

A local constable claimed to have heard her screaming, and gone through the open door of the house to investigate. The woman was already dead. Her husband had been the only one in the room. He was found crouched on the floor next to the bed, raving and incoherent.

His name?

Gilbert Dawson.

The article went on to describe Dawson's defense, which even the tabloid writer seemed to think a feeble one—that he had seen an assailant flee through the window when he came into the room, and found his wife already dead. But the bruises on her battered throat matched the size of Dawson's hands, as had been revealed at the indictment, and it seemed there were clear expectations for what the verdict at the trial the following month would be.

A murderer. The details of the crime made her shudder, but at least this would have to convince Adam that the man was untrustworthy. The article was exactly the evidence she needed. Ellie felt a flash of triumph.

Then she turned to the next piece.

Foreigner Executed for University Slaying.

Dated two months after the first article, this one described how a Russian immigrant had been hanged for the brutal murder of Anne Dawson, wife of the now retired professor of ancient history at Saint Andrews. It detailed how Dawson, originally accused of the crime, had been exonerated after new evidence was brought forward during his trial, witnesses claiming to have seen the foreigner climbing out of the couple's second-story window.

The man did not speak any English. A government interpreter from London had come to the city for the trial, which had been concluded in just four hours. The Russian had offered no alibi or defense.

A government interpreter...

The suspicion was small, just a tiny voice in the back of her mind. It wove together the disparate facts of the articles to draw an impossible conclusion.

An interpreter could say anything he liked, if the man he translated for didn't know English. Witnesses could be bought or manufactured. If someone had wanted Dawson to go free, placing the blame for his crime on a friendless foreigner incapable of speaking for himself was a tidy way to do it.

She thought of the telegram in her pocket, with its obsolete Foreign Office code.

The Foreign Office employed a contingent of interpreters.

Ridiculous.

The British government didn't need to manufacture evidence and false convictions to buy a man's freedom. If the government had wanted Dawson's liberation, they could simply order it. There would have been no need to make another man stand in his place.

But there was something about the story that didn't feel right—that felt deeply, entirely *wrong*. Not that it mattered. It wasn't anything she could explain to Adam and expect him to understand, or believe. She hardly understood her suspicions herself.

To anyone inclined to think well of Dawson, the articles would seem like nothing more than relics of a difficult time in his life.

She hardly needed Adam to feel sorry for him.

Frustrated, she set the clippings aside. There was nothing else in the drawer, and a quick search revealed no secret compartments where something more important might be hidden.

She could hear voices beyond the tent walls, the sounds of

men returning to the camp. The surprise of the explosion must be wearing off now that the fires were under control. Dawson would return any minute. She had run out of time.

She cursed quietly as she thrust the papers back into the drawer and locked it, placing the key back in Dawson's jacket pocket. Her efforts had been for nothing, and she couldn't imagine thinking up a more effective distraction for a longer search. The ball of hydrogen-fueled fire that had shattered the hull of the steamboat would be impossible to top. Her ears were still ringing from the blast, and she had nearly made it back to the shore by the time it happened.

She slipped out of the tent, then looked down the bank to where the tent that served as her prison stood, brushed with flickering light from the flames that consumed the steamboat. Then her eyes moved in the opposite direction, to the promising darkness of the jungle.

It would be so easy to slip away into the night. But then what? Adam was the one who knew which plants were edible and which would make her break out in hives. He was the experienced surveyor who could navigate even when the thick canopy obscured the stars and the sun. And he had the only compass.

She couldn't survive in the jungle without him. If she was going to escape, she would have to bring Adam with her, and that meant she would have to find another way to convince him of the danger they were in. Reluctantly, she turned to the foreman's tent.

Voices called from nearby—too nearby. Ellie ducked quickly around a pile of crates and bumped up against a warm, immovable object.

Adam's hands caught her shoulders.

"Are you insane?" he demanded in a whisper, his features half-lit by the orange glow of the flames from the water.

"There was no one on board—I checked," she protested.

"That wasn't what I meant."

At the sound of a shout from behind, he grabbed her arm and hauled her roughly forward. With a sinking feeling, she saw that they were headed for Dawson and Jacobs.

"Found her," he said, without letting go of her arm. Dawson looked dismayed, while Jacobs frowned thoughtfully. Ellie closed her eyes, preparing for the worst.

"She was making for the jungle," Adam lied smoothly, and Ellie felt a rush of relief, which she struggled not to reveal on her features.

"She'll have to be restrained," Dawson said.

"Apparently," Jacobs agreed coolly. He motioned to a man armed with a rifle who stood waiting behind him. "Take her to the foreman's tent and see that she's confined."

The guard leveled the gun at her, and Adam released her arm. She risked a look behind her as she went, searching Adam's face for some sign of his intentions, but saw nothing. It was like looking at a stranger.

Back in Velegas's tent, the guard pushed her to her knees by the central post.

"Hands forward," the man ordered. She obeyed. The guard pulled them to either side of the tent pole, then lashed her wrists together, effectively anchoring her to the post.

Then he left, and Jacobs stepped inside.

Every instinct urged her to flee. She forced herself not to flinch as he stepped over to where she knelt and crouched down before her.

He gave the ropes around her wrists a leisurely inspection, testing them with a few sharp tugs. Then, still kneeling, uncomfortably close, he raised his dark eyes to hers.

"One of the hydrogen tanks?"

The question took her aback. She blinked, surprised, then nodded.

"Clever," he said. He stood, looming over her. "Very clever."

He smiled. It was not an expression she had any desire to see again. Then he turned and exited, leaving Ellie wondering whether she'd just been complimented or threatened.

She sat down—not an easy task with her arms lashed around a tent pole. Sleeping would be even more of a challenge.

She'd gotten herself into an entirely uncomfortable position, and for what? Her search through Dawson's tent had turned up nothing she could use to convince Adam of the danger he was in. If anything, it had just made her look even more unstable.

But he'd protected her, she reminded herself. Based on where he'd found her, he must have seen her exiting the tent. He could easily have exposed her to Dawson and Jacobs, but he had covered for her instead.

Did that mean there was hope? She couldn't say. She certainly didn't feel hopeful. What she felt was a sense of panic. If all went as her enemies had planned, Adam would be on one of the remaining steamboats first thing tomorrow morning, headed back to Belize City. Ellie was certain he would never arrive. Tonight was her only chance to warn him of the threat, and she was tied to a tent post.

Futility washed over her. She had failed. If she'd just told him the truth from the start . . .

Well, maybe that wouldn't have been entirely realistic, she admitted. But she could at least have corrected the situation while they were traveling upriver on the *Mary Lee*. Instead, she'd let him go on believing a whole pack of falsehoods, misinformation that, unless something changed drastically in the next few hours, might get them killed.

No. She wasn't giving up. There was too much at stake. There had to be some way for her to show Adam the truth of their situation. If she could just reach him . . .

She eyed the tent pole. The base was dug several inches into the ground. The top, on the other hand, was pressed lightly into a connector that attached it to the other poles. If she could reach it, she might be able to push up the connector and slip her ropes through the gap.

She scanned the tent for something she could use, her eyes coming to rest on the chair that sat beside the folding field desk. She reached out with her foot, managing to hook the toe of her boot around its leg. She dragged it toward her and, with a few other extremely awkward contortions, got the chair up against the pole. She stepped onto the seat, then clung to the tent post as the chair wobbled beneath her. Of course, the ground would have to be uneven.

Fighting for balance, she reached up and found the connector. Standing on her toes as the chair bucked beneath her, she gritted her teeth and pressed as hard as she could against the steel.

She heard a rustling behind her. A dark form crawled through the gap she had cut in the back of the tent. Startled, she lost her balance, tumbling off the chair and sliding back down the length of the pole, landing in an uncomfortable pile on the ground.

"You all right?"

Adam frowned down at her. She gaped up at him, too shocked to remember the awkwardness of her position. It flooded back to her awareness quickly enough, and she scrambled to her feet, trying to gather a few shreds of dignity.

"I'm fine," she replied, her chin up.

His gaze moved from her to the toppled chair, then up to the top of the tent post. He shook his head, looking tired.

"How did you know how to get in here?"

"How else would you have gotten out?" he countered. "And while we're on the subject—*what the hell were you thinking?*"

"It doesn't matter," she replied numbly. One look at his face told her clearly the futility of even mentioning the newspaper clippings. All her efforts had won her was a rope around her wrists and an uncomfortable new position on the floor of the tent.

"Do you even realize what you could have done?"

"The boat was at a safe distance from the tree line. There was no way the fire could spread. And there was no one on board."

"You could have killed yourself," he said, barely containing a shout.

"I could not," she retorted. "Hydrogen won't ignite until it reaches the right concentration—and as I'm sure you're aware, it rises. I put a lamp on the floor of the cargo hold and left the hatch open until I was ready to leave the boat. It wouldn't have started building until the room was sealed up. Basic scientific principles. I calculated that I had a perfectly safe window of approximately four minutes before anything burst into flame."

"Unless someone shot you," he snapped back. He shook his head, beginning to pace. "I don't believe this."

"I needed a distraction."

"That was a *distraction*?"

"I needed to search Dawson's tent for evidence. Something that would make you believe me. Please, Bates...you aren't safe here. These men are dangerous. You can't trust anything they're telling you, and if you get on that boat tomorrow—"

"I'm aware."

His response stalled the next words in her mouth, which was just as well, since all she could have done was pleaded with him to trust her. He did not have much reason to do that.

"You are?"

"I'm not a fool, princess." He looked over at her, then away again. "Most of the time."

It stung.

"Adam—"

"*Constance*. I knew it never sounded right." He sat down heavily on the cot. She could see the exhaustion etched into the lines of his face. "Why?"

No more lies. It was the least of what she owed him.

"I was afraid if I told you about Dawson and Jacobs, you might decide the whole business was more trouble than it was worth. And anyway, I had the map. I thought there was no way they could pursue us without it. It didn't seem relevant anymore."

"It would have been nice to be able to make up my own mind about that. But that wasn't what I was talking about. Your name," he clarified, meeting her eyes. There was something unexpected in his gaze, a sort of bleakness.

"It didn't seem important," she protested weakly.

"Your *name* didn't seem important?"

"I was waiting for the right time."

The response sounded lame even to her ears, and Adam turned

away from her. It felt like a closing door—and why wouldn't it? Her excuses were empty. She had lied to him, plain and simple. She couldn't expect him to simply pretend that had never happened. She had no right to ask for his trust anymore.

Which meant that distance she could feel stretching between them, thick and uncomfortable, wasn't going to go away. The realization filled her with an unexpected grief.

"Anything else?"

"What do you mean?"

He turned to her, his expression stony. "Anything else you should have told me before now."

"No," she said firmly, then winced. "Well, maybe one thing. But it's hardly important."

"I'd prefer to judge that for myself."

She ignored the quick hurt of that and pushed forward.

"Your friends from the university—Trevelyan Perry and Neil Fairfax—I sort of . . . know them."

His surprise was genuine.

"You what?"

"We're related. Neil and I."

As the words left her mouth, she realized with horror what they might imply—that her meeting with Adam had been something other than accidental. She hurried to explain. "I swear I had no idea who you were until that night on the boat. The whole thing has just been a wild coincidence."

"How?" he demanded.

"How is it a coincidence?"

"No. How are you related to Fairfax?"

"We're cousins."

He went still. She saw a strange look come over him.

"Eleanora. Ellie." He blinked. "You're his baby cousin Ellie."

"I'm hardly his 'baby' anything," she countered instinctively. "He's only five years older than—"

"You're practically his sister!" he shouted.

"I'm not his—"

"You were raised together!"

"There's no need to get so upset . . . ," she started lamely. But she broke off as she saw a look of profound horror slip across his features.

He dropped down onto the cot again, staring at her.

"I've ruined you."

She felt a flush of heat rush to her cheeks. "You most certainly have *not!*"

"I've been alone with you in the bush for a week. You think anyone is going to believe I kept my hands off of you?" He ran his hands through his hair and gave a half-wild laugh. "I've ruined Fairfax's little Ellie."

She wanted to contradict him, but the words stuck in her throat. He was right. If word of their adventure got back to London, the obvious conclusions would be drawn, no matter how unjustly. Maybe that wouldn't have mattered as much if she had, in fact, been a racy widow, but as an unmarried woman, it was a different story.

Ellie had never wished so badly for a husband, even a conveniently deceased one.

But why should it matter? It was her choice, and she was the one who would bear the consequences. Anyway, how bad could they really be? She was hardly the belle of the social circuit as it was.

Adam would be fine. The world looked differently upon a man who engaged in scandalous episodes. Besides, he spent his days in the bush in a colony populated by criminals and outcasts.

"I assure you I'll be fine. And don't call me 'little,'" she added sharply.

"You will not be fine."

"I will. It's of no consequence what the rest of the world thinks of me. I'm already beyond the pale to most of them. What matters if a few more join the club?"

His gaze darkened.

"This isn't just about you. What about your aunt—Florence, isn't it? Neil used to talk about her all the time. Sounds like a nice lady—not the type who could shrug off being cut out, but you know her better than me. What do you think? Will she be 'fine' when all those nice society friends of hers stop calling? When she hears whispers behind her back every time she goes out?"

Ellie felt her chest tighten.

"It wouldn't be like that."

She knew it was a feeble denial. Adam was right: Those old witches her aunt had tea with would turn on her like a pack of dogs were her ward to be labeled a woman of loose morals. Raising a spinster was one thing, but a *whore*....

Even the kinder ones, those in her circle who weren't simply harpies, would have to close her out to preserve the chances of their own daughters. As though disrespectability were a contagion.

"Oh, yes, it would. And there's the little matter of your cousin to consider, who happens to be one of my oldest friends. How happy do you think he's going to be when he finds out I debauched his adopted sister?"

Ellie felt her cheeks flush.

"You have not debauched me."

"I might as well have."

The intensity of his gaze nearly made her knees give out.

Then a possible escape occurred to her. She clutched at it desperately, without thinking.

"We don't have to tell them. They're all thousands of miles from here. No one has to know anything."

His gaze turned icy.

"I don't lie to my friends."

The words cut. Ellie slumped down to the floor of the tent, feeling defeat wash over her. Of course he wouldn't. He was a decent person.

Not like her.

"So what do we do?" she asked at last, tiredly.

He gave his reply bluntly, and without hesitation:

"We get married."

Shock silenced her. He couldn't possibly be serious. But a single glance at his face told her otherwise. His expression was all cold determination, without a spark of warmth, never mind humor.

Married?

It was ludicrous. And yet it would technically solve their troubles. There could be no scandal, or only very little of one, if the business ended with a ring on her finger. Aunt Florence's friends would simply enjoy it as a juicy bit of gossip, and Neil...well, he would learn to live with it. He might even be happy for her. He'd always told her she wasn't made for a life of solitude.

No. It was ridiculous. Ellie had ruled out getting married years before, but even if she hadn't, she never would have agreed to something like this, something so patently...heartless, she thought numbly.

"Absolutely not."

Something shifted briefly across his expression, a quick flash of what seemed almost like hurt. It was gone before she could be certain, replaced by an even stonier facade.

"It's the only way to fix the mess you've gotten us into."

"By chaining ourselves together for the rest of our lives?"

"We'd hardly need to see each other. I'd come to London just often enough to keep people from talking. The rest of the time we can pretend it never happened."

"You make it sound like a business arrangement."

"That's what marriages are, princess."

"Not all of them," she countered awkwardly.

"I thought you didn't want to be married at all."

"I don't!" she snapped back.

"Then this should be perfect for you. There's far less attention paid to what a married woman does with her days. Take classes. Lobby for the vote. Hell, get yourself arrested again if you want. You get all of the freedom with none of the chains. It's not like there'd be any children."

"No. Of course not," she agreed numbly.

"So it's settled." He moved toward the rip in the wall of the tent, and Ellie felt panic well up inside her.

"Nothing is settled!"

He stopped. Turning quickly, he strode over to where she sat on the floor of the tent and hauled her to her feet. For the first time she could see the anger in him, burning through that facade of cool indifference.

"Yes, it is. You want to ruin your own life? That's fine. But I'll be damned if I'll let you drag anybody else down with you."

"Aren't I dragging you?"

He let her go, stepping back.

"It's what I get for being too goddamned trusting."

Despair washed over her. She fought it. Crumbling into tears would only make the situation even more unbearable. She wouldn't let him see that vulnerability, not if it killed her.

"None of this matters anyway. Those men intend to kill us."

"I'll handle that. You just refrain from getting into any other trouble, and be ready to move when I give the word."

He turned and moved toward the exit. She called out, a quick and desperate instinct:

"Adam—"

He stopped, turning back toward her, but the impulse that had prompted the cry had died incomplete.

"Be careful," she finished instead.

He nodded tightly in response and left.

Ellie tried to feel reassured. Whatever else he thought of her, at least he knew better than to trust Dawson and Jacobs. He would be on the watch for any potential threats and, what was more, seemed determined to ensure her safety as well, even if only for the sake of his friendship with Neil.

She could hardly have expected anything more, after how she'd treated him.

So why did she feel like crying?

15

WHERE WAS SHE? *Someone was screaming....*

The sound resolved itself into the shouting of the men outside her tent, the nightmare fading like a morning fog. She tried to grasp at the last wisps of it. She had been someplace dark and echoing...somewhere underground?

The notion made no sense, but there was no use worrying about it. The dream had already faded into nothing more than the vaguest sense of unease.

Outside her tent, someone started hammering loudly. She tried to sit up and froze at the pain shooting down her neck. Falling asleep with her hands tied around a tent post hadn't been easy. The position she'd finally contorted herself into to escape consciousness for a while was exacting a price in sore muscles and stiff joints. She moved more carefully, wincing her way upright.

Perhaps blowing up that steamboat hadn't been such a brilliant idea. It certainly hadn't been necessary. She had not found anything useful in Dawson's tent. Just those frustratingly inconclusive articles about the murder of his wife.

And as it turned out, no sort of evidence was needed anyway. Adam had not been taken in by Dawson's lies.

Not like he had been by hers...

The conversation of the night before came back to her in all its brutal detail, and Ellie wished she could crawl back to the floor again.

She couldn't blame Adam for the way he'd reacted. Really, she was lucky he felt any obligation at all to take care of her, after how she'd treated him. He would have had every right to walk away without another word to her, and instead...

Instead he'd proposed.

Then again, "proposed" implied a question. Adam's talk of marriage had been less an inquiry and more like an order.

An order she intended to disobey, she determined firmly. Whatever Adam said he felt about marriage, she wasn't going to let him shackle himself into an arrangement with someone he didn't want to be around. He deserved a chance at real happiness, whether or not he decided to take it.

She would find some other way to protect her family from her mistake. She could join a convent, or go to Australia, or...

She'd think of something, anyway.

Adam's face came back to her—the distance she had seen in his eyes as he coldly outlined the terms of their engagement. Remembering it made something twist painfully inside her.

What else could she expect? If anything she should be relieved, but the feeling arcing through her chest was a lot more like bereavement.

It didn't matter. The important thing was that Adam had known better than to trust Dawson and Jacobs.

The flap rustled as a large man entered the tent. She recognized him from the day before, one of the pair who had caught her and Adam in the jungle.

He moved easily, slowly, ambling over to her and nimbly picking the knot that bound her hands. As it released, she sighed with relief, stretching her aching muscles. Then she looked at the big man's face and saw the apology written there.

"You have to tie them again, don't you?"

He nodded. Ellie took his lack of movement as a sign that she could at least squeeze in a stretch first, and she did so as best she could before offering him her wrists.

He tied the ropes firmly but not too tight. At least she wouldn't have to worry about her hands falling off.

How long was this going to last? Would she be tethered to the post again that night? Her sore neck protested the notion, but she'd bombed their boat. They could hardly let her roam free after that.

She remembered the last time she'd spent the day in restraints, chained to the gates of Parliament because she'd let herself go mouth first, brain later. That had been less than a month ago. It seemed like years.

She pulled her attention back to the present.

"Not too tight?"

"No, they're fine," she replied, surprised he would ask. "You're Flowers, aren't you?"

"Yup." He motioned her out the door. She stepped through and waited. He followed a moment later with the cot. A pair of men then began to empty the rest of the tent's furnishings as Flowers folded the narrow metal bed into a tidy package.

"That's your real name? Flowers?"

"Yup."

It didn't seem right. He didn't look like a Flowers. He looked like he should have a massive name to match his massive size— perhaps Thor or Crusher.

"What about your first name?"

"Wilfred."

Flowers it was, then.

"Here's Mendez with your ride," he commented as, behind them, the tent fluttered sadly to the ground. Her ride turned out to be a mule. Ellie eyed it dubiously.

"I'm really fine with walking."

"Well, maybe you are. And maybe this is what the boss says you're going to do. So let's go," Mendez said.

The camp that had sprawled across the banks of the river the night before was gone. In its place was a tumult of men and beasts that rapidly shifted into a sinuous line. Velegas rode up and down the length of the assembling caravan, shouting orders from the back of his quickly trotting mule. It looked bouncy. It also looked like there was very little else left to pack, and therefore no excuse for procrastinating.

Flowers obviously sensed as much. He lifted her easily by the waist and dropped her onto the saddle. She was relieved that at least the mule didn't start jolting her around like poor Velegas.

"Does it have a name?" she asked, frowning down at the animal's ears.

"Probably," Mendez replied.

"I'll call him Thor," she decided. Flowers raised an eyebrow.

"Fine. Let's go, or we'll be left here for jaguar bait." Mendez smacked Thor on the hindquarters, and with an awkward lurch they joined the rest of the expedition.

Adam Bates was moving far more slowly than he was accustomed to. At least it was better than his situation an hour ago, when he hadn't been moving at all. It had taken what felt like an age to get the massive caravan of mules and men organized and mobile, leaving the riverbank for the jungle. Adam could have covered four times the distance they'd gone so far that day on his own. But traveling on his own was no longer an option.

Well, that wasn't entirely true. He could have slipped away if he had liked. He was guarded, of course. Not openly, but his watchful eye had identified a pair of armed men supposedly patrolling the long baggage train whose gazes were on him more often than not. All it would take was a moment of inattention on their part—of which there were plenty—for him to make his escape. Bates had spent enough time in the bush to know how to disappear when he wanted to.

But that would leave Eleanora.

Ellie, he corrected himself. Fairfax's nickname for his cousin fit her better than the ponderous *Eleanora*. Though he was hardly one to say. He obviously knew the woman far from well. Her lies were evidence of that.

The memory brought with it a sense of hurt—quick, sharp, and inexplicable. The anger he could understand. It was safe, sensible.

That wounded feeling was something else. You didn't get wounded by a stranger. You got wounded by the people you cared about.

The implication of that was clear enough, if inconvenient. The woman had gotten under his skin.

It begged the obvious question: What exactly did he think of her?

Instinctively he shied away from it. But this affair he was embroiled in wasn't going to get any easier, and Ellie Mallory sat right at the heart of it. If he was going to get through this in one piece, he might as well be honest with himself about just what cards were on the table.

Given the ponderous pace of the caravan, it wasn't as though there were much else for him to distract himself with.

Time to take a good, hard look at it, then. The first part of the picture came easily enough once he did.

He liked her. He had enjoyed this last week traveling with her, despite how frustrating she could be. And he respected her. There weren't many women—or men, for that matter—courageous enough to make the journey she had, both to British Honduras in the first place and as far as she had into the bush. She had seen the chance for a real adventure and had seized it.

She was also resourceful. She held herself together under pressure. Then there was her sense of wonder. It was palpable in the way she approached everything new to her, from manatees to the crystalline skeleton of a long-dead sacrifice.

When he forced himself to stop and think fairly about it, he couldn't even blame her for the lies. Using an assumed name was a reasonable enough precaution for a woman traveling alone. And once she'd given him that name—which had occurred at a crowded dinner table, hardly the place to blow her cover story— what reason would she have to correct it?

Then there was her failure to mention Dawson and Jacobs, and that business about claiming to be a widow. . . .

The woman was tying his brain into knots, and that was without considering that before long, he'd be married to her.

You make it sound like a business arrangement, she had said. And that was what it should be, wasn't it? A solution to their situation that would save both her and her family from a good deal of suffering and, as he'd structured it, with minimum inconvenience to either of them. What would they lose by entering into it, since they each had no intention of looking for a settled life with anyone to begin with?

He would most likely see her once a year. They would go through the motions of a few social calls, enough to keep tongues from wagging too sharply, and then he'd be off again.

The arrangement wasn't even that unusual. Plenty of marriages worked that way, even if they weren't made under duress. Though his parents lived in the same house, they kept separate rooms. They saw each other at dinner a few nights a week and discussed the running of the household, or which social invitations to return. They weren't atypical in that. Neither would he and Ellie be.

So why did it feel so wrong?

Was he resentful of even that much impingement on his freedom? Did he mind the occasional trip to England that terribly?

No. It was something else, something that seemed embodied in the image of the pair of them sitting at opposite ends of a long, formal table, dispassionately discussing finances or what parties to show their faces at.

He would rather be fighting. Even a good shouting match sounded better to him than that dreary tableau. At least then there'd be some damned passion to it.

Passion. That was the rub of it, wasn't it? Fire. Life. Everything he'd experienced with Ellie Mallory in the brief time he'd known her had been infused with it. The notion of losing that, of seeing it transformed into the sort of bland cooperation his parents embodied, felt criminal. He wanted to wrangle with her. He enjoyed it. And when they did cooperate, it should be like it had been here: her sharp, unpredictable mind challenging him, pushing against his comfortable limits. He didn't want to browse the paper while she sipped tea. He wanted to be drinking rum with her on the parlor floor, or, better yet, out here in the wild, where smudges of dirt would play with those freckles on her nose, her hair matted, her eyes brilliant with excitement.

Dear God.

Adam stopped in his tracks so abruptly, the man behind him ran into his back and bounced off with a curse. He barely heard it. He was too consumed by the revelation that had just shattered its way into his mind.

He was falling for her. The sworn loner with a pathological fear of settling down—he, Adam Bates—was falling for that maddening woman. Head over ever-loving heels.

Well, he thought numbly as the impact of it swelled over him. At least now he knew her name.

By the time Adam's end of the expedition reached the campsite, tents were already set and fires built. The animals were being herded behind a makeshift fence of stakes and rope while pots simmered away with what the men would be eating for supper: rice and beans, from the smell. The place was a buzz of activity, so much so that it took Adam a while to find what he was looking for.

Ellie was sitting on the far side of the clearing, hands still tied, watching as her two guards worked on the little blaze in front of them. He began to walk toward her, then stopped.

What if she didn't want to see him?

He tried to dismiss the idea, but it refused to let go. After all, her reaction to his talk of marriage was still vivid in his mind. Even the idea of being forced to see him once or twice a year had been intolerable to her.

Well, this wasn't London. She was his responsibility for as long as it took him to get her safely out of here, and if that meant closer quarters than she liked, she'd just have to deal with it. Once he got her back to England in one piece, he'd get out of her hair.

Her hair. He wondered what it would feel like to run his hands through it, those short, silken curls twisted between his fingers. . . .

He shook off the thought, cursing inwardly.

He peered at her from across the camp. She seemed safe for now, and as comfortable as she could get with her hands still bound. Had they been like that all day? The thought brought a rush of protective outrage with it, though logically he couldn't fault her captors. She had blown up a part of their expedition.

For me, he remembered. *To try to keep me from being taken in by Dawson and letting my guard down.* The thought filled him with an odd warmth.

Oh, for Pete's sake…

Dawson's voice interrupted his reverie, calling his name. He glanced back to see the professor waving at him from the other side of the camp.

He gave Ellie another look. She had joined her guards in a game of cards. Somehow he had the distinct impression that she'd end up fleecing them. In the meantime, staying in Dawson's good graces was probably a smart move. He put his back to Ellie and answered the summons.

"Over there, by my tent—and careful!" Dawson called to one of the bearers as Adam approached. "Mr. Bates! I trust today wasn't too strenuous for you?"

Only because crawling at a snail's pace is frustrating as all hell.

"Fine, thank you."

"If at any point you would prefer to ride, let me know and I'll see that one of the animals is freed up for you."

"That's very kind," Adam said. Of course, the last thing he planned on doing was riding. The only thing worse than trudging through the bush at a crawl was jolting as slowly on muleback.

"Timber!" The cry was followed by a rush of leaves and crackling branches as one of the pines that towered over the camp fell to the ground.

What were they felling trees for? He turned to ask, but Dawson had other things on his mind.

"How is Miss Mallory doing?"

Something in Dawson's tone sounded a warning note through his head. He shrugged casually.

"Not sure. She's on the other side of the camp, if you want to ask her."

"Ah. You haven't spoken with her today?"

"No," Adam answered shortly.

"But you did speak to her last night?"

There we are.

He hadn't assumed that would go unnoticed, however quiet he tried to make his entrance. Not that he'd had much choice. He had needed to connect with her, to make sure she didn't try anything even crazier. But Dawson had gone to some length the day before to discredit her in Adam's eyes. He wanted his cooperation and his trust to find the Smoking Mirror his obsessive employer wanted so badly. Otherwise, both he and Ellie would quickly become expendable. For now, it was best to let the man think he had both.

"She's very resourceful. And stubborn," he added. He didn't have to act to bring a measure of annoyance into his tone. "I wanted to make sure she didn't try anything that foolish again."

"You needn't have concerned yourself about that, Mr. Bates. As you can see, we have ensured that she cannot cause any more trouble to herself or this expedition."

Dawson looked at him carefully, and Adam knew that his reaction was being measured. "I hope that last night's events went some way further, at least, toward convincing you of the truth of what I said when you arrived at our camp."

Adam had learned to hide his emotions young, in the school of his father's boardroom. It had served him well since at the poker table. He hoped to hell it would hold up here.

"The fact that she hadn't told me her damned name pretty well covered that. I didn't need the fireworks." He sighed. "Look, I don't much like being lied to. Or the people who do it. If I don't have to play nice to keep her from burning the camp down, that's all the better for me."

Dawson looked relieved. *Good.*

It was time for a change of subject.

"So, what's with the landscaping?" he asked as another tree crashed to the jungle floor.

"Ah! That's for a little surprise I have planned. I was hoping to let you in on it."

He turned to a stack of crates. One of the men was busy prying up the tops with a crowbar. Dawson pushed the lid clear and motioned grandly.

Inside lay a jumble of canvas and ropes. Adam frowned and glanced into the next box. It contained a very large basket of solidly woven wicker. He looked to Dawson, genuinely shocked.

"Is this—"

"A balloon," Dawson confirmed.

"You brought a hot-air balloon?"

"It must seem rather extravagant, but I assure you it is not here for recreational purposes. There is a scientific theory I have been wanting to put to the test. Are you familiar with the principles of aerial survey?"

"First I'm hearing of it," Adam admitted.

"The higher the perspective, the more clearly one may see. It is a principle only recently coming into use in the study of geography, but I believe it could apply brilliantly to our discipline as well. Disturbed soil or the presence of anything concealed under the surface means differentiation in growth patterns—differences that may seem random on the ground, but view them from a height . . ."

"And the patterns could become clear," Adam finished. He was intrigued in spite of himself.

"The balloon will need to stay tethered here, of course. There aren't many safe places to set down. And if the map's description is correct, the city won't be visible from here even in the air. But we may catch a glimpse of this 'river of smoke' he talks of marking the entrance to the ravine, and that could save us weeks of wandering around looking for it."

"It's brilliant," Adam admitted. And still excessive. The balloon, the basket, the rigging—all those hydrogen tanks—none of it had come cheap. Neither had the backs needed to get it into the jungle.

Whoever was behind this mess, he wanted his artifact badly.

"Would you care to join me tomorrow when I ascend?"

The thought made the bottom of his stomach drop out. Adam Bates could handle poisonous snakes and sinkholes. He hated heights. But he needed Dawson to trust him, and this was a perfect opportunity to further that aim.

He'd have to handle it. Or at least keep from turning into a shivering mess at the bottom of that basket. That very small, flimsy-looking basket.

"I'd love to."

As Dawson moved on to supervise the rest of the unpacking, Adam turned once more to where Ellie sat with her guards. She looked comfortable enough, but the urge to go to her and see for himself was overwhelming. He fought it back. The conversation he'd just had made it clear that he needed to keep Dawson convinced that he wanted as little as possible to do with her.

He'd play that part—for now. There would be time enough to check on her later. He would just need to think of a way to give them some time alone.

The idea took shape in his mind. Smiling, he went to look for Charles Goodwin and Martin Lavec.

∽

Ellie lay on the cot in her tent and cursed. Flowers had tried to do what he could for her comfort. She was once again lashed to the tent pole, but at least he had pushed the cot up against it so that she didn't have to sleep on the floor. It was an improvement, but she found herself burning with nostalgia for her hammock on board the *Mary Lee*, for its soft comfort and the cool river breezes stirring the mosquito netting, the sound of Adam's even breathing mingling with the gentle lapping of the water. The stuffy atmosphere of the tent was somewhat less inspiring.

She had seen him that afternoon from across the camp and for a moment had dared to hope that he might walk over to her. Instead he'd turned away with little more than a glance and gone to chat with Dawson.

She tried not to let it bother her. It was the most sensible course of action for him to pretend indifference.

If he was just pretending…

She pushed the thought aside, which was easy enough. The awareness of her physical discomfort was happy to take its place. The close air and the ropes weren't the worst of it. That could be laid directly upon her derriere. Ellie wasn't much of a rider. She'd taken the odd turn about Hyde Park on a rented mare before she gave up bothering to entertain would-be suitors. But a day over rugged terrain on muleback had worn out muscles she hadn't known existed. They were now voicing their resentment at the ill treatment. She determined she would coerce Flowers and Mendez to allow her to walk tomorrow.

She started at the sound of shouts outside the tent. There was a crack of breaking glass, then a roar of excitement as a fight broke out. It was a foreign sound to Ellie, but she was hardly surprised. The men who crewed this expedition were clearly a rough crowd. It was likely remarkable that no such scuffles had broken out before. That, or a testament to the level of control Jacobs was able to exert over even such a motley bunch.

She turned, doing her best to shut the racket out and return to the task of ignoring her aching backside long enough to go to sleep. She had very nearly succeeded when the canvas at the tent's opening rustled and someone stepped inside.

She felt a quick flash of fear. Then something in the intruder's size and posture clicked into place in her brain.

"Bates?"

He was staring at her from across the tent. His gaze moved to where her hands were bound at the tent post, forcing her into her current awkward position. His expression darkened, and he reached for her wrists.

"What are you doing?" she demanded, whispering harshly.

"Untying you."

"You can't untie me. What will they think when they come in here in the morning? What are you doing here, anyway?"

"I told you. I'm checking on you," he repeated stubbornly.

"There are guards watching me. Somebody must have seen you."

"The guards are watching the fight."

"How do you know that?"

"That's what I set it up for."

She paused, surprised.

"You set it up?"

"I've got a couple of friends in camp. Not many," he cautioned. "But one of them is a hell of a boxer, and the other has a knack for getting bets going."

"What if he gets hurt?"

"Who?"

"Your friend," she clarified impatiently.

"Lavec will be fine. I'd worry more about the other guy."

He was quiet for a moment, looking at her with an unfamiliar expression on his face.

"We're not escaping now, I take it?" she asked, as much to break the silence as anything else.

"No," Adam replied, seeming to snap out of whatever trance he had fallen into. "Jacobs has men stationed around the outskirts of the camp on patrol. And they're not the sort to leave their posts for a boxing match. This just bought me some time to talk to you, make sure you're . . . you know."

"I'm fine," she said firmly. The man was acting truly odd. It was as though there was something he wanted to say but wouldn't. Tired of waiting for it, she abruptly pushed forward.

"Listen, Bates . . . it's not that I don't . . . What I mean is, I appreciate your concern, especially after yesterday. You've got plenty of cause to hate me right now."

"That's not true," he cut in quickly.

"What?" She shook her head, confused. But Adam's distraction wouldn't last long. They were running out of time, and she needed to get through to him.

"I've been thinking. Yesterday, in the tent, Dawson was trying very hard to convince you they were the ones who had been wronged. He didn't have to. They could easily have shot us both and been done with it. And inviting you to dinner . . . He wants you for something."

"I know."

"You do?"

"He wants me to find an artifact. Something they think might be in the city. That's what this is for, all of it. Whoever's paying the tab wants their hands on this one piece. That's it. Dawson wants me to help him find it. He thinks I'll be able to locate it faster than he can on his own."

"The Smoking Mirror?"

The answer spilled out of her before she could stop to consider its implications.

His expression was unreadable in the near-darkness.

"Yeah. Kind of figured that telegram was more than just a piece of scrap paper."

"I should have told you last night, when you asked if there was anything else I'd . . . I just . . . forgot that one," she finished lamely.

Forgot that one. Because there had been so many other things she'd lied about.

She pushed past it. There was no point in apologizing. The damage was done.

"But you said it's just a name. A myth, not a physical object."

"Apparently Dawson's got other ideas."

The sound of another roar from the crowd outside broke her from the distraction of Adam's news, and brought back her urgency.

"You have to go along with it. Make him think you'll help him. If you don't, neither of us is of use to them anymore."

"I get that."

"And that you believe what he's told you about me. You can't be seen here."

He got up, running a hand through his hair—a sign that he was frustrated. It came as a small shock that she had learned to read his tells that well already.

"Bates—"

"I'm going."

"And when you see me in the camp, ignore me or pretend you can't stand me. It shouldn't be too hard. I've given you plenty of material to work with," she added ruefully.

He looked like he wanted to respond, but he stopped himself. Ellie was grateful. Whatever he would have had to say couldn't have been good, and she had enough to ruminate over as it was.

"Can I do anything for you before I go?" he asked. His eyes fell once again to her bound hands.

She started to decline, then stopped.

"Do you have a knife?"

"What?"

"If you've got friends in the camp, that's the first thing you would've asked them to get you. You must have one."

Adam frowned, then pulled the small blade from his pocket.

"Perfect. I was afraid it would be larger. Unbutton my trousers, please."

He went very still.

"I'm sorry. What was that?"

"I need you to unbutton my trousers. I can hardly do it myself at the moment. Quickly, please. We haven't got all night."

She looked over at him, irritation rising, until she absorbed the shock in his expression and realized what her instructions must have sounded like. She felt the blood rise into her cheeks.

"For the knife! There's a pocket in my drawers. They're less likely to find it there."

The word "drawers" had made him close his eyes, as though pained.

"What do you need a knife for?"

"At some point the time is going to come for us to make a run for it. I'll need the knife to cut these ropes."

"When it's time for that, I'll come for you," he countered.

"And until then?" she pushed on, quickly calculating the best argument to win him over. "What if a snake got into the tent? Or one of those men decided to try something indecent? I am the only woman in the camp, and my position hardly makes it clear whether anyone would bother to protect me."

He muttered a curse and strode to her side. He hefted her upright, then, very determinedly and deliberately keeping his eyes somewhere roughly to the left of her face, tugged at the buttons fastening her trousers.

It was an altogether more unsettling experience than she had anticipated. Adam himself seemed to have gone very pale, his mouth set into a thin, determined line. For her own part, the very near proximity of his solid, looming form and insistent fumbling at her waistband was evoking a riot of rather alarming responses, among them a distinct rise in body temperature and an extremely inconvenient ticklishness.

"Stop. Squirming," he ordered through gritted teeth.

She gathered every shred of self-control she could muster, remained still, and at last the buttons were opened.

"Which side?" Adam muttered, staring somewhere over her ear. She was keenly aware that only his grip on her belt was keeping Tibbord's overlarge garment from sliding down past her hips.

"Left," she replied, throat rasping. It had gone quite dry. Then she leaped at the sudden heat of an unexpected touch, which sent a bolt of hot lightning down her thigh.

"Other left. My left," she stammered, and Adam cursed roundly. The knife found the pocket. He quickly restored the buttons and her belt, cinching it tightly. She stifled a protest, sensing that even that slight criticism might push him over the edge.

He stepped back quickly and took a deep breath, as though he had been holding it. He ran his hands through his hair, disheveling it thoroughly. Then he looked at her, and she saw his features darken.

"How the devil are you going to get it out of there again?" he demanded.

"Don't worry about that. I shall manage it." She felt an urge to straighten her hair and clothes—not that she could have given in to it, with her hands still securely bound. "You should go now, before they come back. That fight can't possibly have lasted so long."

The sound of another cheer belied her assumption.

"Lavec must be drawing it out to buy us more time," he said numbly.

They stared at each other through the darkness, and Ellie was overwhelmed by a rather vivid notion of just what, precisely, they might be able to do with that time, no doubt incited by the riot of feelings the ordeal of the knife had sparked in her.

Perhaps that hadn't been the best idea. It seemed to be having an even more sensational impact on her than Adam's Jamaican rum. She found herself momentarily thankful for the ropes that kept her bound to the tent pole.

"I'll tell you when it's time." Adam's voice seemed to have gone a bit hoarse. "Until then, you stay quiet and keep out of trouble. Understood?"

"Entirely. And, Bates?" she called as he moved to the exit.

He looked back.

"Thank you. For checking on me. I'm grateful for it, even if it is just for Neil's sake."

"You have no goddamned idea," he muttered as he pushed back out into the night.

16

THE ASCENT WAS FAST, much faster than Adam would have liked. The men handling their rigging let the ropes out around makeshift pulleys made from fallen tree trunks, sliding them between gloved hands. It still wasn't quick enough for the balloon, which tugged for freedom as the ground spun away beneath them.

Just don't look down, he told himself. But where else was there to look?

Finally their motion slowed and stopped. They were suspended high above the canopy, and the people of the camp looked like indiscernible dots. He felt vertigo threaten and forced it back. He needed to stay calm. At least he was doing better than Velegas's assistant. The man was huddled on the floor, muttering prayers. It was enough of a spectacle that Adam felt confident no one would notice if his knuckles were a bit white as they gripped the edge of the basket.

"Magnificent view, isn't it?"

Dawson had come to stand beside him, gazing out at the rolling, violently green landscape unfolding before them all the way to the hazy horizon.

"Sure is," Adam agreed evenly, grip tightening as a gust of wind rattled them.

"If the map is right, we won't see the city itself, even from this height. But there might be other patterns. Remnants of a road, perhaps. And just imagine the possibilities this would hold over open countryside. If we were to try it back in England..."

Adam glanced over at the profile of his companion. Dawson's cheeks were ruddy with excitement, his eyes bright. He felt an unexpected respect for the man. Using the balloon was a brilliant intuition. To recognize the value of that change in perspective took a creative and intelligent mind.

He thought of what Ellie had said, that he should try to get close, learn what he could about this man and his past. Perhaps a bit of professional appreciation was exactly the conversation starter he needed.

"When did you come up with this? At Saint Andrews?"

"Yes. Years ago, but I never had the resources to put it to the test until now. Not that I didn't try, of course. I applied for the funding several times. They weren't interested."

"Well, your new employer is more open-minded."

"So it would appear," Dawson answered cryptically.

It wasn't much of an opening, but Adam decided to push on. Talking took his mind off how very far away the ground was.

"Is that why you left the university? I can see the attraction."

"Well," Dawson said quietly, "that wasn't quite how it went."

Adam sensed something behind his tone, a whiff of a deeper story, but his instincts told him this horse would likely shy if approached head-on.

"Sorry. Didn't mean to pry." He returned his attention to the view, being careful to look out instead of down. The cool and casual routine wouldn't work so well if he passed out from vertigo. "Never had any interest in it myself," he added.

"In what?"

"Teaching."

"No? And why not?" Dawson looked bemused.

Adam rattled off the reasons:

"Students. Schedules. Dress code. When do you get the time to get into the field in between all those lectures and meetings?"

"There's more to it than that," Dawson countered.

"Oh, yeah? Come on—look at this." He waved a hand, encompassing the balloon, the mountains, the wide stretch of sky. "You can't tell me you're not better off."

"Perhaps I am. But there are joys to be found in the lecture hall.

Being part of a community of scholars, all those hungry minds…
and you have the knowledge to nourish them."

"Suppose you didn't mind having a comfortable place to come
home to at night, either."

"No," Dawson replied. His tone was clipped, and Adam saw
something dark flicker through his expression. "I didn't mind that
at all."

The basket jolted as the ropes reached their limit. Adam tightened his grip instinctively and resisted the urge to yelp. Dawson
glanced down and waved back at some signal from the men below.

"End of the line." He lifted his field glasses. "Let's see what's out
there, shall we?"

Adam scanned the distant ridges of the mountains as his brain
chewed over Dawson's words—and there it was.

At first it seemed like a shadow, but a shift in the clouds brought
with it a change of light that made it undeniably clear. Marking the
exposed face of a distant cliff was a sinuous black line like a vein of
night-dark stone running through the mountain.

A river of smoke.

That was what the abbot had described on his map, the last
landmark on their route. At its base would lie the ravine that
would take them to the White City.

The mountain itself blocked any glimpse of what might lie on
the far side, even from their current perspective, but that hardly
mattered. The monk from the abbot's story had clearly been here.
If he had gone to that much trouble, and told the truth of what he
found so far, then why would he lie about the end?

It was no hoax. It couldn't be, which meant that the dark line of
stone marked the passage to a place that shouldn't exist, a city out
of myth.

We found it, princess. It's real.

"Dear God."

Dawson's tone was flat with shock, and Adam knew without
looking that he was not the only one who had seen the landmark.

They had found it, all right. But not alone.

Dawson wrestled open a copy of Adam's own map, complete with all of his hard-won measurements and markings. He held it in place against a gust of wind that rattled their basket, sending it for a sickening swing.

"Help me confirm these peaks. This one to the left is here, correct?" he asked, glancing to the place he pointed out on the map. "So that outcropping is part of this elevation. And that means that our goal is... right here." He traced a finger along the paper, then made two swift lines with his pencil. He looked over at Adam, face broadening into a boyish grin. "X marks the spot."

It couldn't be more than three days' walk, even at the expedition's snail-like pace. Three days until they were there, inside that extraordinary place.

Three days until Adam had to either help Dawson find his mirror, or find both himself and Ellie suddenly expendable. They would have to escape, and soon. But even thinking it, some part of him protested. *And never see the city?* Miss the chance to be among the first inside what could very well be the greatest archaeological find on this continent? Wasn't that worth a little risk?

The notion tempted him, until he thought of Ellie. She'd probably be thinking the same thing: that the opportunity to see what they'd already come so far to find was worth taking a chance for. And he'd be damned if he'd let her do that. Even if the place was El Dorado, complete with gold-plated streets, he was getting her to safety before any of them stepped foot inside. He might gamble with his own life, but hers was off the table. Whether she liked it or not, he was getting her out of this mess. As for what happened after that... well, they'd deal with that when the time came.

He needed to come up with a plan—and quickly. Looking at that sinuous black line on the face of the cliff, with all that it promised, Adam realized that he was running out of time.

Ellie was in the ruined city again. The great plaza was quiet this time, with none of the signs of violence that had haunted it before.

It was also, incongruously, covered in snow. White flakes dusted the bare branches of sprawling tropical trees, collecting in drifts on the stones of the plaza like a winter morning in the English countryside.

Except that it wasn't snow.

Ashes, she realized. It was raining ashes.

The gray flakes continued to fall as she watched, thickening on the ground. The air was not crisp and cool. It was sweltering, like standing in the middle of an inferno.

The dream woman waited for her at the bottom of a wide, low staircase. It sat at the foot of a grand facade, rows of white columns framing dark doorways.

"Where have you been?" Ellie demanded. It seemed like a reasonable question, though it shouldn't have been. Ellie had never developed expectations about the inhabitants of her dreams before.

"You lost the key," the woman replied simply.

Ellie's hand went to the place where the medallion should have been, but it was gone. Dawson had it now. Adam had made her give it to him.

"Then why are you here now?"

"Because you have gotten closer to it. Close enough to feel its influence."

The scarred woman extended her small, fine hand, fist closed. Something sifted from between her fingers. It was sand, fine grains of it in an alarming shade of red. It fell in a stream, then slowed, and finally ceased.

"Time is running out," she said. She opened her now empty hand, and on the ground below it lay not a mound of grains but a pool. It looked like blood.

She raised her eyes, meeting Ellie's gaze. "You do not need the key. There is another way. The path of kings. The road that leads through hell."

"But where does it go?" Ellie demanded.

"To darkness—and hope."

The ash was falling thicker now. Where the flakes landed on the woman's skin, her flesh seared and split. She was burning up, one tiny piece at a time, bits of red tissue and bone beginning to show through to the surface.

A fat ash fell on Ellie's arm and she heard the sizzle of it. The flakes swirled around her, obscuring her view of the woman, the palace, even the plaza itself. Her skin charred and smoked from a thousand places. Then the pain began.

The scream tore out of her like it had been waiting, high and full of primitive terror. She carried it with her as the dream shattered apart and the sound of her fear pierced through the still night like a lance.

~

Adam was awake in a breath, bolting upright in the hammock, senses instantly alert. Someone was screaming. As soon as he realized he was hearing it, the sound died into an echo that stirred small birds from the trees.

It had been a woman's scream. And there was only one woman in this camp.

He swung out of the hammock, ducking nimbly under the netting, and ran.

He had marked the place where they'd set her tent earlier that afternoon, and navigated to it instinctively now. When he reached it, he saw two men at the entrance, rifles in hand. They weren't the now-familiar figures he saw with her during the day, but strangers with the hard look of the men Charlie had warned him about, the ones Jacobs was paying tripled rates.

Adam did not slow as he approached them, barreling toward the tent.

"Stop—" the first began, but was cut short as Adam shoved aside the barrel of his gun.

He whisked the guard's machete from the sheath at his belt, then dashed inside even as the second of the pair shouted impotently behind him.

Ellie cursed under her breath. Had she really screamed out loud? What had she seen in her dream that had been so terrible?

Death, she thought, her pulse still racing.

She heard arguing voices outside the tent and tensed. Then the flap flew open, and Adam burst inside, machete in his hand.

"What was it?" he demanded.

Ellie blinked at him, shocked into silence for a moment. She quickly collected herself.

"You shouldn't be here!" she hissed. "How are they supposed to believe you're mad at me if you come barreling—"

"What. Was. It," he ground out.

Ellie momentarily lost her breath. In the near darkness of the tent, with the gleaming knife in his hand and every muscle taut, Adam's appearance was rather thrilling. Then one of the guards burst inside and leveled a rifle at his head.

"A bad dream," she explained hurriedly. "Just a nightmare. See? You shouldn't have troubled," she finished significantly, casting a quick look at the guard.

Adam's expression darkened, something she wouldn't have thought possible given its already murderous state. He stalked toward her, oblivious to the man with the gun following behind.

"Get this straight: You scream; I answer. I don't care whose god-damned rules it breaks. Clear?"

Ellie nodded. Adam turned on the man behind him as Jacobs stepped quietly into the tent.

"Were you just going to stand out there and listen to her scream?" he demanded, his voice low and dangerous. The guard protested.

"Our orders were to—"

"I don't give a damn what your orders were. Someone— anyone—in this camp starts screaming, you go and help them. Is that understood?"

The guard looked helplessly from Adam to Jacobs. It was Jacobs who answered.

"Perfectly," he said, his voice cool and calm.

Adam flipped the knife easily in his hand and returned it to the guard, then left without another word.

Jacobs turned to the pair.

"Are you familiar with what the word 'guarding' means?"

They nodded.

"Then guard her. Until I say otherwise."

"Yes, *jefe*."

They followed Jacobs out of the tent, leaving her alone once more.

The encounter had passed so quickly, she half wondered whether she'd still been dreaming. But no: She had not imagined that fierce protectiveness in Adam's face, the outraged power that had been written into every line of his frame.

He had come for her.

The thought shouldn't have made her heart jump. After all, Ellie told herself firmly, he would have done the same for anyone else in danger. It was one of his basic rules of engagement, as she'd learned firsthand in the bathroom of the Imperial.

But would he have done it so ferociously for someone else?

She thought of the power in his frame as he'd forced his way in, the urgency. It was exhilarating—or would have been, if not for the lingering terror of her dream. And what was it about that vision that had set her screaming? It had been clear as day a moment before but seemed a blur of smoke and shadows now. Not that it mattered.

Adam had just been doing his duty, she told herself firmly. It didn't mean anything. She contorted herself to lie back down on her cot. The thought that followed was even more uncomfortable than her position.

What did she want it to mean?

Walking was heavenly. Ellie had never appreciated using her own two feet back in London, and certainly not over the days when she'd been trudging behind Adam through the bush. But after twelve hours being bounced around on muleback the day before, the chance to move under her own propulsion felt like a gift. She didn't even have the burden of any extra weight to carry. Her pack had been confiscated and was most likely stashed on one of the patient animals that surrounded her. Combine that with the fact that the pace was far from strenuous, and their trek felt a bit like a stroll through the park. Except that in the park, she wasn't usually tied up and under armed guard.

Armed guards, a fleet of mules, and an army of men...Ellie couldn't see the front of their caravan. The length of it was lost in the bush ahead of her. This expedition had to be costing someone a fortune, and they'd mounted the whole thing for a single artifact— an artifact that may or may not even exist. And what would it look like if it did? A piece of reflective glass? An idol?

She had heard of the mania of collectors, men with means who got their hearts set on acquiring prize pieces of history. They were certainly capable of taking extreme measures to get what they wanted. But what kind of collection would this Smoking Mirror belong to?

Something was missing. The parts of the puzzle didn't add up to a complete whole, and there certainly must be a compelling whole to justify all this effort. To justify murder, she reminded herself. She had no doubt that was what Jacobs had in mind when he spoke of disposing of "loose ends." It was what he undoubtedly still had in mind for her and Adam, once Dawson no longer had a use for him.

She was so engrossed in her thoughts, it took her a moment to realize that the caravan had stopped.

Mendez asked a sharp question in Spanish and received a quick reply.

"What's going on?" Ellie asked.

"They found something," Flowers replied.

The words had an unusual weight: *found something.*

She saw the big man make an instinctive gesture with his hand, a motion to ward off evil. She felt a chill and wondered what sort of "something" had ground the whole expedition to a halt.

It was a stela. Adam could see the dark stone peeking out from behind the thick wrapping of strangler-fig vines. Judging by the insistent tugging at the buckle of his belt, it had the same strange magnetic properties as the other stela and the medallion.

There was enough of the monument still uncovered for him to make out the massive figure carved onto the surface. This image was recognizable even through the strange iconography of the men who'd made it: the skeletal visage of Death.

It was fitting, given the tribute that lay at the pillar's feet. The jaguar was a fresh kill, blood barely dry on the ground, flies just beginning to buzz around it. Adam guessed it to have died the night before, or perhaps even early that morning. From the look of it, its passage had been far from gentle.

The animal was butchered. Its belly had been slashed open from throat to tail, the dark red viscera spilled out onto the ground. More gouges marked its back, with particular attention having been paid to the neck, where the mutilations appeared deeper and more deliberate.

"Natives?" Dawson asked. He had dismounted from his mule and was staring down at the corpse greenly.

Adam was saved from the need for a reply to this idiotic theory by Velegas, the foreman, who knelt over the body.

"They wouldn't damage the pelt like this."

"So an animal," Dawson deduced. "But what animal could do this? Another jaguar?"

"Possibly. It's not unheard-of for them to attack their own in territorial disputes."

What the foreman said was true, but something about it didn't sit right. Jaguar kills were vicious, certainly, but could another cat have really ripped this animal open so neatly?

But if it wasn't a jaguar, what else could it have been?

Adam didn't have an answer.

"Remove it before the rest of the men see," Velegas ordered, motioning to a pair of bearers. They dragged the creature off into the brush. It left a dark, wet trail behind it.

"We should get some distance between us and whatever did this before we make camp," Dawson suggested.

"We still have a few hours of light. We'll use them," Velegas confirmed. He rose and brought the caravan back into line with a few sharply shouted orders. The men obeyed, only Dawson remaining behind. He moved to Adam's side, following his gaze to the dark figure grinning out from the half-concealed stone.

"What do you think it is?"

Adam could hear the reply in his mind. It came in the voice of the Mayan from the hidden village, Amilcar Kuyoc.

Because Death lives there. Death and the rest of the old gods. And he and his servants feast on the flesh of those who trespass in their realm.

"A warning," he answered flatly, then stepped past the stela and rejoined the river of mules and men.

17

Ellie woke in the dark. She felt a rush of panic, her pulse pounding, breath short and quick. She tried to sit up, then cursed as her arms caught on the line that tethered her once again to the tent post. She forced herself to still, listening. There was nothing stirring in the tent, no cause for alarm. The truth stole over her, settling her heartbeat. Another nightmare.

She searched her memory for some sense of what had haunted her this time, but she could recall nothing. Maybe it was for the best. Judging by the cold sweat covering her body and the frantic pace of her heart, it hadn't been a pleasant dream. At least this time she must have managed not to scream.

Ever since they had been conscripted into Dawson's expedition, Ellie's dreams had taken a darker turn. She supposed it was understandable. After all, her circumstances weren't exactly promising.

There was also something about this particular jungle that seemed to weigh on her, and she wasn't alone. The mood of the camp had shifted since the gruesome discovery earlier that day. Though the dead cat had been removed long before Ellie passed the spot, word of what had lain at the foot of the massive black stone had traveled quickly down the caravan. Even if it hadn't, the sight of the blood-spattered ground before the stela would have been unsettling enough.

There had been plenty of speculation about what might have killed the jaguar, but no one had an answer. One thing was certain: Whatever could ravage a powerful and dangerous predator wasn't something she was likely to want lurking around.

Then there was the jungle itself. Though they were climbing continually higher into the mountains, the midday heat remained oppressive, if anything becoming even thicker than before. The sky, when she glimpsed it through the canopy, was equally heavy with an uncanny haze.

It was also oddly silent. The bright chirpings and hoots she'd grown accustomed to in the lower altitudes were absent here. There was only a thick buzz of insects. In fact, since they'd passed the slaughtered cat by the stela, Ellie couldn't remember the last time she'd seen any animal larger than a swallow.

These mountain regions must simply be more sparsely populated, but the effect was admittedly eerie. She supposed a few nightmares should hardly be surprising.

She shifted on the cot, trying to settle back down, then groaned. Apparently the bad dream hadn't been the only reason she'd woken up. Her bladder had contributed. She weighed the possibility of simply holding off until dawn, then dismissed it. At least getting up in the dark would give her a chance to stretch her legs and increase the likelihood of catching a bit more sleep before morning.

"Anybody out there?" she called softly. A rustle of the tent flap answered, and she was relieved to see Flowers step inside. It must be nearly dawn if he was already back at his post, and she felt significantly more comfortable with the big, quiet man than she did with the set of rather unsavory fellows who took shifts watching her through the night.

"You need to stretch your legs?" he asked politely.

"Just for a minute," she replied, flashing him a pleading smile.

Flowers freed the rope that held her to the post and motioned her out of the tent. He collected the lantern that sat by the log he was using as a chair and led her from the camp out into the dark of the bush.

A short distance later, he turned his back politely as Ellie fumbled her way through her necessary business, which was significantly trickier with bound hands. She nearly lost Adam's knife in the process, barely catching it before it tumbled to the ground. At least she didn't have skirts to wrangle. Who knew how she would have managed with petticoats?

She buttoned herself back together and turned to Flowers, then froze as a scream ripped through the still night air.

Flowers met her eyes across the small pool of lantern light. He had gone pale, his hand clenched tightly on the rifle as the echo of the scream was swallowed by the thick foliage that surrounded them.

"What was that?" Ellie instinctively kept her voice to a whisper.

Flowers didn't answer. He edged closer to her, his eyes darting around the clearing. She wondered whether she looked as obviously terrified as he did.

"We need to go," he said, voice low and urgent.

A second scream tore through the silence, and continued, howling on in pain and terror.

Ellie turned and ran toward the sound, Flowers hesitating only a moment before following.

The screaming drowned into a thick gurgle as they got closer, and another sound, more delicate, tickled at Ellie's awareness. It was a quick and regular thumping, accompanied by rustling leaves. It momentarily stopped her in her tracks.

I've heard this before.

But that was absurd, she thought numbly. Then Flowers charged through the foliage behind her, nearly knocking into her. She shook off the weirdness and pushed through a curtain of branches.

A man lay on the ground before her, revealed in the glow of the lamp, his rifle lying a few feet away. Flowers scooped it up, slinging it over his shoulder, then adjusted his grip on his own gun as Ellie approached the victim.

From throat to groin, the man's body was a wet, glistening wreck. The flesh around the wound was ragged, as though it had been torn rather than cut. His eyes, white and wide in his blood-spattered face, stared up at the darkened leaves overhead.

Ellie fought the wave of horror that momentarily rooted her to the spot and knelt, pressing her fingers to what remained of the man's throat. She withdrew them a moment later, looking up to see Flowers watching her. She shook her head, half stumbling back to her feet.

They stared down at the dead man.

What could have done this?

There was a sound of crashing footsteps, and men spilled into the clearing. Jacobs came with a trio of armed guards, who quickly aimed their weapons at Flowers and Ellie but faltered as they saw what lay on the jungle floor.

"Make way," the foreman, Velegas, ordered as he pushed past them.

Adam was behind him. At the sight of him, she wanted nothing more than to cross the clearing to his side, letting his solid presence banish the numb, shaking feeling the sight of the corpse on the ground had filled her with.

She forced herself to resist, instead standing still and quiet as he quickly took in the scene, his eyes moving from the man on the ground to where she stood beside Flowers. They shifted down to her hands, which were still red with the victim's blood, and sharpened.

She realized what was coming next and shook her head quickly, warning him off of the demand to know whether she was hurt. That was the last signal she wanted to send with Jacobs standing next to them.

Adam frowned but turned from her and joined the foreman beside what remained of the man on the ground. Behind them, Dawson pushed into the clearing, then went pale as he stared down at the butchered flesh. He stumbled back a step, then caught himself.

"Another jaguar attack?" he asked thickly, his hand over his mouth.

"No," Velegas replied.

"Then what?"

The foreman stood and stepped back. "I don't know."

There was a silence, heavy with unspoken dread.

Jacobs broke it.

"Where is his partner?" He looked impatiently back at the blank stares that answered him. "These men are patrolling in pairs."

Ellie realized that she had been hearing it the whole time: a wet, irregular gurgle, whispering out of the thick growth behind her. She plucked the lamp from Flowers's hand and turned with it, slipping through the branches into a small clearing beyond.

The other man lay spread-eagled on the ground, the dried leaves beneath him stained red. Like his partner's, his body had been torn open. His viscera hung off the branches of a nearby bush like nightmarish garlands. His breath was shallow and wet, the pale white of his eyes visible as they rolled toward her.

Adam brushed past her, Ellie's skin jumping at the unexpected contact. He moved quickly to the victim on the ground, pulling off his shirt as he went. He pushed the fabric against the wound in what Ellie could see clearly was a vain attempt to stanch the bleeding.

She heard rather than saw Jacobs and the others crash into this second clearing, her attention locked on the scene before her.

The wide eyes of the wounded man wheeled to Adam's face. His arm flew up, clamping onto Adam's shoulder like a lifeline. He gasped out a babble of words along with a froth of red film that covered his lips.

"He says it came out of the night," Flowers translated from where he stood beside her.

"What did?" Adam demanded.

The man coughed up the answer in a spray of blood. The coughing continued, degrading into agonized gasps. The sound was horrible, accompanied by sharp twitches of the limbs. She realized it looked as though he were drowning.

Velegas crouched beside the man, his face hard. He studied him for a moment, then pulled the machete from the sheath at his waist.

Adam stepped back. His face and chest were slick with the dying man's blood, his hands red to the elbows.

The machete flashed, and the terrible noise fell silent.

Velegas wiped off the blade, then solemnly returned it to his belt.

Dawson stepped forward, his face pale and sweating.

"What did he say?" he demanded. "What did this?"

"*Los ángeles de la muerte,*" Flowers replied. "The angels of Death."

The gathering of men in the small circle of lamplight went silent, and Ellie felt certain all of them were thinking the same thing: There was something haunting this jungle, something deadly. But for her, there was another implication, one that went beyond the primitive fear of being hunted.

Adam looked at her from across the body of the slaughtered guard. She saw the warning in his eyes and knew he'd realized it, too. There would be no slipping away from their captors, no quiet escape. How could they even attempt it, knowing what was out there in the darkness of the bush, waiting for them?

Or *not* knowing. It was clear from the reactions of the men around her that the violence on the ground had not been the work of a jaguar, or some other familiar predator.

It came out of the night.

Ellie thought of the noise she had heard as she approached the clearing, the one that had stopped her in her tracks until Flowers nearly ran her over.

Wings, she realized. That was what it had sounded like. The beating of mighty wings.

The morning was a blur of tedious motion, the usually boisterous chatter of the bearers strangely subdued. It was not a surprise. Word of the events of the night before had traveled quickly through the camp, a grim murmur that had men casting their eyes to the sky, crossing themselves, and muttering quick prayers when no one else was listening.

Ellie trudged up the increasingly precipitous ground. The night had been virtually sleepless, and she was fighting weariness, almost wishing she had accepted Flowers's perennial offer to saddle one of the mules for her.

Then word began to whisper its way down the caravan. Mendez heard it first and hurried back to them, his eyes bright with excitement.

Ellie felt a surge of nervous energy. *Please don't let it be another body*, she thought.

"They've found it," he announced.

Suddenly alert, Ellie looked up. Ahead of her, the canopy broke, revealing the massive face of a cliff that loomed over their stretch of jungle. The gray stone face of it was marked by a startling, sinuous line of black stone.

The river of smoke.

The open space between the cliff and the jungle was narrow, the caravan crowding it as drovers tried to herd both men and mules into some semblance of order. The wall of stone was sheer, towering some two hundred feet over Ellie's head. Stubborn shrubs clung to its stony surface, while thicker foliage draped its crown like a decaying bridal veil.

At the base of the cliff, the black vein of stone vanished into a narrow ravine.

This is it. Ellie could see the image of the map in her mind. The dark opening in front of her was the final stage of her journey. On the other side lay the place she'd crossed half the world to find.

The White City.

Velegas emerged from the opening, climbing nimbly over a jumble of boulders. He jumped down, dusting off his hands as he approached Dawson.

Nudging her way past a stack of gear, Ellie moved closer.

"There's more rockfall inside, but it looks like the way is clear after that. I won't know for sure until I scout the rest of it."

"I'm going with you," Dawson announced, dismounting from his mule. "You as well, Bates."

Adam stepped past a cluster of bearers. Ellie felt her pulse jump. She hadn't seen him since the night before, and the image of him covered in another man's blood was still sharp in her mind.

Dawson was blithely giving orders. She realized what was happening. He was arranging the team that would scout the way through the passage, the men who would be the first to see the place she'd come all this way to find. They'd be the ones to discover what had survived the ravages of war and disease. Would the temples still be intact? What about the secondary structures? The courtyards and public forums? Was it really all untouched?

Dawson motioned to the men he had gathered. They were about to find out—and were leaving her behind.

She felt a rush of outrage.

The hell they would.

She pushed her way through the crowd, arriving at the opening of the ravine just as Dawson was shouldering his pack.

"I'm going with you," she announced.

"Out of the question," Dawson sputtered. The others around him looked shocked at her appearance, all except Adam. He looked worried, which only inflamed her determination.

"Mr. Bates is not the only trained historian in this camp."

"Mr. Bates did not set off a bomb in one of our boats," Dawson countered somewhat desperately.

"And what am I going to do to you in there? Throw sand in your eye?" She took a long look around the waiting caravan, the sacks of equipment, the crates swinging from the backs of the mules. "On the other hand, I suspect there's far more potential trouble I could get into here."

Dawson looked aghast, then grasped at a quick inspiration.

"You can't get through there with your hands tied," he pointed out.

"I could help her."

The offer came from an unexpected source. Flowers stood behind her. At a look from Mendez, standing among the crowd, he shrugged. "She's light."

To demonstrate, he gripped her belt, and Ellie fought for balance as he hefted her easily off the ground. He set her back down again gently.

She risked a glance at Adam. He appeared to have been consumed by a coughing fit.

"Oh, for pity's sake . . ." Dawson looked to Jacobs for help.

"Let her. If she causes any trouble, we'll shoot her."

The threat was delivered as casually as a comment about the weather, which made it all the more chilling. He would do it, she realized, and with that little concern.

She brushed the fear aside. It didn't matter, anyway. She didn't plan on causing any trouble.

At least, not yet.

Ellie felt the change in atmosphere as soon as she stepped through the entrance to the ravine. The passage was so narrow, they were forced to walk single-file. The high walls let in only thin shafts of light, giving the place a cavelike atmosphere. Thick green foliage clung to the stones, dripping moisture onto her neck as she moved past.

The path twisted and turned. Ellie often lost sight of Adam moving near the front of the team, her view obscured by the trailing vines or the jagged walls of the cliff.

It was eerily silent. Not even the ever-present buzz of insects broke the stillness of the place. The men around her seemed to sense it. They spoke only when necessary, and then in murmurs.

Even the murmurs faded as the ravine widened.

Light spilled down into the space, sparkling off the drops of moisture that clung to the dangling greenery. Dawson and the others had stopped ahead of her and were looking up at a sheer wall of stone.

It was made of the same dark substance as the "river of smoke" that had led them there, but there was nothing natural about the carving that decorated it. Standing nearly three stories high, it was a massive and gruesome relief of the now-familiar god of the people of the White City, the demonlike visage she'd first seen on the medallion.

It loomed over a sculpted mountain of slaughtered men and women like a vulture and held a severed head aloft, a long, serpentine tongue catching the blood that dripped from it.

Ellie found herself grateful that the inhabitants of the city had met their end centuries before. Looking at their monument, she wasn't quite certain she would have wanted to meet them in the flesh.

"We're losing daylight."

Velegas's voice cut through the tense silence, and the scouting team shuffled back into motion, leaving the dark, warning shape of the god behind as they plunged back into the dim, narrow confines of the ravine.

Ellie heard the end of the passage before she saw it, as the awed exclamations of the others echoed back to her. Her heart leaping, she dashed forward, stumbling over a scattering of boulders and spilling out onto a wide, flat ledge.

The landscape before her was an immense, vaguely circular depression surrounded by rugged peaks cloaked in deep forest. There, in the center of it, towers of bright, gleaming stone showed through thick veils of overgrowth. They filled the heart of the place, while, on the outskirts and climbing the steep mountainsides, Ellie could see remnants of terraced farmland.

As she watched, the deep light of afternoon blazed through a gap in the thick clouds bunched at the top of the mountains, spilling across the crowns of the temples and painting their white stones a startling gold.

It's real.

The thought nearly brought her to her knees. The stones before her weren't a myth, or the dream of a frustrated suffragette. They were *real*.

And she had found them.

A flock of rainbow-colored birds rose up, startled by some unseen disturbance. They wheeled over the ruins, flashing red and turquoise against the sky.

Ellie closed her eyes, half convinced that when she opened them, she'd find herself back at her desk in the Public Record Office, staring down at another pile of crumbling tax forms.

No. This wasn't London. She wasn't dreaming. She was *here*.

Adam moved to her side. His profile was gilded by the dying sunlight.

"Congratulations, princess," he said. "Looks like you found El Dorado."

As he spoke, the clouds shifted once more, swallowing the warm rays of light. She felt a breeze brush against the back of her neck, lifting the fine hairs there and stirring the leaves of the trees below.

Velegas's voice rang out across the ledge.

"Let's get the supplies through and set up camp." He turned his face to the wind, the creases of it crinkling with concern. "It smells like rain."

As they descended, the sun dipped lower on the horizon and the clouds thickened, taking on a more threatening air. They followed a narrow track down the side of the mountain, a thin series of switchbacks along dizzying drops. Once they reached the ground, the path quickly widened. Pushing some of the debris aside with her boot, Ellie saw that she was walking on a solid surface of beautiful white paving stones.

It was a road. More than that, she realized. It was a marvel of engineering. The stones must have been precisely laid for its surface to have survived intact after centuries of neglect.

They followed the straight path it made through the thick undergrowth until it stopped at a low, wide stairway. Ellie climbed it as Velegas shouted orders to the men. The intriguing, jumbled piles of stone they had passed on their way had been replaced by larger structures, and as she reached the platform at the top, she realized she was standing in a great central courtyard, surrounded by the mountainous ruins of the city's temples.

That was not what stopped her in her tracks, sending fear through her like a needle of ice.

The fear came because she had seen this before.

The memory was sharp and distinct. The plaza had been free of the creeping piles of vegetation then, the mounds of dry leaves. But she had seen those three smaller temples, and the massive white pyramid that loomed over all of them, dwarfing the other structures with its grandeur. She had stood here, talking to a woman with a scarred face dressed in a gown made of feathers, while voices whispered to her from the shadows.

Impossible.

It had to be a coincidence. A lucky guess made by her dreaming mind. She had looked at drawings of Mayan city layouts in the British Library. There were many variations, certainly, but was the square arrangement of temples in front of her really that unusual or surprising?

There had been other details in that dream. Corpses piled in the rooms of palaces, faces covered in oozing sores. Smoke drifting through the foliage, the sounds of war clashing in the distance.

None of that was here. It was just a ruin—a wildly intriguing ruin. No wonder it was sparking her imagination.

She was letting the atmosphere of the place get to her, and the weather probably didn't help. The sky kept shifting indecisively between slanting light and lowering gray, and bursts of wind rushed strangely through the trees before passing, leaving them utterly still once more.

Flowers stood beside her, watching the men pushing aside piles of debris to make room for the tents. His expression was grim.

"This is a bad place," he asserted.

"They're ruins," she countered. "I'm sure they all feel like this."

She strode toward the site of the camp and tried not to notice her guard's quick gesture against whatever evils he felt lurked in this place.

18

ADAM STOOD HALFWAY UP the steps of the temple, waiting for Dawson to catch his breath. He was torn between two conflicting impulses: first to leap ahead to the enclosure at the summit of the pyramid, and second to rush back to the courtyard, find Ellie, and make sure she was safe.

He couldn't do either, thanks to the man panting beside him. Dawson had wasted no time, quickly identifying this massive structure as the ritual center of the city. He was determined to investigate it immediately, hoping that the artifact his employer sought would be inside.

Presuming it existed at all.

Dawson thought Adam's greater knowledge of Central American ruins would speed up the search, and he was hardly in a position to decline. Until he thought of a way to get Ellie away from the camp, his best strategy was to stay on Dawson's good side. Which meant there was no turning him down to check on the prisoner he was supposed to be mad as hell at.

He could also safely assume that Dawson wouldn't look kindly on being left behind as Adam raced him to the top of the pyramid. In spite of his many causes for concern, Adam couldn't help but succumb to the intoxicating excitement of the discovery.

And it was intoxicating, on more than one level. He could already see that the ruins were startlingly extensive, the remains of an immense and powerful city. Then there was the iconography. Like the medallion and the stelae they'd passed on their way there, it held traces of Mayan and Aztec themes but was also significantly different. The confluence reminded him of Dawson's theory—Dawson's mad, impossible theory—that this city wasn't just another Mayan ruin. That they had stumbled across the remains of an as-yet-unknown culture.

At last, Dawson recovered sufficiently to continue their ascent. As they reached the summit, he didn't pause to examine the remarkable carvings decorating the facade of the sanctuary but instead plunged immediately into the dark, narrow chamber, Adam close behind him.

A face glared at them from the far wall. The carving was done in deep relief, just like the one Adam had seen on the wall of the ravine. It was another image of the ubiquitous god of the city, keeping fierce vigil over the ruins. But it wasn't the idol that immediately caught Adam's attention. It was what sat beneath.

The jars were half-buried in accumulated dust and debris, but Adam could see enough of them to know they were intact, their beautifully painted surfaces unmarred by so much as a crack.

Any grave robber or rogue explorer who had stumbled upon this place would have followed the same course as Dawson had and come straight to this high sanctuary. Once inside, there was no way they would have left those jars intact. They would have been carried off, or at least broken open in search of smaller gold or jade treasures.

The implication stopped his breath. It meant that this magnificent place, this whole city, had somehow managed to escape the ravages of thieves. Everything he saw would be exactly where the inhabitants had left it.

It was unthinkable. In all his years of work in the colony, Adam had never come across so much as a minor settlement that had not been robbed.

There would be no question of securing the funds for a complete and thorough excavation. As soon as word got back to the capital, he'd have more support than he could ask for. An undisturbed find from a potentially unknown culture...

"Is this it?"

Dawson's voice snapped him out of his reverie. For a moment, his awe had made him forget that he wasn't alone here, and that the man beside him was as trustworthy as a snake. Reality set back in like a sack of bricks.

"The interior has to be small to support the roof," he replied automatically.

"But what about the rest of the pyramid? How do we get inside?"

"Any other structures like this that have been excavated were just full of rubble."

Dawson muttered something in response, but Adam was no longer listening. A rustle of movement overhead drew his eye. There, tucked into the stones of the corbeled vault, was a nest of starlings. Except Adam couldn't think of how a few birds could build a nest into solid rock.

He stepped closer and realized that one of the stones of the ceiling wasn't a stone at all. It was a patch of some sort of plaster, crumbling away to reveal what looked like a broken slab.

The startled birds escaped from the sanctuary with a flutter. Dawson was still speaking, but none of the words registered. Adam's attention was completely consumed by a dark space between the plaster and the jagged edge of the neighboring block. An empty space.

He grabbed a pick from the pile of gear the bearer had set down nearby, reversed it, and jabbed it up into the ceiling.

The patch disintegrated, revealing an opening in the roof of the chamber—an opening someone had clearly tried to disguise.

Dawson gaped up at it, then slapped the bearer roughly.

"Get a ladder!"

As the man stumbled out of the sanctuary, shouting down to the courtyard, Adam felt his curiosity reach a breaking point. Quickly assessing the distance, he jumped, caught the edge of the gap, and hauled his body up through it.

He found himself in a sort of attic between the ceiling of the sanctuary and the roof of the temple. The space was narrow and low, forming a tunnel that sloped down steeply. Turning was difficult in such a tight, awkward space, but Adam managed to twist himself for a backward look at the opening through which he had climbed.

He could see oiled ropes, and devices that looked oddly like gears and pulleys. It looked as though the stones that surrounded the opening in the ceiling were connected to some kind of mechanism.

This wasn't just an architectural accident, he realized. It must have been a door, with a trigger to open it disguised somewhere in the room below.

The Maya had never had any sort of technology like that.

But then, this wasn't a Mayan city.

Tulan Zuyua.

He dismissed the thought. Tulan Zuyua was a myth. The place he was climbing through was real.

The tunnel before him sloped steeply down into darkness. There was no way to tell where it ended. He called back to Dawson.

"Tell them to bring a lantern as well. And a rope."

The rope arrived first. After making certain it had been properly anchored to a solid pillar at the entrance to the sanctuary, Adam slowly began to work his way down the side of the vault. After a short distance, the ground disappeared beneath him.

He stopped, bracing himself against the sides of the tunnel. How far was the drop? The space around him was utterly dark, so much so that Adam could barely see the rope he held in his hands. There was no way to tell how far it might be before he reached solid ground again, and the temple was enormous, much taller than any Mayan structure he knew.

The thought that he might be hanging over a sheer drop to its base, like a blacked-out mine shaft, made his hands shake.

For a moment he contemplated turning around and letting one of Dawson's bearers test the way down.

And miss the chance to be the first one inside this place? Not a chance.

Adam forced his fear aside and let himself slip out into the void, keeping a white-knuckled grip on the rope. He found himself wondering whether it would be long enough to reach the bottom of the shaft.

His mind filled with the image of reaching for the next grip, and finding his hand closing on empty air. It was nearly enough to send him back into the tunnel.

Just take it slow. You can do this.

Praying he wouldn't end up dangling off the tail end of the line, he began a careful descent, one hand over the other—and felt his feet touch solid ground.

The space from the tunnel to the landing he stood on couldn't have been more than eight feet.

It figured.

The lantern was lowered to him along a second rope, Dawson following closely behind it. In the lamplight, Adam could see that he stood at the top of a steep, narrow stairwell, descending into the bowels of the temple. It was thick with the misty forms of spiderwebs.

"Be my guest," Dawson said, motioning him ahead.

The stairwell progressed in sharp twists and turns. Though Adam couldn't be certain, his instinct told him that it must closely follow the exterior facing of the temple, winding around at right angles as it descended. The space was barely wide enough for the span of his shoulders. Fat black spiders skittered away from the glow of the lamp as he approached.

After what seemed like an eternity, they reached another landing, one that opened onto a tunnel just high enough for Adam to walk through without crouching.

He stopped in the entrance. He had never encountered anything like this passage in any of his previous explorations. It could lead to anything—the tomb of a great king, some secret altar or offering-place. The utter mystery of it overwhelmed him, until Dawson broke the spell.

"What are we waiting for?"

"Nothing," Adam muttered, and moved forward.

What he saw next nearly made him drop the lamp.

The space before him was immense, so large that Adam thought it must fill the entire interior of the pyramid. The pinnacle of the room, far above, was lost in shadow, the single feeble lantern he held utterly incapable of the task of illuminating it.

The whole structure was nothing more than a shell, one that must have been constructed with the architectural grace of a gothic cathedral. And what it housed . . .

It was too much to absorb at once. Adam's mind reeled with it. First there were the walls, which were entirely covered in vividly colored murals, all of them stunningly well preserved. The images, like the stelae, were both familiar and uncannily different, but they held his attention for only a moment.

Stone tables lined the walls of the room, their contents flashing and glittering in the lamplight. They were covered with a bizarre array of objects. Adam saw grotesque, gleaming idols resting beside other devices that looked more like scientific instruments. Much of it—nearly all—was made of gold.

If he'd had any doubts about grave robbers finding this place before him, they were gone now.

Something about the shining array of artifacts nagged at his attention, but the brief sense of wrongness faded as his eyes moved to the object that dominated the center of the room.

An object that should not—*could not*—exist.

It was a pendulum, shaped something like a massive Christmas ornament, a golden globe that tapered to an elegant point at the base. It was suspended from the pinnacle of the temple by a cable, hanging with utter stillness over the center of a circle inscribed on the floor of the room. The circumference of the circle was lined with tiny, gleaming pins of polished white stone. Perhaps two thirds of them were toppled over, the remaining third waiting in a tidy row like soldiers lined up for review before a battle.

It was bizarre. It was also familiar. Adam had seen the exact arrangement before, on a visit to Paris during a break from his studies at Cambridge. What lay in the heart of the temple was a perfect replica of a system designed to demonstrate the rotation of the earth—the invention of a French physicist by the name of Foucault.

A man who had been born less than a hundred years ago.

It was impossible—more than impossible. Looking at it, still and shining in the flickering light of their feeble lantern, Adam doubted whether he was still entirely sane.

"You see it, too?" he asked Dawson, overcome by the urge to reassure himself that the object wasn't a hallucination.

"Yes," Dawson confirmed numbly. "I see it, too."

Silence reigned as they struggled to absorb what lay before them.

Dawson moved to the tables that lined the walls. On closer inspection, Adam could see that here, too, were artifacts that should not exist in the bowels of an ancient Central American temple. He saw, carefully crafted in gold, devices that looked eerily similar to things he might have found in the observatory at Cambridge. But not all these models were as perfect as the pendulum. There was something that looked like a gyroscope at first glance, but a closer inspection showed him that it couldn't possibly function.

It was as if someone had seen a gyroscope in operation and attempted to re-create it from memory without any real knowledge of how it worked or even what it was.

It made his skin crawl, a sensation that was not improved by turning from the tables to study the paintings that covered the walls.

The artistry was magnificent, the figures depicted both mythically enlarged and yet powerfully human. The work was also startlingly well preserved, making it seem as though it had been brushed onto the plaster the day before.

The paintings were divided into scenes, forming a series—a series about which there was something unsettlingly familiar.

In the first panel, a group of people, primitively dressed, watched a flaming object descend from the sky. In the next, the same group stood around a circle painted deeply black. Waving lines of blue-gray smoke rose from its surface, coming together to form the image of the god of the city, a figure that was somehow both grotesque and glorious. The people who surrounded the god held up their hands as though in offering. Each cupped a small red pool that Adam suspected must represent blood.

It was not an unexpected theme. Both the Mayan and Aztec cultures had included elaborate rituals of sacrifice. Their gods demanded blood—the blood of conquered enemies, criminals, or the innocent—in exchange for boons, including the gift of prophecy.

Small red droplets fell from the cupped, outstretched hands, landing on the dark circle beneath them.

More scenes followed, illustrating the story of the rise of the city, the building of its temples and palaces. But it was a panel from near the end of this visual narrative that caught Adam's eye most powerfully.

In that scene, the people of the city had grown great, as was evidenced by their bewilderingly elaborate finery and the massive size with which they were depicted. They held court over the huddled forms of a few primitive tribes, offering them gifts—a tongue of bright orange flame, a bolt of lightning, weapons, and the glyphs of a written language.

This was it, he realized. He was looking at the story of Tulan Zuyua, as told from the other side. The primitive clans came to seek magic and wisdom from a people who, to them, must have seemed like gods. The image could have been taken straight out of the Popol Vuh.

He was looking at corroboration. The clear evidence that the tale the Mayans told of their movement from primitive tribe to brilliant and powerful civilization was not a myth. It was fact. And he was standing in the heart of it.

The realization nearly brought him to the floor.

Dawson's voice cut through, breaking the spell.

"It's not here," he announced.

"Huh?" Adam was incapable of giving a more intelligent answer, his brain still consumed by the epiphany.

"The mirror isn't here," Dawson elaborated, frustrated. "There must be another chamber somewhere."

Adam involuntarily turned his gaze to the painting directly opposite the entrance to the room. It was the image of the city's dark, grinning god, wreathed in smoke and framed by the painted outline of what looked very much like a doorway.

There was something huddled at the foot of it, something that at first glance had looked like a pile of dried sticks and debris. But as he moved closer, Dawson stepping quickly after him, he realized he was looking not at a bit of refuse but at the remains of a human being.

The dry air of the room had worked to virtually mummify the corpse, turning the skin to brittle brown leather and beautifully preserving its elaborate wardrobe. The robe was made of jaguar hide trimmed with vibrant macaw feathers. The ground beneath the body was scattered with tiles of jade and gold, the cords that had once bound them rotted away long ago. The shaft of a shining obsidian blade protruded from the relic's chest, still clasped in a withered brown spider of a hand.

Dawson ignored the fallen form, moving immediately to the painted frame. He ran his hands along it urgently.

"There must be some way to open it."

Adam looked up from where he had crouched on the floor, examining the desiccated figure.

"I don't see any sort of seam or junction."

"It must be there," Dawson insisted stubbornly. "Why else would they paint a doorway unless it held a door?"

Might as well ask why they painted anything at all, Adam thought irritably, but kept it to himself. He was detecting a touch of desperation about Dawson that made him seem a bit unsteady. It brought Adam's awareness back to exactly how vulnerable his situation was. The wonder of the discovery had almost pushed it from his mind, made him forget that he was a hostage here. And not the only hostage.

Ellie. It was up to him to get her out of this. And at the moment, he hadn't the slightest idea how he was going to do it.

⁓

Ellie sat on a stone block, hands bound, and thought of everything she'd rather be doing. Velegas had the men busy establishing the camp. There was a particular urgency to the business. Since their arrival in the city, the clouds overhead had grown thicker, bringing a premature darkness and a heavy stillness ripe with the promise of moisture.

The rains were coming.

The plaza before her, the one from her dreams, was one of the few parts of the city not broken by the thick trunks of ancient trees or covered in crawling tendrils of greenery. Outside the wide rectangle of neat, close-laid paving stones, jungle and ruin melded together, the bush creeping in across the tumbled stones of promenades and palaces. Ellie could see lights flickering through the trees and pillars. Jacobs had posted patrols of armed guards as soon as they'd arrived. They were another complication, but one she couldn't be entirely unhappy with. The memory of the slaughter she'd stumbled across the night before was still fresh in her mind.

She'd seen no resumption of the normal animal life of the jungle here in the ruins. There were only insects and small, bright birds, which meant this probably wasn't foreign territory for whatever predator had stalked them on the road here. While the armed men would make escape more difficult, they would also, she hoped, keep her from being picked off while she sat on an overturned altar, bound and helpless.

While the rest of the men cleared brush and strapped down tents and equipment, she knew Dawson had taken Adam straight to the top of the tallest temple in the complex. She could see the glow of lamplight from its entrance. Dawson would be looking for the Smoking Mirror, and as soon as he found it, both she and Adam would become expendable.

Whatever he had promised before, Ellie couldn't wait for Adam to come to the rescue. There was no telling when Dawson would give him a chance to slip away. Even if he did have an opportunity, would he recognize it? Or would he be too caught up in the thrill and mystery of the discovery that surrounded them to remember the danger?

She could sympathize. Even now, she was fighting the temptation to examine the fallen stelae cluttering the courtyard, or to delve into the dark spaces between the columns of the palaces. This place was a brilliantly enticing conundrum. Not Mayan, but something else—the stronghold of a new civilization, or a very old one.

If she and Adam got out of this alive, they could come back. Dawson and Jacobs couldn't excavate or even properly loot the city in the middle of the rains. The weather would force them out, and by then Adam could have alerted the authorities. There would be no trouble securing government aid to protect such a monumental find. They would have all the time in the world to uncover the city's secrets—later.

In the meantime, the excitement of the ruins and the threat of the rains would work in her favor. Both were sure to be distracting to the guards. All she needed was the right moment and she would find a way to disappear.

Doing it armed would be nice, she thought grimly, remembering the screams and the blood. Preferably very well armed.

As though the thought had slipped out into reality, the evening silence was shattered by a sharp, panicked cry. Ellie looked to Flowers, who stood a short distance away, hands clenched on his rifle.

He read her expression and sighed.

"After you," he said, and Ellie ran toward the source of the sound, the big man trotting behind her.

The commotion was centered on a long, low building that lined the far side of the courtyard. Rows of pillars framed the opening to dark rooms, and the bush rose up thick behind it, a backdrop of shadowy trees and falling creepers. As Ellie and Flowers arrived, a wide-eyed workman was stammering to Velegas, gesturing frantically toward one of the doorways.

Ellie shouldered through the crowd to the opening, then felt her hair rise at the scene revealed by the lantern light.

The room was narrow, deep, and packed to the ceiling with bones. She caught the odd glimmer of gold or jade shining back at her, hidden among skulls of all sizes, from those of full-grown men to the delicate bones of children.

The dream came back to her, vivid and brutal: the bodies strewn by the roadside and piled in the courtyard, covered in sores or bleeding from knife wounds. The author of the map said that the city had fallen and was ripe for the taking. He had not said how, but Ellie *knew*.

There had been a plague. Smallpox, she thought, remembering the look of the scars and sores in her dream. Panic led to war. They had torn themselves apart. There would have been no time to bury the dead, only to pile the bodies wherever they could.

How? she thought, stumbling back. How had she known this? Another lucky guess of her dreaming mind?

No. It was something more. She had been *shown*.

But why?

Fear forced bile into her throat. She pushed back the instinct to panic and run.

Run, yes.

Grasping at clarity, she looked at the faces around her, all of them transfixed by either horror or greed at the sight of that mountain of bones and gold. This was her chance.

She stumbled back, feigning illness. The crowd parted to let her by. As she reached the back of it, she glanced over the dark, bobbing heads to Flowers, who was just turning as he realized that she had gone.

Sorry, she mouthed, then darted into the shadows.

The shout of alarm was delayed only a moment, but it was all the head start she needed. The gloom had become thick and the brush that grew over the fallen stones of the city was ideal camouflage. It was also treacherous, as she discovered while stumbling over roots and ruined pathways. She heard voices and crashing footsteps behind her, and she glanced back to see the bouncing lanterns of her pursuers closer than she would have liked.

She quickened her pace until a broken pot shattered under her foot and sent her sprawling. She bit back a curse and crawled to her knees. Fumbling with her bound hands, she managed to grab one of the larger remnants of the artifact and, with a silent apology to her own archaeological instincts, threw it as far as she could into the trees, where it shattered noisily. Then she slid down into an open cellar hole beside the place where she had fallen, pushing flat against the ground.

She could hear her pursuers shouting as they moved farther into the jungle, following the sound of the crash. Once they were far enough away, she crawled from her hiding place and slipped along the edge of the ruined structures until she found an opening to duck into. Something cracked and crunched under her feet as she moved inside, and she felt momentarily grateful that she didn't have a lantern. The whole damned city was a graveyard.

She fumbled with her belt and trousers, loosening them at last and pulling out Adam's secreted knife. She crouched down, bracing the knife between her knees and sawing at the ropes until at last the tension gave and she shook herself loose of them. Her unused muscles screamed, joints cracking as she stretched.

She kicked the frayed pile back into the chamber and made a silent, emphatic vow that she would never let someone tie her up again.

Free, she quickly adjusted her clothing, then crept back to the doorway. She could just see the glow of the campfires flickering among the tents of the camp. Steeling herself, she began picking her way as quietly as possible toward her next goal.

It was beginning to make sense—a terrible sort of sense that made Dawson feel queasy and weak, one that his brain struggled to accept. But the evidence was clear and undeniable, hanging behind him from the peak of the ceiling. It was scattered across the tables that lined the walls. This city had clearly been abandoned for centuries, yet some of the objects contained within this secret place in its heart were modern by his own standards.

They should not be here. And yet they were, and the reason for that stared at him from the murals painted on the walls. A black disk, emitting waving lines of smoke that framed the form of a deity of prophecy.

The Smoking Mirror. It was no myth. It was real, as physical as he was, and it was here, somewhere in this city—in this temple.

He accepted it. How could he deny it? Well—perhaps the way he'd denied everything else, all the other pieces of the puzzle that were now, grandly and terrifyingly, falling into place. How had he blinded himself to it for so long? Perhaps his decades of academic training had actually closed his mind, narrowed its perception to what the god Science deemed acceptable. He had refused to see the common link that bound the various objects he had been ordered to study, thinking them the whims of some anonymous eccentric.

But though they crossed cultures and millennia, they did share a common theme.

Power. Everything Dawson's employer had demanded he research was an object purported to possess unnatural power.

That was the thread that wove all of it together, the secret of his master's obsession. Regardless of culture or era, material or origin, he sought artifacts purported to hold extraordinary—even supernatural—power.

The Cauldron of Ceridwen that raised dead warriors back to life again. The bones of an obscure saint believed to cure insanity. The Ring of Solomon that gave its possessor dominion over the nations of the djinn.

That roughly shaped clay in a forgotten tomb in Ostrask that some believed to be the remains of a golem.

Ostrask.

To Dawson, it had been a mere curiosity. The people of the village had believed differently. Of course, Dawson doubted any of them knew the story of Rabbi Eleazar and how he shaped a servant from the raw earth, infusing it with life and inhuman strength that it might protect his people from persecution. They didn't care what the books said, or neglected to say. Their more primitive minds recognized that the thing was an abomination, and they sought to destroy it before it could destroy them.

Damned superstition, Dawson had thought at the time. But then, to him, the artifact, which only barely resembled a human form, like something a child would make out of sand, was a mere curiosity. A fascinating example of a long-dead piece of Hebrew folklore. That the people of Ostrask saw it as a threat had seemed to him a mere inconvenience. That is, until they arrived at the excavation site carrying picks, axes, and torches, vowing that they would not leave until they had destroyed the rabbi's creation.

The scene was seared into his memory. The villagers, perhaps thirty of them—a group that represented nearly every able-bodied male—gathered at the border of their camp, torchlight accentuating the terror in their expressions. Jacobs standing before them, seemingly unperturbed, as though the mob were an everyday occurrence barely worth his attention.

The leader had demanded they turn over the golem. He said if they did not, then they would force their way into the camp and take it. Either way, the thing would be destroyed.

Jacobs had not answered. He had merely watched with perfect calm as the men before him worked themselves up into a holy outrage.

Who is Jacobs? Dawson had often wondered. A half-caste of some sort, that was his best guess, but of what background he could not begin to say. He had heard the man speak Romanian like a native. His Arabic and Greek were likewise flawless, and Dawson was certain he understood everything the men of this expedition said to one another in their various dialects of Spanish and Creole.

Dawson did not know his first name. He had no idea where he lived. His accent revealed nothing. He could not possibly be educated, yet Dawson had learned not to underestimate either his intelligence or his knowledge. Where he had come from was as obscure to Dawson as the name and nature of their employer, a mystery he was not altogether certain he wanted to solve.

As the men of Ostrask prepared to attack what they saw as a piece of the devil's work, the cold night air was broken by the sound of sobs and cries. Around the ridge that separated the camp from the village came the rest of the population of Ostrask—the wives and children of the men who threatened the excavation. They were herded by the roughest of the men Jacobs had hired, who pushed them on with the barrels of their rifles.

How Dawson remembered the sight. The women, lovely and terrified with their dark hair loose about their faces, some in their nightclothes with infants clutched to their breasts. The children clinging to their skirts, eyes wide with fear.

The shouting of the men had died away, the echoes fading off the surrounding mountainsides. By the time the huddled group arrived at the camp, all was silent except for the crackling of their torches.

They would have left, even then. Dawson had seen it in their eyes, how the fury they had worked themselves into was snuffed out like a candle by the sight of their loved ones, barefoot and vulnerable before those harsh-faced mercenaries. All Jacobs would have had to do was say the word, and they would have been gone.

But he did not order them home. He lifted the revolver at his side, pointed it into the group, and fired.

He had barely glanced in their direction, but his aim was flawless. Three of the women went down, as well as a boy who could not have been more than twelve. Then he shifted and, without so much as a moment of hesitation, put a bullet through the forehead of the ringleader of the mob, the man who, a few moments before, had been exhorting them to action.

He had fallen to the ground with a sound like a dropped sack of wheat. Dawson had heard it clearly, because there had been no other sound in that desolate place. No screams. No outrage. Even the children seemed to have sensed that to cry out was to risk making themselves the next target.

On the ground, beside the fallen body of its mother, an infant began to wail. Beside it stood an old woman, twisted with age like a piece of driftwood.

"*Dybbuk*," she said, pointing at Jacobs. She spit on the ground.

Then, as though all of them had simultaneously sensed some kind of subconscious dismissal, they fled, men and women both. They had run down the mountainside as though hell itself pursued them. When Dawson had passed through the village the next day, as they carried off the artifact carefully packed into a wooden crate, the place was empty save a few lean, half-starved dogs. They had gone, all of them, deserted the place they had called home for who knew how many generations.

Dybbuk, the old woman had called him. Devil. Well, men could certainly be devils when they chose, and that night Dawson had seen just how easily Jacobs could put his humanity aside.

And for what? A misshapen lump of clay. A curiosity. Or so he had thought at the time, sickened with the violence he had seen, and with something more—the knowledge of his own reaction.

He had stood by and done nothing. Said nothing as those people had died. He had remained silent throughout an atrocity, consumed by a fear for his own skin.

It had become something of a habit lately, ever since Edinburgh.

Dawson had deserved the gallows.

He remembered that night in Saint Andrews. He had been dizzy as he walked up the stairs to his elegant town house. How had he gotten so drunk? He had gone from a faculty event to a tavern near the university, a disreputable place favored by some of the younger professors. There, he had topped off the brandy he had been sipping at the meeting with two, maybe three glasses of whiskey. It hadn't seemed like too much, but he knew, as his feet stumbled on the steps, that he must be drunk.

He had played the scene out so many times in his mind. He must have been silent coming in, though how that was possible when he was swaying on his feet, Dawson couldn't say. But when he climbed the stairs to the upper floor, the man still lay in the arms of his wife, just as the stranger in the tavern had warned him.

I know you don't know me from Cain, Professor, but as one honest fellow to another...

The dark form had fled, climbing nimbly out the open window. Anne had lain there, mumbling some sleepy, incomprehensible endearment, as though wondering where her lover had gone.

The rage had come in so quickly. One moment he was feeling vaguely ill. In the next, fury filled him, hot and violent. It had been a sort of madness. There was no decision, no rational choice. He had leaped on her like a beast, clamping his hands around her throat.

Dawson had loved her once. She had been lovely, privileged, the daughter of a wealthy factory owner. That she returned his affections had come as a surprise, one he hardly believed.

He wasn't sure what killed it. Perhaps her childlessness. Perhaps it was merely ennui, or the patient accumulation of slights and resentments. But while Dawson knew the decline of his marriage brought feelings of disappointment, boredom, and occasional frustration, it had never really angered him. Anger required passion, and his passion for Anne had burned out years before.

He could remember how the soft flesh of her neck had given way under his fingers. Her eyes looked up at him, thick as though with sleep, her expression one of confusion, then fear, then desperation as she clawed at his arms, mouth gaping like that of a fish pulled up onto the riverbank.

Then she had slipped away. The hands went limp, the eyes vacant, and as the hot fury faded into ash, Dawson looked down and realized what he had done.

Why? Why had he done it? Where had that snarling ferocity come from? Did it really take so little as a bit of drunkenness and an unfaithful wife to turn him into things out of a nightmare?

He should have hanged for it. His guilt was as real and solid as the stones he walked upon. But when offered the chance to live, he had snatched at it as greedily as any beggar. He was still snatching at it now, as he stood before the false doorway in this impossible chamber.

The Smoking Mirror was real.

He had been sent here to retrieve it for a man whose name he did not know, a man who plucked murderers from their just punishment, who did not scruple to hire monsters to achieve his ends. A man whose obsession with powers only gods should possess inspired him to every extravagance, from fixing courtrooms to slaughtering children.

Somewhere in this ruin lay an object that could reveal the technology of the future—and perhaps more. The myth of the Smoking Mirror was of a window into all of time and space. The past, the present, and the future, laid out like sweets on a table.

Every shred of Dawson's remaining decency screamed against letting such a device fall into the hands of a man like his employer. He could not begin to imagine the use to which it would be put, but anything wanted so badly by such a man could not be meant for good.

It didn't matter.

He would go through with it. Dawson knew what the cost of failure would be. That was, of course, why Jacobs had been sent here with him. If Dawson wavered in his duty, Jacobs would see things done.

And Dawson would die.

His life was all he had left. Everything else had died in that room in Saint Andrews, or later, in the filth of an Edinburgh jail, when he had sold out the last fragments of his humanity for a few more years of breath.

He could have spoken up in Ostrask. He might have tried

to stop that loss of innocent life. He had remained silent, afraid to draw one of Jacobs's bullets. And if he could go back to that moment—he would do the same thing again, without a moment's hesitation.

Dawson would find the mirror and deliver it to the ruthless bastard who owned him, regardless of the consequences. He had bought his life dearly, and he meant to keep it, whatever the cost.

Ellie crouched in the darkness at the edge of the camp, making a careful assessment of the scene in front of her. She could hear cries in the distance, the sound of Jacobs's men searching for her. They had fanned out, probing the farther reaches of the ruins. She could see their torches flickering in the distance like will-o'-the-wisps over the moor. No one thought to look for her here, back at the very heart of the camp, which meant getting where she wanted to go would take far less luck than she'd anticipated.

Ellie crept around the perimeter. Using the crates and stacked supplies for cover, she worked her way toward Dawson's tent.

She looked up. A flicker of lightning illuminated a massive spread of thick, dark clouds.

Beside her, the mules shifted in their paddock, braying nervously. They could sense the tension in the atmosphere, the uneasy stillness before the storm.

Ellie waited, tense and silent, as a pair of drovers approached, talking in low voices, then moved by. With a silent prayer to whatever gods might be listening, she dashed across the remaining open space and slipped into the tent.

Moving quickly and quietly, she made her way to the field desk, which sat to the side by a pile of trunks.

She took Adam's knife out of her pocket and held it to the lock of the drawer. She paused, listening carefully for any indication of men passing by outside. Hearing only silence, she hefted a paperweight from the desk and hammered the blade into the lock. It gave, splintering the frame.

She didn't care whether anyone noticed now. By the time they did, she planned to be long gone.

Ellie moved to yank the drawer open, then stopped at the sound of voices outside the tent. She quickly shifted the books on top of the desk to disguise the damage, then ducked behind the pile of trunks just as Jacobs entered the room.

She peered at him through a slight gap in her hiding place. One of his men followed him.

"And when they find her, do you want her returned to camp?" he asked.

"When they find her, I want her shot," Jacobs replied.

It was so matter-of-fact, so utterly without drama, that Ellie nearly missed the import of Jacobs's words.

"But the professor—"

"Only cares about her companion's cooperation. There are other ways to secure that."

Ellie pressed herself back as Jacobs approached her hiding place, but he merely lifted a sack of gear from beside the desk.

"This is what Velegas was looking for. See that he gets it."

"Yes, *jefe*."

The man left, but Ellie caught back her sigh of relief as Jacobs stopped in the doorway.

He turned like a predator suddenly scenting a rabbit, dark eyes surveying the room coldly. They stopped at the desk. Ellie pulled herself back from the small gap, trying to shrink into the trunks themselves.

He stepped forward, and she tightened her grip on the bent knife in her hand. Her hands were sweating, the hilt slipping under her fingers. She felt frantically aware of how useless the weapon would be. But what else was there?

If she could reach the drawer of the desk...

But any movement, even the slightest rustle of her clothing, would draw him like a bloodhound.

If he took another step, moved any closer, then she would have no choice. She just hoped to hell she could move quickly enough.

Another voice called from outside. Jacobs hesitated.

Then, abruptly, he turned and answered, pushing through the flap and leaving her.

She let out a shaking breath, slumping against the trunks. The tone of his voice when he had spoken of killing her had been so easy, as though he were speaking of eliminating a stray cat. And what he'd said about Adam...

The professor only cares about her companion's cooperation. There are other ways to secure that.

The game that had kept them alive for the past few days had apparently changed.

She slipped from her hiding place and returned to the desk, pushing back the books and yanking open the drawer. She shoved the papers aside but felt nothing but the rough wood of the drawer itself, no solid weight of heavy steel.

She pulled the drawer out entirely and dumped the contents onto the floor, but there could be no doubt. The revolver she had seen before was gone.

Adam fought against a rising sense of irritation. Dawson's fixation with the door was getting on his nerves. He had been studying the mural for what felt like the better part of an hour, refusing to acknowledge that there were simply no signs that the painting was anything more than decorative.

The exhaustion and constant tension of knowing that his time was running out certainly weren't helping matters. But he couldn't afford to snap at the man, no matter how justified it might be. He had to stay on Dawson's good side, at least for a few more hours.

"This isn't the sort of problem we can solve tonight. Why don't we go down, finish setting up camp? We can come back and try again in the morning."

Dawson didn't answer. He was staring at the mural, the dust accentuating the dark circles under his eyes.

"If it isn't here, it could be anywhere in the city," he muttered.

"So we keep looking. We've got plenty of time."

Dawson was afraid, Adam realized. But of whom? Jacobs? Or whomever it was who had put this whole business into motion, the mysterious employer with a lust for a mythical mirror?

Dawson opened his eyes, studying the panel again. A new light seemed to come into them.

"What if they walled it up?" he mused aloud.

The notion energized him. He hurried to his bag of gear and pulled out a hammer and chisel, then lifted them to the painted wall.

Shock delayed Adam's movement as he realized that Dawson was about to knock a hole through a piece of history.

"What the hell are you doing?"

"It could just be facing, or maybe a layer of fill plastered over. Before we search anywhere else, we should make certain it isn't here," Dawson retorted stubbornly.

He moved forward. Adam blocked him.

"This mural is priceless."

"Can't you feel it? The rains are coming," Dawson snapped. "We'll be forced to leave before the trail is impassable, and by the time we return this place will have been looted. You really think they'll be scrupulous about a few paintings?"

Dawson's reasoning made him pause, but only for a moment. The city had protected its secrets for centuries. It could keep them for another few months. And that was only if there was no other way to secure the room.

He'd seen too many monuments destroyed by men bent on finding treasure. He'd be damned if he'd stand by and watch this miraculously preserved place fall to the same fate.

He crossed his arms.

"You're not doing this."

Dawson reddened.

"This is what you agreed to."

"I don't recall actually agreeing to anything," Adam drawled in reply.

So much for cooperation, he thought distantly. The game was officially blown.

And all for a damned mural.

You really are a pigheaded bastard sometimes, Bates.

He would be able to get past Dawson. The man was no fighter. Then he would need to find Ellie, fast, and get them both out of here. Make their way back to Belize City and alert the powers-that-be. They might turn a blind eye to many of the colony's shadier activities, but the whole world would be watching once word of this find got out. And Adam would make certain that it did.

It wouldn't save the mural. Dawson would tear that to pieces the minute he got the chance. Adam could see the fear in the man so clearly, he wondered how he had missed it before.

The mural would fall, but at least Adam wouldn't have to stand by and watch it happen.

Dawson tossed the hammer and chisel aside and Adam felt a burst of triumph. It faded quickly as the professor reached into his coat pocket and produced a revolver. He leveled it at Adam's chest.

His grip on the weapon was white-knuckled. Adam absorbed that along with the tenseness of his frame and his determined expression. It wasn't the easy pose of a bluffer. Dawson held the gun like a desperate man, and they were the ones prone to pulling triggers.

"We are going to go up the stairway together. When we get to the top, I am going to call for Mr. Jacobs, and you are going to remain still until he arrives. Is that clear?"

"Perfectly," Adam said grimly, barely containing the urge to charge at him.

Not yet.

His mind churned. He had no doubt what Jacobs's solution would be to the problem he posed. The man would kill him without a second thought, and without his knowledge as a bargaining chip...

Ellie would be no use to them anymore, which made her as good as dead as well. And he'd be damned if he'd let that happen.

Dawson kept the gun on him as they made the long trek back up the twisting staircase and through the tunnel to the narrow sanctuary at the top of the temple. Once there, he pointed his free hand at the bearer who had watched them emerge, wide-eyed.

"Fetch Mr. Jacobs. *Now,*" he added sharply when the man hesitated, turning slightly to give the order.

It would probably be his only chance—and there was only one thing close enough to serve as a weapon.

Wincing inwardly, Adam grabbed one of the beautifully painted, miraculously intact vases, and shattered it across Dawson's skull.

He stumbled back, half falling to the ground. As Adam leaped toward him, Dawson pulled the revolver around and fired.

19

THE BULLET PINGED OFF the ceiling of the chamber, sending chips of stone raining down on the pair of them. Adam moved quickly, knowing he had only a moment before Dawson chambered another round. He threw himself at him, knocking him into the wall. Dawson pushed back, fighting for space to bring the gun to bear.

They grappled, locked like wrestlers, until a sharp, ringing blow to the back of his head sent Adam reeling.

He turned to see the porter drop a shovel and dash out the doorway. He half tumbled down the temple steps, crying out to those below.

The blow threatened to fog Adam's brain. He forced it to clear, whirling to confront Dawson once more, but his opponent had not let the advantage pass. He stood with the revolver leveled, blood streaming down his face from a wound on his forehead where the vase had struck.

"Turn around," he said.

Adam obeyed, standing in the doorway. The brilliant flash of lightning brightened the purple clouds and cast a ghastly illumination over the ruins. A storm was brewing in the darkness overhead.

"You ever killed anyone?" Adam demanded, the boldness of his tone belying the sinking dread in his stomach: dread and guilt.

He had told her to trust him. That he would get her out of this. How would he do that if he was dead?

"Yes," Dawson replied.

It was not the answer Adam had been expecting. The man was a college professor, not some hardened mercenary, whoever he might be spending his time with now. An experienced killer wouldn't have that same look of terror and desperation on his face, and he wouldn't be holding the gun like a life raft.

He had to find a way to get him talking. If he could distract him, get him to let his guard down for just a few seconds...

"Are you really going to do it again for some artifact? Do you want that kind of blood on your hands?"

"It's more than just an artifact. You saw that room. Those tables were covered with pieces of modern technology," Dawson countered harshly. "Objects that the people of this city could not possibly have known about by any natural means."

"I'll admit, it's a hell of a coincidence—" Adam began.

Dawson cut him off.

"Coincidence? Foucault's pendulum in an ancient Central American temple is a coincidence?"

Adam could hear the edge of wildness in his tone. The man was stretched near to breaking.

"What else could it be?" Adam demanded, trying to keep him talking. But Dawson's reply almost distracted him from his own strategy.

"The Smoking Mirror."

"That's a myth."

"It is also the only possible explanation," Dawson retorted.

This is insane.

That the Smoking Mirror might exist as a ritual object he could allow. After all, legends and myths often had their roots in truth. It was possible the people of this city had possessed an actual mirror that became the center of wild religious associations. There were plenty of people who convinced themselves they could be miraculously healed by touching splinters of the "True Cross," likely broken off of someone's discarded coffee table.

But that the mirror actually worked—that it made it possible to see into the past or future, to know what was happening on the other side of the world, or what would be in centuries to come—was beyond belief.

There had to be another explanation. And however far-fetched it was, it'd still be better than suggesting that the people of this city had spied on modern museums through some piece of polished glass possessing magical powers.

He was getting distracted. Jacobs would be here before long. If he was going to get out of this, and stand a chance at saving Ellie, he needed to act.

He started to turn, and his eye fell on the shovel lying on the ground between him and Dawson. His head still smarted from where the porter had struck him with it during their fight. Dawson would expect Adam to run. If instead he moved toward him . . . he could grab the shovel as he rushed, get in before Dawson thought to pull the trigger.

Now or never, Bates.

He whirled, getting ready to leap, but stopped as he saw the gun droop in Dawson's hand.

"All the way to the floor, please," Ellie said calmly. A knife was in her hand, pressed against Dawson's throat. The blade was bent, but still sharp enough to prick his skin.

He obeyed, dropping the gun. Ellie kicked it over to where Adam stood. He bent down and retrieved it. Questions warred for precedence in his brain.

"What are you doing here?"

"I heard a gunshot. I figured it must have been aimed at you." She moved to his side as Adam covered Dawson with the gun. "Are you hurt?"

"I'm fine."

For a moment, Adam thought she was about to check for herself. The look in her eyes was both skeptical and worried. Instead, she stepped back.

"Well. That's good," she said stiffly.

He drank in the sight of her. She had lost her jacket somewhere along the way, but apart from a few scratches, dirt, and a leaf stuck in her hair, she seemed to be intact. The thought filled him with relief.

He should have known better than to think she would be helplessly waiting for his arrival. He glanced down at the battered knife in her hand. What exactly had she been up to?

There would be time to find out later.

As if to punctuate the thought, a gunshot cracked against the stones beside them. Dawson dived to the ground. Adam pushed Ellie to the side, behind the pillars that framed the entrance to the sanctuary. Keeping her behind him, he peered down the temple stairs.

Jacobs stood below, rifle balanced on his shoulder as he took expert aim. Adam ducked back just as another shot sent shards of stone splintering down on them.

"Got any suggestions?" he asked, his back pinning Ellie to the wall.

"Always," she replied pertly, pushing herself free of him and quickly adjusting her clothes. "This way."

She led him to the window cut into the stone of the rear of the chamber.

"He will find you," Dawson called over from where he crouched by the wall. He winced as another bullet pinged off the ceiling. "I suspect he'll enjoy it."

"Let's go," Ellie urged him, and Adam followed her through the window.

The back of the pyramid had no staircase, only massive shelves of stone making up its steps, some half-tumbled into rubble. It looked treacherous in the darkness, and probably was, though Ellie had scaled it quickly enough the first time. Of course, then she had been hurried by the fear of what she'd find when she reached the top.

It had taken her only a few minutes to run to the temple after she heard the gunshot, but her imagination had used them fruitfully.

The silence from above her as she climbed had been terrible, filled with visions of Adam bleeding to death on the floor.

What she had found at the summit was hardly better—him, unarmed and vulnerable, staring down the barrel of Dawson's gun.

If she had been a minute longer, she could have lost him.

The thought made her hands shake.

Almost equally disturbing was the memory of what she'd nearly done once she did save him. She had barely been able to resist the overwhelming, instinctive impulse to throw her arms around him.

It was all terribly confusing—and now was hardly the time to try to sort it out.

"Follow me," she ordered, and began scrambling down the steep faces of the stones until she finally hopped to the ground. An uneasy wind, ripe with the promise of moisture, stirred the dry leaves at her feet as Adam joined her. Thunder rumbled low through the darkness around them, and was then punctuated by more shots pelting them from above.

"Move," Adam ordered, shoving her forward.

They raced along the base of the temple, and Ellie cursed the skill of the city's ancient builders. The paving stones of the temple district had been laid with elegant precision, blocking the overgrowth that had crept over so much of the rest of the ruins. The only cover Ellie could see were the crumbling walls and buildings, and they were uncomfortably far away.

A stone by her feet suddenly cracked, chips of it stinging against her ankle. Another crack sounded to her left, and she saw a small explosion of white shards rise from the ground.

She jumped, dodging to the side.

"How far till we're out of range?"

"Just keep running," Adam ordered, grabbing her arm and hauling her into a sprint.

They bolted across the open courtyard, shots pinging off the stones around them. Voices rose from behind, shouts of alarm that Ellie knew meant the whole camp was being roused against them.

The courtyard ended in a low wall. Ellie mounted it, then hesitated. Below her, the ground was precipitously far away.

Adam turned, grasping the edge of the wall and dropping down to the stones below. He landed with the grace of a cat, then held up his arms.

"Jump."

"You can't possibly expect to catch—"

"*Now*, princess."

The wall six inches from her thigh exploded under the impact of another round.

Ellie leaped.

The rush of empty air was replaced by the grip of strong, solid flesh as Adam caught her. The warmth of the accidental embrace shocked her to silence.

Then her feet were on the ground, and Adam shoved her into motion.

"*Go.*"

The brush had succeeded in encroaching on this lower level of the city. Leaves and branches whipped against Ellie's skin as she stumbled over the uneven paving stones.

She felt a bullet whiz past her ear, and Adam cursed behind her.

"Too close," he snapped. "Faster."

She burst out of the foliage with a snapping of branches and found herself at the top of a crumbling stairway. A bright flash of lightning revealed the space in front of her. It was long and narrow, lined with steep walls more than twice her height. Tiered seats topped the walls, revealing it to be a sort of arena that Ellie recognized from her reading. It was a ball court, the playing field for the ancient American game of war and sacrifice.

She had seen them only in illustrations. The real thing was far more impressive.

On the far side, the jungle loomed, thick and mysterious. They would be able to disappear there—if they could reach it.

"Quickly," Adam ordered, pushing her into motion. Ellie obeyed, half tripping down the stairs.

She reached the surface of the ball court. The flat, even stones were mostly obscured by years of drifting, rotted leaves, slippery with moss. Sharp calls resounding off the stones told her that their pursuers were not far behind. She pushed for more speed, knowing just how vulnerable they would be, caught between the high walls of the court.

Then, with a brittle crack, the ground gave way.

Ellie reached out frantically as she fell, fingers clutching desperately for the edge of the hole that had opened up beneath her. She succeeded in grasping it, stalling her drop. The material under her hands wasn't stone. It felt like thin wooden planking, buried under years of decaying leaves.

Like the cover of a well, she thought numbly as her legs swung helplessly over a deep, empty space.

She scrambled for a foothold but met nothing but air. The plank creaked ominously under her hand.

Then Adam was there, rushing toward the fragile remains of the cover, the determined expression on his face telling her exactly what he intended to do.

"Stay back!" she protested. Then the wood under her hands shifted, tipping precariously. Ellie closed her eyes as she was showered with a fall of mulch and splinters that brushed past her before vanishing into the gloom below.

What sounded like a soft, distant splashing echoed up from some untold depth beneath her.

She shifted her hands, trying to get a better grip on the plank. The wood creaked ominously, and then Adam was throwing himself across the camouflaged boards, flattened out and reaching.

"No, Bates!" she protested. "It's not—"

Her last word was swallowed in a shattering of wood as the fragile platform he lay on gave way and the pair of them plummeted into darkness.

20

SHE LANDED IN WATER. It swallowed her up like a stone, cold and utterly dark. She fought against the instinct to flail and instead let her buoyancy pull her up.

She broke through the surface and took in air with a deep, shuddering gasp. She looked around frantically, her eyes stubbornly slow to adjust to the deep gloom. She swam until she found the wall. The floor of the cavern was shallower there, enough so she could keep her head up without treading water. But the ground shifted and rolled beneath her feet as though covered in some unsteady rubble.

Bates. She had felt him fall with her, knew he must be down here. Her mind flashed through images of his body dashed against unseen rocks, or floating facedown and still somewhere in the darkness around her.

His name rose in her throat, but as she opened her mouth to cry out, a hand covered it, a powerful arm circling her waist and pulling her back.

"Quiet."

Adam's voice was little more than a murmur, hot against the back of her ear. She obeyed, going still, and tried to let her understandable relief at discovering he was intact distract her from the somewhat less comfortable awareness of how very nice it felt to be pulled tight against the firmness of his body.

He continued to hold her, both of them remaining as still and silent as possible as the sound of voices echoed down from the opening above.

"They fell in here, *jefe*."

"Get me a lantern."

There was a shuffling and Ellie looked up to see the opening overhead obscured by a dark form.

She noted the space between her and the distant silhouette. *It's so high.*

The figure pulled back and she heard more talk. A few pebbles were tossed down shortly after. They splashed into the water a few feet from where she and Adam hid. The droplets struck her face.

"Should we call for them?" one of the men above asked.

"He's not a fool." Jacobs's voice was clear, and Ellie sensed in the way his tones rang down that he was speaking as much for them as for his men. "If he is alive, he will stay there and hide rather than reveal himself and be shot."

His shadow moved back and Ellie let herself relax with relief. From Jacobs's last statement, it seemed clear that they were giving up.

She heard a sharp click, the sound echoing down the walls of the cave. Behind her, Adam stiffened, his grip tightening.

"Deep. Breath," he whispered harshly in her ear.

The urgency of his tone overrode her protest. She took in a quick gasp of air and, just as the first bullet cracked against the stone, Adam shoved her down into the water.

She could hear the muffled impact of the shots as Adam pulled her deeper. She felt a sharp sting on her arm as the bullets buzzed around them, a veritable swarm.

Ellie's lungs screamed for air, but Adam's arm was like iron around her, pinning her down. She fought against him but his grip only tightened.

At last, when she felt certain she could stand no more without opening her mouth to the cold water, she felt him push up, bringing them to the surface.

They broke through with a quiet splash that was of a kind with the impact of bits of rubble dropping into the pool around them, loosened by the barrage. Ellie gulped in air as quietly as she could.

She did not need Adam's warning grasp to remind her of the danger. The silence above them had to be deceptive.

It held for a few moments that felt like an eternity, then at last she heard a voice from above.

"I don't hear anything, *jefe*."

"If they were alive down there, that would have finished them," said another.

There was a pause and at last she heard Jacobs's voice.

"It will have to do. Get back to your assignments."

She heard the men moving away, but a single shadow lingered, gazing down into their hole. She felt grateful for the gloom.

At last, Jacobs, too, turned and left. Adam waited another minute, then loosened his hold on her. He turned her around in the water and pulled her to where the light from above shone faintly down onto the quietly rippling surface.

"Are you hurt?" he demanded.

"I don't think so. I— Ow!" she protested as Adam's fingers probed her arm. She looked down and saw a dark stain marking the spot he touched, near a small tear in her shirt.

"You're hit." His voice was oddly strangled.

"I barely felt it," she countered.

Adam put his fingers into the tear and ripped the fabric wide.

"What do you think you're—"

"Just a graze," he said, relieved.

He pulled his shirt off over his head and Ellie forgot to be annoyed. The sight of his bare torso did seem to have that rather inconvenient effect on her.

The impact lasted long enough to keep her silent as he tore a long strip out of the cloth, which he then wrapped firmly around the wound in her arm.

"We need to get you to one of the villages or a mission, someplace we can make sure that's clean."

"It's barely a scratch. And first we've got to find a way out of here. Where are we?"

Adam took a step, then grimaced. He dived down, returning

a moment later with something in his hand. It looked very much like a human femur. Ellie thought of the loose, rubbly feel of the floor below them and felt a chill.

"Is that what I think it is?"

Adam dropped the bone back into the water.

"We're in a cenote. It's a sort of natural well. The Maya thought they were sacred, made them centers of ritual activity. So did these people, apparently."

Ellie felt a twist in her stomach.

"Sacrifices?"

"Try not to think about it."

He began to circle the space, running his hands along the stone walls. The well itself was not wide, perhaps twenty feet in diameter. The walls that enclosed it were higher. To Ellie's eye, the stone sides looked worn and slick.

"Can we climb out?" she asked doubtfully.

"No," Adam admitted.

She looked around for anything that might suggest an alternative but saw only slippery stone and dark water.

"Then what do we do?"

Adam was quiet for a moment.

"I've got a couple of friends in the camp. If they hear what happened and think there's a chance we might still be alive, they'll try to find us."

"And if they don't?"

Adam didn't answer.

He didn't have to. The implication hovered around her in the slick, impossibly high walls and the rolling tumble of bones under her feet.

"I'm sorry," she blurted.

"It's not your fault you stepped on a booby trap."

"No. Not that. The rest of it. You never would have come here if it weren't for me. If I'd just..." She halted, her breath catching. "If I'd just been honest with you at the start about Dawson and Jacobs... if I'd trusted you with the whole of the map...You never would

have let them catch us. And even if you'd decided it wasn't worth
the trouble, at least you'd be safe now in your room at the Imperial,
drinking whiskey and smoking one of those dreadful cigars."

Ellie heard her voice break on those last few words, and realized with dawning horror that she was very possibly about to start
crying.

"Do you really think that's where I'd rather be right now?"

Adam's voice was almost disembodied in the darkness, his tone
ambiguously dark.

"At least you'd be alive, and not about to drown in some hole in
the ground."

There was a particularly mortifying quaver on the word "alive."
Ellie took a deep breath, refusing to dissolve into hysterics.

"I should have trusted you with all of it. Right from the beginning. I was wrong. And I'm sorry. I'm so very, very sorry."

She waited for a reply. And waited.

There was nothing, only silence and the ominous sloshing of
the water. It was worse than his recrimination would have been,
worse than the curt dismissal she deserved—that thick, humming, dreadful silence.

When he finally spoke, his voice came from perilously close by,
and Ellie realized that he had moved, coming to stand no more
than six inches away, a deeper shadow in the darkness.

"Say it again." His voice was a rumbling growl, coming from
deep in his chest.

"I'm sorry?" Ellie offered weakly, his nearness making her painfully unsure of herself.

"The other part."

She swallowed thickly.

"I was wrong."

Warm hands gripped the sides of her face, pulling her closer.
The hard, wet planes of his body were only a breath away from her
own, radiating heat and solid, barely contained strength.

"I. Don't. Care," he said, grinding out the words with startling
ferocity.

"You don't care that I lied to you? Bates, I deliberately misled you. I lied about the map, about Jacobs. . . . I didn't even tell you my name. How can you possibly say you don't—"

The last word was abruptly muffled as Adam pulled her to him and kissed her.

It was a thoroughly remarkable sensation. First there was the water, the strange buoyancy of it and how easy it made it for their bodies to meld together like pieces of a puzzle. Then there was the heat. Adam's body radiated it, from the hands running over her back to the whole long, muscular length of him pressed against her.

And she could not dismiss the potency of her own response. The pressure of his mouth, the taste of him and his raw, animal smell opened something inside her like the floodgates of a dam. She was filled with such a powerful *want* for an even deeper embrace, more heat, more skin, more of that delicious pressure that built inside her till it threatened to burst her apart.

"Dear God, that's lovely," she exclaimed when he freed her mouth to explore other regions.

"And about damned time," he growled against her ear as his teeth pulled at her lobe.

Something of the implication of his words managed to penetrate through the haze of bliss and desire obscuring her brain.

"You mean that you've been waiting for this?"

He pulled back and looked down at her. Lightning flickered overhead, and the light danced across his face. He was desperate, earnest, and more than a little lost.

"You really have no idea, do you?"

Words deserted her. Something else took their accustomed place: an awareness of feeling. It was deep and powerful, hopeless and ecstatic, and so complete, so unalterable, she wondered how she had ever managed to ignore it for so long.

"Oh, my," she said softly, and he embraced her with a new roughness, a fierce passion that she matched now, fueled by the startling epiphany of what she felt for him.

"This is not at all what I planned," she protested feebly as she clutched at his shoulders, her legs coming up around his waist.

"It wasn't exactly on my agenda, either," he retorted, his hands gripping at the seat of her trousers and bringing her even closer.

The explosion of *that* sensation threatened to overwhelm her reason entirely. But she clung to a last fleeting scrap of it like a drowning sailor as his mouth moved from her neck to her collarbone.

"Bates," she groaned, then snapped herself to attention and called more sharply, taking his head in her hands and forcing it back. "Bates! We have to get out of this!"

"I'm just getting started," he grumbled in reply, and returned his lips to their work at the skin revealed by the loosened buttons of her shirt.

"No, not *this*." She moaned, tangling her fingers in his hair. "The well. We've got to . . . can't just . . . Oh, bloody hell . . ."

She succumbed, that last fragment of rationality escaping like dandelion fluff on a spring breeze. She gave her mind over to the sheer pleasure of what he was doing to her, and the surrender felt like heaven.

Then he stopped.

"No. You're right." He pulled back from her. She nearly hauled him in again but mustered restraint as he gently tucked a curl of her cropped hair behind her ear.

"You're right," he repeated. He released his hold on her rear, and Ellie felt herself slide down off of him. "We have to find a way out of this. We can't bank on Charlie or the others coming to our rescue, and I'll be damned if I'm going to let you die in some god-forsaken hole in the ground. There will be plenty of time to finish what we've started once we're safe."

"Finish?" she echoed weakly, her brain still struggling to catch up.

"Oh, yeah," he replied, a dark and hungry note coming into his voice. "We're going to do a whole hell of a lot of finishing."

Adam very carefully set her at the edge of the water, where it was shallow enough to stand.

"Cenotes are wells," he said, moving farther out and exploring the space. "Ritual wells. Naturally formed. A depression in the bedrock. Usually limestone. Limestone…"

Her own focus was beginning to return, now that the immediate distraction of his touch was past. She found herself gazing at the water or, more precisely, at the slow movement of the debris of rotted wood and thatch slowly circling on its surface.

"Adam, this well has a current," she announced evenly.

"Wait here," he ordered. Then he dived down beneath the surface.

The water rippled at the place where he had vanished, then stilled. She felt a quickening of panic, the impulse rising to dive after him. Before she could succumb to it, he surfaced, grinning.

"Caves. Limestone means caves," he said, eyes bright. "There's a tunnel."

"We've got to try it."

"Not we," he countered.

She felt a rush of indignation. "I'm entirely capable—"

"Cave diving isn't like a swim in the pond. If you don't know what you're doing, it's a quick way to get yourself killed."

"And you know what you're doing?"

He answered with an eloquent look.

"I'll be back." He took a long, deep breath, then vanished once more beneath the surface.

Ellie waited—and continued waiting. Fear began to creep in. She held her own breath, testing, then let it out in a rush.

Too long, she thought.

She couldn't lose him. Not after just discovering what he meant to her.

She would go after him. It didn't matter what the risks were. She'd dive into that hole, and one way or another would find him. As to what she'd do then…well, she'd figure it out when the time came.

She took a deep breath, then another, and Adam surfaced in front of her with a splash.

"Where the devil have you been?"

"There's an opening," he said before she could castigate him any further. "It leads to some sort of cavern. It could be part of a larger system."

"A system with an exit?"

"Possibly," he cautioned.

"Well, possibly is better than waiting around here for a rescue that may not be coming."

"It's a long swim. There are a couple of pockets of air along the way. You'll have to follow my lead. And don't panic."

She stiffened.

"Have I given you any reason to think I am the type to panic?"

"You blew up a boat to get me to listen to you," he replied bluntly.

"That was not panic," she protested. "That was a perfectly logical strategy."

He didn't bother to respond.

"Deep breath. And stay with me."

She nodded. They inhaled deeply, then dropped under the water. She followed Adam's kicking feet down into the deep center of the cenote, then felt it—a gap in the stone, opening into a smooth-sided tunnel. She swam into it, following in Adam's wake.

The darkness was impenetrable and long. Her lungs began to ache for air. She forced herself to keep moving. Adam was swimming swiftly. She kicked furiously to keep up. At last, as the urge to inhale grew overwhelming, she felt a hand grab her shoulder and pull her up.

She broke the surface, and only Adam's grip on her arm kept her from hitting her head on the low ceiling. There were a mere six inches or so of space between water and rock. But the air tasted fresh, and she drank it gratefully.

"That was the worst one. Can you keep going?"

"Well, we can hardly reverse, can we?"

He grinned at her, then took another breath and dived.

They passed through two more air pockets, nearer than the first—and she had to wonder about that one. If it hadn't been there, how would Adam possibly have made it back to her? She would have to talk to him about that, once they were safe.

At last, the tunnel ended. They broke through the surface of a still lake. The space around her was lost in complete darkness, but Ellie could tell from the echoes of the rippling water that they had emerged in a larger cavern. Following the sound of Adam's splashing movements, she paddled forward until she felt solid ground beneath her feet. It sloped up, the water growing shallower until they found themselves on dry land.

It was hardly ideal, but it was still an improvement compared to treading water over a pile of bones.

Adam pressed a metal box into her hands.

"What's this?"

"My match tin. Open it—carefully. The striker is inside the lid. When I say, light one and look for anything at all that might serve to get a fire going."

Ellie fumbled with the box in the dark and got it open. Careful with her wet fingers, she plucked up one of the tiny slivers of wood.

"Ready."

"Do it."

The match hissed to life, and a flicker of light illuminated the space, just enough for her to see that the cavern was indeed vast. What lay at its edges was impossible to discern. All too quickly the flame burned down to her fingers, and she dropped it.

"Light another."

Ellie obeyed, and in the light saw Adam holding what looked like a resin-soaked torch.

"Where did you get that?"

"Are you going to light it or not?" he asked as the second match snuffed itself out on her fingers. Ellie muttered a curse.

It took a third match for it to catch. The torch flamed to life.

The basket stood beside them. It was made of woven branches and leather strapping, and inside was a bundle of torches. And beside the basket, something else.

Ellie bent down for a closer look. It was a small pile of flints, the sort used for starting fires. It was as though someone had put the whole arrangement there for them, anticipating their arrival.

It looked like they weren't the first ones to find this cave.

Adam handed Ellie his torch, then took another from the basket for himself. The combined glow cast a bit more light on their surroundings, and shimmered strangely off the floor of the cave.

Very strangely, as though the ground itself were moving.

Ellie took a step forward, then stopped as the flame caught more of the pitch and brightened, revealing what lay before them.

It wasn't the ground that was moving. It was a field of glittering black bodies, pouring into the space from every crevice of the walls. Scorpions—large ones, their tails dangerously curved.

❧

Adam pulled Ellie back into the lake, the water sloshing around their knees as the insects crawled toward them.

It seemed like black, shining bodies were pouring toward them from every direction. But that made no sense. No species of scorpion Adam knew was that aggressive. At best they were indifferent to humans, if not afraid. So why did it look like these were desperate to get to them?

They reached the edge of the lake and Adam thought furiously.

Not every species of scorpions was dangerous, but a rare few could be fatal. It was possible he'd recognize the ones swarming toward them if he could give one a closer inspection.

Then again, maybe not. And the circumstances weren't exactly ideal for a thorough study.

What the hell are they attracted to?

He glanced at the torch in his hand. On a whim, he tossed it onto the shore.

"What are you doing?" Ellie protested.

He didn't answer, watching the insects react. Those nearer to the torch wheeled in their tracks. They charged toward the flame, climbing into it like moths after a lamp. The sheer numbers of black bodies smothered the torch.

"They're drawn to the light."

"We can't see where we're going without the torches," she countered.

The river of black creatures surged forward into the dark water, climbing over one another as Adam and Ellie splashed back.

"Are they dangerous?"

"I don't know," he admitted.

"Adam..."

"I'm thinking."

They needed a source of light big enough to attract the bugs, leaving them a way to get out of the chamber.

He looked to the basket packed with resin-soaked torches.

He sloshed up to it, yanking out two. He pushed them into Ellie's free hand.

"Hang on to these for a minute." He nodded toward a dark opening in the stone at the far side of the chamber, one from which the insects did not seem to be issuing. "That look like a good option to you?"

"Option for what?"

He hefted the bundle of reeds. It was heavier than it looked, but not too weighty for what he had in mind.

"Give me your light."

She handed Adam the burning torch. Her eyes widened as he thrust it, burning end down, into the basket.

"Are you insane?"

He picked the whole package up and, twisting his body, heaved it toward the far end of the cavern. It landed in an explosion of sparks that quickly turned to flame. The conflagration grew, fueled by pitch and dry wood, and the river of scorpions turned toward it.

Adam held Ellie's arm, stilling her, and watched as the creatures seethed toward the flames, leaving open a path to the promising mouth in the wall of the cave.

"Come on," he said at last. They picked their way along in the gloom, avoiding stray or straggling insects until the tunnel swallowed them.

They paused at the edge of the light. Adam faced the darkness and thought about what he was about to do.

Plunging into an uncharted cave system was a chancy business even at the best of times. Doing it in the dark was insane. There could be pitfalls in the floor, branching tunnels leading off into an unending labyrinth.

Not that they had any choice. He couldn't risk lighting another torch until they were safely out of range of the swarm. He would just have to move carefully—*very* carefully.

He would feel for air currents, follow them if he could, and if he couldn't, choose a direction and stick with it until they reached a dead end.

"Let's go."

Slowly, cautiously, they made their way forward, creeping along the length of the tunnel. It twisted and turned but did not branch. Far from the light of Adam's bonfire, they were consumed in a complete blackness.

Ellie stopped.

"Do you hear that?"

"Sounds like water," Adam replied.

"Is that good or bad?"

"Let's find out."

They rounded a few more bends and the sound became immediate. With it came a strange smell, acrid and unpleasant.

"Stay here for a second."

Adam took out the match tin and gave another silent thanks for the thing. It had proven reliably waterproof many times before, but never quite so urgently as now.

"Still have those torches?"

"Of course." He struck the match, Ellie's dirt-streaked face coming into view in front of him. He touched it to the resin-soaked wood she held out in her hand and a flame flickered tentatively to life.

"Watch out for any more of those bugs," he ordered, then moved forward, Ellie following close behind.

They stood on a rocky ledge leading down to a quickly moving river. In the torchlight, the water showed a strange, opaque shade of red that looked eerily like blood. It bubbled darkly over boulders worn slippery smooth, filling the space before them. On the far side, Adam could just make out the opening of another tunnel.

"What's that smell?" Ellie asked.

"Cave waters often have high mineral content," he replied. "At least it doesn't look too deep. I'll try heading across. You wait here until we know what we're dealing with."

"I might not be able to do that." Ellie's voice was tight. Adam turned and saw a trail of dark insects trickling in from the mouth of the tunnel. His bonfire must have burned itself out, or else other nests hidden in this part of the cave had been roused by their presence.

One approached Ellie's boot and she kicked at it, sending it down to the edge of the water. It landed with a soft hiss.

Adam moved in for a better look, Ellie close behind. The scorpion writhed on the ground, trying futilely to pull itself out of the water with its remaining legs. The rest appeared to have been burned away, along with the bottom half of its body.

"That's not water," Ellie said numbly.

"No. It isn't."

Acid. It made a sort of sense. After all, that was how caves like this were formed. Acidic water ate away at the soft limestone over thousands of years, slowly carving out the tunnels, chambers, and bizarre mineral formations that surrounded them.

This was different. There was nothing mild about the acidic content of the water in front of him. It was harsh enough to burn through the exoskeleton of the scorpion. Adam doubted his boots would fare much better.

A skittering behind them reminded him that the creatures were still coming. They were running short on options. Ellie realized it as well, her face pale but determined.

"We'll have to cross on the rocks," she said firmly.

Adam took in their smooth, shining surfaces. One slip, and her foot could end up in that soup. Dealing with a graze from a bullet while trapped underground was one thing. A chemical burn was another.

He contemplated carrying her, but even if she would let him—which he doubted—it would only make their passage more dangerous.

Ellie kicked another scorpion away and hopped onto the nearest rock. The acidic water swirled inches from her feet.

Adam gritted his teeth and stepped forward onto the neighboring stone.

"I go first," he ordered. "Stay within arm's reach if you can. That way if you slip, I can catch you."

"Or I could catch you," she retorted.

He looked forward at their path. Though slick and wet, the stones were evenly spaced in the stream, almost as though someone had placed them there on purpose. Though it hardly made their passage safe, it was certainly less dangerous than it would have been if they'd had to leap from one island to another.

He moved forward, testing each rock as he progressed, painfully aware of Ellie following precariously behind him.

The safety of the bank was only a few feet away. Adam became more confident. He turned back to give Ellie a reassuring smile, then watched as the stone beneath her foot gave an unexpected wobble.

He saw her slip, her balance gone. He lunged forward, grasping the fabric of her shirt. His legs spread between the two stones, he hauled her to him, catching her body against his own.

She looked up at him, her face inches away.

"Thanks."

Adam's mind momentarily went blank. Then he realized his heel had slipped into the stream.

"Go," he said, pushing her toward the larger, secure boulder. She stepped over, then leaped nimbly across the remaining stones to the bank.

Adam pulled his boot from the river, trying to shake off the corrosive drops. He hurried to join her.

He stopped, turning back to look the way they had come. The opposite side was a mass of undulating black, an army of scorpions drawn toward the light of the torch but warned by some instinct from touching the deadly water. Adam looked around for any sign of the creatures on their side of the stream, but saw none.

As risky as the acidic water had made their crossing, it seemed to provide a barrier between them and the hordes of light-seeking insects. Had it not been there, he and Ellie would have been forced to try to find their way through the caves in the dark.

It wasn't a pleasant prospect.

He took the other torch and lit it, handing it back to Ellie, then turned to the dark opening behind him.

"Let's hope that was the worst of it," he said, and led them on.

With the bugs held at bay by the ruddy stream, the tunnel around them seemed to be safe.

Well, perhaps *safe* was an exaggeration. They were still wandering through a large, unknown cave system.

Out of the frying pan . . .

There had to be a way to the surface somewhere. The basket of torches proved that. Someone had been here before, and they could hardly have brought all that in the way he and Ellie had come.

But why had they left the basket there? It was almost as though they had expected someone to make their way through that treacherous tunnel in the cenote, one he and Ellie had barely had the intuition to discover.

It was a mystery, a damned intriguing one—the latest in a series of them he'd stumbled across since finding this place.

Looking for answers to any of them would have to wait, though. His first priority was to get himself and Ellie safely out of this.

Ellie . . .

He could sense her behind him, hear her boots scraping against the rock as she followed him down the sloping track. He could recall all too vividly the way she had felt when they'd embraced, how she had tasted. . . .

The intensity had clearly not been one-sided. Her response had been just as visceral as his own.

Which meant what, exactly?

Maybe everything. Maybe nothing. She was flesh and blood, after all, and with the rush of their escape in her veins, the threat of death looming over her head, she could easily have gotten caught up in the moment.

After all, he couldn't forget the way she'd reacted to the notion of marrying him, even just in name.

The signals were more than mixed. They were incomprehensible, and his own emotions further clouded the picture. How could he trust his judgment of what Ellie was feeling when his own heart was such a mess?

Figuring it out would have to wait until they'd discovered a way out of this underground maze. And as Adam found himself facing a pair of dark gaps in the stone, that effort got a touch more complicated.

"There are two ways forward," Ellie said, coming to his side. Her voice held only the slightest bit of apprehension. Good, Adam thought. Neither of them could afford to panic. This was sure to be just the first of many such choices they'd have to make to find their way to the surface.

He took a few steps into each of the two openings, enough to see that they did indeed lead away into darkness, instead of dead-ending abruptly. But which one to choose?

Ellie was making her own examination and came to a quicker decision.

"This one leads up. It seems to me that we're more likely to find an exit the closer we are to the surface."

"Possibly," Adam admitted, less certain. He stood in the mouth of the second tunnel, feeling as though something important were calling for his notice. Just not quite loudly enough.

"This one slopes downward," Ellie noted.

"Caves can be deceptive," Adam replied absently, still chasing that nagging sense of missing something. "You never know where they're really leading you. This system could be a labyrinth."

"Well, if we can't trust up and down, what other options do we have?"

"Someone else was here before us," Adam pointed out with a glance back at the torch she held in her hand. "Maybe they left some bread crumbs."

"Bread crumbs?"

"Like Hansel and Gretel." His tone was vague. His attention had moved to the ceiling of the downward-sloping tunnel. Like the one they had just passed through, it was low, with barely enough room for Adam to stand upright.

He ran his fingers over the stone, then looked down at the residue that dusted them. From beside him, Ellie looked from his hand to the stain that darkened the stone above.

"What is it?"

"I think they're scorch marks," he replied.

Her eyes widened at the implication. She looked to her torch, the flames tickling at the roof of the cave.

"Bread crumb?"

"Looks like it," Adam replied, and they started down the deeply sloping path.

The tunnel was steep but short, quickly emptying out into another chamber. The walls lay far beyond the range of the light cast by the small flames they held, but Adam could tell by the echoes of their footsteps that the place was vast.

It wasn't a comforting notion. At least in a tunnel, there was only one way to go. Here, who knew how many options might present themselves, or how hard it might be to find signs of someone else having made the passage.

Adam cursed softly under his breath.

"We'll have to follow the wall. Make a note of any openings and decide which looks the most promising once we make it back here."

"But how will we know where here is?" Ellie asked.

"We'll just have to mark it somehow."

Adam turned to consider their options, and went silent. The

opening behind them was far from unmarked. The stone around it was elaborately carved, shaped expertly into the blockish forms of gargoyle demons or gods, their expressions grotesque. The blocks formed a rectangular frame around the tunnel entrance that was further accentuated by a roughly painted border of some viscous black substance. It gave off a sickly sheen in the firelight.

Adam let his eyes follow the track the painted substance made as it moved from framing the doorway to running along the floor, hugging the base of the cave walls to either side of the opening until it receded into darkness.

He moved closer to it and rubbed it with his fingers. A bit of the stuff came away. It was sticky. He gave it a sniff.

"Smells like petroleum."

"But why would they paint the door with it?"

Adam shrugged, then, on an instinct, touched the flame of his torch to the strange substance.

It caught. Flames spread quickly along the track of it, framing the door and then accelerating around the chamber. The stuff had been painted around the entire circumference and, in the flickering glow, illuminated three other elaborately carved doorways, and something else: a great mural in the center of the chamber floor, its sinister colors of black, white, yellow, and ocher accentuated by the circling flames.

They died back as quickly as they had come, their strange fuel spent. Adam and Ellie stood alone and silent once more in the feeble glow of their small torches.

"Bates?" she asked softly. "What is this place?"

He took a moment to reply, his mind still struggling through the impact of that elaborate arrangement, from the carved doorways to the vivid images painted onto the floor.

"I think it might be hell," he replied at last.

21

THE SCENE DAWSON STOOD IN was something out of a nightmare. Workers swarmed around him, clanging hammers and chisels into every wall. Little remained intact of the original murals, just fragments and splashes of color visible through the thick haze of limestone dust that floated around them like a fog. Their sweating bodies were white with it, turning them gruesomely ghostlike, and the clouds of fine stuff stung at Dawson's watering, red-rimmed eyes. He stood back, watching them work, breathing through a handkerchief he kept pressed to his face.

It had started with a hole—just one little gap chiseled into the surface of the painted doorway. He had chosen a spot that would least damage the priceless art of the mural. He did not want to destroy such a precious find, but he had to know, beyond doubt, that the image was simply that, and nothing more.

Behind the plaster he'd found only stone and rubble. No opening, no promise of another chamber hidden in the temple.

That was where Jacobs had found him, peering into the gap. He had entered the room so quietly, Dawson hadn't realized he was no longer alone. It was the fear, quick and familiar, that alerted him.

He had tried not to let it show. Not that it mattered. Jacobs knew; he had no doubt about that. Jacobs had a preternatural instinct for another man's fear.

"Tear all of it down," he had ordered, taking in the entirety of the painted history. "Make certain it's not here before we move on."

Horror had overtaken terror at the notion of the destruction Jacobs was ordering.

"But the other walls..."

"All of it."

So here he was, supervising an army of workmen made ghostly by the dust of what was once an astonishing relic, chipping away the very walls themselves in search of the entrance to a chamber that might or might not exist.

It could have been worse, Dawson reminded himself. Much worse.

A figure moved toward him through the haze. Even if Dawson had cared to learn their faces, the man would have been unrecognizable to him under his heavy coating of gray grime.

"We've punched through," he reported.

"And?" Dawson asked unhopefully.

"Rubble."

Dawson absorbed this glumly. "Move eighteen inches left and up, and start another."

They had all turned up rubble, every one of the holes piloted through the facing stones since Dawson's first. But there was no choice but to keep working until the whole room had been torn down to gravel. Then they would move on, taking the entire city apart stone by stone to find the mirror.

Dawson prayed it existed. The alternative was too miserable to contemplate.

There was a call from the stairwell, the words obscured by the din of the hammering. One of the nearer men turned his ear, then shouted over to where the professor stood.

"What is it?" Dawson snapped, pushing past the swinging arms and dusty bodies to the entrance.

"They have a prisoner," the man replied blandly.

A prisoner? Dawson could think of only two people in the vicinity of the city who weren't in Jacobs's employ.

"Is it Mr. Bates or Miss Mallory?"

"No. It's some Indian."

Some Indian...

Dawson's mind quickly leaped through the potential implications.

What Indian would be wandering in this remote place? What if he wasn't wandering?

What if he lived here?

It had never occurred to him that the city might still be inhabited. The idea made him distinctly uncomfortable. He looked at the destruction that surrounded him and tried to imagine what a resident of this haunted place would think of it. Nothing good, he was certain.

He shook off the idea. The city was clearly a ruin. Even if the captive did "live" here, he was a descendant so distant he could have no knowledge of its secrets.

It wasn't his problem, anyway. Prisoners, he decided, were clearly Jacobs's area of responsibility.

But what would Jacobs do to an interloper—any interloper?

It didn't matter. It wasn't Dawson's affair.

"Bring him to Mr. Jacobs."

"We don't know where the *jefe* is."

"So hold the Indian until you find him!"

The man turned, calling over his shoulder, and Dawson realized with horror that the prisoner he spoke of was standing on the other side of the room.

He stood between two guards who towered over him like giants. He was an old man, brown and wrinkled. His head was bald, save for a few white tufts of hair, which made the scar that marked his forehead stand out starkly against the rest of his skin.

He was not dressed like any native Dawson had ever seen. Over his homespun shirt and trousers, he wore what looked like a bizarre homemade armor. It was a breastplate of dry reeds, bound together with twine. The effect was that of a Mayan Don Quixote.

His expression was unreadable as he stared at the pulverized masterpieces that surrounded him.

Dawson searched for words. What was he supposed to say? *You can't be here. This is a closed excavation.*

This wasn't an excavation. This was a crime against history.

But would some ignorant native peasant really understand that?

He was being ridiculous. He was in charge here, not this withered Mayan. The man was a prisoner.

Dawson opened his mouth to give the order that would see him dragged back out of here to someplace where he could become Jacobs's problem again, but the Mayan spoke first.

"Looking for something?"

His tone was calm, his English surprisingly clear. Dawson sputtered for a response.

"We're archaeologists. We're—"

"Perhaps I could help you," the native cut in smoothly.

Dawson gaped like a fish for a moment, then clamped his mouth shut.

"Why would you do that?"

"So that you will pay, of course."

Dawson felt a moment of ambiguity. Pay? Then the implication clicked into place.

Money. The man wanted money. He was a mercenary, like the others who surrounded them, willing to desecrate the graves of their ancestors in return for a generous salary.

No, not like the others. There was more in this old man's eyes, something deeper. A comprehension Dawson didn't see in the dust-clad figures that surrounded him. But it was more than just intelligence. This man *knew* something.

"Who are you?" he demanded.

"I am Amilcar Kuyoc," the man replied.

The camp was quiet. Only a few scattered fires broke the darkness, flickering in the quick gusts of wind. Small groups of figures gathered around them. Flowers knew that many men were still working in the great temple, and that others were with Velegas and the *jefe*, Jacobs, securing the site. But those did not account for all the absences, and he wondered how many had been drawn by the lure of treasure to explore the ruins under cover of darkness, and how many others, feeling the same foreboding that tossed like quicksilver in his stomach, had slipped away into the bush to find the narrow ravine and the road back home.

They were fools. Flowers knew what waited in that jungle. He had seen what it could do. It was a vision he would never forget.

The words of the man dying in the jungle came back to him.

It came out of the night.

Flowers did not run. But he had nothing else to do. No one gave him any orders. The bosses seemed to have forgotten that there wasn't anyone to guard anymore.

He thought of the sounds the gunshots had made, echoing among the trees and stones. The first two had put a vise grip on his insides. The volleys that followed had loosened it again. But eventually a rough group of men had come back into camp with rifles slung, and Flowers had known by the laughing, proud tone of their jokes what the outcome had been.

Guard the woman, he had been told.

He had failed. He had not guarded her, and now she was lost.

He wanted to run, but he was afraid. And he had someone to answer to first.

He skirted the edges of the camp, avoiding the glow of the fires, looking for the one he sought. He was so focused on the search, he nearly ran into the man who stepped from the dark brush to his right, buttoning the fly of his trousers.

He was short but strongly built, his face bruised around the dark growth of his beard. Seeing Flowers, he flashed him a grin that was half grimace, accented by a pair of missing teeth.

"You look like someone pissed in your lemonade."

Flowers hung his head, ashamed. Martin Lavec released a stream of tobacco-stained expectorant toward the ground, then nodded toward a fire on the far edge of the camp.

"Your cousin is over there."

Resigned, Flowers walked to the place Lavec had indicated. The fire was set apart from the others, surrounded on every side by the rustling darkness of the jungle. It glowed cheerily for the moment but would not last for long. The sky overhead flickered with lightning, and the distant rumble of thunder punctuated the stillness of the night.

Charles Goodwin sat by the blaze, his head resting in his hands. He looked more tired than Flowers had ever seen him, his sadness a palpable thing.

The guilt was a stone in his chest.

Charlie was his hero. He always had been, since Flowers was a boy who had to look up to see his face, instead of towering over him. Failing him, especially in something so important, was a pain like a knife.

He hung his head.

"I'm sorry."

"Wasn't anything you could have done," Charlie replied. "Bates got in over his head."

Lavec ambled up behind him, collapsing onto a tumbled stone and pulling a packet of snuff from his pocket.

"Going to miss that bastard." He put a pinch into his cheek and sneezed. "So what now?"

Charlie stood. He looked weary. The night seemed to have grown heavier, and the wind rippled the fabric of his shirt.

"Now we go home."

"We haven't been paid yet," the Québécois pointed out.

Charlie's gaze darkened.

"Would you take their money?"

Lavec sniffed in reply, but Charlie had made his point.

He kicked dirt over the little fire, dampening the flames.

Lavec frowned at him.

"Shouldn't we wait till it's light out? Start moving in the dark and we might never find our way out of this hole."

"We're not going into the bush," Charlie replied.

"Then how do you propose we get home, eh?"

"You'll see."

The elaborate painting covered a circular area of ground in the center of the vast chamber. Ellie knelt beside Adam as he studied it in the red light of their torches.

The wild rush of fire that had raced around the room when Adam ignited the dark pitch by the doorway had expired as quickly as it burned. The outer reaches of the chamber were lost in shadows once more.

The air was cool here, more so thanks to her soaked shirt and trousers. But that wasn't what made her shiver. It was all that dark, open space at her back, the sense that anything could be hiding there, watching them.

She shook the notion off, focusing instead on the images before her.

The mural was divided into sections, each depicting a different scene. All of them were dark and violent. In one, a pair of figures wrestled with a great spotted cat. In another, a severed head, dripping blood, hung from the branches of a tree.

"What do you think it means?" She nodded toward the medallion of color on the ground.

"Looks like something from the Popol Vuh."

"Tulan Zuyua again?"

The notion had been tickling at the back of her mind since she'd arrived in the city. The words on Dawson's telegram came back to her. *Candidate for Tulan Zuyua.*

The city above her wasn't Mayan or Aztec. It was something else, something different. A place with its own history and culture.

If their circumstances were different, she would dig trenches, some under the central courtyard and others farther into the outskirts of the settlement pattern. She would carefully unearth each layer of remains, looking for ways to date what she found. If she could establish that this city had been inhabited in the centuries before the rise of the Mayan world . . .

She could bring the archaeological world to its knees.

Even if she couldn't find that evidence, the city was still a discovery of shattering importance. It would change everything scholars thought they knew about Central American history.

"This could be it. Couldn't it?"

Adam glanced over at her, his face deeply shadowed in the flickering light.

"Possibly."

Ellie forced her attention away from what that revelation might mean, focusing instead on the puzzle before them.

"What are we looking at?"

"In the Popol Vuh, there's a tale of a pair of twin brothers who venture into the land of the dead—Xibalba—to try to rescue their murdered father."

"Like Orpheus and Eurydice?"

"Not quite so pretty," Adam countered, frowning down at the image of the severed head. "All Orpheus had to do was sing a song and keep his eyes front. The tests the twins were subjected to were a lot nastier."

"Such as?"

"Well, before they even got to the gates of Xibalba, they had to cross a river of scorpions."

Ellie looked up, surprised.

Adam met her eyes evenly. "Then a river of blood. Our acidic Amazon back there was a bit on the ruddy side, as I recall."

Her skepticism flared up in protest.

"You can't possibly think that this is some sort of mythical realm."

"No. But I think it might be someone's attempt to replicate it. It could have been used as a sort of initiation, part of the ascension into kingship or the priesthood."

The path of kings.

The dream came back to her in all its vivid strangeness—the city, the scarred woman, and her words. Words that were now beginning to make a terrifying sense.

Ellie had already been compelled to acknowledge that the images haunting her brain for the past few weeks carried in them some semblance of truth. The city itself had forced that upon her. It was a reality that her waking mind couldn't possibly have guessed at, but that appeared in her sleep with all the clarity of a vision.

But to think that she had known, somehow, that she would end up here, in this ritual nightmare buried beneath the ground...

The road through hell.

Ellie didn't know what to make of it. She didn't *want* to.

She looked from the mural to the elaborately carved doorways that lay around them, beyond the reach of their feeble torchlight.

A rite of passage. A test to prove a leader's worth before his ascent to power.

"What happened to the twins?" she asked. At her feet, the pair of youthful figures clung together as dark shadows surrounded them.

"Once they got into Xibalba, they had to pass through a series of rooms. Each one housed an ordeal they had to survive in order to reach their goal."

"Did they make it?"

"Not exactly," Adam replied from where he crouched by a particularly gruesome panel. He looked up at her from across the painting. "You see what I'm getting at?"

She looked down at the scenes of blood and darkness below them. "If this is an initiation, then they'll have built those rooms down here somewhere. Like booby traps."

"Tests," Adam confirmed. "We want to follow this route, we'll have to get through them." He met her eyes. "You want to do this?"

"What's the alternative?" she countered.

"Not sure we've got one."

"I thought as much." She stood, holding up her torch and surveying the room. The four doorways were mouths of deeper darkness, barely visible in the gloom. "So one of these is our ticket to hell. And the others?"

"Could go anywhere," he replied. "Most likely they lead deeper into the caves. There's no telling how big this system is. It might be fairly self-contained, or it could be immense."

"You mean that we could get lost down there."

"It's a possibility," he admitted frankly. She thought of the chill currently goose-pimpling her skin. It would only get worse farther underground, and then there would be hunger to contend with, and the need for water. Safe water, she added mentally, thinking of the deadly stream at their backs.

"Well, then," she said forcefully. "We'd best choose the right door."

He grinned at her proudly, then sobered. "If this is an initiation, there will be a goal at the end."

"Our way out."

He nodded. "We just have to pass the tests. You ready?"

"Certainly," she asserted curtly.

"Then let's go." He started toward one of the doors. It was framed with dark smears of black paint, its frame of carvings crowned with a particularly fearsome-looking god.

"Hold on," she called. "How do you know this is the right one?"

"You want to visit the land of the dead, you follow the sunset. West." He pointed.

"But we're underground. How do you know this is west?"

"Come on, princess. Haven't you learned to trust my instincts by now?"

Ellie was unmoved. She crossed her arms, planting her feet.

"You want me to trust both of our lives to your instinct?"

"How about this, then?" He held up a compass, then answered her muttered curse with a grin.

The temple's inner chamber was a hot cloud of fine white dust. Amilcar Kuyoc could make out bodies moving in the haze, coated white with pulverized stone and sweat. The atmosphere was so dense, so obscure, he could catch only the slightest glimpse of the walls through the thick of it. Only fragments of the magnificence the room had once contained were visible, the rest being pulverized, inch by inch, by the servants of the Englishmen.

The destruction hurt him all the more because Amilcar Kuyoc remembered well what the murals had looked like whole and intact, as they had been the first time he had seen them.

He had stumbled through the ravine half-starved, on the run for his life. It had been after San Pedro Siris, after he had seen the village he had come to call home obliterated by the army of the overlords. He remembered the children clinging to the bodies of their mothers, who had collapsed from smoke inhalation or burns. He had seen the crops smoldering and had known the hunger that would result. A lesson, they had called it. Punishment for the hospitality and support San Pedro Siris had shown for Kuyoc and the man he followed, Marcus Canul, the one with the temerity to demand that the men and women who had called this land their own for millennia be given a fair stake in it. The notion was beyond the pale for the Englishmen. For Canul's "arrogance," San Pedro Siris burned.

And Amilcar Kuyoc ran, the breath of his would-be executioners hot on his neck. Alone, devoured by guilt and terror, he had plunged deeper and deeper into the bush.

The jungle could be generous, but he was a single man with no more than a knife to hunt with. Hunger had deviled him, so when a hare crossed his path, there had been no question as to whether he would follow it.

He stalked the creature for miles. Always it remained just beyond his reach, then lingered as though waiting for him to catch up. The animal had turned into a torment, until at last it led him out of the jungle to the base of a sheer cliff marked with a sinuous vein of night-black stone.

The hare vanished into the ravine at its base, and Kuyoc, half-mad with grief and hunger, followed it into the city.

He wandered the ruins for weeks. The land had once been cultivated, and he found remnants of orchards, heavy with fruit. Some of the crops had survived, slowly returning to the wild but still edible. And the small animals here had not seen man in centuries, making them easier prey for the traps he set.

When he was not seeking food, he explored the city's dark chambers and corridors. He found its caches of corpses, its abandoned weapons, collapsed storehouses, and deserted plazas.

And other secrets.

When he first descended into this room, he had only a single light, a primitive lamp he found in the city, fueled by lizard fat. In the feeble, sooty flame, he saw the stunning beauty of the paintings, the powerful expressions of the men and women frozen there; preserved so much more eloquently here than in mere bones and rotted cloth.

He had seen the artifacts, golden mysteries, and that great, silent machine.

He had passed through all of it to the door that led him to the city's true heart, its animus—the object he now knew with certainty these Englishmen hoped to acquire.

The mirror.

When he fled San Pedro Siris, he left behind his clarity. Once he had been so full of purpose, so certain in his course. But the sight of the suffering of the innocent, punished for his banner, had cast him into irreparable doubt.

The mirror changed that.

At first it seemed like a blessing from the gods. The power that it offered…Absolute knowledge. The past, the present, and the future, laid out like maps on a table. He needed only desire, and the path to its fulfillment would be made his.

Desire, and offer sacrifice.

With such power at his fingertips, who could stand against him? Everything his people fought for could be theirs, their enemies toppled like palms in the fierce winds of a storm.

Then he remembered San Pedro Siris. He remembered the flames and the silence and in a moment of wisdom understood what the power he contemplated was in truth: a great mouth, hungry and merciless, that would devour the world if it could.

Because no cause stood in absolute justice, and every victory came with a price paid in blood.

He left the city, and he worked to keep any other from stumbling across the dark secret it hid.

Kuyoc had always been a storyteller. But where once he had seeded stories of hope and insurrection, now he sowed rumors of death and horror. He quietly, carefully draped a pall of fear over that corner of the mountains, so that even his own people would avoid the place.

It had not been hard. Long before his arrival, rumors of horrors hidden in the mountains kept all but the most intrepid at bay. Nor were those rumors baseless. There were monsters here, things out of a nightmare. Kuyoc had met them, getting close enough to win the scar that jagged across his forehead and the teeth he wore around his neck.

He had been lucky.

But white men didn't hear such stories. Like mosquitos, they were without boundaries, went everywhere and took what they desired. When the surveyor and his woman came, Kuyoc knew that the day had arrived, the moment for him to take up a cause again and all that it would cost him.

Those two, perhaps, would have left it as he had, recognized its threat. But these others, the men he had seen capture them, whom he had followed, silent and subtle, along their crashing way through the jungle—they would have no such sensitivity. He had known that before he descended into the chamber and saw how they had rampantly destroyed beauty in their search for power.

The men around him slowed their working, turning to stare. They were astonished by his strange appearance, these figures like ghosts with their dark eyes staring out of chalk faces.

Their leader was sweating, his pale face caked with dust. Kuyoc could smell the fear on him. He was weak, a blade of grass that would flatten in the slightest breeze.

He could see the man thinking, struggling to come to a decision about Kuyoc's fate. As though as small a man as this could control so great a matter.

"We don't need more workers," he said at last.

"I did not come to work."

"Then what are you here for?"

He ignored the Englishman's words. Instead he made a show of slowly circling the room, pushing back the anger he felt at the obliteration of the graceful limbs and faces. He paused before the remains of the painted doorway, looking down at the desiccated corpse that lay at the foot of it.

He knew who lay there. He had dreamed her face in the fullness of its beauty, the scar that marked her only adding to her nobility. She deserved more than what he was about to do, but there was no time for reverence anymore.

Callously, he kicked her remains. The move exposed a part of the floor that had been concealed behind the body. A strange carving was set into the stone, surrounded by glyphs.

"Looks like a keyhole," he said, pointing to it. "Needs a key."

Once, he had held such a key. He had come across it around the neck of a corpse, a skeleton encased in the regalia of a high priest. It had lain in a rubbish heap at the outskirts of the city, along with countless other dead.

He had taken the dark circle of stone and placed it in his pocket. There had been something about the object that sang to him, whispered promises of desires fulfilled.

The dreams had begun shortly after. They had shown him the secret door in the roof of the temple sanctuary. The mechanism that once controlled it was long rotted away, but a hammer had sufficed to break it open. The dreams led him down the long, twisting staircase into this room of glittering mysteries.

She had shown it to him. She had led him here, to the place where she had died. She had shown him the hidden door, and the secret that lay on the other side, the danger buried in the heart of this ruined place.

That key was gone. Kuyoc had destroyed it himself, shattered it into sharp fragments.

He had hoped then that it had been the only one, but fate was not so kind. He was pained, therefore, but not surprised when the Englishman reached into his pocket and removed a medallion of dark, shining stone.

He saw how he held it, cradling it as though it were something precious.

The Englishman heard its song as well, Kuyoc realized.

The foreigner pressed the medallion into the carved space in the floor. It fit with a click, one magnet calling to another. He turned it and a hidden latch released. The slab of stone shifted with a rattling clank. He looked to the old man, amazement vying with suspicion.

"How did you know?"

Kuyoc shrugged, the reeds of his breastplate rattling.

"Lucky guess."

He saw the question in the Englishman's eyes, the flicker of doubt. Greed and the urgency of his purpose overrode it.

"Watch him," he ordered a pair of armed men. Then he set the rest to push.

The slab in the floor slid aside on well-oiled machinery, revealing a set of steps descending into the earth. The men poured inside, lanterns in hand, and Kuyoc accepted that this battle would not be won easily. But that was all right. He had come prepared to do what must be done. Silently he followed his enemy down into the bowels of the temple.

22

ELLIE WAS COLD. The air in the dark tunnels she moved through was cooler than that aboveground, significantly so, and her clothes were still damp from the plunge into the cenote. The torch lent feeble enough light, never mind warmth. But for all the discomfort, her overwhelming feeling was one of excitement. She and Adam were moving inside of one massive artifact, a ritual maze built by hands vanished centuries ago.

They were undoubtedly the first human beings to see these tunnels in hundreds of years. Even then, this would have been a sacred precinct, known only by the most holy and powerful. The path of kings, and she was walking it.

Adam led the way. His clothes were also damp—what was left of them, at any rate. He had already sacrificed his shirt to the scratch on her arm, and his trousers sported a new tear down the side. The sight of him in the torchlight, traveling with her through this ancient and mysterious place, was moving, to say the least.

Her thoughts turned to the cenote—or, more specifically, to what Adam had done to her in the cenote. That kiss. It had not been like the kiss that she'd once received from a determined if dull suitor. That experience had been less exciting than a night at home with a new issue of the *Journal of the Anthropological Institute*.

No, Adam Bates's kiss had been something else altogether. There had been heat, an explosive heightening of the senses, and some hitherto unknown pressure building inside of her like steam in the boiler of the *Mary Lee*.

They had gone straight from that to navigating deadly submerged currents, dodging scorpions, and leaping across acid streams. Following him down the twisting, narrow tunnel, only the crunch of their footsteps and the quiet crackle of the torches breaking the silence, was the first moment she'd had for reflection, to pause and consider the whole business—what she thought of it, and what it meant.

The latter question was a rattling one. It was impossible to consider what the kiss had meant without stumbling across the uncomfortable question of what she hoped it had meant. What did she want the significance of that embrace to be? The answer was clear enough but confused the devil out of her.

She wanted it to mean that he was deeply attracted to her, that both her mind and her body inflamed his passion. She wanted that because the unsettling truth was that his presence was having precisely that effect on her. It was all she could do to keep quietly walking behind him and not reach out to demand a more thorough introduction to the world he had revealed to her in the cenote. But where would that lead?

She hoped her hunger was merely for sensual experience. The alternative was too frightening. It seemed to her it could only go terribly wrong. Admittedly, Adam had proposed to her, but his motives had hardly been romantic.

Did she want them to be romantic?

Marriage would mean everything she had fought all her life to avoid: the loss of her freedom, her independence, her control over her own destiny.

Or would it? a tiny voice inside her asked.

The question sparked a tremulous but potent little flame, a shocking hope.

He is different, the tiny voice said.

He couldn't give a toss for the strictures of society, and she had seen already how he treated her as an equal, an intelligent and capable partner with inexperience, not gender, her only handicap.

Maybe it would be just like this, the little voice offered.

Just like this, but with more of what she had tasted in the stirring waters of the well. Ever so much more . . .

Except that, until that moment in the well, she'd been fairly certain he despised her, and with good reason. Did the embrace mean she'd been wrong about that? Or had it just been an irresistible impulse, fueled by a close brush with death?

The whirlwind of thoughts was building to an intolerable buzzing, an overwhelming need to ask, though she hadn't the foggiest notion what the question was.

She realized that they had stopped. The tunnel had ended with a wooden door. It was fitted neatly into the opening with mortared stone, held closed with a simple latch.

Adam glanced at her. "Shall we?"

She studied his face, trying to find an answer in the way he looked at her. It was a futile effort.

Instead, she lifted the latch and pushed open the door.

They stepped into another chamber. Lining the walls in an evenly spaced circle was a ring of monsters, massive figures seated in thrones as tall as her head.

There were thirteen altogether, each with a visage out of a nightmare. They were silent, still, and fearfully lifelike.

"What are they?" she asked. The question was barely above a whisper, as though she feared that speaking louder would cause the terrible heads to swivel and fix them with grisly stares.

"The Lords of Xibalba," Adam replied. He, too, spoke in hushed, reverent tones. "The gods of death."

He explained the rest to her as they moved slowly toward the center of the room, pausing to inspect the great statues in the flickering torchlight.

"This must be the council chamber."

"So it's in the story?"

Adam nodded. "The brothers had to get past it in order to continue on their journey."

"And how did they do that?"

"They had to tell the real gods from the false ones."

The light of his torch flickered eerily across the snarling face of one of the great statues. "Some of the figures in the room were statues, perfect replicas of some of the lords of death. If one of the twins addressed a piece of wood instead of a bona fide deity, it constituted an insult, and the gods would have the excuse they needed to tear them apart."

"If they're gods, why did they need an excuse?"

Adam smiled thinly.

"Rules, princess. There are always rules. Even for gods."

The light of their flames danced across the carved faces. There were jaguars with bloody jaws, grinning skulls, and a figure that held its own decapitated head on its lap. The artistry was vividly lifelike, the painted colors still bright and fresh.

The exit was at the far end of the gallery, another door of wood closely fitted into the rock. As they approached it, Adam handed her his torch.

"Hold this." He stepped back and unleashed a powerful kick at the boards. They barely shuddered. In the firelight, the wood gave off an oily sheen.

Adam took back his torch and searched for hinges.

"They must be on the other side."

"So there's no way to open it?"

"There's got to be a way to open it. But it must have something to do with them." He turned back to the circle of figures.

"It's a test."

"Looks like it."

"But how does it work?"

He shrugged. "I'm open to suggestions."

They moved quietly around the room, studying the sculptures. Each one was elaborately decorated in carved, brightly painted robes. The artisans who made them had been fanatics for detail. Every nuance of their expressions was artfully rendered, and in the flickering, uncertain torchlight, they almost seemed alive.

"It's got to have something to do with these," Adam said. He had his foot on a lever of stone protruding from the base of one of the thrones. Ellie realized a similar mechanism could be seen on each of the figures.

"So, we think we've got a real god, we flip the switch?"

"That's my guess."

"And if we get it wrong?"

"Whatever mechanism was here, it's been neglected for centuries now. Let's just hope it still works if we get it right."

Ellie felt uneasy. The place had the air of something built to last a very long time.

"What was the punishment in the story?" she asked as Adam inspected the lever, then moved on to study the elaborate robes and adornments covering the grotesque figure in the throne.

"They were roasted alive," Adam replied, grasping the eye sockets of a carved skull on the throne. He used it as a hold to haul himself up. Bracing his feet on the polished surface of the statue's knees, he stared the monster in the face.

It was some sort of animal. Dark fur was artfully rendered by the carved wood. Pointed ears rose from its head, and its snout was lined with razor-sharp fangs. Then Ellie saw the wings, wide and webbed structures that spread out on either side of the throne, blending into the wall of the cave.

It was a bat.

She thought back to the cave on the Sibun, the final resting place of a sacrificed girl. There had been paintings on the walls like this, dark winged figures with bloodthirsty eyes. What had Adam called them?

"Camazotz," he said, frowning at the statue. Then he lifted the hand he had braced against the figure's chest, rubbing his fingers together. "There's some kind of oil on the wood."

"Probably a preservative." It would explain why the wood had held up so well over the centuries in the damp of the caves.

"It stinks," he commented. Then he shifted his footing, leaning in for a closer look.

"You know, princess, I'd almost swear these teeth were—"

The rest of his words died as his boot slipped on the oiled knee of the statue. Adam tumbled to the ground, landing on the lever at the figure's base.

It snapped backward.

"Damned preservative is slippery," he said, brushing himself off. "Maybe I could hoist you up for a look. I'm almost sure those were real teeth in that—"

"Shh. Do you hear that?"

The hissing started low and sibilant, but as they listened, the volume grew, becoming unmistakable.

Adam stepped past her, frowning. He raised his torch and the flickering light fell across a crack in the floor of the cave. Steam was rising from it in thick white clouds.

He extended a hand into it, then pulled back with a quick curse.

"Let me guess," Ellie said, her stomach sinking. "It's hot."

Adam grasped her elbow. "Let's discuss it somewhere else."

A grinding crack sounded behind them. Ellie turned to the door through which they had entered just in time to see a heavy slab of oiled wood drop into place.

A geared mechanism, she thought, judging the sound. It must have been triggered by the lever. More technology the people of this city shouldn't have had.

"Fascinating," she murmured.

"Damned inconvenient," Adam retorted, striding to the door. He ran his hands over the surface. "Solid. I guess a handle would have been too much to hope for."

He felt along the sides, then knelt, probing the place where the wood met the stone.

"It's fitted into the walls and floor of the cave. There's nowhere to get leverage."

Her wonder at the cleverness of the device faded, and Ellie turned her attention to the rest of the room. It was not a vast space. The walls and ceiling were free of tunnels and fissures. Smooth, seamless stone surrounded them. With both doors tightly closed, it would not take long for the steam to fill the room. Already she could feel it getting warmer.

Not roasted, she thought. *Poached.*

Without much hope, she pushed the broken remains of the

lever at the bat-god's feet back into place. The steam continued to pour in.

Adam kicked a massive grinning monkey in the shin, cursing.

"If the trap still works, so will the release. We have to solve the puzzle," she asserted. Her voice sounded calmer than she felt. "In the story, how did the twins get out of this?"

"They were saved by a mosquito."

"A mosquito?"

"It offers them help. Comes into the council chamber and bites each of the lords of death in turn. The ones that complain it knows are real. The others are fakes. The bug goes back to the twins and reports the results."

"A mosquito," Ellie repeated flatly.

Adam paced the circle, glaring at the dark, immense figures. She could already see the sweat starting to bead on his brow. It was getting hotter.

"There has to be a trick." He knelt at the foot of a grinning sculpted corpse, running his hands over the slick surface of the wood. "Something that gives away the real from the false."

"It could be anything. It could rely on ritual knowledge on the part of the initiate, or a glyph hidden on the thrones. But we can't read the glyphs."

"Make them speak," Adam retorted, grimly determined. He kicked the corpse god soundly, shouting, "Hey!"

Ellie closed her eyes. She took a deep breath, trying to force back the panic. The room felt like a sauna. London was never this hot, not even in the height of summer.

Make them speak. . . .

How hot did it need to get to kill them? First would come confusion, delirium. Then loss of consciousness. It was already getting hard to think. Could they plug up the gap in the floor? Slow it down somehow?

Make them speak. . . .

She stared at the grinning face of the death god in front of her. In the shifting torchlight, the shadows crawled across its face.

One shadow remained still, a dark circle at the base of the statue's throat.

Ellie scrambled up the surface of the gruesome figure, slipping on the oiled wood. At last she managed to brace herself on the throne, bringing her face level with the monster's own. It was hotter here near the ceiling of the cave, the wet air almost too thick to breathe.

She lifted her torch. The dark circle she had seen from below was a hole carved into the base of the figure's neck. Acting on instinct, she shifted her grip and peered behind the creature's head.

Something protruded from the back of the god's neck, a slender wooden tube with an oblong cut at the far end. It looked like the mouthpiece of a flute.

Aunt Florence had once signed Ellie up for flute lessons, after she had proved herself hopeless at piano. It had been one of her last efforts to spark Ellie's interest in something more ladylike than mummification techniques and Ancient Greek.

She'd been terrible at it, but she remembered enough to know how such a mouthpiece worked. *Press your lips to the side, blow across...gently, gently...*

She wedged herself awkwardly into the space between the statue and the throne. The wood of the pipe tasted bitter against her lips, and Ellie hoped sincerely that she wasn't poisoning herself.

Then she blew.

The sound whispered out of the throat of the statue, an eerie, lingering note.

She didn't know the language. No one did—no one living, at any rate. But she had no doubt that what she'd just heard was a word.

More than that: a name.

Adam was staring up at her from the base of the statue, his eyes wide with astonishment.

"They're instruments," Ellie repeated weakly. He responded by yanking the lever at the base of the statue.

There was a loud ticking sound as ancient gears moved forward. The door at the far end of the room rose an inch from the floor.

Adam raced over to it. He wedged his fingers into the narrow gap and hauled, the cords standing out on his neck.

The door didn't budge.

Ellie half slid, half fell off the statue, ignoring him as she hurried to the next figure in the circle. This one was scaled like a lizard, glossy, inhuman eyes glaring red in the torchlight. She pulled herself up, feet scrambling for purchase. She found the pipe at the back and blew.

Nothing.

"Fake," Adam said from below. He moved past her to the next figure, climbing as Ellie descended.

"How the hell does this work?" he shouted down.

"It's like a flute. Blow across it, not into it," she called as she dropped back to the ground.

She stumbled against the next statue, catching herself. It was so very *hot*. The clouds of steam were a veil she fought through, one that invaded her brain, making it hard to think.

A clear, haunting phrase sounded behind her, cutting through the fog.

"We have a winner," Adam announced from his perch.

Just find the pipes, she ordered herself grimly, and started to climb a giant skeleton. But at the top of this statue, there was no pipe. Only a broken stub of wood, the mouthpiece snapped off centuries before.

"This one's broken," she called, her voice cracking.

"Skip it and move on. If we reach the end and the door is still closed, then we'll know whether or not to pull the lever."

She nodded, though Adam was no longer looking, and worked her way back down to the floor.

The rest of the circle passed in a blur. Every success ticked the door up another hairbreadth, but it was still not enough for anyone larger than a child to squeeze through, not enough to relieve the mounting pressure of the steam that poured into the room.

Finally, only one figure remained, the largest in the room. The face before her was human but twisted. The sickly yellow skin was crossed with fat horizontal lines of black. Wings rose from behind it, and one arm was replaced by a coiling serpent. In the center of its chest was a black disk, flat and shining. The strange preservative caught the torchlight and threw it back, casting eerie reflections.

It was a face she knew. The god of the medallion. The Smoking Mirror.

Her head throbbed. Her muscles ached. Nausea welled in her guts, the heat choking her. And it seemed like the monster before her shifted, turning its black eyes to her, and smiled.

It will swallow me whole, she thought distantly.

Then she shook herself. She was hallucinating. The heat had nearly overcome her. She needed to *move*.

She scrambled up the statue, her limbs sluggish, as though she fought her way through water. At last she reached the top and stared down numbly at the back of the statue's neck.

There was nothing there.

Just as with the skeleton on the far side of the circle, the delicate wood was broken here as well. There was no mouthpiece, no way to make the monster sing.

"Princess, we need to hurry."

Adam looked up at her from the base of the throne. Sweat streamed down his chest. His eyes were hollow.

"This one is broken, too."

She slid down the statue, landing awkwardly on the floor.

Adam's eyes were closed.

"Two broken. The door's still stuck," he muttered. "At least one of them must be real. How the hell do we know which one?"

The light danced around her. It seemed like all the gods of hell had turned to gaze at her, their faces contorting into monstrous grins.

Hallucinating. She was hallucinating.

"We have to choose," she said thickly.

"And if we choose wrong? We can't afford for it to get any worse in here."

She stared at him across the lever. The rest of the room was dissolving into twisting, ghoul-haunted shadows. Only Adam seemed solid, exhausted and gleaming in the torchlight.

Then even he faded, the darkness at the edge of her vision narrowing to consume him. She felt the tendons of her knees quiver, then give way. She slipped toward the floor.

There was a sharp curse. Strong arms caught her, gathered her up. She felt Adam's body shift as he gave the lever before them a sharp kick, snapping it into place.

She was only vaguely aware of the crunching of ancient gears, but the blast of cool air that followed—that she felt in exquisite, almost painful detail.

She was carried into it. The heat melted away, replaced by blessed cold. Then she was half spilled to the ground as Adam sank down beneath her, letting her fall to his side as he slumped against the wall of the next chamber.

He was barely visible in the flickering light coming through the doorway, the remnants of the torches they had abandoned. Steam poured through the opening, but Ellie could already see it thinning.

Adam leaned back against the wall of the cave, eyes closed.

"How did you know?" Ellie asked.

"Know what?"

"Which one was real."

He shrugged. "I figured a fifty-fifty shot was better than a one hundred percent chance of getting cooked."

The implication dawned on her.

"You guessed?"

"Didn't have time to flip a coin."

She felt both horror and admiration.

That had been close—far too close.

The caves that surrounded them were more than an initiation. They were a death trap. The tests they would have to pass to get through this maze were meant to take the life of anyone unworthy. Only someone with a lifetime of training in the myths and sacred knowledge of this culture should be able to pass.

None of which they possessed.

Adam climbed to his feet. He ducked through the low doorway back into the council chamber and returned with one of their torches. It was burning dangerously low, but another basket beside the door provided replacements. As the new flames caught, Ellie took a careful look at their surroundings.

The space around them was narrower than the others they had passed through. A jumble of rock formations protruded from floor, walls, and ceiling to create a sort of half-finished jigsaw. Moving in any visible direction would mean ducking and dodging, twisting around and under massive obstacles.

It was impossible to discern a path or make out more than what lay a few yards away through the maze of stone. The location of the exit was a mystery.

"Which way do we go?" she asked.

"We start left and follow the outer wall until we find a way out."

Torch raised, Adam ducked around a thick pillar, resting a hand on a narrow, oddly twisted stone. He jerked back with an exclamation of pain.

"What is it?" Ellie said, hurrying to him.

"Damned sharp rock," he retorted. She saw him give his hand a pained shake and she caught it, then flashed him a warning glare when he started to pull it free.

"Don't move," she ordered, then muttered a curse of her own. His palm had been sliced neatly across, nearly four inches from side to side.

"It's a scratch," he declared firmly when she looked up at him, wide-eyed.

"It needs stitches," she countered. He would not talk his way out of this so easily.

"You got a needle?"

She turned her shoulder to him.

"Tear off the sleeve," she ordered.

"What?"

"My sleeve. Tear it off," she repeated impatiently.

He was still staring at her with a sort of numb, shocked look.

"Oh, very well," she snapped, tugging at the sleeve herself. Her efforts seemed to give Adam the picture. He snapped out of the trance he'd been in and ripped the seam with one sharp yank with his good hand.

"Thank you," she said curtly, taking the fabric from him. She lifted his hand and bound the wound, tying the makeshift bandage tightly.

"That will have to do for now," she announced, then frowned. Adam was staring at her bare shoulder.

"Is something wrong?"

"Stay still."

He slipped carefully past her and took a closer look at the stone that had wounded him. Peering around him, Ellie could see the dark stain where he had been cut, and something else, an odd patterning to the rock. It was a sort of regular faceting. She frowned, studying it more closely. There was something familiar about the look of it.

"It's been knapped," Adam said.

"Knapped?" she echoed, frowning.

"Like a piece of flint. Someone made this sharp on purpose."

Ellie raised the torch and took a closer glance at the other rock formations. Once she knew what she was looking for, it was easy to see them: bladelike edges, man-made, glinting from every surface of the cave. Adam followed her study, and his expression darkened.

"Xibalba was supposed to contain a room called the House of Razors," he said, brushing a fingertip carefully across one of the knifelike edges.

"Another test."

He nodded.

Ellie eyed the uneven ground, covered in tumbled stones. All it would take was one misstep, and either of them could fall against knives of stone. The slice on Adam's hand could easily have been a severed artery.

"How do we get through it?"

"Very carefully," he replied.

The place was a maze. The stones of the floor shifted precariously under her feet, and more than once Adam's quick reflexes were all that kept her from tumbling against some razor-sharp blade of rock. Low archways forced them to make awkward contortions, ducking and weaving beneath glittering edges of stone. After the fourth time she'd been forced to crawl across the floor to avoid some knife-sharp obstacle, Ellie stopped.

"Where's the bloody door?" she demanded.

"Over there." Adam nodded. Ahead of them, the ground gave way on either side. Only a narrow ridge remained, lined on either side by a dark pit.

Ellie moved closer, letting the light of her torch fall on what lay below. Daggers of rock like the fangs of some enormous beast shone back at her.

On the far side, a wooden door sat in the flat face of the cave wall.

Adam turned her face to his. His words were calm and even, as though he were speaking to a horse about to bolt.

"You'll want to move slowly. Don't. It's harder to stay balanced when you're standing still. Hold my hand, and walk like there's a temperance group with a petition behind you. Got it?"

"What happens if one of us—"

"Time to move."

Adam grasped her arm with his uninjured hand, pulling her onto the ridge. Her instinct roared at her to pull back, but doing so would only upset his balance. There was no choice but to let him drag her forward.

She could feel the peaked stone crumble under her boots. They tilted on it like the fulcrum of a seesaw. She forced herself not to look at the stone daggers below her, instead following as Adam hauled her along.

Then it was over.

She stood on solid ground on the far side of the pit, looking at another heavy door set into the wall of the cave.

Then she noticed something odd about their exit.

"Shouldn't there be a latch?"

Like the last door, this one had no visible knob or hinges. There was only the smooth, oiled surface of the wood.

"There must be a release mechanism here somewhere. Look for it."

Adam turned his attention to the door, feeling along the frame. Ellie was drawn to the surrounding walls of the cave.

There was an opening to the right of the doorway. It seemed no more than a shadow at first, but she lowered the torch for a closer look. The hole was deep and narrow, no wider than eight inches across. When she held her torch at just the right angle, it seemed to her she could see something on the far side of it.

"Bates?" she called. "I think I've found a lever."

He peered into the space.

"It's lined with razors," he announced. "Might need your other sleeve by the time this is done."

He reached for the opening.

"Of all the idiotic..." She caught his hand and pushed it back. She thrust her torch at him and began rolling up her sleeve.

"If you think I'm going to stand here and let you—"

"Your arms are twice as broad as mine," she countered crisply. "This maze was designed for Mayans, or people very like them— a slight people. Now hold that as close as you can. I need to see where I'm going."

Adam was obviously unhappy with the situation, but Ellie knew he couldn't argue with the logic of her point. She stood a much better chance than he did of coming through unscathed. And the man was battered enough already, she thought, giving him a quick look. His trousers were torn, skin scraped, hair wild.

Not that it lessened his appeal one bit.

She shook her head clear of the thought and focused on the task before her. That other edge had sliced Adam as neatly as a scalpel. She was sure these would be no different. She could not afford so much as a tremble in the wrong direction.

Hand elegantly folded, she slowly, painstakingly threaded it into the gap. She realized that the torchlight would be of little use.

She would have to rely on feeling, holding her arm carefully to the center until she had cleared the far side.

She breathed deeply and steadily, trying not to think of how very easily this could go wrong. Cut the wrong vein, something that couldn't be easily stopped up, and she might bleed to death here on the cave floor.

Stop that.

She paused, badgering her uncooperative mind until it begrudgingly cleared, then continued.

Straight and still, nice and easy...

After what seemed like an eternity, she felt her fingertips brush against a staff of wood, warm and smooth under her hand. Gripping it, she pulled it toward her, arm kept ramrod straight and carefully centered.

There was a clicking of gears, then a shudder and a clang as the door gave way, creaking open a hairbreadth. Cool air poured into the gap. She let out a gasping laugh of relief, allowing herself that much release before returning her attention to carefully withdrawing her arm from the hole.

At last, she was loose. Adam grabbed her hand and Ellie started, wondering whether he had noticed some new threat. Then she realized he was studying the bare skin, making certain she hadn't been injured.

"I'm fine," she assured him.

"I can see that."

They stared at each other in the torchlight, and Ellie felt her unanswered questions bubbling back to the surface.

"Ready?" he asked, breaking the tension.

"Of course," she countered, and pushed past him into the next room.

She lifted the flame and looked around the vast, empty space as Adam entered behind her.

23

THE GAP IN THE floor opened onto a short set of stairs, and from there a tunnel sloped gradually down. Dawson trudged along it with shoulders hunched to keep his head from bumping against the low ceiling. He kept a few steps behind one of the dust-covered workmen. He had seen enough of the technical skills of the vanished people of this city to consider booby traps a possibility, and preferred that someone else be the one to discover them. The workman, happily, was oblivious to that threat, being more concerned—based on the tight grip he kept on the crucifix around his neck—with the possibility of evil ghosts.

Luckily for the hapless fellow, the tunnel was free of hidden dangers. It ended at a pair of wooden doors that swung open without so much as a single lock, revealing a vast, dark space that smelled of damp and stone and time.

The men came in tentatively, raising their lanterns.

It was a tomb, but one utterly unlike any that Dawson had seen before. The chamber was a natural one, a vast limestone cavern threaded with delicate pillars. The walls were vividly painted, though their imagery was unsettlingly different from the graceful figures he had smashed to pieces in the room above.

There, everything had been light and elegance. These paintings told another story—one of darkness and sacrifice. Some of the scenes they depicted were so lifelike they made his stomach lurch.

He turned away, looking for something to distract his attention. His eyes fell on stacks of folded bark that sat below the murals.

No, not just bark. They were books, Dawson realized, recognizing their similarity to those few that remained from the Mayans. The sight of them put the murals right out of Dawson's head, sparking his archaeological fervor. These were more precious than any pile of gold might have been. All the wisdom of this place, all its secrets— they had survived.

But the room was not meant to be a library. It was a graveyard. Massive stone sarcophagi rested in a circle around him, each one elaborately carved. Atop them, larger than life, were portraits of the powerful men who lay within. The greatest kings of this lost place, the masters of a hidden empire...and they were sharing a tomb.

It was unheard-of. In no culture that Dawson had studied did the ego-mad leaders condescend to share their final monuments. Tombs were singular. Great men wanted their own memorials, bigger and more impressive than those that had come before. And here were more than a dozen of them, lying together as equals in this cave.

Dawson knew better than to think it was by preference. There was only one reason such men would give up dreams of their own temples or pyramids, and that was because there was a greater power in this kingdom than their own. And that power, it appeared, lay in the center of the cavern in a round depression in the floor.

It was a massive, perfectly flat disk, polished to a flawless gleam that echoed every detail of the room, from the lamplight of the workers to the stone pillars dripping down from the roof. Dawson could not tell whether the thing was made from stone or metal, only that it was cool and smooth as a lake on a windless day, and utterly, completely black.

It was a mirror, he realized—*the* mirror. The Smoking Mirror, glass of Tezcatlipoca. The Eye of the Gods. The object he had been sent here to retrieve at all costs, an object he now knew was no mere curiosity.

It was Power, shining on the ground before him.

Tentatively he approached it. It lay in a shallow declivity carved to fit it. A moat surrounded it, feeding into a channel that ran to a narrow crevice in the floor of the room. Both were stained a dark, rusted hue—blood, Dawson realized.

The whole arrangement suddenly became clear to him, the realization fueled by the horrific scenes on the walls around him.

Sacrifice. It made perfect sense. The ritual virtues of blood were not strange to the Mayans and the Aztecs. Blood celebrated victories, placated angry deities, and it also opened the gates of prophecy. The blood of animals, of enemies—the precious fluid of self-mutilation . . .

It was no small leap to deduce it. The mirror would be fed, the priests offering it birds, beasts, maybe men. In exchange for life, it granted them knowledge.

The idea made him ill.

He forced himself to move closer, crouching down beside it. The disk wasn't embedded in the floor of the cave, but only rested on it. It was at most an inch thick. Not that it mattered. It was still enormous.

How the devil am I supposed to get this to England?

"Get the photographic equipment," Dawson ordered, and a pair of his men turned and hurried up the ramp, glad for an excuse to leave. A few others were eyeing the big stone sarcophagi greedily, but most hung near the entrance, looking uneasily at the murals covering the walls. Dawson could understand why. A longer examination of them revealed depictions of even more horrific brutalities.

He forced his mind back to his work. They would need images of everything, and the camera was much faster than waiting on the skills of an artist. The books, the walls, the coffins, and the mirror—all of it would be photographed in situ before they began packing it up. His employer had asked only for the mirror, but the scholar in Dawson insisted that as much of its context as possible be preserved as well. If the object was worth all this trouble, then the information would undoubtedly be appreciated eventually, and so would the man who had thought to save it.

He called for a camp stool and began taking notes. The surface of the mirror was clean. In fact, not even a speck of dust marred its perfection. But then, perhaps the cave was very stable. Certainly there had been no humans here to shed their skin and hair into the atmosphere.

Or had there? He noted that the stained surface of the channel around the mirror was darker in one place. And there, at the base of the nearest pillar, just in its shadow... Dawson rose and walked over to it. It was the corpse of a bird, a particularly spectacular macaw. Dawson could see the wide, dry flap where the creature's throat had been cut, skin turned to leather by the atmosphere of the cave.

Why was this one bird left when the rest of whatever victims had once been offered to the mirror had clearly been removed? Had they been in such a hurry at the end? Or...

Dawson bent over the bird, peered more closely at its feathers, its delicate bones. How long had this corpse been here? Was it less faded than the body they had found in the chamber above? What if they weren't the first ones to find this place since its abandonment? He thought of the broken stone that had given away the entrance to the temple's secrets. If someone else had stumbled across this place, someone superstitious enough to try the mirror's magic...

He stepped back, frowning. He glanced around the room, his gaze stopping on the figure of the strange Mayan, who sat at the foot of one of the sarcophagi with eyes closed as though napping.

It was only the merest suspicion. And the man was unarmed. But Dawson told himself he would watch the newcomer carefully.

The chamber Ellie stood in was not far across, but it stretched wide and dark to either side. And it was a cold space, startlingly cold. The impact of the frigid air was heightened by the dampness of her clothes, which quickly wicked away her natural heat, starting her shivering.

Before them, a narrow bridge of land stretched from the door through which they had entered to the exit, which was clearly visible. On either side of the bridge were the still, greenish waters of a pair of underground lakes. Any doubts she may have had about whether the chill of the room was a trick of contrast with the warmer, closer space they had just left were put to rest by the sight of the ice rimming the still waters of the ponds.

"Where are we now?"

"I'm guessing the Rattling Room." Adam's words came in a fog of breath. "The Room of Shaking Cold."

"It's certainly that," she noted.

"They must be tapping into some subterranean air current, something from farther up the mountains," Adam said, answering her unspoken question.

"But it's summer," she countered. "It wouldn't get this cold even at the highest altitudes."

"Well, they're getting it from somewhere," he retorted.

That she could not argue with.

"Shall we try the door?" she offered.

"Can't hurt."

They crossed along the narrow land bridge, the waters utterly still on either side, reflecting back the light of their torches. The exit was like the others had been, a door of solid wood lacking a visible knob, latch, or hinges, carefully fitted into the opening.

Adam glanced around the cavern, keen eyed. "There must be another lever hidden in here somewhere."

"Hidden where? There aren't exactly many places we can get to."

The waters of the two ponds were flush with the cave walls on either side of each doorway. There were no other paths or ledges to explore, only a platform before each door and the bridge that connected them.

She saw him frown. His gaze moved from the bridge to the pale waters beside it. She read the thought before he voiced it, and fear leaped up into her throat.

"That's madness."

"Nowhere else to look," he replied. He knelt down and began to untie the laces of his boots.

"The water temperature must be near freezing. You'll black out if you're in there for more than a minute."

"I'm not planning on hanging around."

"There's got to be another way."

"I'm all ears."

He looked for her response, but she had none.

"We can't spend much longer in here. Not like this." He nodded toward her damp clothes, then went to work on his boot. She knew that stubborn cast to his expression. It would be futile to try to reason with him. What she needed was to think of an alternative before he got those boots off and tossed himself into the deadly waters.

She turned from him, examining the door frantically. There had to be some kind of trick, but the surface revealed nothing. No holes, no gears, nothing that could hide a secret release.

Logic was not going to avail her here, she realized. She didn't have enough time for precision. In another moment Adam would be plunging into those ice-cold waters, and she wasn't sure he would make it out again. She needed a leap of intuition.

She took a long, deep breath, forcefully clearing her mind, shoving back her awareness of the sound of Adam tossing the first boot aside. She gazed at the door, the whole of it.

What's different?

She glanced up. There was a dark black stain flaring up from the top of the door, shadowing the stone. *Smoke*, she thought. *There has been a fire here.*

Fire defeats cold. She noted the oily sheen on the surface of the wood as, behind her, Adam moved to the water's edge.

"One minute. I won't be any longer," he said.

Ellie did not bother to turn to him.

"You may want to step back," she said, and tossed her torch at the door.

It was as though she had thrown it into kerosene. Flames roared up and out, the entire surface exploding with heat. Adam grabbed her and pulled her along the bridge.

"Head down," he ordered as the smoke poured across the chamber. But the space was wide, and the same mysterious system that spilled cold air into the chamber functioned to ventilate it, so that where they stopped by the far door, the air remained clear even as the blaze continued.

It took no time at all for the treated wood to crumble, giving way. The door collapsed onto the ground, where it continued to crackle and smolder.

They crossed the bridge to the remains of the door, and, after retrieving his boots, Adam used his hands to scatter some water over the hot embers that glowed in the tunnel mouth, cooling them with a hiss of steam. He shook the droplets off and thrust his hands under his arms for warmth, then looked down at the icy pond.

"Pretty glad I didn't have to go for a dip in there," he commented. "How'd you figure the door would go up like that?"

"Women's intuition, Mr. Bates. You should learn to listen to it every once in a while," she replied haughtily.

"Yes, ma'am," he answered, with a telltale crinkling of his eyes. Then he gestured widely at the opening. "Ladies first."

She proceeded into the tunnel, the damp sleeve of her shirt pressed to her nose to cut the still-lingering smoke. The way twisted once, then back before the low-ceilinged passage ended at a closed door. This one had a latch that was clearly visible. Ellie put out a hand to open it, then hesitated.

"What other tests were in the Popol Vuh?"

"Damned if I know," he replied easily.

"Didn't you read the whole book?" she demanded.

"Ages ago. And the trials of Xibalba were only a small part of it. Hell, even the twins made it through only a handful of them."

"Whatever is behind this door was meant to possibly maim or kill us. It'd be nice to have a little bit of warning."

"We'll manage," he tossed back, and, reaching around her, pulled the latch. The door swung wide and their torchlight spilled into a high-ceilinged chamber, quiet and smelling of dust. Another basket of torches sat at the entrance. Adam lit one to replace the one she'd sacrificed in the Rattling Room. They lifted both high and their combined light fell across a pile of bones.

They were all in a jumble, skulls and femurs and smaller, more obscure bits and knobs, stacked in a heap at the base of a near pillar. Some were clearly animal. Ellie thought she recognized dogs and monkeys. Others—fewer, but assuredly present—were human.

"What did that?" she asked quietly, feeling fear tickle at the back of her neck.

"I think they did," Adam replied. His tone was solemn. Ellie turned and saw that he was gazing down at a pair of skeletons that lay a few steps farther into the room.

They were intact, perfectly arranged on the floor of the cave. The bare ribs gave onto gracefully angled limbs, the backbones extended out in a long curve that had once been a tail. In the skull, rows of wicked fangs glimmered dully in the torchlight.

"Jaguar."

Adam confirmed it with a nod. He moved forward a few steps and his flame illuminated another of the long-dead beasts, crumpled under a ledge of stone.

"They must have been trapped down here with no way outside. They would have to have been fed, watered. And when there was no one left to do that . . ."

"They starved," she finished for him. The notion made her stomach clench. Surely even in the chaos, someone could have remembered, could have taken a few extra moments to open the door, to give them a chance.

Adam touched her arm.

"Let's go."

The room was large, broken here and there by tall, graceful pillars. The sound of their footsteps echoing off the high walls as they walked reminded Ellie of passing through a cathedral. The hollow echoing was the same. It was appropriate. The place was, after all, a tomb.

Like the last one, the door on the far side was closed with a simple latch. Opening it was not meant to have been the challenge.

Getting there at all would have been the meat of it, when the guardians of the place had still been alive and hungry.

The tunnel into which the door opened quickly narrowed, lowering within a few yards to the point where the pair of them were forced to crawl, torches awkwardly suspended in front of them. It felt as though they were moving deeper into the bowels of the cave system, farther than ever from a way out.

Then there was the smell. It was faint at first, just a noxious hint to the atmosphere, but it grew stronger and richer as they progressed, until at last Ellie followed Adam through the mouth of the tunnel and stood, only to feel her feet sliding out from underneath her.

Adam grabbed her arm, tugging her upright before she could fall. She saw that he had braced himself against one of the stones. The floor of the chamber appeared to be covered in some sort of thick slime—a very smelly slime. She took a careful step to better balance herself and something crunched lightly under her boot. It was an altogether unpleasant sound. Glancing down, she saw what looked like small animal bones protruding from the sludge.

"What on earth—" she began, but Adam cut her off with a hand clamped over her mouth. She started to protest, but he only shook his head, his expression deadly serious. He put a finger to his lips, then pointed up, straight to the roof of the cave.

Ellie followed his gesture and felt her stomach knot. The ceiling, which was not nearly as high as she would have liked, was covered in hanging bodies of brown fur and thick, leathery skin.

Bats.

But these were not the pests that inhabited church belfries back in England. They were monsters. Ellie estimated that they were roughly four feet in length, with wingspans broader than a man's outstretched arms. They clung to the roof of the cave with massive black claws. As she watched, one of them yawned lazily, revealing an array of knifelike fangs, yellow and wicked.

She realized she had been hearing them since she came in, a sort of gentle sighing, the subtle stirring and murmuring of a thousand sleeping monsters.

Adam yanked her back into the tunnel. They crouched there together, and she felt her hands start to shake.

"What are they?" she whispered hoarsely.

"They're a goddamned myth," he muttered. His voice was just the slightest bit unsteady. "Camazotz."

Camazotz. She remembered the name. Back in the caves they'd passed through on the *Mary Lee*, they had been an ancient painting scribbled onto the wall, a story told to frighten children.

The creatures sleeping overhead were no myth. A myth wouldn't reek of refuse and rot.

"But how have they survived down here all this time?"

"They must have a way out to feed."

Feed.

It came to her in silent horror. She remembered the two slaughtered guards in the jungle, the blood staining the leaves, the look of wild terror in the eyes of a dying man.

They came out of the night.

The angels of death.

The monsters that had caused that slaughter were sleeping in legions over her head.

Because Death lives there. That was what Amilcar Kuyoc had said, back in the village. Death and his servants, who feasted on the flesh of trespassers.

She forced herself to calm. Panic wasn't going to help.

"How did those twins of yours get past them?"

"They didn't," Adam muttered.

Her fear was as real and sharp as the stench.

"Can we go back?"

Adam's answer was an eloquently raised eyebrow. Ellie winced, thinking of everything they had come through already. Cold, knives, acid, and poison. And at the end of it, a long, dark swim to a hole in the ground they could never escape from.

No, there was only one way to get out of this alive, and it led through that room full of demons.

"We'll move quietly," Adam said.

Very damned quietly, Ellie thought in response.

Still gripping her arm, he led the way as they crept slowly across the floor, feet sliding in the thick slime of guano and crunching over small bones. Ellie winced with every crackle, painfully conscious of the mass of horrible brown bodies suspended over their heads.

She thought of the jungle they had passed through, how conspicuously absent of animal life it had been. Of course. These things had been hunting it for centuries, feasting and breeding down here in the dark.

She moved carefully, trying to watch the ground for obstructions or anything that might cause noise. The crackle of the torches, even the hush of her own breath, sounded painfully loud to her ears.

She took another step forward, and the stone beneath her foot sank several inches into the ground.

Ellie froze.

"Bates!" she whispered fiercely. He turned back to her. "The floor just moved."

He came closer, so close that she could feel his body in the dark. His voice was low and dangerous.

"What do you mean?"

"I mean…that I think I've just stepped on some kind of mechanism."

His curse was barely a whisper, but was no less virulent for its lack of volume. She felt him kneel down, his hands running down her leg to her boot. They probed at the floor where she stood.

"It's square. Too regular to be natural. It's dropped about four inches."

"Maybe it's just meant to trip me?" Ellie offered weakly.

"Yeah. Maybe."

She thought of the other tricks the people of this ancient place had played on them. Doors dropping into place. Steam pouring from the ground. Ice and heat and monsters.

Whatever the stone beneath her foot triggered, she knew with a sinking certainty that it couldn't be good.

Adam rose. She felt his hand on her shoulder as he looked steadily into her eyes.

"First I'm going to pull you off of it. Then we're going to run."

"That's your solution?"

"Do you have a better suggestion?"

Ellie opened her mouth to reply, but words failed her. What was the alternative? Stay where she was until the beasts overhead woke up for a snack?

She felt Adam's hand slide to her arm, gripping her tight.

"On my mark. One...two...three..."

Adam pulled her off the stone.

She felt it rise under her foot, and a high-pitched whistle shrieked through the room.

The sound was so abrupt it stopped her in her tracks, freezing her in place like a startled animal.

For a moment the chamber was deadly silent. Then it erupted into a chaos of squealing screams and beating black wings.

"Down!" Adam shouted, and shoved her toward a tower of stone to her left. Her knees slid in the slime coating the floor, and she scrambled for traction, using both her hands and her feet to claw her way forward. She skated through the filth, coming to a stop under an outcropping. Adam crashed in beside her and they huddled together as leathery wings whipped past them, the air shattered with inhuman screams.

"What now?" she demanded.

"I'm open to suggestions," he shot back as they both flinched away from a particularly low-flying monster.

He glanced around their hiding place, then pushed his torch into Ellie's hand.

"Put them in there for a second," he ordered, pointing to a deep crack in the rock. Ellie didn't relish the idea of making their situation any darker than it was already, but obeyed. Adam had the air of a plan about him, and she was fresh out of ideas.

The cave went dark as the flames were concealed. Adam waited, listening, then suddenly thrust his head out from under the ledge.

She resisted the urge to haul him back, and he returned intact a moment later.

"There's an opening in the roof. That's how they get out," he reported.

"Can we climb to it?"

He shook his head. "There's got to be a trick to this one, just like the others. I'm going to go out and take a look for it. You just... stay put."

No—not again.

In the past few hours, she'd watched Adam risk his life over and over again, each time coming within a hairbreadth of being lost to her for good. Now he was about to head out into a maelstrom of demons. She had seen firsthand what those creatures could do to a man, and here was not just one or two but hundreds of them. It was entirely possible that Adam would leave their precarious shelter and never come back.

For the first time, Ellie acknowledged how that made her feel— and what that feeling meant.

It hit her with all the impact of a freight train. What was happening in her heart went beyond a physical attraction, beyond the respect of colleagues, or even friendship. Losing him would mean losing everything that mattered to her.

Ellie grabbed his shirt, pulling him back under the overhang, and kissed him.

Everything else melted into static—the screaming of the predators circling around them, the stench of the filth covering her clothes. There was only the glory of touching him resonating through her, setting her buzzing like a tuning fork.

The kiss broke. The dangers around them came roaring back, and with them an even greater sense of urgency. It drove the words from her mouth before she had time to fear or second-guess. She grabbed his face in her hands, turning it toward her and meeting his eyes with desperation.

"I love you," she cried over the racket that surrounded them.

She saw his eyes widen with shock, then melt into what looked—rather surprisingly—like relief.

"Thank God!" he exclaimed.

She had been bracing herself for disappointment the moment the words had come out of her mouth, for a look of pity or awkwardness. His actual reaction was far more confusing.

"What's that supposed to mean?" she demanded.

"It means—"

His explanation was cut off by a cacophony of outraged screams and a thunder of beating wings. The monsters outside had passed so close, Ellie could feel the wind of their passing. Adam pulled her to the farthest reaches of their shelter, putting himself between her and the threat that surrounded them.

The monsters passed, and he put his hand behind her neck, fingers tangling in her cropped hair. His face inches from her own, he stared into her eyes in the near darkness.

"How about I get us out of this mess, and then I'll show you what it means?"

"Fair enough," she said weakly.

"Don't move," he ordered. Then he kissed her again, this one quick and urgent, and disappeared into the maelstrom.

The room was a whirling nightmare. Moving blindly, Adam half dashed, half skated across the floor, keeping as close as possible to the more immobile shadows. He swung around one, a massive stone cliff, and pressed himself against it as the bats buzzed past him.

In that moment of rest, it came home to him in a giddy rush.

She loves me.

Though of course the woman would have to wait until now to reveal it. The circumstances weren't exactly amenable to his showing her just exactly what he meant to do with the knowledge that his feelings weren't one-sided.

Once he got them out of this, he promised himself, he would make it up to her. Thoroughly.

He forced his attention back to his task. He wasn't sure what he was looking for. He just knew there must be something, a key to this puzzle like there had been to the others. Pressing himself to the stone, he took a slow, careful look around him.

There it was—a slight glimmer flashing at him through the darkness. It was barely discernible from where he hid, so he risked another dash, moving across the slick floor, rolling under a swooping great dark thing and coming to another small shelter. From there, he could see clearly what he had only glimpsed before.

It was a painting, glowing softly in the darkness with an unearthly greenish light. It was like the glow he'd sometimes seen on the beaches of the cays at night, an eerie phosphorescence. The image was of the pale outline of a vaguely familiar figure. He had seen something like it before, carved into temple walls or marking stelae. It looked like Huracan, the Mayan god of wind. In the dark, Adam dodged another swooping monster. It was time to stir things up in here.

Ellie waited alone in an active and vicious darkness, surrounded by rushing bodies, choked by the stink, and wondering what the devil was taking Adam so long. Every extra minute brought a hundred different visions of what might be happening to him out there in that nightmare of a cave.

How about I get us out of this mess, and then I'll show you what it means?

He'd better, she thought fiercely. She would be damned if she was going to let him slip away from her.

Then something clattered on the ground before her hiding place.

Ellie froze, her instincts screaming.

A great black body flopped awkwardly in front of her. It hovered at the entrance and sniffed.

Then sniffed again.

Ellie muttered a silent prayer that she was sufficiently covered in bat slime to disguise her scent. The creature let out a high, piercing screech and took to the air with a heavy flap of its wings. She felt a brief moment of relief.

Then the bat swooped in shockingly low and fast, coming within a few inches of the ledge.

It flew at her again, wings slapping against the stone as it reached into the nook with its daggerlike talons.

Ellie pressed herself back against the rock and kicked out as hard and quick as she could. She felt her boot connect with solid flesh and the bat fell back, flopping awkwardly on the ground before flipping itself over and taking flight once more.

She rolled over and pulled the torches from their hole in the stone. The flames were still burning brightly. She smiled grimly. Whichever of those monsters came at her next was going to get more than a boot.

Then the space around her filled with a roaring, and she fell back as she was hit with a fierce gust of wind. The whole chamber was consumed with it, an impossible storm that sent the bats, screaming in protest, out their far skylight and into the night. The torches blew out, leaving her in virtual darkness.

Ellie waited, trying to hear some sign of Adam's approach. There was nothing but the roaring wind.

She crawled from her hiding place, gripping the stone to keep herself upright. Looking up, she could see black winged forms spilling through the star-studded gap in the roof.

"Bates!"

A hand gripped her arm, propelling her forward.

"Time to go," Adam said.

"What did you do?" she shouted over the wind as he pulled her along.

"Found a door marked 'Storm God' and opened it," he replied, and hurried her around a bend. They ducked as a disoriented bat dipped over them, then turned to face another of the maze's many doors. This one, too, featured a simple latch. Adam opened it and pushed Ellie inside. He shoved it closed behind them as Ellie protested.

"The torches..."

There was a heavy clank as the door sealed. She felt frantically for a latch, and failed. There would be no going back—not that she was all that eager to try.

"Hold on. I'll get a match. You look for something else we can burn. There might be another basket of torches nearby."

Ellie nodded, then realized the gesture was meaningless. While the open roof of the last chamber had offered at least a feeble illumination, the darkness here was so complete, she couldn't see her hand an inch from her face.

She heard Adam rustling in the dark; then with a scrape and a hiss, one of his matches flared to life.

She had just enough time for a comforting view of his filth-streaked face before, with a soft draft like a whisper from the cave itself, the flame blew out.

"Damn," Adam muttered. She heard him fumble for another match.

Scrape, hiss, light—and with a quick and ghostly sigh, it was also extinguished.

"Bates?" she said.

"Yeah?" came the reply from the darkness.

"This is going to sound a bit daft, but did those drafts seem a bit...convenient?" She heard the quaver at the end of her own words, and recognized it as fear.

"Caves are notorious for drafts."

His answer was somewhat less than satisfying.

"How many matches do you have left?"

She heard the sliding of the tin again, the wooden scratch, and another flicker of light.

A rustling breath and it was gone.

"Not enough," Adam replied, and, hearing the nuance of his tone in the sense-sharpening blackness, she realized she wasn't the only one afraid of this darkness.

24

FLOWERS DID NOT LIKE walking in the dark. This uncanny place was fearful enough with the comfort of lanterns. With only the occasional burst of lightning filtering down through the trees, the world became a horror of shifting shadows and imagined threats. But Charlie had said they could use no lights. They couldn't risk being spotted, and so the lamps they carried were closely shuttered.

Flowers kept his nervousness to himself. He would not let Charlie think him weak. Flowers might be twice his size, but Charlie was the older one. He had always wanted to impress Charlie. He would ignore the way the shadows unnerved him, though it was all he could do not to cry out when one of them detached itself from the others and came soundlessly toward them.

It was Martin Lavec. The man could move like a panther when he chose, a habit acquired during years of fur trapping both here and back in his native Canada. He came up to the pair and sat down on a block of stone.

"Found it," he announced.

"Far?" Charlie asked.

Lavec shook his head.

"Guarded?"

Lavec smiled, flashing stained teeth. "Not anymore."

"Well, then. Let's move along." Charlie rose and turned with Lavec toward the deeper part of the ruins. Flowers held back, confused.

"But the ravine is that way." He pointed backward.

"We're not going to the ravine," Charlie explained as Lavec snorted and spit.

"I thought we were leaving," Flowers said.

"We are. But if we're going without any pay from these sons of whores, we're taking the easy way," Lavec retorted.

"There's an easy way?" Something in Lavec's tone and the wicked glint in his eye was making Flowers's stomach twist.

He felt Charlie's hand clap onto his shoulder.

"You're going to love it," he asserted.

They turned to walk once more, and the silence of the night was shattered with a chorus of screams. They were high-pitched, sharp, and utterly inhuman, rising from the central courtyard.

They echoed among the tree trunks, then bounced distantly off the surrounding mountains before fading to a tense silence.

"What was that?" Lavec hissed.

Charlie silenced him with a gesture, crouching low in the bush. Flowers followed his example, a primal terror having replaced his unease.

That noise...

Silently, cautiously, Charlie crawled forward toward the source of the unearthly screeching. Only his even greater fear of being left behind pressed Flowers to follow.

They reached the edge of the brush at a ruined wall that bordered the courtyard. They could see the whole of it and, at the far end, the dwindling fires of the camp.

The wind whipped past them, wet and cold. Flowers looked up as lightning cracked across the sky.

Then he saw them.

Dark shapes, massive, wheeling through the air on black wings. He knew what they were, heard their name in his mind in the guttural tones of a dying man.

Los ángeles de la muerte.

The monsters screamed at another sudden flash of light, then swooped, diving at the figures huddled in the camp.

More screams filled the air—screams of men. Another spike of lightning made the slaughter stark, the black beasts tearing at the bodies of the bearers.

Then the rain began.

It poured out of the sky, drenching them in seconds. The ground beneath Flowers's feet turned instantly to mud, tiny rivers running around his boots.

Charlie slid back behind the ruin, Flowers and Lavec following. He looked to the Québécois, his face pale and sober through the downpour.

"How far was it?"

"Sixty yards, due east," Lavec replied.

"We'll get things started." He met Lavec's gaze meaningfully.

"I'll find guns," the other man replied, and slipped away into the storm.

The tomb of kings, the sacred heart of the city: Dawson could see all of it now.

They had brought in bright, high-powered kerosene lamps, and their glow illuminated all but the most narrow and shadowy of corners.

The space clattered with activity. Flash powder exploded, the camera recording all of the gruesome images on the walls. Behind him, workers were carefully packing the precious books into straw-filled crates. Meanwhile, another four men by his feet were crafting a peculiar crate of their own. Very wide and flat, it would be just the size to accommodate the artifact and keep it protected on the long journey back to England.

Jacobs stood beside him. He was looking down at the flat, shining surface of the mirror.

"Are you certain that's it?"

Dawson's hackles rose. What else could it be? An object of such ritual significance that the tombs of the kings were arranged around it—did Jacobs think perhaps some other trinket might be the one they were looking for? And who was Jacobs to question

Dawson's conclusions anyway? Nothing more than a hired thug. A very clever thug, certainly. An extremely clever, very capable thug. But he was not a tenured professor of ancient history.

"This is it," he replied in cold, clipped tones. Jacobs accepted the response without so much as a nod and turned his dark gaze to the men packing the books. He frowned.

"We'll only be taking back what's absolutely essential."

Dawson felt another flare of rage. As if a treasure trove of books from an unknown culture were of anything but the most profound importance. But Dawson suspected there was only one set of terms by which Jacobs measured "essential."

"Those very well may contain vital information about the artifact."

"Fine," Jacobs allowed after a moment's consideration. He turned to the four working on the floor beside the mirror. "Make certain that crate is reinforced."

One of Jacobs's armed men stumbled down the ramp. He was soaked through, and Dawson realized that aboveground, the storm that had been threatening since they arrived must finally have broken.

His face was white with fear.

"There are devils coming out of the sky!" he called.

Jacobs pulled his pistol from its holster, then pointed to a pair of men boxing books near the entrance to the tomb.

"You two, pick those up." He gestured to a set of rifles on the ground nearby. "Anything tries to come through this door, shoot it," he ordered flatly, then stalked through the exit.

⌒

The darkness was perfect. Ellie had been in dark places before—the glade around a country house on a moonless night, a lampless room with heavy velvet curtains. But even then, the gloom had not been impenetrable. There had been forms, variations. If she had let her eyes adjust long enough, she could have seen her way to a door or window.

This was different. This was blindness. She could wave her own hand back and forth in front of her face and catch no glimpse of it. All was ink, thick and impenetrable. It filled her with raw fear. She had to fight the urge to demand that Adam light another match, just to know for a moment that a world still surrounded them, that they had not fallen into some unspeakable void.

"Where are we?" she asked instead.

"I don't know," Adam replied, his voice eerily disembodied. "Some kind of room of eternal night, I'm guessing."

"Should we try another match?"

There was a pause.

"No. I don't think so."

Adam's words stirred the fear in her again. The air around them now was as still as a grave. The drafts that had extinguished the matches they had lit before had been convenient and abrupt.

Ellie found herself unable to avoid the sense that there was something intentional about those subtle exhalations.

It was irrational, of course, almost certainly an invention of her own fear. But then again, there were living things that had survived down here through the long centuries. What they had encountered in the last room was proof of that. If something similar was hidden here, something silent and old, countering their feeble efforts to fight the dark... well, they would hardly be able to see it, would they? Anything could conceal itself in this thick, black night.

She could hear the soft rustle of Adam's clothing as he turned, uselessly surveying what lay around them. "There will be another door somewhere. I think we should choose a direction, follow the wall until we find it."

She nodded uselessly, then answered. "Agreed."

"I'll lead. Stay behind me and watch where you step. I'll be testing the way ahead, but there could be pits in the cave floor that I miss. Keep close and be careful."

She felt his hand connect with her arm. She gripped him back and he started moving slowly from the door.

They walked without speaking, but even the grinding of boot

on stone, the brushing of cloth on skin, sounded loud as a thunder crack in the stillness and darkness of the cave.

They rounded a bend, and the ghost of the place returned again. Ellie felt it as a soft breath in her hair. Then came a distant murmur, a whisper like that of faraway, distorted voices. They were barely discernible, but they chilled her.

It could be water, she thought. A trickle of running water somewhere nearby. Or just her ears playing tricks on her in the dark. The breeze shifted, brushed her again, and then the sound was gone. She hurried forward, keeping close as Adam continued his painstaking progress around the room. Abruptly he stopped, and with her hypersensitive ears she could hear the difference in the texture under his fingers, smoother and hollow.

"I think we've got it," he said. She joined him, running her hands over the door, feeling the edges. Like the others, they were flush, tightly fitted. And after a moment, it was clear their escape would be more difficult than it seemed.

"No latch, no hinges," Adam growled. "It's another one with a trick opening."

Ellie sat down, feeling despair wash in. Who knew how big the cavern was? The release could be anywhere. It might take days to find it, days in the dark with no food or water....

She sniffed. Her stream of panicked thought stumbled to a halt, arrested by a strange instinct. There was something about the smell of the air here, something important.

Phosphorus. The place where they stood reeked of it.

She ran her hands over the ground as, behind her, Adam continued to curse at the door. It took only a moment to find what she was looking for. She rose, fumbling until she found him, and pressed it into his hand.

"What—"

"It's a matchstick, Bates."

He groaned as the implication dawned. "It's the same door."

"We're back where we started," she confirmed. She heard him begin to pace.

"The exit must be somewhere else. Not the walls. Maybe the floor. Or overhead. If there's someplace we can climb up, get closer to the ceiling..."

She remembered the uncanny draft, the haunting whispering. A suspicion took shape.

"Come with me."

She took his hand and led him around the cavern once more, feeling her way along the wall. She opened her senses as she moved. She was rewarded when she once again felt the hairs blowing gently on her head and neck, caught in a strange draft. Another step, and there were the whispers—intermittent, quieter now, but unmistakably there.

"I need you to boost me up."

"Watch your head," he replied. She bit back a yelp as she felt something press against the backs of her thighs.

"What are you—"

"Just hang on."

She slipped back as he rose, lifting her on his shoulders like a child. She barely kept her balance, only just remembering to raise her arms to ensure that her head wasn't about to knock into the roof of the cave.

Fortunately, the ceiling was high.

"I wasn't expecting that," she said primly.

"You said you needed a lift."

"Yes, but I didn't mean—"

"Princess..."

His tone carried a warning. Biting back her reply and orienting herself again, she reached out with both arms, groping.

"Closer to the wall, please."

He stepped in and her fingers brushed stone. She explored it, probing in every direction. Then her right hand slipped into nothingness.

"To the right," she ordered excitedly, and he moved. Both of her arms extended into a void, then found its edges. The breeze was blowing softly in her face, emanating from some mysterious source.

"Hold still," she said, and climbed awkwardly off his shoulders, hauling herself up into the opening. Once inside, she laughed aloud. Then she remembered herself.

"Here," she said, scrambling. "I think if I brace my feet, I can give you a lift."

"Just show me where the edge of the gap is."

"I'll reach down to pull you up," she said, extending her hands, her feet braced against the mouth of the tunnel.

Adam's hand brushed briefly against her own, then disappeared. Ellie felt a quick flash of irritation.

"I'm perfectly capable of—"

Her words were cut off as Adam backed up, then ran and leaped, grabbing the ledge. He pulled himself up, spilling into the tunnel right on top of Ellie.

"Oof." She gasped as the impact squeezed the breath out of her.

Adam rolled clear of her. She tried to corral her scattered wits as she dusted herself off. It was a futile effort, given that she was fairly covered in bat guano.

The tunnel was low, perhaps three feet in height, and curved immediately up and to the left.

"Let's hope this is it," Adam said, and led them forward.

The climb was long. They alternated between crawling on all fours and moving in a slow, awkward crouch along a narrow path that twisted, turned, and doubled back on itself.

The tunnel turned once more, and at last Ellie was able to stand upright. Light, dim but discernible, spilled into it from somewhere ahead. She could see Adam twist, cracking his back with a groan of relief. His greater height would have made the journey up the tunnel even more cramped.

He grinned at her.

"Nice to see you again."

She appreciated the sentiment. Being able to make out the familiar shape of his face once more filled her with relief.

"You, too."

She turned to examine their surroundings.

The tunnel ended on a platform that hung over a vast chamber. The light came from an opening in the ceiling, spilling down along with the voices they had been following, which were clearly human now. But it was what lay on the floor of the cavern that left both of them speechless.

Bones. They were piled upon one another in a mass that made the ancient carnage in the jaguar room look like nothing at all. It was a mountain, an avalanche of the dead. There were bones of all types from animals large and small, but even from the height of their perch, Ellie could see that the greater part of them were human.

There had to be the remains of thousands of men and women down there. Children as well, she realized, noting the diminutive size of some of the skulls below.

"What is this?" she asked in a whisper.

"I think they're sacrifices," Adam replied softly.

They stared at them together, awed to silence by the sheer enormity of the dead.

"Is this normal? Do they find this in other cities?"

"No."

"But the Mayans and Aztecs did conduct sacrifices."

"Not like this," he countered soberly, looking out over the charnel house before them.

"Then why...?"

"I don't know." His tone, the vista before them, all of it sent a chill through her. She thought of the monsters they'd encountered below—the thick-bodied scorpions, the nightmarish bats. Had the men who designed that hell simply stumbled across such creatures? Or had they made them, bred beasts out of myth?

The graceful architecture, the beauty of the city she had seen from the overlook at the ravine—it was nothing but a gilded surface. Everywhere she peered beneath it, she found horror and death.

"There's something wrong with this place," Adam said.

Yes, Ellie thought. That was what she had been feeling since the moment she had stepped into that impossibly familiar courtyard. This place was *wrong*. Beautiful, mythic—almost certainly the archaeological find of the century—but wrong. The mountain of bones in front of her only made it undeniable. For all its elegance and wisdom, something rotten lay at the core of this place. It had been festering there for centuries, demanding tribute in the lives of the dead piled before her.

"This way. Quietly," Adam warned with a glance at the hole in the floor, the light and the voices emanating down. They followed an open ledge that curved around the pit of bones. It ended at a crevice in the rock. Ellie squeezed through it and found herself standing at the bottom of a narrow staircase, roughly but deliberately hewn from the stone.

She started climbing. As she climbed, the voices grew stronger and clearer.

When they reached the top, they became familiar.

"Carefully—carefully, I said! Do not let it drop."

The voice was Gilbert Dawson's. And as she joined Adam at a narrow crack in the wall, she saw the figure to match it, wildly gesturing his arms as a group of men, sweating with effort and concentration, hefted a massive, weirdly flat disk between them, carrying it toward a similarly shaped crate lying on the ground.

No, not a disk. The surface was dark, polished, reflective.

The Smoking Mirror.

It had to be, based on the anxiety in Dawson's face and the care with which the men were handling it. She and Adam had crawled through their hellish maze only to drop right into the heart of Dawson's excavation. If that was what it could be called. Ellie saw none of the activity she would have expected from a legitimate scientific effort. No one was measuring, drawing, or surveying. Men were leaning tiredly against priceless murals on the walls, and the books...

She gazed at them with mingled wonder and rage. There were

piles of them, every one of unspeakable potential importance. The possible keys to unlocking the secrets of an entire civilization, and Dawson's men were dropping them into crates without so much as an inventory.

"He's not an archaeologist," she muttered to Adam, who watched from beside her. "He's a bloody grave robber."

"Right now, he's mostly an obstacle," Adam countered in a quiet tone.

Ellie knew he was right. In her survey of the room she had identified only one possible way out, an opening leading to a ramp located directly across from where they hid. It might as well be on the other side of the world. High-powered lamps had burned away any gloom or shadows they might have hidden themselves in. There was no way they could reach it without being seen.

"We'll have to wait until they go," she concluded, noting the number of men who carried pistols at their belts or had rifles slung across their shoulders. Behind her, Adam muttered something that could have turned her ears pink, but his lack of any other protest told her that he, too, saw the impossibility of their position.

Since there was no telling how long they might have to wait, she gave her attention to a more thorough examination of the room before them. Even an untrained eye would have marveled at it. The high ceiling seemed to be held up by lofty pillars of stone, giving the whole space the feeling of a cathedral. Then there were the sarcophagi. She counted thirteen, each one massive, twice the length of a man. The stone was covered in glyphs and carvings, too detailed to make out at this distance, but clearly of stunning artistry. But the walls—that was artistry of a different matter. She felt her stomach clench and thought of the sea of dead beneath them.

"Bates, look at the murals."

"A little different from what they put upstairs," he commented flatly.

The images, massive and expertly painted, were of scenes from a nightmare. Men dangled from nooses, their entrails pouring out like a gory cascade. Grinning demons stood atop piles of decaying corpses, and a king mounted steps of victory holding a bouquet of human heads by their long black hair. All was violence, death, and blood.

She tore her attention away from the paintings and looked for something else to focus on. She stopped at the sight of a small, eccentric figure moving across the cavern to the open crate that held the mirror—a familiar figure wearing what looked like a child's mock armor.

"Is that Amilcar Kuyoc?" she said disbelievingly. Adam came to her side to look.

The Mayan turned. His gaze moved indiscriminately from Dawson to the other men in the room. His voice rang out in clear tones.

"If any of you want to live, leave this place now."

She turned wide-eyed to Adam. His expression was grim.

"He's going to get himself shot," he said. Then he slipped through the opening, dashed silently across a stretch of open ground, and ducked behind one of the massive sarcophagi.

Ellie bit back a curse. What was he thinking?

"Shoot him if he moves," she heard Dawson order furiously. He pushed two armed men roughly into position on either side of the Mayan. He pointed to another pair by the door. "Fetch Jacobs. Now!"

They turned and ran up the ramp, glad to escape the tension of the tomb.

"The rest of you should follow," the old man said.

Dawson whirled, shouting, "All of you stay exactly where you are, or you'll pay for it later."

Ellie saw the men hover, locked in indecision. They were clearly less convinced of Dawson's authority than they were that of his colleague. Kuyoc also seemed unmoved, continuing to gaze at Dawson steadily.

"Look," Dawson tried. "Just step away from the artifact, and we can talk about it. No one needs to get hurt."

"Yes," the old man countered. "Someone does."

Adam crept from one of the massive coffins to another. So far no one had seen him, their attention gripped by the drama unfolding between Dawson and Amilcar Kuyoc.

How on earth did he get here? And why did he come?

It was as much a mystery to her as Adam's plan was—if he even had one. It would hardly be out of character for the man to go barreling into things on impulse, figuring he could make up the rest as he went along.

That was one habit she'd have to break him of. She could hardly have him risking his neck at every turn.

She caught herself. Who was she to break the man of anything?

Well, he did ask you to marry him.

The thought stopped her short.

That had been entirely different, of course, simply an expedient way of solving the social tangle she'd gotten them into.

Though there'd been nothing expedient about the passion he'd shown her in the cenote, or in the cave of the bats…right after she'd told him she was in love with him.

The memory made her stomach drop, bringing with it an agonizing vulnerability. What was it that he had said in response?

Thank God.

Which meant what, precisely? That he felt the same? If so, why hadn't he said so?

Perhaps because he didn't.

The thought made her sick.

Why did all of this have to be so bloody confusing?

Adam made another dash, moving to a sarcophagus even closer to the drama unfolding in the room before her. Whatever his intentions toward her might be, one thing was certain: He was doing a rather brilliant job of trying to get himself killed.

Whatever mad plan—or lack thereof—was motivating him, he was almost certainly going to need help.

She checked the men in the room. They were still looking at Kuyoc, watching him and Dawson like spectators at a Roman circus. Good.

She slipped through the crack in the wall and hurried to the nearest sarcophagus.

Not everyone missed her move. Adam was glaring at her from his hiding place.

Stay. There, he mouthed urgently.

Ellie nodded. She would stay—at least until she figured out what her next move should be.

⁂

The fluttering, panicked feeling in Dawson's core was increasing as the old man continued to stand there, his bizarre attire making him look even more clearly like a lunatic.

He could see the doubt in the men around him. They were frightened. The atmosphere of this place was getting to them, making even the absurd threat of an old man in a homemade suit of armor seem real. What could the Mayan possibly do to them?

To Dawson, on the other hand…

If he intended some harm to the artifact, and succeeded in accomplishing it, Dawson knew who would be held responsible.

"Listen to me," he said slowly, stepping closer. "My partner is on his way here. And when he arrives, if he sees you by that mirror, he is going to shoot you."

"That would be very foolish."

"Why?" Dawson burst out, frustration rising. "What are you threatening us with?"

The Mayan gave him a slow, sad smile.

"I suppose it's time to show you," he said, and reached into his pocket.

There was a crack, sharp and awful. The old man's head snapped back. He crumpled, falling across the mirror as Dawson felt tension turn to horror. He whirled.

"Who was that? Who shot him?"

"You said if he moved…," one of the men, loosely holding his rifle, protested weakly. Dawson felt rage grip him. It obliterated reason, fueled by panic. He ripped the gun from the man's yielding hands and swung the butt of it against his jaw.

"Not on top of the artifact!" he screamed.

The man fell to his knees and spit out a tooth with a mouthful of blood.

Dawson staggered back.

No, he thought. *Not again—not like Saint Andrews...*

He still held the rifle. He dropped it like a poisoned thing, his hand shaking. The rage-fueled passion, horribly familiar, was already gone, extinguished in the cold water of his fear.

The mirror...

He whirled toward it. The body of the Mayan was sprawled across the surface. Blood pumped from the wound in his head, staining the stone a vivid red.

It will clean, he thought, fighting the rising sense of panic. *Remember the bird, the bloodstained channel in the stone that surrounded it. They sacrificed to it like a god. This can't be the first time.* There had been no stains on its perfect surface, which meant it must be capable of being washed. No one would need to know, not even Jacobs....

Jacobs. He had sent for Jacobs.

The men were watching him, faces wary. They must sense it, how he was losing control. He had to regain it—quickly.

"You two," he snapped. He forced authority into his tone. "Move him off of there. You"—he pointed to a third—"fetch water and rags."

They obeyed him. Dawson watched them move with a sense of profound relief.

He would get through this.

⁓

Ellie watched, hands shaking with shock and anger, as the men Dawson had screamed into action hurried over to Amilcar Kuyoc's corpse. It had all happened too quickly. There was supposed to be time, a chance for them to intervene. If they could have reached one of the more inattentive men, seized his weapon... They were supposed to be able to help, not sit crouched in hiding while a single bullet snuffed a man out like a candle.

But why? she wondered. Why had he come? Why wasn't he safely back in his village where he belonged?

The village. Someone would have to tell them. She and Adam—
they could find the place again. She thought of Kuyoc's grandson,
Paolo. There was Cruzita, and his stoic, hardworking sons. Ellie
would have to tell them what had happened to their father.

Assuming she and Adam got out of here without getting shot
themselves.

Something was happening by the body. There was a hissing,
eerie and serpentlike. Where Kuyoc's blood spilled across the dark
surface of the mirror, thick white smoke was billowing up, rapidly
rising and spreading.

It reached the men Dawson had sent to remove the corpse. They
coughed, waving it away from their faces. Then, abruptly, they
sank to the ground.

The sheer surprise of it nearly brought her to her feet.

What was going on?

She watched as the pale smoke spread farther into the room,
and more men dropped to the ground. Those still standing began
to panic, shouting and running for the exit.

This was it—their chance. That is, if they could slip through the
crowd without running into the apparently toxic smoke.

What on earth was it? And what had it done to the men who
had fallen? Were they dead, or simply unconscious?

There would be time to consider it later. Now they needed to
move.

She shifted around the sarcophagus, putting herself in Adam's
sight line. He was tying something around his face. It was the
sleeve she had torn from her shirt, still damp from their journey
through the caves. He had taken it from his wounded hand. Seeing
her, he motioned urgently toward the narrow gap in the wall, the
entrance to the labyrinth.

No, she thought. *Not that way.*

They needed to make for the other door, the way out....

Then the smoke reached her, and she sank into darkness.

25

ELLIE WOKE UP IN the bathroom.

Not just any bathroom. It was the bathroom of the Imperial Hotel, with its cool white tile, luxurious towels, and massive tub.

The light of a golden afternoon filtered through the high, narrow windows. It was quiet, clean, and peaceful.

Ellie did not have the foggiest notion how she'd gotten there.

"That's because you aren't really here."

The voice came from behind her. Ellie climbed quickly to her feet and turned.

It was the woman: the one with the scarred cheek, the Mayan cast to her features, and the sadness in her eyes.

"Oh. I'm dreaming."

The thought came with some dismay. Ellie really might have preferred to be near an actual tub.

"No. You are not dreaming. You are *seeing*."

"Seeing what? A bathroom?"

"What you desire," the woman replied simply.

She was wearing the plain gown of a Mayan peasant. Her hair hung down her back in a long braid. She sat in a chair at the back of the room, her hands folded in her lap, looking as though she had never been anywhere else.

What she desired...

Ellie looked down at herself. Tibbord's shirt and trousers were torn, caked with mud and bat guano. So was the rest of her. She reached toward her hair, then stopped, grimacing. She wasn't sure she wanted to know the state of it.

And then there was the smell.

Yes, she supposed if she wanted anything right now, it was probably a bath.

Beyond that, none of this made any sense.

"How did I get here?"

"You aren't here," the woman replied. "You are in the mirror."

The mirror.

Ellie could vividly recall how she had last seen it. The body of Amilcar Kuyoc had been crumpled on its smooth black surface, his blood pouring onto the stone.

Pouring, and then hissing like water in hot oil where it touched.

A reaction. A chemical reaction. That was the only explanation. The stone of the mirror looked like hematite, the same material that made up the medallion and the stelae they had passed on their way to the city, boundary markers or perhaps threats set in stone, warning away would-be trespassers.

But it couldn't be. Ellie hadn't specialized in geology, but she knew enough to say with certainty that there was nothing in the substance of hematite that would react with human blood like that.

Though even that theory had a flaw. If the stone was the substance reacting, there would have been scars or pockmarks on its surface, not that smooth, uncanny perfection. It was more as though the blood itself was reacting to the stone, not the other way around.

Which was even more impossible. There was nothing in human blood with even the slightest potential to become that volatile.

Ellie shook her head.

"I'm fairly certain this is a dream," she countered stoutly.

The scarred woman was unmoved.

"It doesn't matter what you believe. All that matters is what you *want.*"

The door to the room opened. Ellie whirled toward it and watched herself walk in.

She was carrying Constance's peacock-blue robe. Ellie watched a look of surprise dance across her own features as she took in the room, the size of the tub and the hot-water tap. She remembered that delight at finding a place like this in a second-rate colonial hotel. How delicious the prospect of a soak had felt after a long journey at sea.

This was weeks ago, the afternoon she arrived in the city. The moments before she met Adam Bates.

The Ellie of before tossed Constance's robe over a chair, then turned the hot-water tap. She shook a box of lavender soap flakes into the water, oblivious to the snake curled up on the tile underneath the tub.

But the Ellie of now was no longer paying attention. Her thoughts were elsewhere, with Adam.

When she'd last seen him, he'd been pressed against the carved stone of one of the massive sarcophagi that circled the mirror, trying to work his way closer, to intervene before something happened to Amilcar Kuyoc.

He had failed. They had both failed.

But what happened to Adam?

The white tile blinked from view. The tub, the robe, her former self, all of it winked out in an instant, and Ellie was someplace else. Someplace dark.

No, not completely dark. Light filtered down from above. Ellie looked up and saw rock. A fissure in the stone opened overhead, letting in the deflected glare of the lanterns.

She realized where she was: inside a crack in the floor of the cavern.

Adam was beside her. He had wedged himself into the tight space, his shoulders pressed against one wall, his legs braced against the other. The bandage from his wounded hand was wrapped over his nose and mouth. He breathed heavily through the wet cloth.

She could see his muscles straining with the effort of keeping his body suspended and wondered why he didn't just let himself down to rest.

Then she looked at what lay beneath them.

Nothingness. A vast drop, and then, barely visible in the faint light filtering through the fissure, bones. A mountain of bones.

Ellie remembered looking up at that mass grave from below, when she and Adam had finally stumbled out of the deadly maze beneath the city. Adam had wedged himself into the gap in the floor of the tomb of kings, the same opening countless generations of priests had used to discard the remains of their sacrifices.

She heard voices above.

Jacobs was shouting orders. Men babbled in panic. Through all of it, Adam held himself in uncomfortable readiness, and Ellie wondered what the devil was going on.

The world blinked again, and she was in the cavern above.

The mirror lay before her like a dark pool, the dead kings surrounding her in their heavy stone coffins. The rest had changed. There were no men scrambling about, no tools and crates, no Dawson and Jacobs. The cavern was silent with the stillness of centuries.

Torches flickered from sconces on the walls, and the scarred woman stood in the midst of all of it, but not as Ellie had ever seen her before.

She was fierce and resplendent, dressed in a strange and ancient finery. Her chest was covered by a breastplate of linked, overlapping tiles of jade and gold. A gold headdress sat on her brow, crowned with standing feathers in bright hues of green, blue, and red. Bracelets hung from her wrists and ankles, and the skin of a jaguar served as her skirt.

It was the garb of a queen or a priestess. Perhaps both. It revealed the woman before her, illustrated her strength and the power that filled her slight frame. Ellie had to resist the overwhelming urge to kneel or curtsy.

The impulse was lightened by a healthy dose of righteous indignation.

"Who are you?" Ellie demanded.

"The echo of a sacrifice," the woman replied. It was the same answer she had given Ellie before. It was even less satisfying the second time around.

"Stop being vague. *I want to know who you are.*"

The shadows around her flickered. The woman shifted with them. She stood before Ellie naked, barely more than a girl. She was trembling, covered in filth. A red, raw, bleeding cut ran jagged across her cheek.

Something about the sludge covering her skin looked familiar.

Ellie's mind flew back to the bats, the monsters waiting in the darkness beneath them. She knew what she was seeing. The girl was a young initiate, one who had only just crawled out of the maze of death hidden below.

A ring of figures surrounded her, shadowy men made larger by the elaborate plumes of their headdresses. One of them stepped forward, holding a white kitten in one hand and an obsidian knife in the other.

The girl accepted them both with shaking hands. She held the mewling animal over the dark mirror and, after only the slightest pause, neatly cut its throat.

The shadows changed again. Ellie saw her older, one of a company of figures who hovered around the mirror with blood on their hands. She watched her slaughter a goat. A snake. A beautiful emerald-green bird. Saw her lean into the smoke that poured from the mirror's surface, breathing deeply. Heard the low, strange drone of her voice, reciting the content of her visions.

The images flashed by like slides in a stereoscope, forming and dissolving and resolving again into something new.

The woman, her scar faded, knelt by the mirror with the knife in her hand, and the shadowy men behind her brought forth a child.

The shift in her expression lasted only a moment, but Ellie saw it—the flash of recognition, of dismay. The boy was no more than three, his ankle and foot twisted with some deformity. Ellie saw her hesitation, the quick glance she flashed back at the ranks of priests watching from the darkness behind her.

She saw hesitation become resolution. The knife clattered to the ground and she turned away.

Another glided forward to take her place. The boy's blood was spilled.

Then the shadowy chorus was gone. Only one other figure remained. He was a pale, thin, rat-faced man with a scraggly goatee, dressed in the tattered habit of a Dominican monk. He looked at the woman with terror and disgust.

The torchlight flickered again, and he, too, was gone. Only the woman remained, tired and worn with grief.

"You were a priestess," Ellie said, still recovering from the barrage of visions.

She nodded.

There were so many questions, so much Ellie didn't know or understand. One tumbled its way to the fore.

"Why am I seeing all of this?"

"This is the mirror." The priestess nodded to the dark, still stone that lay between them. "It is a window to anything that is, was, or might be. Whatever of the past, present, or future you most desire to see, it will show you."

"That's fairy-tale nonsense," Ellie blurted.

The priestess shrugged. "Stories hide truth."

Ellie struggled to absorb it. Past, present, and future...the power of prophecy? No, it was more than that. It was virtual omniscience. It was...

Impossible.

Her rational mind pushed back desperately. She was a scholar, damn it. A scientist. She didn't believe in magic mirrors.

And yet...

She felt the pressure of it, pushing at the seams of her tightly built world. The realization that there was something *more*. Something greater and stranger than periodic tables and Newtonian physics. It had set its hooks in her weeks before, in Mr. Henbury's office, when a pile of papers tumbled to the floor and revealed a crumbling book with a wild secret hidden in its core.

It was in the uncanny dreams that had haunted her, in the myths she had dismissed as cultural curiosities but now knew to be fact.

Tulan Zuyua was real. She was standing in the heart of it, talking to one of its initiates, to a woman who had been dead for centuries.

It's just a hallucination.

But the protest was a weak one.

What did a scientist, a true scholar, do when confronted with facts that contradicted a carefully constructed theory?

Revise the theory.

This was more than a revision. It was a revolution. No—that wasn't it. Revolution implied forward movement. To admit there were things in this world that defied every law of physics Ellie had come to hold as true was a step backward, a collapse into the ages of human history when magic was as real as gravity.

It was unthinkable. And yet, all of science had seemed like magic once, before years of painstaking study had revealed the secret rules that governed atoms, motion, and the void between.

Something sang to her, a call that seeped through the rapidly forming cracks in her comfortable view of the world.

Imagine, it whispered. *Imagine the possibilities.*

Past, present, and future. The power to *know*. The hidden location of any ancient city, the fate of the suffrage movement. The identity of her true enemy, the person who commanded Dawson and Jacobs.

That only scratched the surface.

Knowledge was everything. Knowledge was the weaknesses of a rival. The compromising secret of an authority. It was the strategy to win every battle.

Power. Absolute and total power.

The implication was staggering. The call became an urge, as fierce and primal as any thirst she had ever suffered.

Ask. Want. Desire.

All Ellie had to do was wish it, and it would be hers.

The priestess waited in solemn silence on the far side of the mirror.

Ellie took a deep breath, struggling to regain the rational calm of a scholar as the potential of the object before her screamed through her mind.

"How does it work?"

"Blood," the priestess replied simply.

It was a shock like a slap in the face. She remembered the ancient, rust-hued stains that colored the stone surrounding the mirror. The bones that lay beneath them, the remains of countless thousands of slaughtered men, women, children, and beasts.

"You sacrificed to it."

The priestess nodded slowly. "That is the price it demands." Her voice was sharp, bitter. "We grew rich on it. Wise, beautiful. We saw the path to greatness, and over and over again we took it. We were like gods." Her eyes flashed, and Ellie wondered how she had ever thought the woman small. She looked magnificent.

But her words made the mirror sound like a tyrant, a savage king roaring for the flesh of his subjects. The image reflected the vicious paintings that surrounded her, with their vivid portrayals of gods and men feasting on slaughter.

Ellie shook the thought away. It was simpler than that. She had seen the reaction herself. Blood combined with the stone of the mirror to form the smoke that had brought her here, through some yet-unknown chemistry.

It was still a deeply strange notion, but at least it retained the outward form of rationality. More so than the idea that the dark, still object before her possessed a will, an identity. A drive and thirst of its own.

"Blood meets the stone. Creates a reaction. Then what?"

"It shows you what you want to see. Not what you think you want, or what you ought to. Your true desire. It reads your heart like a book." Her eyes darkened, her expression becoming fierce. "Do you understand what that means?"

"That you don't really control it," Ellie blurted. "Desire isn't rational. It's...it's animal. Instinct."

"Almost always," the priestess agreed softly. "And it is never satisfied."

Ellie looked down at the mirror. In that moment it looked like a vast, black eye, staring coldly out at the world.

It was like a cancer. A disease rotting away the core of this beautiful place. Desire wasn't everything. Wanting something didn't mean you should have it.

But her own desires were different. Weren't they? Rights for women, the equality they had so long deserved. For herself, professional respect. The freedom to pursue a career that wasn't limited to typing or housewifery. Those desires weren't evil, weren't a lust for power or glory. They would benefit not just her but millions of women struggling for the right to look up, to dream.

But would I kill for them?

Because that was what it would take. The price the mirror demanded.

It wouldn't have to be human blood. There were smaller bones in that pile below. Birds, monkeys...

Things that hardly mattered. Things she wouldn't have thought twice about if they showed up on her dinner plate. Surely that wasn't too much to ask to release an entire gender from virtual slavery....

The priestess watched her, silent and still, her black gaze impenetrable.

The mirror glittered on the floor in front of her, dark with promise and possibility.

Such a small thing to ask, it seemed to say. *Just a little life or two.*

Ellie stumbled back, horror rising in her throat, nearly choking her.

That was only how it would start. Little things, things no one cared about. But that wouldn't be enough. There would always be more—more she could do, more she could want.

Bigger prices to be paid.

Across the cavern, the priestess looked older, worn around her edges.

"Yes. You understand."

A buzzing began to whisper around the walls of the cavern. It sounded like a broken machine or the rapid, distant hum of many voices. It penetrated Ellie's mind, itching at her. She climbed to her feet, grimacing.

"What is that?"

"You are waking up. We are running out of time."

"But I have so many questions. Where did the mirror come from? Was it always like this, or was it made, somehow— transformed into what it is now? Is it electrical, or some kind of psychic phenomenon?" An even more startling idea occurred to her. "Are there other things out there like this? Pieces of myth that aren't just stories?" She shook her head, overwhelmed. "There's so much I need to know."

The voices grew louder. She could feel the room shivering. The priestess was right: There was no more time.

"Ask the most important question," she demanded.

The most important question.

Her mind spun. She felt dizzy and sick. It was too much, too big a mystery. How was she supposed to know what question to ask?

The voices rattled at her. Some of them were almost beginning to sound familiar. But running around and between them was something else, a sort of tugging at her soul. She could *feel* it, sense it pulling at her like a fish on a hook.

What do you want. What do you want. What do you want.

It was a whisper, a demand, a promise. Anything in the world, anything she could dream of... Desire, and it would be shown to her. Want, and it was hers.

This wasn't the priestess. It wasn't the voices from the real cave, the one she'd collapsed in, instead of this reflection of it lost somewhere in the distant past. The call came from the dark stone in front of her, from the mirror itself.

Want want want

Back there, in that other room, Ellie was outnumbered, surrounded by enemies. Powerful enemies who had pulled out every stop to acquire this *one thing*, the single, impossible object that lay before her.

What happens if they get it?

Ellie didn't know who Dawson and Jacobs really were, who pulled the strings behind their actions. The employer who used government codes, ordered murder and deceit to achieve his aims. The person powerful enough to scour ships' manifests, probe her obscure past, and track her to the far side of the globe, hiring an army to set against her.

Were the mirror to fall into hands like that, hands that wouldn't hesitate to pay it the blood it demanded . . .

She looked to the murals that haunted the walls, celebrations of victory drenched in death. Power run through with viciousness.

She had to stop it.

She couldn't let Dawson and Jacobs bring the artifact back to their master. Somehow, outnumbered, unarmed, and temporarily unconscious, she had to stop them.

But even that wouldn't be enough. Amilcar Kuyoc had been right, she realized, her heart sinking. Where one foot had trodden, others would follow. If it wasn't Dawson or Jacobs, someone else would find this place and claim the secret that lay before her.

The world would never be safe until the mirror was no longer part of it.

The thought was a splash of cold water. It hit her with perfect clarity, the question she had to ask. The thing she needed to *want* before she lost this moment.

The historian in her gasped with outraged horror and keeled over. But the woman, Eleanora Mallory, latched onto the notion with fierce determination.

"Show me how to destroy it," she called out.

The priestess sighed, her whole being seeming to release some mighty tension. For the first time, Ellie could almost swear she saw her smile.

Then the cave winked out, replaced by a quick, blinding succession of images. Amilcar Kuyoc standing over the mirror, reaching into his pocket. A shed with a padlocked door on the outskirts of a mountain village. A silver tin in Adam's hands, and the flash of light in the darkness. She saw herself, for a moment, her hands covered in blood, holding a burning match in between her fingers.

It could all be a dream, a hallucination. The ravings of her own unconscious mind.

But if it wasn't?

She felt it, a seed inside of her. Doubt—small, perhaps, but solid. Undeniable.

If it wasn't . . .

Then darkness swallowed her, and spit her out again into a blinding glare.

Ellie coughed violently, pushing herself up from the floor of the cave.

"There's another over here!" someone shouted. Rough hands grasped her arms, pulled her up, and dragged her into the center of the room she'd left moments before, the tomb crowded with men and tools and the last, lingering wisps of smoke.

She was dropped by a stone pillar, her legs shaking with strange weakness, her head spinning. A familiar figure slumped against a sarcophagi across from her.

"You," Dawson said, staring at her with red-rimmed eyes as he turned from choking down a mouthful of water.

"Interesting," said a dryer voice from above. She lifted her head and saw Jacobs looming over her, his dark eyes coolly assessing her face.

26

Dawson wanted to be sick.

Sickness would have been a relief. His body churned with horror, rebelling against and repulsed by the things that he had seen, the knowledge that was now his.

It's real.

He had known it, of course. Recognized it in the impossibility of the artifacts he saw in the chamber above, the pendulums and gyroscopes, clocks and telescopes. But forming a rational, if terrifying conclusion was one thing. Experience was something else.

The smoke had held him, and he had *seen*.

He had seen the man in the tavern in Saint Andrews slip something into his drink, a gray powder that dissolved into the whiskey, leaving no trace. He saw a shadowy form bent over Anne, pulling the stopper from a vial under her nose. He saw her wake, her eyes glazing, the frantic fear becoming a drugged indifference.

Since that night, Dawson had wanted nothing more in the world than to understand how he could have lived his whole life unaware of the murderous potential that waited inside him.

He had his answer.

It was a setup.

They had both been drugged, manipulated into acting out a drama someone else had written. A drama where Dawson was meant to play the murderer, and Anne his victim.

But why? Why would someone go to such trouble, just to compel a man to kill his own wife?

And as the question formed, the answer presented itself—and

with it revealed the key to another puzzle that had tortured him since that day in the Edinburgh jail.

He saw Jacobs standing behind the tavern, handing the man who drugged him the envelope of powder.

He saw Jacobs in his bedroom, looming over the drugged body of his wife. Playing the part of a lover who slipped out the window, leaving his paramour to the jealous rage of her husband.

Jacobs had done all of it. But Jacobs had a master. Jacobs followed orders.

The rest had come in a quick succession of images, flashes of insight mingled with the rising cacophony of calling voices and coughing men.

He saw an office, a nondescript room with a print of Queen Victoria mounted on the wall. There were files on the desk, telegram slips, and scribbled notes.

It looked like a government office, the sort that packed the buildings that lined Whitehall. And Dawson's name was on one of the files.

Familiar hands flipped through the pages. The man he had met only once, in a stinking basement jail cell, closed the folder and handed it to Jacobs, who stood waiting on the far side of the desk.

"This one."

Dawson's vision had narrowed. It focused on a ring. The man wore it on his right hand. It was a heavy brass signet, ancient-looking, engraved with the sign of a rock rising from tumultuous waters. A motto surrounded it, carved in Latin.

Pro Albio.

For Albion.

Then the angle shifted. He looked not at the ring but at what lay beneath it. A piece of letterhead, neatly embossed and clearly legible.

Office of the Foreign Secretary, it read.

Five words that shattered every assumption Dawson had made about the man who owned him. He thought he had imagined the possibilities. His employer must be the head of a vast criminal network, or some avid wealthy collector.

But he was looking at a civil servant.

Then gabbling voices had risen like a wave, sweeping the vision away and replacing it with the cold stone of the cavern floor.

He crawled to his knees, retching. His limbs shook, his world shattered. He wasn't a murderer. He was a pawn. And the man who moved the pieces sat behind a desk in the British Foreign Office.

***

Ellie couldn't stand. Her knees were weak, her mind too thick to respond to what was happening around her as Jacobs's men quickly and roughly bound her hands in front of her. Only a handful of them were on their feet. The rest lay on the ground, still recovering from the effects of the smoke.

The body of Amilcar Kuyoc was beside her. The dead Mayan had been carried from the mirror and unceremoniously deposited next to a massive pillar of stone that ran from the chamber floor to its distant roof. On her other side, propped up against one of the carved sarcophagi, sat Dawson. His face was pale and glistened with sweat.

His gaze shifted to Ellie. "I thought you were dead."

"Apparently not," Jacobs replied. "Which means the other is most likely here as well."

"He's not," Ellie protested thickly. She forced herself to meet Jacobs's eyes. "He drowned in the well."

Jacobs stared at her darkly, his expression unchanging.

"Search the room. He won't be far."

No, Ellie realized with a jolt. He wouldn't be. In fact, she knew exactly where Adam was. The mirror had shown her.

Impossible.

But her eyes still moved to the crevice in the floor of the cave, opening to the mass grave beneath them. She could see Adam vividly in her mind, braced between the stone walls of the fissure, gritting his teeth and waiting.

A handful of men hurried to obey Jacobs, carrying lanterns to the farthest corners of the cavern. Some plunged into the tunnel through which she and Adam had entered the space, the one that led back to the maze.

The rest sat on the ground uselessly, looking weak and wide-eyed. Ellie moved her legs and discovered that she wasn't feeling altogether steady either.

Across from her, Dawson was pale, his eyes closed, face glistening with cold sweat. He looked worse than the rest of those affected by the smoke.

The smoke that had triggered her visions.

The memory came flooding back to her with painful clarity. She saw the woman with the scarred face—*priestess*. Saw past and present and the threat of the future.

She remembered its song, that siren pull at her heart. *Anything you want. Desire and it is yours.*

She tried to dismiss it. Her waking mind fought for that simple solution to the problem. Label it all a hallucination and brush it away. But the content of the visions lingered with disturbing clarity.

Her gaze moved to the body on the floor beside her.

Amilcar Kuyoc.

The corpse of the old Mayan had been dragged off of the mirror. It lay crumpled nearby, ignored now that all of the attention was on the search for Adam.

Kuyoc was still wearing his strange breastplate of reeds, though the helmet was gone, along with the better part of the man's head.

She felt her stomach heave and shifted her eyes away from his face. They rested instead on the dead man's hand. There was something clutched in it.

She glanced over at Jacobs and the others. The men in the room were either busy following his orders or still too absorbed in their own confusion to take any note of her.

She crawled along the floor to the body and pulled the unknown object from Kuyoc's fingers, then quickly shifted back to her original position. She checked the room once more. No one had seen her.

Satisfied, she looked down at her prize.

It was a tin of matches, not unlike the one Adam carried in his pocket.

The one she had seen in her vision.

But how could she possibly have known, even in her unconscious mind...

The seed of doubt inside her sprouted, grew tendrils.

It brought with it the memory of all she'd realized in her vision—all she had been forced to see about the world she'd thought she knew.

She felt the edifice of her intellectual defenses crumble. The truth spilled in, with all its dark implications.

The mirror was more than a stone. More than a ritual object. It was real, and it was dangerous.

And she had to make certain it never left this chamber.

She tried to call back the easy certainty of the moment before, to label it all "hallucination" and go back to comfortable denial. She couldn't. The doubt was here to stay, and with it came a terrifying responsibility.

She could just see the mirror from where she sat, the black surface peering over the sides of the crate. It was like a pool of ink, or a hole in the world, swallowing everything.

A match. She remembered the sight of the flame from her vision. But how was a single match supposed to help her? She didn't see any convenient hydrogen tanks nearby.

There had been something else in that quick succession of images, something besides the old Mayan in his makeshift armor and a single tiny flame.

A locked shed on a hillside.

She remembered that shed. It was just outside Amilcar Kuyoc's village. They had passed it on their way to his house. When he was asked, he told them easily what it contained.

Dynamite.

She looked at the fallen man's body once more. Why *had* he worn that bizarre breastplate? He must have known it wouldn't stop a bullet. He would have been better protected from the weapons of Jacobs's men by silence and stealth, not rattling reeds.

The armor was a burden, an unnecessary weight, and Ellie knew firsthand that one did not carry unnecessary weight into the jungle.

So why had he brought it?

She looked at it more carefully. There was something odd about the cords. Thick and stiff, one protruded from each of the reeds. They were cleverly woven together to form a single cable running up the side of the breastplate. But the cable was not attached to anything else. It served no practical purpose that she could discern, and could hardly be considered decorative. So why was it there?

She looked more closely at the place where the cord vanished into the reeds. There was something in there, she realized. The reeds were no longer hollow.

Checking the attention of the others once more, she gave one of the cords a tug. It resisted her efforts, but then some inner adhesive gave way and the contents slid toward her.

She needed to see only a fragment to recognize it. The sight set her pulse pounding.

Apparently tree stumps weren't the only thing Kuyoc intended to use explosives on. He had stuffed the breastplate full of it. The cords were fuses, carefully woven together. Light the business end, and Amilcar Kuyoc could easily have taken out the better part of the tomb.

She carefully nudged the dynamite out of sight and crawled back. It was all she could do to resist the urge to retreat to a safer distance.

He had come prepared to destroy something, and to give his own life in the process. But what? If it was Jacobs and his men, he could hardly hope to get all of them gathered in a single place. And anyway, he had not gone into the camp making threats. He had found his way here, to the tomb—had stood before the mirror when he took the matches from his pocket.

He had known about it, she realized. Had known of its existence back when she and Adam had visited the village, and for who knew how long before then. She remembered what he had told them about the region they intended to explore, how he had tried—futilely—to scare them off. He must have known that the city was their goal and either followed them or made his own way here, prepared to destroy himself if necessary to keep them from acquiring the mirror.

He had known what it would mean if such an object of power fell into the wrong hands—so much so that he'd been willing to die for it.

She felt an unexpected surge of admiration, mixed with grief.

Of course, this meant that technically, Ellie was sitting next to a bomb.

"Nothing, *jefe*," she heard one of the men say. He was standing by Jacobs, who did not look perturbed by the news.

"You're certain?"

"There's nowhere else to look," the man protested.

"Then let's see what happens when we do this."

Jacobs strode to where she sat and grabbed her by the hair. He hauled her to her feet with it, the pain bringing tears to her eyes, and shoved her to the center of the room. She managed to slip the matches into her pocket before Jacobs pulled his gun from its holster and pressed the barrel of it to her temple. It felt hot against her skin, as though recently used.

"Mr. Bates!" he called loudly, his voice ringing off the far corners of the room. "If you do not wish to see me shoot this woman, I suggest you show yourself before I reach the count of three. One," he began, and clicked back the hammer.

Her mind worked furiously. The dark fissure in the floor of the cave was several yards away, on the far side of the place where the mirror lay in its crate. Adam was too stupidly chivalrous to resist Jacobs's challenge. It was only a matter of seconds before he showed himself and promptly got them both shot, which meant it was up to Ellie to figure a way out of this—and quickly.

"Two," Jacobs counted, and a pair of guards stepped back as a figure crawled up from the crack in the floor of the tomb.

Adam had pulled the damp cloth away from his face, and the wound on his hand had reopened and was dripping blood. He looked savage, battered, and—she was forced to admit with a rush of pride and pleasure—utterly magnificent. Too bad the damned man was going to get himself killed.

He stepped forward but stopped on the far side of the mirror. He held his hands out.

"I'm unarmed."

"Good," Jacobs said. "This is getting farcical."

She felt the barrel of the gun leave her skin and knew precisely where it was being redirected. She waited only a breath, then slipped her leg behind Jacobs's ankle and twisted into one of her wushu maneuvers.

It was perfect.

Ellie felt his balance shatter. He was thrown to the side, tumbling to the ground.

Adam dived as the shot pinged off the stone behind him. Ellie gave the gun on the ground a swift kick, skidding it out of Jacobs's reach. It was all she had time to do before he regained his feet and grabbed her.

"Cover him!" he shouted to two men who stood gaping nearby. He kicked Ellie's legs out from underneath her, throwing her to the ground. She struggled, but there was no wushu maneuver for getting out of this one.

Then he grasped her throat and began to squeeze.

She tugged at his fingers. They were like stone. He was stronger than her, pure and simple. She wrenched with her legs, but they were securely pinned. Her only remaining option wasn't very sportsmanlike, but with her lungs screaming for air and her vision narrowing, there was little else she could do. Forming her fingers into a claw, she thrust them into Jacobs's eye. Then pulled.

Adam pushed for purchase but his hand slid from beneath him. That damned gash on his palm had opened up again, and he had fallen on something slick and smooth.

He had been biding his time. Waiting until their attention was elsewhere, until a lone guard stood by his hiding place. Then he could have crawled out, disabled him, and taken the gun. The rest of the plan was rather vague, of course, but he figured it was a start. And he'd always had a knack for improvising. But Jacobs had forced his hand—Jacobs, who was currently screaming.

Adam's head snapped up. The dark-haired man was standing a few yards away, blood streaming through a hand he held clamped over his eye. He spat an order and two of his men grabbed each of Ellie's arms, hauling her to her feet. Her face had gone pale, he noted, and angry, red marks were springing to life against the skin of her throat.

Jacobs's hand dropped as he turned, and Adam saw only raw emptiness where his eye had been.

Damn.

Ellie pulled against the hands that held her, but her efforts were useless. Jacobs's expression had gone even colder and more vicious, something Adam hadn't thought possible.

He was going to kill her, he realized, then wondered even more slowly—*Why aren't I moving?*

He looked numbly down at his hand, resting in a smear of blood on a flat black surface. It sizzled against the stone, hissing like water on a hot skillet.

The mirror, he realized. *I've landed on the damned thing.*

There was a jolt, a surge that ran like electricity from his hand to every bone in his body. The world around him went still.

A few yards away, Jacobs moved toward Ellie purposefully. But it seemed as though he crawled through water, his foot suspended over the stone in a step that took an eternity.

All of time had slowed, turning the cave into an exceptionally vivid tableau. Something whispered at the back of his mind, insistent and alluring. It murmured, promised, demanded.

What do you want?

The answer was simple.

To save her, Adam thought fiercely, without really understanding what he was answering.

Then the scene spun out before him like a waltz.

He saw the two men approaching him from behind, one armed with a shotgun, the other with a revolver. He saw his hands clasp the hammer and the piece of wooden planking that lay discarded at his feet. He watched how all of them came together—hammer, wood, flesh, gun—as elegantly as a ballet. It was a perfect, violent choreography.

Then, with a snap of awareness, it was finished.

His instincts screamed, his mind sharply focused.

Now.

Time snapped back into play. As the world began to move again, Adam rolled to his right. He flipped over the side of the crate and scooped up the hammer and the plank, one in each hand. He pushed to his feet, turning as he rose. The plank thrust up the barrel of his first attacker's weapon; then the hammer connected smoothly with his knee. Adam felt the perfect momentum of it, heard the bone snap, and the man crumpled.

The dance was flawless, executed with impossible control. Adam felt every muscle, sensed every nuance of his surroundings. Intention connected seamlessly to action.

This was what being a god would feel like, he thought distantly.

The shotgun fell into his hand. He swung it solidly into the temple of the second guard. The man loosened his hold on the revolver as he fell back. Adam caught it left-handed but felt how it was already balanced perfectly in his grasp.

He turned, both weapons ready. He pulled first one trigger, then the other, and the men at Ellie's sides both collapsed to the ground.

He dropped the shotgun, moving both hands to the revolver. He leaped easily over the body of the man whose knee he had shattered and leveled the weapon at Jacobs's head.

The dance ended. The trance he had been held in shattered, leaving him at a loss for the next step. He was in the process of inventing one when Ellie did it for him.

She had scrambled to where Amilcar Kuyoc lay. Kneeling beside the corpse, she pulled a match tin from her pocket.

There was a scratch and a hiss, and her voice rang through the chamber, clear and calm.

"This man has roughly two dozen sticks of dynamite strapped to his chest. I'm about to light them. I suggest you vacate the premises."

Her hand wanted to tremble. She couldn't let it. Ellie was many things, but a munitions expert was not one of them. She had no notion of how much time the length of fuse on Kuyoc's armor would buy her.

She suspected it wasn't much.

But there was no time for hesitation. She knelt by a corpse in a cavern full of men holding guns. She was armed with only a match. There wouldn't be a second chance.

She might be killing all of them.

Across from her, Dawson snapped out of his trance, scrambling to his feet. But she looked past him, her eyes seeking Adam. He looked so solid, so real, though he had just pulled off a series of maneuvers that made him seem like a piece of myth. He was bloody and strong and *hers*. She didn't want to lose him. Not yet. Not ever.

She could feel the mirror, its dark presence in the center of the room like a cancer in the heart of the city. She could sense the ones that lay beneath her, the relics of countless dead, sacrificed in the name of power. She thought of how many more would join them if this thing found its way back to England, the seat of an empire.

She focused on Adam. She could see the surprise on his face. He didn't know—couldn't know—what the mirror was. He couldn't possibly understand what she was doing. But there was something else in his gaze, something more than shock.

Trust.

She saw it, felt it. He might not understand what she was doing, but he *trusted* her. Despite everything. Despite how little she deserved it. He trusted her to do the right thing.

He nodded. It was barely perceptible, but it was all that she needed.

The match burned low in her fingers. She touched it to the fuse.

She knew a moment of triumph, captured in the surprised *O* of Dawson's mouth. Then the steady hiss of the quickly burning fuse registered and her heart clenched.

"Bates!" she shouted. She saw him whip the gun across Jacobs's face. He fell and Adam raced toward her, grabbing her arm and propelling her toward the door.

"Move!" he ordered, but she was already racing up the dark and narrow passage.

The tunnel spilled them through a carved doorway into a room full of wonders, a vast chamber lined with glittering objects and dominated by an enormous pendulum. Ellie had only a moment to absorb what she saw before Adam was pushing her across the room and up an endless, twisting staircase.

The stairs ended at a blank wall and Ellie knew a moment of panic. Then she noticed the ladder. It led up to a dark opening in the ceiling.

"Climb," Adam ordered, pushing her toward the ladder. She hurried up the rungs and climbed through the hole. It opened into a low, narrow tunnel that sloped sharply upward. A short, quick crawl brought her to another opening, a gap in the floor that she half fell through.

She landed roughly in a small, bare room that she recognized as the sanctuary at the temple's apex, where she'd saved Adam from Dawson a few hours before.

It felt like years.

Adam landed beside her. He pulled her to the exit, and she found herself looking down at the massive stairs that covered the face of the pyramid.

It was raining. The water pelted down, soaking her instantly. Ellie hesitated for a moment as a burst of lightning illuminated the landscape before her.

She caught sight of something utterly unexpected and entirely out of place rising above the canopy to their left, something very like the upper curve of a great, pale sphere. Then Adam had her hand and was dragging her down the stairs, so quickly she wondered whether she was running or falling.

They had nearly reached the bottom when the explosion shook them. The stones seemed to leap under their feet. Ellie tumbled down the remaining steps as the sound of the blast echoed violently off the ruins. She risked a glance behind and saw more men from the tomb spilling out of the top of the temple, clinging to the shaking pillars.

Ellie thought of the room she had passed through so quickly. It must have taken up the entirety of the pyramid. The whole building was nothing more than a hollow shell—a shell that was about to come down.

Adam scrambled to his feet and pushed her across the courtyard. She pulled back.

"This way," she shouted, and pointed. She saw him frown but didn't stop to argue, dashing away and leaving him to follow. She was nearly to the edge of the wide, paved plaza when the second explosion rippled through the ground beneath them.

The world shook. Ellie fell to her knees, Adam beside her.

"What was that?" she shouted as they pulled each other up. The sound of cracking and crumbling stone drew their attention and they turned to the temple.

Men were still climbing down its stones even as the crown of the pyramid began to fall. The whole structure was swallowing itself from the inside, crumbling into a void at its core. As they watched, a great section of the courtyard split, a dark, jagged gap opening in its center.

"The caves," Adam said grimly. "The explosion must have destabilized them. The whole system is collapsing."

As though in confirmation, another boom resounded through the night, deep and hollow. The gaps in the courtyard multiplied and she stared in wonder and horror as a huge section tilted and slid down into a dark abyss.

"Time to go," Adam said.

She didn't need to be told twice. They turned as one and leaped into the bush, heedless of the thorns and snapping branches. The ground trembled violently beneath her feet, urging her forward still faster until they spilled out into a clearing.

Astonishment stopped Adam in his tracks. But Ellie had known what their goal was and pulled him toward the fully inflated hot-air balloon.

Three men stood beside it, gaping at them as if seeing a pair of ghosts. Ellie recognized Flowers but not the other two.

They wouldn't be able to overcome the men, not in their current battered state. She would have to convince them—somehow, and quickly. . . .

"Bates?" one of them said, squinting at them through the rain. "That you?"

"I think so, Charlie," Adam replied.

"Where the hell did you come from?"

"Who cares?" Lavec growled. "Just get in the basket."

Ellie moved forward but Adam held back, protesting.

"You can't fly that thing in the storm. It'll act like a damned lightning rod."

"Storm's passed," Lavec countered flatly.

"Then why's it still raining?"

"Given the current state of the ground, I think we'd best take our chances with the sky," Ellie cut in. She grasped his arm and hauled him forward as a series of bangs like a giant's firecrackers bounced off the surrounding ridge, and another violent quaking shook the stones beneath them.

Despite all of it, Adam paused at the side of the basket, eyeing it queasily.

"Are you sure there's no other—"

"In. Now."

She pushed him to the side, where Charlie and Lavec grasped his arms and hauled him over. Flowers did the same for her, easily lifting her inside.

"I'm glad you're not dead," he said as he set her down.

"Thanks," she replied awkwardly.

Charlie and Lavec sawed at the ropes that tethered them. The balloon quivered, pulling upward as another crack resounded off the trees.

A dark gap opened at the edge of the clearing. It widened, moving closer.

"The ground's disappearing," she called nervously.

Adam glanced over her shoulder, then cursed roundly. Beside him, Flowers hefted the machete in his hands and brought it down on the rope with all his might.

It snapped, and the basket tilted precariously as the free side rose from the ground.

"The other ropes!" Charlie ordered.

"They're too stinking thick," Lavec growled.

The ground rumbled again, the crack creeping closer.

"I'm going to regret this." Adam sighed. Bracing himself against the basket, he hefted the gun. "Everybody duck."

He fired in quick succession, the bullets striking the knots holding the ropes to their anchors.

With a jolt that threw Ellie to her knees, the balloon leaped up, ascending with a stomach-lurching rapidity. Winds buffeted them, making the basket swing like a child's toy.

Lightning cracked across the sky before her. In the flash she could see dark, whirling specks moving away from them, and knew they must be the nightmare residents of the caves below, carried off by the storm.

The balloon slowed, their ascent going from rocketlike rise to a more gentle drift. Climbing to her feet, Ellie gripped the side of the basket. Looking down, she was able to see the full scale of the destruction she had wrought.

The ruins were gone. As they rose, the last of the temples gave way in a tumble of stones. In place of the city was a massive depression, its depths concealed by smoke and dust. She thought back to their escape from the herd of boar, the great sinkhole they had swung out over. One very like it seemed to be forming before her eyes, taking with it the last remnants of an entire civilization.

And the mirror. There was no way it could have survived this. It was shattered, buried beneath impenetrable tons of rubble, as were the books, the murals—all the secrets of a myth made real.

But not the men, she realized. A line of lights danced along the edge of the collapse, moving quickly toward the safety of the surrounding ridge.

A pair of field glasses hung beside her. She snatched them up, peering down at the figures.

She could just make some of them out in the light of their torches. There was Velegas, the foreman, motioning and shouting. She shifted her view, and another form came into focus. It was Dawson, hurrying along, while behind him another figure stopped, turning toward her. She could make out only the lean frame and dark hair, and a stain that streaked down his face to mark the front of his shirt.

Jacobs had survived.

He watched their ascent calmly, as though unmoved by the chaos that surrounded him.

At last he turned and continued up the ridge with the rest.

Adam was beside her. His knuckles went pale on the side of the basket as a gust of wind shook them, then died away again. She knew without asking that he had seen the trail of men as well.

"They got out?"

She nodded.

She couldn't wish it otherwise. Enough people had died in this place. But the idea that Dawson and Jacobs were now making their way back to civilization wasn't a comforting one.

They were only the tip of an iceberg. A very powerful, very dangerous iceberg. One that would still think of Ellie as a loose end.

She knew nothing about them. But they knew everything about her. Her name, her address. Her childhood friends. And they would be looking for her.

She couldn't go home. Or at least, not as Ellie Mallory. Her old life was lost to her irretrievably. The thought should have grieved her, but instead she felt something entirely unexpected—a sort of relief. And excitement.

"So much for our big discovery," Adam said, looking down at the still-crumbling landscape below them. The temples and palaces were gone, even the silvery road dissolving into a widening abyss.

Ellie's heart lurched.

She hadn't realized it until that moment, utterly consumed with their escape. In destroying the mirror, she had lost the city, and with it the chance that had sent her out on this adventure in the first place.

She had found a mystery, a place that would have revolutionized archaeology in Central America, changing the whole history of the world. And she had destroyed it.

"What have I done?"

"What you had to," Adam replied, putting his arm around her. She leaned into him, then pushed back, remembering.

"Bates—that thing...the Smoking Mirror..."

"More than just a rock, wasn't it?"

She nodded.

The significance of that still shook her. It changed everything about the world she had thought she knew. Physics, history—the limits of the human brain. If an object with such unnatural power could exist—wherever it might have come from—what other dark secrets might be out there, buried beneath the earth, waiting to be dragged into the light?

"Do you realize what that means?" she asked.

"Right now, I'm not sure I care."

"Not sure you care? How can you possibly be so indifferent to..."

The words died in her throat as he grabbed hold of her.

"Do you know how close I came to losing you back there?"

"I admit that things did look a trifle uncertain for a while...."

Something in his look made the words trail away. It was a sort of desperation, one so intense it silenced her. Then he laughed, shaking his head.

"Telling you to never put me through that again would be an exercise in futility, wouldn't it?"

"It's not as though I intended to nearly get myself killed," she countered primly. "And you took more than a few risks yourself, if I might remind you."

"You may," he replied. "You may remind me as often and as frequently as you like. As long as you're *here*."

"I shouldn't think you wanted to remain in this basket any longer than necessary," she noted.

"I'm not talking about the basket."

"I didn't think so," she admitted.

"Princess—"

"You know, I really did despise that name."

"You want me to stop?" he asked in all seriousness.

"I...No. No, it's rather grown on me."

"Has it?" He pulled her closer. Ellie wondered absently whether their weight was going to upset the basket.

But only absently. The rest of her awareness was taken up with a far more pressing question.

"Bates—back in the caves, when I said that I...That is, we were in peril for our lives, and I thought that I might not actually see you again after you went out into that room with those monsters...That is to say..."

Her words stumbled. His gaze had grown intense, the sheer depth of it making her thoughts turn to water, running through her fingers. She fought against it, seizing for boldness. What was the use of equivocating? She was suddenly tired of hiding her feelings, and the fears that came with them, from him—and from herself. If there was ever a time for boldness, this was it—the moment to declare all, and damn the consequences.

"Adam, what do you want?"

"You," he replied, clear and sure.

"In—ah—what capacity, exactly?"

"Any. All. Whatever you're willing to give me." She saw the struggle in his features as he searched for the words. "Damn it, princess—there's nothing else like you. Don't you get it? If you said the word, I'd give up all of this. The bush, the surveying—put on a suit. Play nice at parties. Whatever it takes."

"That sounds absolutely ghastly," she said baldly.

Something in his face started to break, and she moved quickly to prevent it.

"I mean you wearing a suit and playing nice at parties. If we went to a party I wouldn't want you to play at anything at all. I'd rather you shocked everyone by being entirely yourself. And don't you dare talk about giving up your work."

"No?" he asked. The man almost looked amused. She felt her temper begin to flare.

"Of course not," she snapped. "As a matter of fact, if I could have my say, I'd be doing it with you. As long as you promise not to turn into a tyrant when we're chasing down your ruins, and not ones I've got half the map to."

He cracked a smile. "Tall order."

"My intelligence and my academic background are in no way inferior to yours, and you know it. There's only the matter of my inexperience to consider, and I assure you that will be remedied very promptly."

"Yes," he agreed, pulling her closer and leaning in. "I plan on remedying that first thing."

His lips had nearly reached her own when a throat was cleared purposefully behind them. Ellie felt her cheeks turn what she was sure was a rather awkward shade of red. Adam merely cursed.

Charlie was watching them with an air of wry amusement, while Flowers appeared to stare very determinedly up at the balloon. Lavec looked up, chuckled, then returned to polishing his knife.

"Sorry to interrupt," Charlie apologized blandly. "But does anybody know how to steer this thing?"

The rain had died back, and so had the dark, heavy clouds of the storm. Ellie could see it drifting away from them, illuminated by a breaking light from the east. The rainy season had started, but this particular squall was on its way out. A fresh wind had picked up and was blowing them briskly over the distant tangle of the jungle below.

"Where are we going?" she asked. She turned from the horizon to Adam. The dawn light fell across that rugged, familiar face—sun-stained, covered in stubble, and, at the moment, rather becomingly filthy—and she felt something tugging deep in her chest.

It was a good feeling, one with which she hoped to become increasingly familiar.

"Well, princess," he replied, slipping an arm around her waist. "How do you feel about Mexico?"

THRILLINGLY GOOD BOOKS
FROM CRIMINALLY
GOOD WRITERS

CRIME FILES BRINGS YOU THE LATEST RELEASES FROM
TOP CRIME AND THRILLER AUTHORS.

SIGN UP ONLINE FOR OUR MONTHLY NEWSLETTER AND BE THE FIRST
TO KNOW ABOUT OUR COMPETITIONS, NEW BOOKS AND MORE.